Kill the
Farm Boy

Kill the Farm Boy

THE TALES OF PELL

DELILAH S. DAWSON

AND

KEVIN HEARNE

DEL REY

NEW YORK

Published in the United States by Del Rey, an imprint of Random House, a division of Penguin Random House LLC, New York.

DEL REY and the HOUSE colophon are registered trademarks of Penguin Random House LLC.

Map drawn by Kevin Hearne.

Hardback ISBN 978-1-5247-9774-4
Ebook ISBN 978-1-5247-9775-1

Printed in the United States of America on acid-free paper

randomhousebooks.com

2 4 6 8 9 7 5 3

Book design by Caroline Cunningham
Frontispiece goat illustration: iStock/duncan1890
Title page border: iStock/jcrosemann
Title page and chapter opener ornament: Vecteezy.com
Space break ornament: iStock/mxtama

To all the mouthy goats out there: You're extraordinary.

Trust us. We're writers.

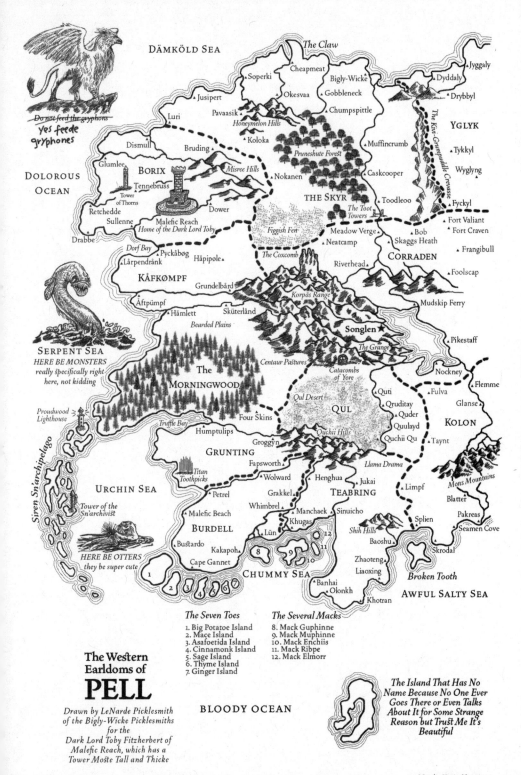

Do not feede the gryphons
yes feede
gryphones

DÄMKÖLD SEA

The Claw

DOLOROUS
OCEAN

Soperki
Jusipert
Luri
Dismull
Glumlee
BORIX
Tennebruss
Tower
of Thorns
Retchedde
Sullenne
Drabbe

Cheapmeat
Bigly-Wicke
Okesvaa · Gobbleneck
Pavaasik · Chumpspittle
Honeymelon Hills
Koloka
Bruding
Misree Hills
Nokanen
Dower

Pruneshute Forest
Muffincrumb
Caskcooper
THE SKYR
Toodleoo

Jyggaly
Dyddaly
· Drybbyl

YGLYK
· Tykkyl
Wyglyng

The Kiu-Grumpuddle Crevasse

Fyckyl
· Fort Valiant
Fort Craven

Malefic Reach
Home of the Dark Lord Toby
Dorf Bay
Pyckåbøg
Lårpendrånk · Håpipøle
KÅFKØMPF
Åftpümpf
Håmlett · Sküterländ
Bearded Plains

Figgish Fen
The Coxcomb

Meadow Verge ·
· Neatcamp
Riverhead
Grundelbård

Korpås Range

The Toot
Towers
· Bob
Skaggs Heath
CORRADEN

· Frangibull
· Foolscap
Mudskip Ferry

SERPENT SEA
HERE BE MONSTERS
really specifically right
here, not kidding

Proudwood
Lighthouse

Siren Sn'archipelago

Songlen ★
The Grange
Centaur Pastures

The
MORNINGWOOD

Truffle Bay
Humptulips
GRUNTING
Titan
Toothpicks
Four Skins
Groggyn
Fapsworth

Pikestaff

Catacombs
of Yore
Qul Desert
QUL
Ouchii Hills

Quti
Qruditay
· Quder
· Quulayd
Quchii Qu

Nockney
· Flemme
· Fulva
Glanse

KOLON
· Taynt

URCHIN SEA

Tower of the
Sn'archivist

HERE BE OTTERS
they be super cute

Petrel
· Malefic Beach
BURDELL
Bustardo
Kakapoh
Cape Gannet

Wolward
Grakkel
Whimbrel
Manchaek
Khugas
Lün
8 9
10
11
12

Llama Drama
Henghua · Jukai
TEABRING
Sinuicho
Shih Hills
Baoshu
Zhaoteng
Liaoxing

· Limpf
Mons Mountains
Blatter
Splien
Pakreas
Seamen Cove
Skrodal

Broken Tooth

CHUMMY SEA
Banhai
Olonkh
Khotran

AWFUL SALTY SEA

The Seven Toes
1. Big Potatoe Island
2. Mace Island
3. Asafoetida Island
4. Cinnamonk Island
5. Sage Island
6. Thyme Island
7. Ginger Island

The Several Macks
8. Mack Guphinne
9. Mack Muphinne
10. Mack Enchiis
11. Mack Ribpe
12. Mack Elmorr

**The Western
Earldoms of
PELL**

Drawn by LeNarde Picklesmith
of the Bigly-Wicke Picklesmiths
for the
Dark Lord Toby Fitzherbert of
Malefic Reach, which has a
Tower Moste Tall and Thicke

BLOODY OCEAN

The Island That Has No
Name Because No One Ever
Goes There or Even Talks
About It for Some Strange
Reason but Trust Me It's
Beautiful

Map by Kevin Hearne

CONTENTS

Contents

Kill the
Farm Boy

1.

In a Foreboding Tower, Glowing with Portent or Possibly Pollen

Many moons ago in a principality far, far away, a hirsute lady slept in a tower that was covered in thorns. In general, such an occurrence would not be considered worthy of note, for people slept in towers all the time regardless of their current level of hair growth.

But in this particular case, it was not just the lady who slept. Almost everyone in the castle was magically sleeping, including the earl and countess and even Oxnard the guard, sitting in the kitchen with his mouth open, eyes closed in bliss, forever eating a piece of cherry pie, thereby creating with each passing minute a new world record for extended pie eating. Dogs, horses, children, knights, the bathing woman with soap in her eyes—everyone stood or sat or lay as if frozen in midaction, even when such actions were wildly inopportune.

The sole exception to the rule was the owner of a lonesome, warbling voice that could be heard every so often singing songs about remembered conversations, and how awfully quiet sleeping people tended to be, and how if someone didn't arrive with groceries soon, a certain someone would go to sleep and wake up dead, because

Oxnard the guard didn't have the keys to the tower door on him and they were nowhere to be found, plus the door itself had turned into solid stone, and all the other exits and castle walls were likewise impossible to manage and food was getting rather scarce, especially cheese.

There was little else of note besides the roses peeping out from the thick blanket of vines. The plush fuchsia blossoms were as beautiful as the thorns were sharp, and there was an abundance of them both, together with a cloying scent of attar and some dizzy, happy bees that seemed to possess a particularly charmed ability to not succumb to sleep and thereby patter to the ground like furry grapes.

There was also an abundance of portent swaddled about the place. Oodles of it. A surfeit, even.

Something would go down there soon.

But for now, the lady slept.

And drooled a little, probably.

2.

In a Squalid Barnyard in Borix, Redolent of Feces and Angst

The very worst part about drudgery, Worstley thought, was all the blasted drudging one had to do. Nothing joyful or fun or frolicsome around the corner for a lowly farm boy like him to look forward to. Just more drudgery of a mind-sapping, soul-sucking nature—and on a good day, no cause for involuntary upchuckery.

At least he'd become somewhat accustomed to cleaning up the barnyard after his older brother, Bestley, had been stabbed in the heart by Lord Ergot for being too handsome. Some said barnyard duties were a step up from scrubbing the chimney, but Worstley wasn't so sure. It had been almost nine months since he'd last vomited at the smell of assorted animal dung, but it was a constant struggle. It was still his least favorite chore, and he had to do it every other day: walk out there with a shovel and a sack among the goats and the pigs and the chickens and those dratted geese that goosed him whenever they could and scoop up whatever foul turds they had excreted since the last time he'd cleaned up. And after that, the stables awaited the same routine. Only then could he have a sad waffle with no syrup on it for breakfast. He didn't think his mother made them properly: rumor in the village had it that waffles weren't supposed to be gray.

Like most cheerless days in Borix, the sky was the color of his mother's waffles. Worstley sighed at the clouds, exasperated. "Would it kill you to let the sun shine through every once in a while?" he said.

The demon geese honked at the sound of his voice and waddled his way, hissing, wings extended in a threat display. Worstley raised his shovel in front of him protectively. "Go on, now. Shoo!" he said.

As he fenced with their snapping beaks for a few seconds, he couldn't help muttering, "There's got to be a better way to live than this."

Had he been in a musical, he thought, right then would have been the perfect time to sing a sad song about his woeful lot in life while emphasizing his eternal optimism and plucky heart. Although he'd been born in this very barnyard—right there by the bucket of lumpy slop—he'd always felt that he was meant for greater things, for some important purpose in the larger world. But there wasn't so much as a gap-toothed troubadour around to strike an obliging opening chord rhapsodizing about his shining future. Lord Ergot had hanged them all for singing a little ditty about his poky short sword on his wedding day.

The geese fended off, Worstley checked the position of the black billy goat that occasionally found it amusing to ram him from the blind side and bleat a laugh as he clutched his back and winced. So far the goat was staying still—Gus was his name—but he was watching Worstley carefully from the other side of the barnyard near the fence. Or at least Worstley thought Gus was watching him; it was hard to tell. The goat's eyes never seemed to point in the same direction.

"Don't even think it, Gus," Worstley called.

Gus bleated, lifted his tail, and ejected a fresh pile of pellets out his backside.

"Oh, great. Why do people think animals are cute?" Worstley wondered aloud. "They're just nasty."

"Aw, you got it easy, kid," a voice called from the fence to the right of the billy goat. Worstley's eyes slid in that direction and spied a diminutive form perched on a post. "Goats ain't nothing. You want a dangerous pile of poop, wait until you get a load of dragon dump. It's hot and sulfurous and will burn the hairs right out of your nose."

"Who are you?" Worstley asked. "Better yet, *what* are you?"

"C'mere, kid. We gotta talk."

Keeping a wary eye out for attacks from geese and goat, Worstley drew closer to the fence to get a better look at the speaker.

Whoever she was, she had a set of double wings like a dragonfly's branching from her back, thin and translucent and veined with iridescent colors. They were the most beautiful things Worstley had ever seen. But the owner of said wings wasn't precisely the image of a proper fairy. A rather large mole with three stiff and proud hairs sprouting from it was rooted on the side of her left nostril. She had two black holes where teeth should've been, and the three remaining molars were capped with gold. A single eyebrow not unlike a furry caterpillar wriggled about on her forehead.

Worstley would've expected a glittering dress, dainty as a flower, but such was not in the offing. She wore a shirt that looked more like a used handkerchief, possibly swiped from someone with the plague. Her dull red pants ballooned over the thighs with the right leg bunched at the knee, revealing one blue threadbare sock. Her left pants leg fell to her ankle, but that foot was sadly sockless. Dirt rimmed her toenails, and she radiated a powerful funk that might've been fungal in origin.

In short, she resembled a fairy about as much as Worstley looked like a prince.

"Are you all right?" Worstley said.

"Of course I am. I mean, apart from it being too blasted early, I'm fine." She belched robustly. "Ah, that's better."

Worstley blinked. "Right. It's just that you don't look—"

"Like what? You'd better not say a fairy, kid," she said, pointing a warning finger at him. The finger appeared to have a booger affixed to the tip. "I'm a pixie. Name's Staph."

"Staph?"

"That's what I said. I'm here to change your life, so we should probably get on with it so I can do something more productive with my day than talking to some scrawny cheesehole."

Worstley took a step back and looked around, suspicious. He'd always dreamed of seeing a fairy, but never one that smelled quite so terrible. "Is this a joke? You can't be a pixie."

Staph blanched and looked over her shoulder to make sure she still had wings. The motion made her wobble unsteadily on the fence post. "Wings are still there. I'm a pixie. What the puck else would I be? A bogie?" She waggled her booger-tipped finger threateningly at him and cackled.

"Are you drunk?"

"Not as much as I'd like to be. Now look, kid, I'm here to tell you something important. The good news and the bad news is that you're the Chosen One. You have a destiny, and I'm here to bless you with it. Or curse you, whatever. Anoint you, let's say."

"This has definitely got to be a joke. Who put you up to this?"

The pixie rolled her eyes. "Gahh, enough with that, all right? Nobody cares enough to play a joke on you, farm boy. This is destiny, all gen-u-wine and bona fide. What's so hard to believe?"

"I thought pixies were supposed to be named Butterblossom or something, and they're, like, I don't know . . . clean."

Staph's eyes bulged, and she held up her boogery index finger to scold Worstley. "First, Butterblossom is a no-talent harpy who invades homes at night and eats little kids' pet hamsters." She held up another finger. "Second, clean people have no fun and they only bathe because they can't think of anything better to do. But me, I've seen some right bloody business and I know things."

Worstley shrugged and sighed and shouldered his shovel as if to say that if he had to deal with someone else's crap in the barnyard, it should at least be the physical rather than the metaphorical kind.

"Don't believe me? Okay, I'll prove it to you." The pixie hawked up a loogie and spat it at his feet. "I've got more magic juice than a poisoned apple orchard in Chumpspittle. That's an ordinary goat over there, right?" Staph pointed at Gus.

"He's kind of annoying, but otherwise, yeah."

"Watch this." Staph glared at the goat and thrust out a hand in a clawed gesture. The billy goat rocked back as if struck and began to choke and spit, its yellow eyes rolling back in its head. The pixie produced a tiny wand and added some extra oomph to whatever she was doing, and the goat fell over.

Worstley dropped the shovel. "Hey, what are you doing to Gus? Stop it!"

"Already done," Staph said as she lowered her hands and put the wand away.

Kneeling by the fallen and unbreathing billy, Worstley was unsure how to give mouth-to-mouth to someone with such thin, filthy lips full of such snuggled yellow teeth. Fortunately, Gus's round belly puffed up with air, and he rolled over and onto his callused knees, coughing.

"You okay, Gus? C'mon, buddy. If you're dead, Mom'll kill me. Or, actually, that might save me a step . . ."

"My name," said the goat, newly gifted with speech, "is Gustave, not Gus. Get it straight, Pooboy." His voice was more cultured than Worstley's and filled the boy with rage that only made him sound more the bumpkin.

"What did you—?"

"That's your name, genius. Pooboy. As in the boy who scoops up my poo."

Worstley bristled and said, "That's so juvenile, you—" but Staph cut him off before he could finish.

"Look, will you forget the goat and listen to me now? He's not important, but I'm for real, and I'm telling you that you're the Chosen One. You have a special destiny. You're going to do great things."

"Why me?"

"Hey, it wasn't *me* that chose you, okay? I just got sent here to do the deed. If I'm gonna choose a hero, you can be darned sure it's not gonna be some whiny, pathetic punk named Pooboy."

"That's not my name! It's Worstley!"

"Whatever. Like that's any better. Anyway, you're hereby anointed, so get to it, will ya?"

"Get to what?"

"Saving the world. Or changing it. Or both. The aura kind of takes care of everything, and it's not my problem anymore. All's I need is a drink and the occasional night of debauchery at the local halfling bar and I'm good. But you're not good, right? You're a pooboy named Worstley living in the most wretched earldom in Pell. Time to move on, don't you think? Find your destiny, get some songs written about you. Do something worth singing about."

Staph turned to go, and Worstley yelped and reached out a hand, although he chickened out of actually touching her. They were short on soap around the farm, after all.

"Wait, that's it? I mean, what have I been chosen to do?"

"Gadzooks, boy. Or zounds. I don't know which is more appropriate in this case, and I get them mixed up."

"Me, too," Worstley admitted.

"But I do know one thing: you gotta figure out your destiny your own dang self."

"But I'm really new to all this. Don't you have a suggestion about where to begin?"

The pixie shrugged, scratched idly at her belly, and pointed vaguely to the southeast. "If you amble along that way a while on the road to Tenebruss, you'll come across the earl's tower. His castle, too, but the tower's the thing."

"So?"

Staph blew out a frustrated sigh. "So people don't go to the trouble of building a tower unless they want to protect something they think is valuable inside it. Odds are you'll find some treasure in there. Either that or the patriarchal son of a nun is trying to protect the virtue of his daughter. She'll probably be clean and boring, in which case I bet you'll take a shine to her. Go thou, verily, forsooth, swear by your troth or something. Or just do your chores here in the muck for the rest of your life. Doesn't tweak my tuppence either way. I'm done here." She turned her back on Worstley, blasted him with a powerful if squeaky fart, giggled, and flew away in an unsteady looping trajectory, leaving a trail of dull glitter in her wake.

"Wow. Did that just happen?" Worstley gagged, trying to wave away the pixie's parting gift.

"Sure did," the billy goat said. "Say, why don't you begin your quest to change the world by giving me something good to eat for a change. Go in the house and fetch your father's boots. They smell delicious."

At the sound of the goat's voice, Worstley whipped his head around so fast that he heard something pop in his neck. "So I wasn't imagining it. You really can talk now."

"Boots, Pooboy. Now. Read my lips."

"Your lips don't match your words very well."

"Goat lips are different, aren't they? Now hurry up."

Worstley wasn't about to argue with a goat—no, wait. He totally was.

"Forget that noise! You heard Staph. I'm the Chosen One. That means I'm done with this barnyard. Done with you. Done with this life! I'm going to go to that tower and things are going to be better. I'll be able to go up to the baker in town and ask for a slice of real cake! The fancy kind, with frosting and no mold!"

Gustave snorted. "You really ought to think that one through, okay? You have trouble defending yourself against me and a couple of geese. You have no weapons and no armor. You're like, what, ninety pounds? World out there is gonna crush you."

"Nah, it'll all work out. I was *chosen*. I have a *destiny*. You'll see."

"No, I really won't. I'm staying right here, where it's safe."

"Okay. Stay if you want, but my parents are planning to eat you in a couple weeks. Mom won't shut up about all the curry recipes."

Gustave stared at Worstley so long that the farm boy thought the goat had lost the ability to talk.

"You know what?" the goat finally said. "I'm tired of this barnyard, too. Can't remember the last time I saw a she-goat. Maybe they're all in that tower we're supposed to go find. An entire tower of goatly delight. Sweet nannies galore."

"Yeah! Let's go! I just need to pack a few things."

"Don't forget your father's boots."

Worstley's parents, unfortunately, were less than understanding about his announcement that he was off to seek his fortune as the Chosen One, anointed by Staph the pixie. A bit of flailing and wrestling ensued as they tried to lock him up in the root cellar "for his own good," but when Gustave intervened and told them to let him go, they tried instead to set the goat aflame.

"Evil magic!" his mother shrieked. "Evil in our home! Kill it with fire!"

Worstley's father let him out of a choke hold and dashed to the hearth, fetching out a burning branch.

"Get thee gone, demon!" the decrepit and toothless thirty-two-year-old man shouted, waving his torch.

"Y'all are intense," Gustave said, backing out the door and dropping a batch of emergency plops in self-defense. Worstley's father followed, and then came Worstley himself, all gangly limbs and wild eyes, clutching a loaf of bread and a jar of pickled herring. The goat and the boy quickly outpaced their elders down the road toward the village.

"That's all you got?" Gustave said, eyeing Worstley's bundles and trying very hard to frown but lacking the proper facial musculature.

"I just grabbed what I could on the way out the door."

"You could have gotten the boots!"

"He was wearing them, and he wanted to burn you alive."

"That's no excuse. You just had your arse anointed by an honest-to-gods pixie. You ought to have better luck than this."

"Well, I'm sure we'll do better in town. Look at the sky. The clouds are parting for once! It's an omen, Gus!"

"Or it's just weather. And again, the name is Gustave."

"Fine, Gustave it is. But I think you're both right and wrong. You're right that I should have better luck. And I will, when there's something I truly need. I don't need my father's boots—"

"Yes, you do. You need to give them to me."

"No, I don't. I need to go to that tower and score the first notch in my hero's belt. And once I've got that experience, you know what I'm going to do? I'm going to find Lord Ergot and make him pay for killing Bestley. Because a Chosen One sets things right."

"I thought a Chosen One just leaves a trail of blood and chaos behind him."

"What do you know about it? You're a goat! You're wrong about that—and wrong about the weather, too, which is what I meant to say before you interrupted me! That break in the clouds is an omen! Of justice! Of light beating back the darkness! Of the dawn of the age of Worstley! Does that not sound noble?"

"It sounds like an era of shame and incontinence."

Worstley scoffed. "You have no ear for poetry."

"Maybe not, but I have an ear for nonsense."

"I was *chosen*. Wait and see."

"I don't have to wait to see that you're putting too much faith in a drunken pixie."

"Wrong again."

But Gustave was right—about the weather, at least. It soon began raining in a very nonmagical style. There were no rainbows, no leprechauns, and, after a few brief moments, no gleaming sun parting the clouds. Just a boy and his goat taking their first muddy steps toward a moist, squelching destiny.

3.

In the Tower of Toby, the Dark Lord, He Who Dreams of Artisanal Crackers

The Dark Lord took a break from studying the esoteric movements of the magical spheres of portent and went to the cupboard for some crackers. Lo, he found none. And he was very angry.

"Dementria, where the gadzooks are the crackers?" he shouted into the night, and then wondered if he should have said "zounds" instead.

When no answer wafted his way, he glared at the hourglass, forgetting when last he'd turned it. It was probably past six, and his wizened servant had already departed for the night.

"The world is a terrible place," Toby said to a hedgehog squatting sadly in a cage on the table. "What's the point of being a potentially all-powerful wizard if you can't even have cheese and crackers when you really, really deserve them?"

The hedgehog merely tightened into a bristly ball and said nothing, seeing as how Staph had not visited and bestowed the gift of speech upon it. Even if she had, the hedgehog mostly would've whimpered, having been the subject of Toby's wizardly attentions all day. And then the hedgehog would've uncurled, poked a tiny finger in the wizard's chest, and explained that hedgehogs and box turtles couldn't mate, and even if they could, shoving them at one another and shouting at them for hours wasn't exactly considered seductive. The turtle, for his part, was playing dead, and rather convincingly. The hedgehog liked the turtle better that way, but she still had a boyfriend back home in the garden and wasn't interested.

"I AM THE ALL-POWERFUL DARK LORD, AND I WILL HAVE CRACKERS!" Toby shouted, green bolts of magic issuing from his fingertips and leaping to a nearby platter, where something almost exactly like crackers appeared in an artistic sort of arrangement. Unfortunately, one of the green bolts also hit the cage, and its energy traveled all along the metal and wound up shocking the nethers of its occupants. The hedgehog squeaked in anger. That was not the way to turn anyone on. The turtle, for his part, just crackled a bit. Turning away from his recalcitrant captives, Toby fetched a wheel of cheese from his magical cabinet and began paring off slivers to eat with his almost-crackers.

"If you two would just breed like reasonable creatures," he said to the hedgehog, "I'd have the magical familiar I require to fully access my abilities, and then I could conjure real crackers. The kind with seeds placed on them by artisans. Or maybe the seeds were grown by artisans. Regardless, they'd be artisanal. Because I'd have an armored, spiny, talking turtlehog familiar, and my magic would be boundless, and I could lure the finest cheesemongers to my very door. No more ordering from catalogs!"

He took a bite of cheese and pseudo-cracker and munched thoughtfully, almost-crumbs peppering his almost-beard. He stroked it—what few pathetic hairs there were—and his spirits sank. If only he had a beard, he wouldn't need the turtlehog. He would already have the magic he desired, and he'd be able to summon true crackers from the aether—and a lot more. Darkness! Storm clouds! Storks! But he had to admit, at his ripening age, that such a beard would never be his unless he managed to stumble across a particularly hirsute dwarf corpse while holding a very sharp knife in an area with little foot traffic.

There were many such ways to become a true wizard if one was born with the knack, but they all depended on something random, dangerous, or impossible. Among them: connect with a mystical animal that agreed to be your familiar; grow a stupendously long beard; find a crystal wand; be blessed by a pixie; fall into a vat of glowing green spiders; or climb a beanstalk and steal a golden goose. Thus far, Lord Toby had utterly failed to secure the means to really pump up his power and make his dreams come true. He'd never left this little corner of Pell, as he'd heard the ill-kept roads were chock-full of highwaymen and unsavory halflings. Even his decently fat purse wasn't enough to secure a true crystal wand, and so he'd spent years trying to breed strange animals while hunting for beard oils and unguents to encourage follicle growth, but it was all for naught. His oily little goatee would barely look respectable on a billy goat. And he hated billy goats, except to eat.

It might be time, he thought, to figure out some other career. His father—the elder Toby, a true Dark Lord with a luxurious beard—had died in a freak pitchfork accident, cutting short a life of macabre magnificence, and Toby was now that same age and had accomplished not nearly half so much. All his life, Toby had longed to follow in his father's dread footsteps, save for the last one on the pitchfork. But until his magical powers were secured, he couldn't print DARK LORD on his stationery without summoning the wrath of the Council of Merlins. Privately calling himself the Dark Lord, however . . . well, that would be hard to give up. He might have to grow accustomed to being merely an Ominous Adept. And perhaps he needed a convertible carriage with a bespoke leather interior to distract him from this disappointment.

Just then, a sonorous bell rang, echoing around and up the jet-black stones of the Dark Lord's tower. Toby perked up, straightening his robes and smoothing the crumbs from the embroidered stars on his velvet lapels.

"Ah," he said, drawing himself up tall and looking very wise. "'Tis the mail."

Ignoring the traumatized creatures in the cage, he clambered down the stairs of his tower, noting that towers were really a very stupid kind of building, as they required three times as many steps as anything else, and one day, if all went well, he would be a white-bearded wizard and fall down and down and around and break his back and die in a puddle of wizard blood. This time, at least, he made it down all six hundred thirteen steps to throw open the carved oaken doors to reveal neat rows of roses and hedges and a very angry male hedgehog and an Unwelcome mat.

"Who dares disturb the might—"

But the mail carrier was long gone, considering it had taken Toby nearly half an hour to navigate his own home. There on the step he found a packet of missives filled with dark tidings, including several bills and foul solicitations for charity. One letter stood out, and he slit the wax seal with a particularly creepy pinkie nail he'd grown out long for just such an occasion.

"Dear sir or madam," it began. "Dost thou have the power to kill thine enemies? For I need just such a wizard." Toby brightened considerably, pleased that word of his powers—or almost-powers—had spread. But when he read, "Payment shalle be in chickens," he ripped the letter in half and set it on fire with a candle guttering in a sconce in his foyer. He hated chickens. The ones in his barnyard were exceptionally awful. They wouldn't breed with hedgehogs, either. The only worse payment than chickens was exposure, and Toby didn't like to talk about his seamy past in the Lordling of the Month calendars.

The last letter seemed rather promising, being heavy in the sort of way that indicated it might contain actual currency, but Toby quickly noted that it was addressed to someone else, a "Grinda the Goode Witche" who lived at Malefic Beach, whereas Toby lived at Malefic Reach; it was a simple enough mistake. Weighing the bundle in his hand, Toby stroked what little beard he had.

"The Dark Lord does what he will," he finally said, and there was no one around to suggest that perhaps the Dark Lord shouldn't open someone else's mail.

Unfortunately, the letter's weight wasn't owing to a bundle of writs or deeds or the secret recipe for Glandalf's Great Goatee Growing Grease. No, the envelope, in fact, held the most horrific thing the Dark Lord could imagine: a very detailed letter of woe. "My Dear Systere Grinda," it began. "Woe unto Usse, for Worstley hath runneth offeth. He is our last remaining Sonne, and who shalle now Clean up the Dungg?"

Normally, Toby would've stopped reading immediately, but something caught his eye in the next sentence: "He hath told Usse he is the Chosen One and taken with him our Laste Foine Goat, which is truly an Evil Creature, as it hath begunneth Talking, and spraying mine floore with Panic Shite."

Mesmerized, Toby read on, wincing at the horrible grammar and utter abuse of capital letters and extra *E*s. After several pages of ranting and bemoaning her many recipes for goat stew that would never be used and the loss of an important bottle of fish, he had learned one fact that now overshadowed even his need for crackers and a proper turtlehog empire: the boy, Worstley, had been designated the Chosen One. Toby was very familiar with Staph the pixie and her proclamations. It was she who had first suggested that he "go home to grow his beard and fiddle with his pillar," which was obviously a reference to his future as a wizard living in a properly terrifying tower.

He had followed her suggestion immediately, and he still wasn't done fiddling with his tower. He had many improvements to make, in fact, and assumed he'd be fiddling with his tower and grooming the shrubbery around it until he was a doddering old man and his tower was falling down.

Staph, for all her unpleasantness, was never wrong.

And that meant . . . there was a Chosen One.

And one of the many unusual ways to become a fully puissant wizard involved possessing the heart of a Chosen One.

It seemed like a ghastly way to breed magic, but Toby wasn't complaining. After all, there were other benefits to killing a Chosen One, so he'd be doing a public service.

For one thing, Chosen Ones were very bad for business. One couldn't have them mucking about, seeking their destinies and screwing up everything for the hardworking folk who didn't think they were the center of the world. Whether or not they succeeded on their quests, Chosen Ones upset the status quo, and Toby the Dark Lord was rather happy with the status quo at the moment. Maybe not as related to crackers, hedgehogs, and turtles, but when it came to the current political climate, the common man was prospering. On one side of Toby's tower, the king of Pell was a silly, unambitious man who paid more attention to liquor and horses than to his actual kingdom. And on the other side, the fatuous Earl of Borix was resting, as it were, under a sleeping spell. Lord Ergot of Bruding was mostly running things while the earl was napping, and Lord Ergot was quite easily bribed when one needed a wee favor, at least in regards to building codes and tower improvements.

Peace and quiet and magic. That was what a Dark Lord wanted. Or quiet and magic and a thriving market for crossbred animals. Get a bunch of Chosen Ones running about unchecked, and one of the lot was certain to start gunning for the Darkest Lord around, assuming he had all sorts of terrible plans to call forth demons from the underworld and steal princesses and . . . honestly, that was just a lot of work. Toby was quite content, and that meant he now had one goal: kill the farm boy.

For the general economy, of course. For the good of the people.

And if the Chosen One's heart should disappear, most likely no one would notice.

They'd be too busy cheering to have the wicked little busybody safely out of the way.

"Poltro!" Toby shouted, stepping carefully over his unwelcome mat to glower in the direction of his barn.

Part of the Dark Lord's contentment stemmed from a tidy insurance settlement (they paid double for pitchfork accidents) that had financed many improvements in his demesne, as well as a few servants bound to his land. Dementria went home at night to soak her bunions, but his own un-Chosen farm boy shared the hayloft with his sister, Poltro. The girl appeared now, cutting a charming figure as she leapt from the barn's double doors. Her livery was all black, her sword and dagger hanging at her side as her cloak swept dramatically behind her. Her hair, dark as a raven's wing, rippled back from an olive brow, her eyes as sharp as an eagle's. Toby had paid handsomely to have her fostered to a huntsman named Cutter, and as he watched her approach, he felt that his money had been well spent.

Right up until she tripped over a chicken and fell on her face in the muck.

"Cor," she muttered, sitting up on her knees to wipe chicken dung from her lips. "I bloody hate chickens. Stealthy things, they are."

Toby's fingers twitched, but he used his hard-won control to firm them up into a fist.

"Poltro, I've a job for you," he said, sounding mysterious and magnanimous.

She stood, wobbling, and tried to wipe the various stains from her costume. "Hope it ain't chickens," she said. "Never trust 'em, what with their poky beaks. And their buttfruit. I tell you, sire, it's unnatural, eggs is." She cocked an eyebrow. "But if it's eggs you want, I have a source." Her eyes slid over to a chicken coop. "You didn't hear it from me, but I find a bucket of eggs by the henhouse every morning. I do suspect foul play."

Toby swallowed hard and counted to ten. Between her brother and Poltro, Poltro was still the better bet. And the job he had for her was a tricky, delicate thing. He beckoned her closer, and Poltro managed to make it across the yard without tripping on another chicken, although she did have quite a standoff with a sheep. Finally, she stood before him, cloak thrown back to undulate in the wind.

"What is your will, m'lord?" she asked. She meant to kneel in respect but misjudged the distance and ended up with her face just a little too close to Toby's crotch.

He cleared his throat and backed away. "My huntsman, I command you to find the Chosen One, take his life, and bring me his still-beating heart," he said, sounding just as grand as he imagined he would.

In the silence afterward, a few chickens clucked, and the one Poltro had fallen on sort of fluttered to indicate it was trying.

"A fine errand for a Tuesday, m'lord! But, uh. Just so there's no misunderstanding, do you mean, like, kill him, and then bring you his heart? Because I was fairly certain that when you killed someone, their heart stopped beating. Cutter led me to believe it was a sort of cause-and-effect thing and no way around it. So I feel like I could bring you his not-beating heart, or maybe I could like tie him up and bring him, and then kill him in front of you, and you'd know his heart was still beating right up until he died?"

Toby considered that and was frustrated by how much sense it made. When Poltro started talking sense, it usually meant one had drunk too much.

"Fair enough. I then command that you kill the Chosen One and bring me his heart. Not beating. But if it was, that would be okay, too."

"But it won't be," she argued.

"Fine. Just . . . the heart."

"Why his heart, my lord? Could a kidney work, or maybe a lymph node?"

Toby barely stopped himself from spluttering. "Because . . . well . . . I need to know he's dead."

"Oh, so my word isn't good enough for you? I tell you someone's dead, and you would doubt that? My lord, I find your lack of confidence very insulting."

Toby's fingers spasmed and his voice cracked, but he most certainly did not shoot green lightning at Poltro, because even if she was terribly clumsy and rather annoying, she was an excellent and effective tracker who would soon have this Chosen One in hand, as long as he wasn't a chicken.

"A Chosen One," he said slowly, "is a very tricky thing, my dear. I will need his heart for . . ." He almost said "personal reasons" but realized that sounded a bit creepy. "Magical reasons," he finished, but afterward realized that sounded equally stupid.

"Magical reasons," Poltro repeated. "Well, can't argue with magic. What can you tell me of this Chosen One, my lord?"

Toby squinted at the sheaf of papers in his other hand, trying to remember the pertinent details drawn from the pages and pages of purple prose he'd read. "His name is Worstley. He smells of dung. He's traveling with a black goat that may or may not talk. Worstley is eighteen, white as milk, and tall and strong with wavy blond hair and earnest blue eyes that sparkle with a call to greatness." He paused to wrinkle his nose. "Gadzooks, who writes this trash? He was last seen in a jerkin and breeches the color of mud and smeared with barnyard waste, with a cloak to match, headed out with a jar of pickled herring to save the world while breaking his poor parents' hearts. Honestly, he sounds terrible."

"He sounds like every other lad about the countryside. Pickled herring is right popular for good reason. But the talking goat might give me an edge," Poltro mused. "Where will I find him?"

"The return address suggests he lives somewhere to the west, so I suppose this tower he's headed toward is the earl's—the one all covered in thorns and whatnot. Only a Chosen One would be foolish enough to try to penetrate that wily thatch."

Poltro rose to her feet and struck a proud pose, with one boot pointed. "Head toward the tower entangled in a wily thatch, find the Chosen One, and kill him. Got it." She took a few stalwart steps, then turned back around. "What about the goat?"

Toby shook his head. "What about the goat?"

"Do you want its heart, too, and if so, can I eat the rest of it? And if so, will you be wanting some? I mean, how are we going to divide this guy's goat friend? And how do you feel about curry?"

Rubbing the place where a headache was brewing, Toby said, "You may keep whatever parts of the goat you wish. I just want this farm boy's heart."

"So the rest of him is up for grabs?"

"The rest of the goat?"

"No, the rest of the . . . yeah, the goat. The goat. Good eating, goat."

With that, she saluted him with the wrong hand and set off toward the west. Toby watched her go, feeling a lightness in his heart as the huntress hopped over the fence and landed on her face. As she stalked into the sunset, he called after her.

"Poltro?"

From far away, she turned, cape billowing in the early evening wind.

"Yes, Dark Lord?"

"Did you want to take your horse?"

She shouted a very rude word and jogged back toward the barn to saddle her coal-black steed. Toby waited, watching his chickens and sheep, all black as night, peck at the ground. When Poltro finally rode out of the barn, her stallion prancing, the Dark Lord walked up to her and held out a small bag he'd untied from his belt.

"What's this, my lord? Provisions?"

"No, Poltro. You can take your own provisions from the larder in your quarters. These are a few potions to aid you on your journey. They are carefully labeled and sealed with wax. One is an invisibility potion that will hide you from any enemy. One is a sleeping potion; taken in its entirety, the victim will sleep for a year. And the third is a healing elixir that will heal any wound or sickness."

He didn't mention it, but he'd purchased them through a mail order potion purveyor and was too frightened to use them himself.

Poltro took the bag and peered inside as her horse snorted and danced. "How do they work?"

"Read the labels."

"But do I drink them? Or do they go . . ." She made a poking motion with one finger. "Up the other way? Me mum used to give us one like that."

"Read the labels. None of them are to be taken rectally."

"Good," she said, nodding and tying the bag onto her belt. "Anything else, my lord?"

"Just kill the farm boy, Poltro, and bring me his heart. When you return, you will be well rewarded. What will you claim as your bounty?"

Her chin raised as she looked off into the sunset, a fierce creature with eyes always on the horizon.

"A world without chickens," she breathed.

"I could probably build you a lean-to in the south pasture," he said. "But you'll have to keep the chickens out yourself."

"Such is my fate. Onward, Snowflake!"

Digging her heels into the black stallion's ribs, she took off at a mad gallop before stopping short at the gate, dismounting, fumbling with the latch, opening the gate, remounting, riding through the gate, dismounting, closing the gate, catching her horse after he wandered off to crop grass, and remounting. With another ferocious war cry, she kicked the horse again and galloped off into the outer reaches of his estate, completely forgetting to take any provisions.

There were three more gates to navigate before the road, which required an obscene amount of mounting of both the re- and dis- varieties.

Toby gave up and began the long climb upstairs. For just a moment, he considered going after the Chosen One himself. But he'd never left his tower before, and the papers and best-selling books he ordered seemed to suggest that life happened on the other side of the doorstep and that said life generally involved a lot of getting robbed and killed. One of the lovely things about being the Dark Lord was that one could choose to stay at home, masterminding various dark deeds from the comfort of one's own armchair. Even if one always felt a bit left out and couldn't quite manage the right sort of crackers. Home had been good enough for his father, and home would be good enough for Toby.

The Chosen One was, for the moment, out of his hands.

But maybe the hedgehog could still be coaxed.

4.

AT A TIME AND PLACE WHERE A GOAT PROVES TO BE REMARKABLY PRESCIENT

One of the many downsides to chain-mail bikinis, Fia thought, was their utter uselessness as protective gear against a tower of thorns. To be sure, they were utterly useless as protective gear against most things, including inclement weather, and this blasted gloomy northern province had been rainy and cold for days. Her skin had developed long-standing goose bumps the size of angry pimples. But her purse was more than unusually light as she'd put down a significant sum with a blacksmith for some real armor, and whatever she found in this tower was going to pay off the balance of it. Fia had recently ventured north and west from the warm eastern lands to seek her fortune, and her dark brown skin, impressive height, and ability to pound xenophobes to pulp had already become legendary. She'd even gotten a hot tip from a shady halfling in the capital that most everyone inside this castle was asleep. It was ripe for the picking.

Fia had challenged him on that point. "If it's so ripe, why hasn't it been picked already by someone else?"

The halfling ordered another pint on her tab before answering, but he didn't dodge the question. He leaned over the table at the inn, his foul breath making Fia curl her lip in disgust, and for the first time that evening looked her in the eye. "I'll walk you through it, my tall drink of mead. Most people do not appreciate the extent to which thorns truly suck. If you have just a single rosebush to deal with, then they're no big deal. You just go around, right? But the entire tower is covered in thick vines—heck, the entire castle is—and each vine bristles with thorns that can only be described as deluxe, and you have to climb the tower to gain access through a window. The door is impregnable. Invisible, actually. No one can find it."

Ignoring the paradox of an architect who forgot to include such essentials as doors in his designs, Fia adjusted her chain-mail wedgie and said, "I don't see the problem. Bushes and vines are flammable."

"True enough! That's no lie. But if you start a fire, you're asking for other trouble. You lose all hope of stealth, for one thing. You might wind up burning down the stuff inside you want to steal, and besides that, fire always brings the neighbors outdoors to see if they can help put it out. You don't want witnesses, now, do you? And there's evidence that not everything sleeps inside that tower. There's someone—or something—most certainly, definitely, indubitably awake in there, and whoever or whatever it is, they are not afraid to sing horrible songs."

Fia scoffed. "What do I care about songs?"

The halfling grinned. "Oh, these are no mere ditties. The melodies are laced with magic of a most powerful and potent nature. And the singer of said songs *never* sleeps. We have confirmed this through long observation."

"Why don't you just fly to the window on one of those giant eagles or a dragon?"

The halfling's casual amusement vanished, and his voice grew intense. "Do you have access to any creatures willing to perform such services? Because if you do, I assure you we would pay well for an introduction."

"Who's 'we'?"

The halfling waved the question away. "A consortium of like-minded individuals." He looked pleased with himself, as if he'd just learned the word *consortium* the day before and had been waiting for an opportunity to use it.

"Well, no, I don't know any flying creatures, sorry." The halfling deflated, and his eyes drifted down from her face and toward the tiny triangles of her top, perhaps in an effort to cheer himself up. Fia resolutely ignored this, adding, "And I guess you don't know any either. But how about a ladder?"

The halfling picked up his pint, which was nearly the size of his head, and answered with the cup to his lips, making his voice ring hollow: "We've tried that. Three times. We sent out *teams* with ladders. Ropes and grappling hooks, too, before you ask. Real quality stuff. None returned. As I said, these are truly deluxe thorns."

Well, Fia had listened to that halfling, and she had taken what he said to heart. She now wore a pair of rose-repelling metal gauntlets as she stood right at the base of the aforementioned tower in the middle of a ferocious and properly dramatic downpour. The halfling had been willing to lend these so-called deluxe gauntlets to her for an outrageous forty percent of whatever she got out of the tower. He'd first demanded eighty percent, but she'd pointed out that she'd generously allowed him to stare at her chest all night without smashing his brains into pudding, and that should be worth something. To protect her feet, she had wrapped up the soles of her boots in belts of the toughest leather she could find. Now she just had to get past the deluxe thorns in the cold rain while still mostly naked. No big deal, she told herself. Although . . . up close these particular thorns seemed a step up from your average rose thorns in the way that a rabid wolfhound seemed a step up from a pug.

The halfling, against his better nature, had been telling the truth.

The vines had been growing for so long and had wrapped themselves so tightly around the tower that they could serve as a natural ladder, providing a convenient way to climb up—convenient, that is, apart from the thorns. Because there were many smaller, thinner vines flourishing and flowering on top of the thick, trunklike ones, forming a dense thicket of doom. A tricky tangle, Fia thought, for she'd have to reach in there with clever fingers. A most wily thatch concealing the tender flower she so desired.

And to think: she was doing all this for a single rose.

As it turned out, the two things Fia most wanted in the world were armor and peace. If everything went according to plan, the heart rose of this enchanted tower would give her both, thanks to a generous prize to be awarded at the celebrated Pell Smells Rose Show. With the heavily perfumed bag of gold in hand, she'd be unstoppable. Or more stoppable, actually, as she would finally be able to stop fighting and settle down. A prizewinning rose garden in a quiet hamlet where nobody knew her past, and the ability to defend said garden from anyone who wanted to take it from her: that was Fia's idea of earthly paradise.

But first she had to get inside.

She noted a small collection of rusty hatchets at the base of the tower. Not stacked neatly; they looked as if they'd fallen there randomly from the sky, although even in this strange place, it didn't generally rain basic lumberjack supplies. A few frogs here or there, but such was weather. Fia had brought a hatchet, too, expecting to clear away some of the branches, but now she reconsidered, thinking of the halfling teams that had never returned and noting that there were also a few assorted bones mixed in with the hatchets, as well as some rotting pieces of wood that had no doubt, at one time, formed a ladder. Squinting up through the rain, she saw scraps of blue and yellow cloth snagged upon some of the vines, along with a sprinkling of tarnished metal medallions. And there were pale flashes of white caught in the boscage, which proved to be the latticed rib cages of other thieves, forever imprisoned in verdigris and roses. That was not merely gruesome; it was strange.

"If they died while trying to climb up," Fia mused, as she often talked out her problems, "they'd have to fall. Especially if they were on ladders. There's no way a few thorns can hold up that much dead weight. I should be seeing full skeletons down here. So that means the vines had to overgrow them … *while they were still alive.* Trapping them. Hells, that'd have to be a quick-growing bush. But it's not growing now, is it?"

It most certainly was not. At least not visibly so. That meant that something had triggered the rapid and clearly fatal growth. And that something was probably the collection of hatchets at the base of the tower. Hack at the magical vines and they would quickly respond with a thorny embrace, hugging you close until something vital was pierced or you simply bled to death.

Hugs shouldn't hurt, mighty Fia thought. Much less kill you.

Fia added her hatchet to the pile but kept her sword lashed to her back in its leather scabbard. She also had some pocket shears hanging from a belt in case things got snippy. Reaching out one steel gauntlet toward the thicket, she laid hold of a thick rope of vine and heard the dull click of a thorn snapping beneath her hand. She paused, grimacing, waiting for the vine to strike like a snake, but the vine just did what normal vines do, which is not much. And that was good.

She looked down, seeing that there was still a smidgen of space between her body and the mass of thorns. Such was the benefit of being seven feet tall with an impressive reach, and such was the supportive power of chain mail. She grinned in the rain and took a deep breath of the rosewater air. The blossoms beyond the vines must truly be remarkable.

Fia had neglected to tell the halfling that she wasn't there for gold or kisses or the usual booty. No, all Fia wanted was that heart rose. With her large green thumb, she could create a hybrid that didn't want to murder everyone but still promised bright blooms and strong stems. Unfortunately, a small clipping from the tangle simply wouldn't do; no, she needed the heart rose, which was almost certainly inside. And she'd happily suffer some scratches to get it. The leering halfling scum could have forty percent of her cuttings if he wanted; he wouldn't know what to do with them. Fia, though, would turn those cuttings into profit. And turn that profit into a snug little house to come home to, surrounded by sensible fortifications and prizewinning roses. Any scars she earned in the process she'd wear with pride. Wenches, after all, dug scars.

Best be about it. She couldn't maintain her distance while she climbed, so she would necessarily need to hug the wall a bit during her ascent and get stabbed and scratched. She could mitigate that, though, by sucking in her belly and carefully collecting and pushing thorny branches back to the wall with her metal gauntlets as she searched for a new handhold.

Purposely beginning to one side of the window so she wouldn't have to climb over halfling remains dripping with cheap jewelry, Fia grunted and cursed as she slowly worked her way up the tower, her leather-wrapped boots finding protected toeholds among the vines but the rest of her getting finely shredded. The pain gave her a boost of energy on top of her already formidable strength, and she found the rain refreshing instead of oppressive. She wasn't getting tired; she could take her time.

Once she'd cleared the topmost collection of halfling remains—perhaps only a third of the way up—Fia shifted over so that she was directly underneath the window. Only then did she notice a couple of things that had not been obvious from the ground.

For one thing, the thickness of the vines diminished considerably as they climbed the tower. They wouldn't be able to bear her weight much longer and probably would snap or break off in her gauntlet. Fia imagined that if that were to happen, it would be no different from taking a hatchet to the plant: it would respond with prickly, deadly force.

But she spied a potential solution to that problem just a few feet above: a frayed, braided rope dangling down from the window, hidden beneath the leaves and blossoms and thorns, invisible until now. If it was fastened securely to the interior, she'd be able to use that to climb up the rest of the way.

A few more careful minutes and it was in her grasp. She held on firmly to a thick vine with one hand and tested the rope with the other. It had some give to it, but only a few inches, and then it was solid. She pulled hard, and it didn't budge. Excellent.

Fia grinned into the rain and said, "Oh, yes, my lovely magic roses, you will be mine!" Grabbing on to the rope with both hands, she braced her feet against the wall and started to walk up. The rope pulled away from the tower reluctantly, entwined with vines here and there, and in some cases Fia saw fibers get torn away by thorns. They didn't behave like proper rope fibers, though. They were much finer than any rope she'd ever seen before. And now that she looked at it closer, the braid didn't really look like a standard rope twist or even smell like a rope should. It smelled like scented soap, like—

"Hair! Oh! Ick!"

Fia's hands jerked open in revulsion. A split second later, she realized quite literally the gravity of her mistake. She fell from the tower, thinking this was going to be a stupid way to die, and commenced to plummeting. She was just expecting an explosion of pain when she landed on something that wasn't the ground and that made several disturbing noises all at once: a cry of pain, the dull pop of bones breaking, the tinkle of shattered glass, and the squelch of blood spurting from torn flesh.

"Gah! You killed Pooboy!" a man's voice exclaimed. "I mean Worstley!"

"What?" Fia rolled off of whatever had broken her fall and discovered that she had broken a pale and rather malnourished young man, together with a jar of pickled herring he must have been carrying. His eyes stared unblinking into the rain, and the sharp edges of snapped bones stuck out of his ruptured skin here and there. "Oh, no. I'm sorry!" she said to him, and then spoke to whoever she'd heard speak earlier. "Maybe he'll pull through."

"I don't think so. That was wild, though! One second he's talking about the treasure he's going to find in that tower, and the next, POW! I told him the world was going to crush him, but I didn't think it would happen exactly like that, you know?"

Fia turned toward the man's voice for the first time as he finished the sentence and realized it wasn't a man speaking at all. "Gah! You're a talking billy goat!"

"Yeah, but never mind that." The sodden goat craned his neck up at the sky. "It's raining humans around here! Used to be you only had to worry about lightning, but now you can get struck by women! I didn't realize the weather would be so severe once we left the farm. What do you call this kind of storm? Is it a hurricane? But actually, like, a her-icane? I understand now why people speak of them with such dread, because they're obviously deadly."

"What? No. It's not weather. I just fell from the tower. Don't you even care about your friend here?"

"Who? Worstley? I wouldn't say he was a friend. His mother was going to eat me, you know, which means he would have eaten me, too, when she called him in to dinner, and once somebody confesses they have plans to eat you, it tends to dissolve any emotional bonds you may have had. You're not going to eat me, are you?"

"No. I'm a vegetarian. I don't eat things with faces."

"What about when you have two eggs and a piece of melon for a smile, and it kind of . . . ?"

"Ew. No. Eggs are just faces that haven't learned to smile yet."

"But you're okay with leather?"

She glared at him. "Leather doesn't have a face."

"Ah. Okay. Well. I'm sure we'll get along fine, then. My name's Gustave."

"I'm Fia."

"Nice to meet you, Fia. I notice you have a whole lot of extra leather wrapped around your boots. You don't really need all that, do you? Because I'm hungry." Gustave drooled a little, his yellow goat eyes going all dreamy.

Fia studied her scratched-up leathers and itty-bitty metal bikini. "Well, I do need it, actually. I have to get back up that tower."

"The one you just fell from? Look, you seem nice for a human, but I'm not going to stand underneath you to break your next fall, okay?"

"No, I mean there might be a way to save Worstley."

"That's fascinating, because to my eyes he appears beyond saving."

"Well, maybe not. There's magic up in that tower."

Gustave gave a very goatish snort. "More magic. How do you know?"

"You can't see it, but there's a rope of living hair dangling out of that window. And that means it's attached to someone. Someone who didn't wake up and scream when I yanked on it. Which means someone up there is frozen in time. Suspended until the spell is broken. I've heard this place is under an enchantment. So if I take Worstley up there with me, maybe he'll be suspended, too, until we can get help."

"Help to bury him or . . . ?"

"Help to revive him! Heal him. Fix him somehow! I don't want his blood on my conscience. I feel terrible."

And she did. The whole reason she'd left home and traveled to Borix was to bring an end to the violence that had plagued her entire existence. When you're taller and more muscular than all the men in any room, you tend to get into a lot of fights. Although Fia preferred peace, she'd made her first kill . . . well, accidentally. And her second also accidentally, just trying to defend herself from some knuckle dragger who'd been ogling her body. She had slain quite a few more people accidentally, but no one wanted to believe they were accidents. She couldn't physically shrink or escape her growing reputation for violence at home, so she'd fled to the west, hoping to find some isolated spot where she could live unmolested and far away from potential victims. But now, out here, alone, she'd still managed to accidentally kill a guy, and without even drawing her sword.

"Look, you might feel terrible," the goat said, sounding very reasonable for a goat, "but Worstley doesn't or he'd be complaining, believe me. So you don't have to worry about it."

"Yes, I do. I have enough guilt and can't live with any more. I have to try."

Rising to her feet and wincing at some new aches—she'd definitely bruise up—she took the opportunity to stretch and work out some tightness in her muscles. The rain obligingly slowed to a drizzle.

"Dang. You're the tallest human I've ever seen. Are other humans usually afraid of you?"

Fia eyed him suspiciously, waiting for the tall joke. "It tends to manifest itself in different ways, but . . . yes."

"Good. Can I tag along with you, then, and have you fall on anyone who wants to eat me?"

Fia snorted. "Sounds like a lot of work. What's in it for me?"

"Well, you get to walk around with a talking goat, which means you're distinguished at the very least, but more likely venerable and maybe even illustrious."

"I don't need that. People already respect me. Or at least they respect my ability to administer pain." She grimaced. "Eventually."

"Right. Negotiation! That's great. You do what you need to do up in the tower and I'll wait here and think up something to sweeten the deal."

"You don't want to . . . say goodbye to your friend?"

The goat rolled his eyes and coughed, resigned to at least pretending to be polite. "Goodbye, Pooboy. Your shirts tasted pretty good. Sorry your destiny didn't work out. Hey, wait a minute." Nudging Worstley with his nose, Gustave waited a few moments for any response. When none came, he pulled off the boy's poo-covered boots with his teeth and daintily lipped them with a small moan of pure ecstasy.

"You done?" Fia asked. "Because this is getting weird. Can I take the poor boy up to the magic tower now?"

"Sure. You do that. I'll enjoy some private time with his boots. To remember him."

Fia bent down, picked up Worstley, and slung him over her shoulder so that his bottom half was draped across her front. That meant Worstley's backside and legs would shield her from the worst of the thorns. She just hoped the rain-slick vines would hold their combined weight long enough to allow her to get to the hair rope again.

The grunting and cursing as she climbed were louder this time, and she felt her strength drain away with every inch of progress. But she'd done this before and some of the vines were already smooshed flat from her first trip, so it went faster. Once she shifted over to where the hair rope was, she felt the vine in her gauntleted right hand begin to give way. She let go and lunged for the wet golden braid, breath labored now, fully grossed out by the boy bleeding on her and the hair presumably attached to someone's unconscious head. It was hardy stuff, though; the owner clearly had fantastically strong roots and ate a lot of collagen.

Stuffing Worstley's body through the window with one hand while thorns snagged on his clothing and she held on desperately to someone's hair with the other hand was worse than anything Fia had ever done before, and she had once vomited chunks of fried okra while wearing a tightly fitted mask. Her arms trembled with fatigue, and her frustration and guilt welled up and spilled out of her eyes. Fia hadn't really let herself cry since the day her mother had been eaten by a Yilduran shockfrog, but now, in the rain, uncertain if this caper would ever pay off or just leave her scarred if not dead, she wept.

When she was done crying, she managed to lever the rubbery, blood-slicked body of the farm boy over the wide windowsill. His legs ensnared in thorns, she crawled over him and crashed to the floor inside, her eyes scanning the room as she took deep gulps of air. Rolling to her back, she allowed herself one drop of a healing potion, which at least made the many scratches go from red to pink. The healing potion, a cheap brand called NyeQuell, tasted of licorice and unconsciousness, but Fia had to stay awake. There were roses to be plundered, a peaceful future to be secured by force of pruning shears.

The room was surprisingly warm and cozy like a winter blanket despite the cold rain outside and the open window. Fia looked around, wondering if the peculiar scent riding the air was a curse or too much varnish, as the walls and floors were carved of knotted hardwoods that seemed to glow from within. Tapestries covered two

of the walls with scenes of frolicsome unicorns happily disemboweling white men while maidens looked on with ill-concealed delight,
just a few slim fingers failing to cover their wide grins. A promising
sort of door waited on the wall opposite the window, but Fia's attention was caught by a huge poster bed shrouded with thick velvet
curtains. The thick rope of hair was threaded through a hole in the
center of the bed's headboard, but Fia couldn't see the occupant yet.

"Hello?" she called out, but received no answer. Rising to her feet,
she took a few steps forward to see what could be seen, peering
around the corner of the bed. "Oh! Uh. Well, that's different."

Something akin to a young white woman rested on the bed, her
blond hair pulled away from her face and through the hole in the
headboard, head pressed up tightly against it rather than centered
comfortably on the pillow. Fia grimaced; she had been responsible
for that.

The woman was dressed in blue velvet embroidered with gold
knots around the neckline, but she must have been lying there for a
good long while, since her face and neck had sprouted long, fine hairs
that wreathed her face like a lion's mane and also a lion's beard, and
her fingernails had grown past the point of claws into long, curling
monstrosities. Fia briefly considered using her pocket shears to clip
the nails but decided against it. She didn't know, after all, if they had
grown during the woman's long slumber or if she'd been put to sleep
that way. It wasn't Fia's place to judge standards of beauty. Neck-
beards and impractical fingernails might be a mark of extraordinary
hotness in this woman's culture, and Fia wasn't originally from Borix
or anyplace near it.

There was nothing of value in the room unless one counted the
stunning tapestries. No jewelry on the woman, no tantalizing chest
secured with an iron padlock. No large blue key foreshadowing future usefulness. No helpful instructions, either, on how she might be
awakened. But the woman appeared to be glowing with health, and
that was a good thing.

Her mind made up, Fia tugged at Worstley's still form until his pants tore free of the thorns and she could carry him to rest beside the enchanted hairy lady. He looked much worse for the wear, but she told herself that she'd make it right somehow. She'd also make right the ragged cloak she was borrowing from his corpse, because although this particular room was warm, the province as a whole was a little colder than she was accustomed to, especially considering the chain-mail bikini.

Seeing that there was nothing more she could do for him, Fia turned toward the door, ignoring the large wardrobe on one side of the room, which doubtless was full of gowns and other items belonging to the sleeping lady. Fia had no desire to rob the innocently slumbering lady, especially considering that she'd pulled rather hard on her hair just to get into the tower. It was time to leave the sleepers and her guilt behind to find the heart rose.

There had to be something else in this castle worth all this trouble. And it had to smell better than the farm boy's feet.

5.

NEAR A ROSE MOST SCARLET
AND EFFULGENT

"Five years asleep my master's been
And all his mice and all his men
Until the lady wakes and then
The spell shall make everyone else also wake up as well—"

"Potzblitz!" Argabella cried, throwing down her lute, but very softly and onto a pile of cushions, because she was running out of lutes. "You'd think that with five long years to perfect a song, I wouldn't still be hung up on the first stanza. What rhymes with *then*? Sin? Hen? Winter wren?" She huffed through her wiggly pink nose. "All I wanted was to be a boring, respectable accountant and count beans, but no, Father wanted me to go to bard school and be Tuneful. Well, here I am, Father. Are you proud?"

She nudged her father with a fuzzy toe, but he didn't respond. He was asleep, just like everyone else in the tower and castle and, according to her song, the mice. That was pretty convenient when it came to leaving out bits of cake and bread overnight but not at all convenient when you hadn't spoken to another waking creature in several years. Just the other day, Argabella had found herself talking to a candlestick, which didn't seem at all strange until the candlestick talked back and told her to stuff it. She'd thrown the candlestick across the room, where it had bounced off the red nose of the Earl of Borix himself. He hadn't so much as grunted, which was also pretty convenient considering how *off-with-her-headish* and Killful the earl had been when awake.

The thing about curses was that they could be quite Loneful, Argabella thought.

With a heaving sigh, she picked her lute back up and girded her loins, or at least gave a convincing and confident shimmy. "You're going to do it this time, Argy," she said. "You're going to be Tuneful. I can feel it in my ears." She strummed a soft opening chord and begain to sing: *"Five years asleep—what was that?!"*

Argabella went still as a shrew in a hawk's shadow. She'd heard something loud coming from the tower, something that definitely wasn't ensorcelled thorns slowly and madly growing or the candlestick being rude. She stood, her hold on the lute going from *let's have a nice song, then* to *maybe I'll split your skull, Intrudeful Stranger.* Tiptoeing silently, she crept from the throne room, out into the keep and behind a fountain showing buxom mermaids spitting water in a way that seemed much more suggestive now that the fountain had run dry. Ears up and quivering, she focused on the sound.

There! A cloaked figure emerged from the tower onto the parapet that connected it with the rest of the castle, running with acrobatic grace along the stones. A Threatful figure that was most definitely not asleep. A figure that had most likely not come to hear a certain bard's song about nearly permanent narcolepsy.

Edging back into the throne room, Argabella slipped a crossbow from the side of Oxnard, one of the earl's best guards. Argabella had to admit that even asleep, Oxnard had done his duty: no one had assaulted the earl, the countess, or the lady in all this time. Sure, maybe it was the millions of seemingly sentient vines crawling over the castle like nightmare monsters and whispering to Argabella in her sleep. Or maybe it was Oxnard's mighty bulk and ever-ready bow. Which was now in Argabella's altogether more noodly arms. She'd never worked a crossbow before, but there were lots of things happening for the first time today, weren't there? With the entire castle asleep, it was up to her, Argabella the cursed bard, to defend the castle's treasure.

Her watery eyes followed the figure nimbly jogging along the stone, and she immediately knew where this thief, this burglar, this *larcenous villain* was headed. Not toward the castle coffers, deep underground and brimming with dusty gold, and not toward the throne room, where the countess's jewels glistened around her alabaster neck thanks to Argabella's thoughtful quarterly polishing. No, the intruder was headed toward the one room Argabella wouldn't let him breach: the Rose Room.

Darting across the keep, Argabella was careful to keep hidden, skidding behind a slumbering horse here and a wagon there and carefully skirting the frozen, wizened dingus of the old man who'd been preparing to pee on the same patch of mud for many years. As she neared the steps up to the Rose Room, which had once been the countess's sitting room and the site of a rather dastardly curse by a very diabolical but annoyingly glamorous witch, she slowed and checked to see if the arrow was properly positioned in the little clippy thing on the crossbow. It seemed to be, so she pointed it away from herself and took a deep breath, her heart hammering and her buck teeth chattering. She smelled something, a strange stink, not unlike when dogs get their anal glands impacted and start butt scooting all over the cobbles, much to the embarrassment of any area wolves. Whatever was in the queen's room was far more beast than Argabella was, and that was saying quite a lot.

She steeled herself and swung into the doorway.

"Halt, knave!" she cried, but it came out as more of a question.

The cloaked figure looked up from where it crouched over the heart rose, which is what Argabella had named the beautifully glowing flower from which all the poison-green vines grew before multiplying and snaking away in their quest to envelop the castle. With a gasp, the figure withdrew from the rose and unfolded to stand.

And kept unfolding. It was, in fact, a very tall figure.

"I don't wish to hurt you," the figure said in a husky but female voice that promised violence. "But I must have this rose."

Flipping back the hood of her cloak, the figure revealed acres and acres of woman, her clipped black hair nearly brushing the stone ceiling. Her golden eyes, the eyes of a cat, met Argabella's eyes, which were more like the watery eyes of a patchy rabbit that preferred to live in a cage because free-range grass could be scary. Slowly, carefully, the woman knelt and unhooked shears from a belt that didn't fasten around a tunic, hold up a pair of pants, or appear to serve any function except to hold those shears and a bottle opener. She honestly wasn't wearing much under her muddy cloak, and Argabella winced to think of how cold the poor girl must be. As Argabella watched, the woman's thick, callused fingers stroked the velvet petals of the heart rose most scarlet and effulgent, and—

"No! Don't touch it, I said." Argabella swallowed a ball of fear. "Please."

"I will have it."

"Absolutely not!"

"Then fight me."

The intruder's grip on the shears changed subtly, and she brandished them in a decidedly less horticultural and more murderous fashion. Argabella went cold all over as she considered her own brief, failing forays into the realm of violence. She couldn't even properly destroy a lute.

The figure flipped her cloak onto the ground in a cloud of stink, which cleared up one of Argabella's big questions. But her next question was something along the lines of "How do I not get murdered just now?" because the woman began twirling the shears around her branch-sized fingers and growling.

Argabella squeaked, and she might have accidentally hit the switchy thing on the crossbow that made the bolt do the thwacky thing, which it did, with a *thwack*.

She'd barely muttered, "Sorry!" before the intruder rolled smoothly out of the arrow's path and came up with the shears in one hand and a sword in the other. The arrow, for its part, thudded into the countess's favorite dog's favorite ottoman and quivered, shedding its remaining kinetic force.

"I said fight me, not shoot me while I was preparing for battle! You're supposed to wait your turn. There are rules for this sort of thing. Initiative and all that. Or are you a coward?"

"Uh." Argabella's toe claws raked over the stone in embarrassment. "I am a coward, actually, but please, still, don't touch the rose, maybe?"

Argabella blushed and fought tears as the figure looked her up and down, perplexed. This was a new sensation, for no one had seen Argabella since the witch's curse had . . . changed her. She was a beast now, and it spoke to the intruder's fortitude and courage that she hadn't immediately run away screaming. Argabella had been shy and insecure before the curse, but now she felt as if anxiety and nervous twitches ran in her very blood.

"What are you supposed to be?" the intruder asked. "A . . . like a giant bunny?"

"Uh," Argabella said. "Kind of."

Because although she was a beast, she was nothing like a werewolf, a bear, a lion, or even a slightly frightening badger. The castle mirrors had revealed long ago that she looked more like the thin, fidgety woman she'd once been, mixed with a sickly rabbit, all watery eyes and dandelion-puff fur and quivering ears and an adorable if awkward poofy tail. The first time she'd beheld her own visage, she'd growled in rage and attempted to break the mirror glass, but she'd only succeeded in bruising her hairy knuckles. She'd been neither pretty nor ugly before, but now she just looked like she needed to be put out of her misery. The intruder was watching her carefully, still twirling her shears, so Argabella dropped the empty crossbow, and her claws clicked together fretfully.

"My name is Argabella. I'm the court bard. Sort of. And I honestly don't know what will happen if you take the heart rose, but I suspect it will be terrible, considering that the witch who laid this spell sent a postcard saying something to that effect."

"Which witch?"

"Why?"

"Why which witch?"

"I don't see why it matters which witch was the witch which cursed me."

"I know some witches, and I'm curious."

"Grinda the Sand Witch."

The tall intruder shook her head. "Never heard of her."

"She lives to the south at Malefic Beach," Argabella added helpfully, having learned as much from the letters she'd been reading all these years as the postman just kept tossing them through the letter slot in the wall. He never took her letters crying for help, though, merely scrawling "Insufficiente Postage" on each envelope and tossing it right back. She'd run out of stamps ages ago, and he refused to accept gold pieces without proper change.

Argabella had dashed off several strongly written letters to the Postale Service, but the postman predictably refused to deliver complaints about his Jerkful behavior.

"Well, then. Greetings, Argabella the bard. I am Fia, a fighter for hire. And an amateur rosarian." Fia shrugged, looking much less lethal. "I wasn't going to take the whole rose, you know. Can I just take a cutting?"

Argabella collapsed inward like a blancmange, clawed fingers over her eyes. After five years of complete silence, this was all a little much. "I don't know, but I can't stop you, so go on. Go on and kill us all. Over a leggy little species with a slightly crumpled heart."

"Wait," Fia said, rising to her full seven feet of slabby muscle. "You . . . speak flower?"

"Kind of hard not to. Thanks to the curse, I can't wake anyone up, and I can't leave, and I must protect the heart rose until the lady wakes and the spell is broken. So here I am. I've read all the books in the library on flowers, trying to better understand this cultivar, but it's honestly more magical than sensible. Still, I think you'll find, if you look closely, that it's an imperfect specimen."

Fia raised an eyebrow and knelt, making a show of hanging her shears back on her belt. Argabella noticed that they were rather a nice pair of shears and that someone with such well-honed blades probably knew their way around a flower or two. She relaxed a little and stopped with all the claw clacking as Fia inspected the rose and stood again, her brow drawn down.

"You're right. It's not as perfect as it seemed."

"Not much reason to lie. I'm doomed either way."

Fia paced around the room, considering the vines that twined through the windows and doors and pried between bricks and stone flags like a greedy child sticking their fingers in the lattice of a pie. "So why are you . . ."

"Furry?"

"I was going to say 'cursed,' actually."

Argabella shrugged and fetched the countess's watering can, giving the rose just enough water so that she had something to do instead of just standing there being stared at.

"Like I said, I'm the court bard. The countess didn't invite this Grinda the Sand Witch to the lady's sixteenth birthday party, so the witch just popped into the room in a cloud of sand, right when they were cutting the cake."

Fia winced. "Ew. So sand got in the frosting?"

"Exactly. It was awful. And then the witch suggested that she should've been invited to the party, and the countess said that she *had* been invited, and Grinda said that her postman was very forgetful, and the countess sympathized because her postman was also wretched—which is totally true, he's super Rudeful—and so the countess asked the witch why she'd messed up the cake over a simple postal mishap, and Grinda said the cake wasn't the point, and . . . honestly, I'm surprised they didn't start pulling each other's hair. In the end, the postman somehow never got fired but the lady was put under a spell. The witch said that one day the lady would prick her finger on a rose thorn, and then she'd fall into an enchanted sleep until awakened by true love's kiss. So the countess and the earl ordered everyone to destroy all the roses in Borix. But some absolute fool who'd been out of town during the party gave the princess a single rose they found lying about on the ground in the keep."

Even though she was fighting the tears, they welled up, and Argabella started to snivel as her claws scratched the stone.

Fia shook her head sympathetically. "It was you, wasn't it? With the rose?"

Argabella fell to her knees, pulling her long ears and moaning. "Yes! But she was always so kind to me and said my songs might actually be not terrible one day, and I'd been away at bard school, and I didn't know! Nobody meets you at the door on your way home to do laundry and tells you roses are suddenly public enemy number one! It was just lying there!"

"So you gave her a rose . . ."

"You can guess the rest. There was a thorn, then a bead of blood, and then she just fell over asleep. As did everyone else, exactly where they were. I picked up the rose and ran to bring it to the countess and tell her the lady had some sort of rose allergy or clotting disease, but her room here was empty. Everyone was in the throne room to celebrate the destruction of every rose in the kingdom. The flower fell from my hands, right here, and it put down roots and spread, and here it's been ever since."

"So the fur . . . ?"

"Nobody told me that part, either! The witch sent me a brief postcard beginning with, 'Welcome to being a scapegoat!' and warning me of the terms of my curse, but everything else I pieced together by reading everyone's mail! Even though that's illegal! The curse has marked me a beast, a lady killer, a mail thief, a castle ruiner, a bad bard, a very very very bad bard—"

Fia caught Argabella's hands before she could shred her own long ears with her claws.

"Hey, now. It's not your fault. Nobody accidentally curses a lady for fun."

"Except witches."

"Well, yes. Except them. But look at the bright side. You have this amazing rose!"

Argabella snorted. "It's not the nicest one I've seen, anyway. Toby the Dark Lord has much nicer roses, and he's been able to breed some amazing hybrids, but he's never shown them because he doesn't leave his tower."

"Toby? The Dark Lord?"

"Oh, well, he's not that dark. He's really quite nice. I call him the Crepuscular Lord, and he's never even hit me with lightning for doing so. His tower is halfway to the bard school, and I often stopped to bring him bits of mail that had accidentally been sent to the castle instead. And cheese. He's very fond of cheese. I hope he's still alive and not cursed." Argabella blinked back yet more tears. "I don't know how far the curse goes. I haven't seen anyone I like in five years. Haven't had a bit of cheese for most of that time because I ate that first. I wish I were asleep like everybody else." Clattering across the room, she threw herself dramatically on the countess's divan.

"So let's go see him."

"See who?"

"Whom."

"Bless you. But really, who?"

"This Crepuscular Lord with the cheese and the roses. I need a rose to take to the annual Pell Smells Rose Show so I can reimburse this halfling, and I've already paid the entrance fee because I was counting on this rose, and . . . never mind. Let's just go. This place is pretty creepy. I think I can actually hear the thorns growing."

"Wait until they start whispering."

"Never mind that." Fia's face lit up. "Because if this Toby is a real wizard, maybe he can wake up . . . your sleeping hairy lady. And this boy, Worstley, who is also currently sleeping in her tower."

"There's a boy in the tower?" Argabella perked up, hopeful. "A boy who might wake the lady with true love's kiss?"

"Yes, but he's mostly dead."

Argabella deflated again. "But I'm not supposed to leave, so I can't take you to see the Dark Lord. I must guard the rose."

"Or else what?"

"Or else I don't know, but it could be bad."

Fia knelt in front of the divan and gave Argabella a sad but beautiful smile. "Can it possibly be worse than being stuck alone in a creepy tower with a bunch of sleeping people and absolutely no cheese?"

Argabella's heart lifted. Something about Fia emboldened her. Made her dream again of a world of cheese and properly delivered mail and songs that just naturally happened and didn't require weeks of work and headaches and calluses. She suddenly realized what would rhyme perfectly with *then: Again*. Also *Sven* and *glen*, but that wasn't as useful.

"It probably can't get worse than that, no."

"So let's go."

"Should I bring my lute?" Argabella asked with some trepidation, for her father had always warned her that no worthy adventurer left home without a bard to herald her path.

Fia considered, hand on her chin. "Do your songs wake bravery in the hearts of heroes, heal wounds of the flesh, and help strength bloom in the souls of the weary?"

Argabella jumped up, now filled with nervous energy and a strange feeling that she soon recognized as hope. She hadn't felt hope in a long time.

"No, not really. Not yet. That's more graduate-level stuff. My songs are mostly about roses and dairy products and sleeping people."

"We can work on it," Fia said. "Now come on."

Together, they retrieved Argabella's nicest unsmashed lute and hurried up the steps to the lady's tower. Argabella did her best to tamp down her guilt and instead tried to take some pride in the lovely set-up she'd created so the Lady wasn't slowly suffocated in her tangling hair. She showed Fia the lady's closet full of lovely thick cloaks that didn't smell like goat dung, and they each selected something warm for the road. Argabella looked upon Worstley and agreed that he was indeed rather dead and would pose no threat to the lady and the heart rose as he was. And then Argabella climbed onto Fia's broad but feminine back and clung to her as the mighty fighter climbed down a braid of the lady's magically preserved hair. It was a very intimate sort of feeling that woke new sensations in the bard, but the fact that they were both yelping with pain as thorns shredded their flesh kept some of the awkwardness at bay.

At the bottom of the tower, scratched and torn but exhilarated by the upcoming adventure, Argabella leapt to the ground amid a puddle of thorn-scratch blood and old halfling bones and laughed a mad laugh.

"What's so funny?" Fia asked.

"I'm out of the castle, and nothing horrible is happening. The thorns aren't reaching for me, and the halfling bones aren't turning into angry skeletons to haunt me. I'm not even becoming more rabbity! I'm out! I'm free! And I'm apparently hallucinating a goat. A bedraggled and bony billy goat."

"My name is Gustave," the goat said. "And honestly, you're not one to go insulting people's looks."

Argabella skittered behind Fia, terrified and trembling, but Fia just sighed.

"Goat, why are you still here?"

"Again, it's Gustave, and I've been napping and eating old halfling boots and pooping little halfling boot poops. But now that you're back, I still think I'll go with you."

"But you don't know where we're going," Fia said, sounding altogether more annoyed than she'd sounded with Argabella, Argabella noticed.

"Does it really matter? I'm a goat on the move, and I might as well go with someone more likely to protect me than eat me. Besides, I'd make a great spy for whatever sort of adventure you're on."

"How can a goat be a spy?" Argabella asked.

The goat looked her up and down as if assessing the nutritional value of her clothing. "People always suspect goats might have eaten almost anything they can't find at the moment, but they never expect goats to be listening in on their conversations. They reveal their most horrid secrets. And now I can tell them to you."

"Oh, I like him," Argabella said.

"You've been locked in a castle for five years. You'd probably like anybody," Fia said, but not unkindly.

It was probably true. But Argabella wasn't about to argue with someone brave enough to walk around in a chain-mail bikini.

6.

In the Darkness Surrounding a Small Camp in a Verdant Pasture

Poltro dismounted from Snowflake some distance away from the flickering campfire and patted her stallion's ebony flanks with affection, picketing him for a little gourmet grazing in this fine pasture. It smelled fresh and clean and safe, and it was all of those things, Poltro thought . . . at least until she arrived, the dangerous huntress of the dark nighty night. (Or was it supposed to be *knighty* night with a silent *k*? She was never sure except that she would sure like to make homophones illegal and lock up the person who thought silent *k*s were a good idea in a dungeon most dank and stank. She would tie him up in *nots* with an *n* instead of *knots* with a *k*, because he would *not* be getting away.)

Poltro allowed herself a grin as she threw the hood of her cloak over her head. It had stopped raining, but the clouds still obscured the stars and moon. Nobody would see a black stallion in such a profound absence of light, and she could infiltrate the camp ahead in complete stealth and stealthily purloin information like a gopher smuggling ale into subterranean oblivion.

Wait, should that have been kale? No. Again, this *k* was silent.

Her footsteps made only the barest whisper in the grasses, like the secrets of caterpillars. The turf under her boots was soft and springy like the jiggly bellies of middle-aged men. Her mental prose was as purple as a very purple thing. She advanced on the camp, cloaked by her actual cloak of mystery and menace but also by the night, two cloaks that cloaked great together, providing her near invisibility, an impenetrable fog of stealthy stealth as she—

"Hey there," a man's voice said, and Poltro froze. He couldn't be talking to her. She was a shadow in the darkest pit, unknowable to any—

"Yeah, you. The one skulking around in the cloak and hood. What're you looking for?"

Poltro flailed in surprise, took two steps back, and stumbled over a tiny tricksy pebble, one that had obviously lain in wait to ambush her in a moment of vulnerability. Pebbles were like that, always tripping her up, even worse than chickens sometimes.

"Gah! What?" she said. She couldn't see who was talking. Was it a god or some restless spirit of the night?

"You're clearly looking for something," the voice said. "Did you lose a coin purse, maybe, made of stitched and oiled leather, utilitarian yet delicious?"

Poltro scrambled to her feet, stepped on her cloak, and fell down again. "No," she said, her breath coming fast as she peered into the darkness for the speaker. All she could see was the fire some distance away. She put a hand over her heart and tried to will herself to relax, to slow down, buy some time. "I'm looking for a farm boy. People around these parts are calling him the Chosen One."

"What do you want with him?"

"Oh, well, not to kill him, ha ha!" she said as she fumbled at her waist for her dagger. "Certainly not that."

"Too bad. I could have made you happy there. Because he's dead already."

Poltro froze again. "The Chosen One . . . is dead?"

"I know, it sounds impossible, right? The evidence suggests someone made an astoundingly poor chosening. Say, do you really need that cloak? Seems like it just gets in your way."

"Why, do you need a cloak?"

"I could use it, sure. This grass is a bit rich for my blood, and I like high-fiber foods."

"Pardon me?" The conversation had turned so sharply around a corner of strangeness that Poltro couldn't follow where it had gone. Nor could she see who was talking. "Who are you? Where are you?"

"My name's Gustave," the voice replied. "Come on, let's head over to the fire. I'll introduce you to the others and you'll be able to see."

Gathering her cloak carefully from underneath her feet this time, Poltro succeeded in standing up and locating her dagger. She didn't pull it out, but she kept her hand on the hilt the way she'd learned from Cutter, although he had mostly just advised her to run away and say the target had gone underground while gazing into the distance, her eyes narrowed and haunted. With her cloak balled up in one fist and her dagger's handle in the other, she'd be ready for trouble if this Gustave fellow intended to give her any—or if his secretive and sneaky friends did.

"Who's over at the fire?" she asked.

"An unusually tall human and a sort of rabbit thing."

Poltro thought it odd that the man specified there was a human there but ignored that bit to ask, "A rabbit thing?"

"Once you get used to the twitching nose, she's not so bad." Gustave's disembodied voice rose as he called out: "Hey, Fia! Argabella! I found someone out here who's looking for Worstley!"

Two silhouettes stepped out of the dark to stand in front of the fire, and one of them was indeed unusually tall, as was her unusually tall sword. The other was thin with fluffy rabbits' feet and whiskers and some long ears drooping down from the top of her head.

"Who is it?" the tall one asked.

"Oh, some human lady with the kind of cloak that would ruin your diet."

"My name is Poltro," the rogue called ahead, her voice crisp and confident in the night. But that confidence didn't stick around; it migrated south in search of sunlight after she got close enough to see who she was dealing with.

"Well met, Poltro. I am Fia the Mighty, and this is Argabella, the bard."

"Almost bard. Still two credits short," Argabella mumbled.

Fia the Mighty was a wall of muscle barely restrained by a chain-mail bikini, the firelight lending bronze highlights to her dark brown skin. Poltro noted that she had a sword *and* a high-quality pair of shears and what appeared to be a truly wicked bottle opener. Deadly things, bottle openers. Poltro let her hand fall to her side lest Fia think she was going to pull that dagger.

The other person, Argabella, displayed a hybrid of human and rabbity features that Poltro thought the Dark Lord Toby would appreciate, since he was so interested in crossbreeding animals. She had no visible weapons, but Poltro thought her claws might be nasty up close, and her chattering teeth could probably crunch through bones. Argabella didn't appear to favor violence, however. She looked terrified, which was gratifying. Then again, she looked like looking terrified was her default. Must've been the rabbit blood.

The owner of the rich male voice turned out to be a black billy goat with a coat as dark as Snowflake's—no wonder she couldn't see him in the night! And she realized that Gustave must be the talking goat that Lord Toby had told her about. The goat she was allowed to eat if she completed her mission. He licked his goat lips and stared at the hem of her cloak, obviously imagining how it would taste. That was okay; she was imagining him in a stew pot brimming with spices from Thyme Island. But business would have to be concluded before dinner.

"Great to meet you all. So!" Poltro clapped her hands together and kept them clasped. "This Chosen One. What happened to him?" She saw a flash of shame in Fia's expression before the fearsome fighter turned hostile.

"Why do you care?"

"Well, I'm told that Chosen Ones tend to have quite a bit of magic about them. Lots of folks are interested in that."

Fia snorted. "He had no magic ability whatsoever, I assure you."

"Well, what about his heart?"

"What about it?"

Poltro didn't think it would be wise to ask her if it was magic, so she said, "Do you know where it is?"

Fia's reply dripped with scorn. "Inside his rib cage, of course."

"Do you think he's still using it?" The fire popped and hissed, and Poltro felt the weight of three heavy stares and an awful silence. "I mean, being dead and all, he's probably a bit disappointed with it, or he would be if he could feel disappointment anymore, and so he wouldn't mind if someone borrowed it for a while, if he was able to mind anything, that is."

"Borrow it?" Gustave said. "You want to *borrow* his heart? Cut it out of his body and return it later?"

"No, no, you're right," Poltro admitted, realizing her mistake and relieved that they were simply concerned with semantics. "He probably wouldn't be a stickler about me returning it. What are deadlines to a dead guy, am I right?"

Poltro was pretty sure she was right, but another uncomfortable staring session stretched on and she couldn't think of what to say to make it stop. Just as she was going to deliver a prosaic compliment to Argabella on the length and utility of her whiskers, Fia spoke in a flat voice.

"You can't have his heart," she said. "He's going to be needing it later on."

"For what?"

"For beating, of course."

"He's going to beat his heart?"

"No," Fia said through clenched teeth, "his heart is going to beat and he'll be alive again."

"Oh! Oh, I see now. Yeah. That'll be great, no doubt. But that sort of thing—returning to actual life—that's, uh, kind of rare, isn't it?"

"We're going to find a wizard to make it happen."

"That's right!" Argabella chimed in for the first time. "We're going to see the Crepuscular Lord, Toby."

"You mean the Dark Lord?"

"Right. He might be able to help."

Poltro did some quick calculating and broke into a smile. "He probably can! You know, I just came from his tower! I work for him. I can take you there if you like—I know the shortest route."

"You work for him?" Fia frowned. "So he's the one who wants the heart of the farm boy?"

"Not if he's still alive!" Poltro hastened to reassure them. "I'm no expert on manners, but I'm pretty sure that would be rude, and Lord Toby's very polite. It's just that his heart might be worth something, magically speaking, if the poor boy doesn't need it anymore. One man's garbage heart is another man's treasure, right? But things are different now. I'm sure you can work out something with Lord Toby."

For Poltro was quite certain that if there were three things in all the world her master could appreciate, they were a magically talking goat, a cursed rabbit woman, and news of where the Chosen One's unbeating heart might be quietly doing nothing of use.

"Great. Let's go," Fia said.

"Now?" Argabella's whiskers drooped. "But we just got here. I was going to forage for lettuces."

"We don't have time to waste. What's your name again, rogue?"

Poltro beamed. A proper recognition of her skills, that was. Professional courtesy. "You can call me Poltro."

"Well met, Poltro," Fia said, and kicked dirt onto the fire. "Lead the way."

"Oh." The rogue turned in a circle, uncertain.

"What's the matter?"

"Well, it's mighty dark out here, isn't it? I can't find my horse."

7.

Over Something Fried in Duck Fat with a Piquant Dipping Sauce

Gustave swiftly found Snowflake, for not only did beasts have an uncanny need to smell one another's bums, but the horse was positively riddled with bits of dangly leather.

"Is he being eaten by a blanket?" Argabella asked.

"A proper huntsman requires a proper costume and kit," Poltro explained. "The Dark Lord says that makes it more legal."

Fia squinted at the accoutrements doubtfully. "It looks like he's being ridden by a jellyfish."

The goat made lip-smacking noises. "It looks delicious."

Gustave sidled up to the stallion and delicately reached for a bit of saddle ornamentation. From Snowflake's point of view, he was being attacked in the night by a coven of monstrous beasts intent on lipping at his pendulous bits. In the way of stallions and cowards everywhere, he squealed, spun, and galloped away, taking his decorative blanket and ornamental trimmings with him.

"Cor," Poltro shouted. "He's got all my food—that I totally forgot to bring with me, dang it!—plus my weapons and that special box the Dark Lord gave me for . . ." She trailed off. "Um, fresh herbs."

Argabella perked up. "Fresh herbs?"

Poltro nodded, in no way lying now. "Oh, yes. Lord Toby adores fresh herbs. He makes the loveliest rosemary butter, and then he uses a sort of squeezy bag to make butter stars on these things that are almost crackers."

Fia looked around. The first flickers of dawn shone pink at the edge of the forest. She put her mighty hands on her goose-pimpled hips. "It is nearly morning. Perhaps we should venture forth to see this Dark Lord."

"We kind of already were," Gustave said after swallowing the tiny bit of leather he'd nibbled from Snowflake's harnessing. "That's why we're standing and sort of headed in that direction over there."

Fia's brow rumpled. "I was just making it official. Four people stumbling about in the forest means someone has to take the first steps. And I say they go that way." She pointed at the rising sun.

"Well, Toby's demesne is more that way." Poltro pointed a bit to the right.

"To the east?"

"No, to the right. And down a little."

Nodding wisely, Fia shielded her eyes with her hand. "Then that is where we go." She lifted her boat-sized foot to take a step.

Gus sighed heavily. "Yes, we're trying to, but you keep stopping us to make pronouncements."

"Um," Argabella said hopefully, "perhaps we should make sure the fire is totally extinguished first? And fetch our bags?"

"That," Fia said loftily, "is what I was going to say next."

"Good gravy," Gustave muttered. "People." He wasn't sure that being able to talk to them now was an improvement. They didn't seem to want to hear anything he had to say, and being understood and ignored was little better than bleating incomprehensibly and being dismissed as a dumb animal. In fact, he was beginning to suspect it might be worse.

With Poltro in tow, they hurried back to their campsite. Fia stamped out the last few stubborn smoldering coals while Argabella collected the makeshift bag she'd fashioned from her fine cloak, which was now full of the carrots, vegetables, and herbs she'd rummaged for along the way. Fia had appeared frustrated with her at first, stopping all the time when they were clearly on a schedule to revivify the farm boy before he got even deader. But every time Argabella froze, sensitive nose twitching, and threw her arms out as if to halt the world in midsentence, she seemed to find some sort of gastrodelectable gold. Leeks and ramps and sunchokes and rutabagas and . . . well, Fia didn't complain anymore except when they found Gustave innocently sidling toward the stored veggies, drooling a little. The humans seemed quite capable of hiding their desires, but he had not yet gained such powers.

While Fia and Argabella broke down the campsite, Poltro did her part by protecting them from rogue chickens and other dire threats, or at least holding out her dagger and hopping around a bit. Gustave flopped down on his callused knees, closed his slitted eyes, and took a quick nap as green foam oozed out the side of his mouth. Soon the sun was completely up, and the entire group was ready.

"It is time—"

Gustave interrupted Fia's next pronouncement with a sneeze as he wobbled to his hooves, shaking his shaggy head. "I was dreaming of cake," he said. "Nasty dream. Wretched stuff. It had sprinkles. That bit of leather must not've agreed with me."

"—to go."

They walked all morning, discussing mainly the weather, which everyone agreed was nice, and the current political state, which no one knew anything about but on which topic everyone had much to say. Around lunch, Poltro pointed out a pitch-black tower rising into the sunny blue sky.

"That's the Dark Lord's demesne," Poltro said with great seriousness.

"Why do you keep saying that? What's a dem-ez-nee?" Gustave asked.

"It means his territory, the land attached to his tower thingy," Poltro explained, bending down to help make Gustave feel that they were on the same side and that she had many valuable things to teach him.

"It's pronounced 'do-main,' and you're an idiot," the goat said, then coughed up some cud and chewed on it, rolling his eyes.

Poltro stood straight and pointed at the goat with a shrug that said, *Can you believe this ungulate?*

"He's right, I think," Fia said. "I've always heard 'domain,' sure enough."

"Those scribes do love their extra *S*s," Argabella added. "The castle scribe back home spelled Argabella with three of them. Looked very pretty but sounded like a cat with a hairball."

They hadn't stopped walking all through this exchange until Poltro froze suddenly to sniff the air, taking in a deep lungful. Her stomach made noises like growling dogs. Gustave took a whiff and caught something savory and oily that was making the rogue's stomach grumble.

"The Dark Lord's domain," she said, nose tilted up to catch the breeze, "is up ahead. And you're in luck, as it smells like Lord Toby is throwing one of his grand luncheons."

"A grand luncheon?" Fia said, catching up to her in a few strides. "So there will be others there? Strangers? High society?"

"He's not the most sociable sort, our Dark Lord, but it's possible he might have some turtlehogs at the table," Poltro admitted.

"I don't have anything fancy to wear," Fia said. "Think I can get away with just closing the cloak?" She pulled said cloak around her body and buttoned it down the front. She was so tall and broad that she somewhat resembled a velvet-wrapped armoire, and Gustave briefly considered calling her Chester Drawers for a laugh but then remembered he kind of needed Fia to be on his side so as not to wind up as part of somebody's grand luncheon.

"Wardrobe shouldn't be a problem," the rogue said.

As Poltro led them along, they soon found neatly kept cobbles under their feet and hooves, respectively, leading them down a hill toward the dark tower of Toby, its black stones glistening in the morning sun as it stood proudly, surrounded by well-trimmed ornamental shrubbery and several circular stone walls. Fia's earlier nervousness subsided immediately after she spotted a rose garden inside the outer wall. She turned to Argabella to share her excitement, murmuring, "Those roses!"

But she found the rabbit woman's eyes wide and soft with wonder as she beheld the inner walled garden planted in neat rows of green plants bursting with life, the scent of flowers and rich black loam floating on the air.

"Those vegetables! I'd noticed them before, but now that I'm . . . different . . . oh, they smell wonderful!"

"There's leather down there, too," Gustave assured them. "And a nice pile of rotted melons."

"And chickens," Poltro growled. "Of an indeterminate amount. 'Tis a dismal day indeed."

"So is this Dark Lord going to mind us being here?" Fia asked, self-consciously pulling the cloak more carefully about her.

"Nah." Argabella was almost skipping a little. "I told you—he's very nice. Takes him a while to get to the door, but as long as you bring him something useful, he's generally glad for the company."

"Beware, though. The Dark Lord," Poltro intoned, "does not suffer fools gladly."

"But he suffers foods just fine. And he's going to like the young asparagus I picked this morning. His always turns out a bit woody. I only wish we could've found some cheese."

Poltro sighed and deflated a little. "I had some gold tied to my saddle. For food like that. But my nightmare steed is gone, vanished in the—oh. Wait. There he is. Good pony!" Snowflake waited patiently by the gate as if he were accustomed to having it opened for him by the local pooboy so that he might crunch upon his morning grain, a sentiment Gustave deeply understood. Poltro soon had the bag of gold off the saddle and the gate opened, although it was a bit dicey, what with Gustave trying to eat the saddle again and the chickens pecking at Poltro's breeches for their own breakfast. The huntress eventually untangled herself from the reins, gates, and chickens but did require some help.

Now armed with gold, the group ventured into the nearby town of Dower, just a terrifyingly dark and poisonous wood away, where Argabella sniffed out the best cheese shop and crafted a gift basket of fragrant cheeses, dainty grapes, and the artisanal crackers she said Toby enjoyed most. Finally they stood on the doorstep of the tower, a respectful foot back from the Unwelcome mat, which Poltro claimed was a trapdoor to untold evil and/or the jam cellar. Before they could knock, a postman appeared, dropped a wad of letters on the mat, rapped on the oaken door, and fled before anyone could get a proper look at him.

Argabella reached for the letters, but Poltro stopped her with a hand.

"It is not wise to touch the Dark Lord's mail."

Argabella's nose twitched. "I was just going to hand it to him, helpful-like."

Poltro shook her head. "The Dark Lord found me rooting through his coupon flyers once." She lifted her hair to show a jagged cut in her ear that left the lobe in two unattractive flaps. "Once."

"And he slit your ear for that?" Fia bellowed, the veins standing out on her forehead in rage.

"Naw," Poltro said, letting her hair fall back down. "He yelled at me, and I tumbled off the steps and landed on my back, and one of the chickens tried to pull out my earring, and I jerked away, and there it is. Mangled for life. You mess with the mail, you get mutilated by those clucking horrors."

All this time, the sound of spectral footsteps could be heard, tapping down stone stairs as aged and somber as eternity, their middles bowed with the passing of the slippered feet of Dark Lords long past. It really did take an awfully long time, and several attempts at polite conversation were made, but then the sound of tripping and cursing would interrupt, and honestly, only so much time could be spent talking about what a lovely day it was before the day entirely ceased to be lovely.

At last, the sound of a lock snapped on the other side, and the carved wood door creaked inward just a crack.

"Who dares disturb my dark ruminations?" a voice croaked, deep and heavy with foreboding.

Everyone looked to Poltro, but the huntress had skulked around behind Fia and was busy staring at her black-rimmed nails. Oddly enough, it was tremulous Argabella who spoke first.

"Good morning, Crepuscular Lord, sir. I know it's been five years since I've been around to visit, but you won't believe the asparagus I've brought, along with other fine vegetables—"

"Give him the basket," Fia whispered out the side of her frozen smile.

"Oh, right. The basket!" Smacking Gustave away from the fine ribbon he was chewing, Argabella picked up the now ribbonless basket and held it out to the yawning chasm of shadow.

"Is that—" The voice within coughed, cleared its throat, spat into the bushes, and then spoke in an utterly normal voice that wasn't scary at all but rather smooth and affable like warm milk. "Is that manchego?"

The door opened farther, and out stepped a man who looked to Gustave, judging by his childlike excitement regarding the basket and his general body language, bereft of menace. The Dark Lord was slight and middle-aged, and his skin was pleasantly tawny with copper undertones. He had practically no chin, although something that very much wished to be a beard clung to a tiny moon of flesh that had grand aspirations of chinniness. His eyes were a cheerful if dull brown, not at all the lightning-lit violet or lava-rock black one might expect. Above them, his eyebrows were apparently trying to race his beard for supremacy, as they were bushy with antennalike bits waving around.

"It is manchego," Argabella said. "And some of those crackers you like with the seeds placed on them by artisans. And a little pot of something jammish, possibly made with dragonfruit."

She held out the basket, and the Dark Lord took it and giggled. "Oh, goody! This'll be the perfect amuse-bouche for the grand luncheon upstairs. If you'd all care to join me?"

He looked around from face to face and settled on Gustave, who swallowed the last of the ribbon like a noodle and said, "You're going to amuse us with boots? Now we're talking."

The Dark Lord's eyes lit up as much as dull brown things can.

"Did that goat," he asked, "just talk?"

"How observant of you," Gustave answered. "The name's Gustave. Now about those amusing boots?"

"Toby, might I introduce my, er, friends," Argabella said, sounding more confident than she had thus far. "Fia, Gustave, and I believe you already know Poltro."

Toby's face abruptly contorted as if he'd been painted by a Cubist living on nothing but weltschmerz and absinthe. "Poltro! Where are you hiding, girl? And did you bring me the farm boy's—" He paused, his lips twitching. "The farm boy's *herbs*. In the *specially made herb box*." As he said it, he made little quotation marks with his fingers.

Fia stepped aside to reveal the cowering huntress.

"Ah, yes, my Dark Lord. Well, no, actually. Don't know much about herbs, to be honest. Argabella found some greenish things, though, so maybe that'll do you."

Toby shook his head and stepped closer. "No, Poltro. Remember how I sent you out on an errand to find a certain farm boy who thought he was The Osen-chay One-way, and you were supposed to bring me his ill-stay eating-bay eart-hey?"

Poltro looked befuddled and in profound need of rescue. Gustave rose to the occasion. "He means the dead kid's heart. And no, we didn't bring it, because that's nasty."

"And rude," Fia added. "Especially since we were hoping you might bring him back to life."

Toby raised an eyebrow. "But I wanted him dead."

Fia also raised an eyebrow. "Well, he is. For now."

Toby's face lit up like a firefly's fundament. "Excellent! Poltro, my huntress, we must celebrate! We must feast! This is your first major success!" He wrapped an arm around Poltro and steered her toward the stairs, shoving her upward. She skittered up a few steps like an ant avoiding the crush of a merciless heel, and he followed, so she kept on skittering. The entire party trotted behind, curious to see how things would play out and if there might be any extra cheese to go with the delectable smells wafting from the top of the tower.

The stairs were so many and so steep that no one had the breath to explain the farm boy's current situation further. Whether for fear or asthma, Poltro didn't admit that the farm boy's demise was not reflective of her murderous capabilities. Upward and upward they labored, hundreds and hundreds of stairs. Gustave clattered up behind them, helpfully ejecting a trail of pellets out his back door in case someone should get lost and require a reminder of the way out.

Halfway up the tower, the scent of the food reached peak deliciousness and pulled the humans forward with more alacrity. When at last they burst onto the floor of Toby's dining room, there was some confusion as to whether or not they'd all simultaneously died of exhaustion and landed in the same heaven.

The long, wooden table was simply covered in food, drink, and unnecessarily ornate candelabras. Flagons of wine twinkled like liquid gems, and greased-up birds were suggestively splayed on pewter platters, onions and apples spilling from their assorted orifices. An entire peacock somehow had been emptied out, cooked, and stuffed back inside its own gorgeous plumage, and it didn't look particularly happy about the situation. A centerpiece of artfully arranged hedgehogs and turtles quivered but did not seem edible or interested in mating. Tiny moist quails, lollipops of lamb, and a pile of baby chickens that appeared to have been fried whole, feathers and all, lolled on their plates. Quivering cubes of meat sat upon particularly small plates, and wee whole fish rested upon large plates scribbled over with glimmering sauces. Watermelons carved as warships carried bananas in full armor, sailing on seas of aspic and gelatin and compote. Truncheons of roasted vegetables, cauldrons of savory dips, skulls of fondue, and tureens of glistening soup waited, their ladles practically begging to be used. Pâté jiggled, pork gelatin wiggled, and fig jam figgled.

"Where are the blasted boots?" Gustave complained. "This is the worst lunch I've ever seen."

"It's magnificent," Argabella breathed, her nose quivering with keen arousal. "Toby, you've really outdone yourself this time."

"Where are the other guests?" Fia asked, clutching her cloak to her chest and trying not to drool.

"Other guests?" Toby sat down at the head of the table and looked up at her curiously. "What other guests?"

Fia gesticulated at the laden table. "This is enough food for an army."

"This is enough food for *me*," Toby said warningly. "Be glad you brought the cheese and crackers."

The party gazed at him with existential despair as he sat down, stone-faced, and tucked a napkin into his neckline before a spread that was many times the size of a human stomach. Eventually he could bear it no longer, and he laughed, pointing at them. "You should see your faces! Priceless! No, of course you must join me. Please, be seated and fall to!"

And then they dined.

Fia asked so many questions regarding what was and was not fried in animal fat that Toby cast an enchantment enrobing all the vegan items with a greenish glow. She began with an assortment of blistered folk seaweed, inhaled a sublimated plum bun, then annihilated a platter of sheltered orecchiette. Her every action was shrouded in some sort of violence.

Poltro took advantage of the glow to freely plunder the many meaty delicacies, such as the ox marrow bombs glazed with snail paste and exploded salt, the sungold fish dumplings steamed in butter smoke, and the invigorated ham jam for which Borix was famed throughout Pell. The Dark Lord demanded that she put on a lobster bib when she threatened to destroy her fine costume with a distressed anchovy dressing.

Argabella made no beef about her current disinterest in meats but instead quietly joined Fia in enjoying the vegetarian offerings. She started with a winter acorn and hand-rubbed arugula toss, followed with a naïve kimchi medley, then graduated to a frightened farfalle swimming in tormented eggplant liqueur and surprised truffle drippings. She nibbled and moaned in turn, her whiskers twitching happily.

Gustave was given an old boot, once bespoke and very chic but now used and soleless; the Dark Lord claimed it was too expensive to be thrown out even though its mate was long gone.

"This is the finest boot I've ever beheld or smelled," Gustave whispered. "I can practically taste the brains in which the leather was tanned. And there's a soupçon of foot sweat impregnating the uppers. Mmm."

"What are these?" Fia asked, pointing to a big platter of circular breads topped with savory fillings and crumbles of cheese.

"I call them take-Os," Toby said proudly, rolling one up and stuffing it in his mouth. After a moment of chewing, he sighed blissfully. "Because they're circles that you can take with you. My own invention."

"They're called tacos, and you didn't invent them," Gustave said, midboot.

"I can turn you into gravlax," Toby warned.

"Bleat," Gustave said. "Or baa. Whatever. I'm very impressed with your take-Os."

At some point, they all fell back in their chairs, clutching their bellies and groaning. Only Toby continued in his gustatory glory, drowning something fried in duck fat in a piquant dipping sauce accented with a sprinkle of fondled pine nuts.

"Now that you've dined, I have bad news, my friends," he said between bites.

"There's another course?" Fia moaned.

"Or another curse?" Argabella asked. "It was in the food, wasn't it? And it's going to turn us into newts?"

Toby smiled, gratified to finally have someone besides hedgehogs and turtles to share his meal and also pleased that they thought him capable of turning them into newts. "Neither. It's just that . . . well, if I understand correctly, this farm boy, Worstley, is dead?"

"Really dead," Fia said.

"Like, ostentatiously dead," Gustave added. "Eyes open. Tongue hanging out. Bones in places bones shouldn't be. Smells worse than normal."

Lord Toby rubbed his hands together with glee.

"And Poltro, this was your doing?"

All eyes looked to the huntress, whose face was smeared with an expressed sardine and ramp reduction. "Er," was all she managed.

"I fell on him," Fia finally admitted, "while trying to enter the sleeping castle. It was an accident."

"And he just died, easy as that?"

"Well, judging by the bones poking out of his mushier bits, I don't think it was easy for *him*," Gustave said.

Toby licked a finger and held it up, cocking his head as if listening for a far-off song. "Yet I sense that the winds of destiny have not changed course. Which means that either this Worstley was not actually the Chosen One, or that he's not really dead, or that whoever proclaimed him Chosen was lying."

"It was Staph the pixie," Gustave offered. "And honestly, she didn't strike me as particularly trustworthy. She had only one sock."

Toby stroked the thing that he probably thought of as a beard. "Her fashion shortcomings are legendary, but when it comes to the bequeathal of auras, Staph is never wrong. The boy must be revivified. Alas, my powers are not yet strong enough to accomplish that sort of thing. If I consorted with the darkest of forces, I could probably turn him into some sort of shambling, brainless zombie—"

"Nature beat you to it," Gustave mumbled under his breath.

"But that sort of creature could never fulfill the destiny of the Chosen One. I will require an influx of power." Toby cracked his knuckles and turned to Gustave with an air of destiny. "Goat of many magicks, will you agree to act as my familiar?"

"What does that entail, exactly? More boots?"

Toby grinned a dark grin. "You will be bonded to me, body and soul, our auras merged in the service of the Dark Lord's otherworldly powers."

"Um," Gustave sputtered. "How about no?"

Looking flustered but still somewhat hopeful, Toby looked to Argabella. "Would you, Argabella, consider cleaving yourself unto me?"

"I think maybe you're getting a bit *too* familiar," Fia growled.

"What? Toby, no," Argabella said, drawing back from the table. "Gross."

"But if I had a true magical familiar," Toby started, sounding pretty whiny for a Dark Lord, "I could bring the Chosen One back to life! Be a real necromancer! Grow a real beard!"

"We're people," Argabella argued. "Not animals. I'm sorry your turtles and hedgehogs never worked out their differences, but . . . that body-and-soul-binding business just sounds icky. I like you, but not in that way."

Toby's shoulders slumped, which seemed to be their normal mode. "Well, then. The bad news is I can't help you."

"That's okay," Argabella said, a dark look in her eyes. "We'll just go see Grinda the Sand Witch instead, and perhaps she has the right sort of powers. She's the one who enchanted the castle, after all, so she owes me. Waking up a farm boy should be nothing for someone that impressive and powerful."

The look on Toby's face suggested that he was considering smiting her for assuming that Grinda was more powerful than he was, but then he started thinking out loud, which made Gustave deeply uncomfortable. When humans began to think out loud, they often confessed their interest in doing horrible things, especially to nearby succulent goats.

"Hmm. I can't smite the rabbit girl, considering how often she used to bring me mail and cheese before the whole curse thing. But this Grinda is definitely a problem. Grinda. Hmm. Where have I heard that name before? Grinda . . . Grinda the Sand Witch . . . Grinda the Sand Witch of Malefic Beach, aunt of the Chosen One and possessor of a terrible postman!"

"So you know her, then?" Gustave asked.

"No. Of course not. Whatever gave you that idea? Silly goat. But she sounds like a real treat," Toby said, but what he probably really meant was that she sounded like someone who needed to be taken down a few pegs right before a certain Dark Lord plundered her library and laboratory for the pearls of arcana locked within. Gustave had always been good at reading the menacing body language of humans, and the way Toby was wringing his hands and snickering darkly spoke of either ill intent or a dire need for lotion.

"Would you want to go with us, then?" Argabella asked, her watery eyes filled with hope. "We could use magical protection. And maybe you'll be able to convince Grinda to help you, too."

"That would be just lovely," Toby said.

And he really did seem to mean that, which made Gustave a little nervous. For although Lord Toby possessed the finest of boots and seemed a genial host, there was something off about him. His smile was a bit mad, his bland brown eyes twinkling with something a bit too greedy and murderous. The thought of being the man's bosom friend, much less his familiar, made Gustave's cud go sour. And of course Gustave couldn't forget that earlier slip about how the Dark Lord had sent a rogue to cut out the pooboy's heart. Gustave hadn't been too fond of Worstley, but his most sinister plans had included kicking the boy in the junk, not sawing out his internal organs for nefarious wizardly reasons. Gustave wasn't sure what he wanted now that his life had changed forever, but he was fairly certain it didn't involve having his own heart roasted in Toby's oven and topped with a cardamom soufflé.

He would have to watch this warlock carefully.

"You must be tired and ready to sleep off that meal," Toby told his guests, ringing a bell. "I'll summon my servant, Dementria, to show you to your quarters. Why don't you take your ease this evening, let me make some arrangements for provisions, and we'll depart in the morning on a pleasant perambulation."

They all belched their agreement except for the turtles and hedge-hogs forming the centerpiece. Lord Toby muttered a phrase, sketched a sigil in the air, and splayed the fingers of one hand suddenly to their maximum extent, waggling it three times. The animals disappeared from the table, and Gustave desperately hoped they found themselves safely deposited in the lush gardens surrounding the tower to enjoy their freedom, mate with their own kind if they wished, and be amazed by their good fortune. The Dark Lord, Gustave noted, was in an uncommonly good mood. And to a goat, that remained quite worrisome.

8.

At the Scene of a Richly Deserved Punch in the Kisser

It was a rare sunny day in Borix when the party set off to the south with light hearts and a wagon groaning under the weight of victuals and Lord Toby's potion and feast ingredients, all fastidiously labeled to avoid mixing the deadly mushrooms with the edible ones or the salamander eyes with the salmon roe. Since Fia couldn't really ride horses without crushing them or having her feet drag the ground, and also because cardio is important, they all walked alongside the wagon, which was being pulled by two sturdy oxen named Moxie and Doxy. That was all right by Toby, who'd never actually ridden a horse before and wasn't entirely prepared to look a complete fool. He knew he'd be able to ride at least as well as Poltro, but that wasn't saying much.

As he locked the tower door and left a note for Dementria to keep things tidy while he was gone, he couldn't help gazing up at the top of his home. He looked up and up and up and up to the tiny window where he spent much of his time watching life pass by using an enchanted spyglass. He'd grown so accustomed to the lofty view that the world seemed quite large and strange when viewed from his doorstep.

"Coming, Lord Toby?" Argabella called.

She stood with the others beside Toby's oxen. He'd never met the oxen before or been close enough to smell their meaty musk. Poltro's brother kept track of the beasts, using them to cart groceries in from some hamlet or other. Now Toby realized how very big oxen were and how very moist their noses looked, and that somehow made him realize how very big and terrifying the world could be.

"Er," he said, pressing his back against the solid comfort of his door.

His door, he understood. Everything else was still up for discussion.

"We're losing travel time," Fia added.

"Hey, you look a little green," the goat noted. "Are you dyspeptic or homesick?"

If he was being insulted by goats, Toby clearly had to pull himself together.

"I am merely laying an enchantment about my demesne," he said. "Pay me no mind."

"Keeping the chickens out." Poltro nodded. "Quite wise, m'lord."

As Toby looked beyond his new companions and his wagon, the road seemed to disappear into the horizon. He could well imagine the terrors that awaited: monsters, larger monsters, entire cities bereft of cheese. Yet that way might also lie his dreams: the means to becoming a true Dark Lord replete with powers beyond his current ken. All he had to do was step off his own porch and keep walking—and in the company of a rogue, a fighter, a bard, and a talking goat, no less. Surely he could do that much.

He stuck out his foot, for the first step was surely the hardest part—

And Poltro put a hand against his chest.

"Not on the Unwelcome mat, m'lord," she reminded him.

Grateful for the timely reminder, Toby stepped over the mat, saving himself a troubling and sticky afternoon in the jam cellar. His boot landed in the dust, and he smelled his fine roses, which were kept trimmed and fertilized by Poltro's brother. He took another step and another, right up until he was close enough to pluck a rose from its bush.

"These are pretty fabulous, aren't they?" he asked, holding the rose out to Fia.

She took the flower, but not as if it were a gift from a fine wizard. Turning it around carefully, prying its petals apart, and picking off the thorns one by one, she considered it. "Better than most, but I think the bushes toward the center of the circle are more true. Within a few generations, with the right care, I do believe they could win a prize." Bowing, she held the flower out to Argabella, who laughed lightly and blushed, tucking it above her ear.

Fia started walking, and everyone followed her, including Toby. By the time he realized it was happening, his tower was far behind them, obscured by a cloud of dirt and methane from the oxen. He told himself this "going outside" business wasn't so bad and began to sweat.

They headed almost due south toward Malefic Beach, straight through the pristine realm of the dwarves, who mostly lived in the Korpås Range and left the largest part of their lands open and unspoiled, concentrating their population in a few cities and building economies around the shampooing of beards. Poltro commented that their route was likely to take them through the wondrous demesne of the elves, being very careful to pronounce the word correctly this time. A quick roll call revealed that none of them had ever beheld the magical elven Morningwood before, home to the proudest stands of timber anywhere.

Argabella realized that it was the perfect moment to perform her bardic duties and maybe make Lord Toby more comfortable, as he kept gazing back in the direction of his tower and sucking worriedly at his lip like a small child who'd lost his favorite doll. She pulled her lute around front, strummed an experimental chord to check that it was in tune, then plunged into a cheerful riff, improvising a happy song about cheese that was sure to be a hit with her audience.

"Oh, there's nothing quite so hearty
As a huge hunk o' Havarti
When I'm going to visit the elves!

I'd sure like to take a crack
At a wedge of Colby Jack
When I'm going to visit the elves!"

The rest of the party quickly caught on and joined in on the last line of each verse.

"Yes, I'm the kind of fella
Who'd like some mozzarella
When I'm going to visit the elves!

A thick slice of Swiss
Sure wouldn't go amiss
When I'm going to visit the elves!

Just toss some Gorgonzola
Into my cheesehole-a
When I'm going to visit the elves!"

Fia threw back her cloak and danced along with heavy steps as she walked, straining the ability of the chain mail to contain her metaphorical milkshakes. Although everyone noticed and enjoyed her enthusiasm, Lord Toby took an especial, perhaps salacious interest in her movements. Fia had kept her cloak fastened all during yesterday's epic luncheon, so he had not realized she was in such fantastic shape or that she had so very little clothing underneath the cloak. It took only another couple of verses before his hips began to gyrate and thrust in an unfortunate simulation of rhythm, and a single verse after that he had shimmied up to Fia in what he thought was a deeply sensual dance of seduction but really wasn't. He puckered his lips and stood on tiptoe to give her a kiss and the goat called him a jackass, and something happened to the sun because it completely disappeared and the music stopped and—

Toby blinked and moaned some time later. "Where am I?"

"About a foot away from my fist," Fia growled. "Would you like to try that again?"

Toby's vision snapped into focus, and he saw said fist and the snarling face behind it. Beyond that was the blue sky, and he realized that he was flat on his back in the dirt. His teeth did not feel securely anchored in his gums, and he tasted blood. "No, no," he assured her through mashed lips. "Once was enough."

"Good. Delighted to travel with you, Lord Toby. You have been kind and generous with your provisions, and I promise I will have your back if there's a fight. But if I—or anyone else, for that matter—wants anything more than a traveling companion, we'll let you know with words we speak out loud. Do not assume otherwise."

"Got it. That's very clear, thank you." Toby coughed once and spat blood to the side. Fia beamed at him, unclenching her fist and offering an open hand to help him up. He took it, and she hauled him easily to his feet.

"Excellent. Then we can continue without further delay. Perhaps our bard knows a healing song to help you feel better."

Argabella's ears drooped. "I know one called 'The Ouchie Song,' but that's it."

"Practice makes perfect," Fia said, and the bard strummed the opening chord.

Gustave noted with private amusement that Fia still had a bottle of NyeQuell on her belt but had seemingly forgotten it was there. Perhaps looking like a pummeled pudding would remind the Dark Lord that consent was more important than magical ability and being born among the landed gentry.

9.

IN THE LUMINOUS PRESENCE OF THE ELVISH MORNINGWOOD

As the afternoon wore on to dusk and the party continued perambulating and singing about cheese and fond fantasies of fabulous fair folk, a funny thing happened. Everyone started sneezing, even Gustave. Poltro in particular began to swell up and look a bit puce about the gills. Fia was at her side in an instant, but she couldn't find anything wrong with the rogue—nor could she stop sneezing herself. Fortunately, the Dark Lord never traveled without a trunk of handkerchiefs, doilies, and antimacassars, and he generously supplied everyone with a bit of linen he'd embroidered personally and with very little skill.

"Do you have a potion for this malady, my lord?" Argabella asked hopefully, whiskers twitching and, truth be told, a little moist.

Toby flicked his fingers, in no way trying to get rid of a persistent booger. "Alas, there is no spell to staunch the common cold."

"Not even NyeQuell can touch that beast," Fia lamented.

Argabella sneezed explosively. "Perhaps the elves have something. A dainty posset of flowers and berries to soothe the—ah—ah—achoo!"

"Yes," Fia chimed in between sneezes. "The elves are known for their healing powers and wisdom."

"And their beauty and art and songs," Argabella added.

"And their skill at killing things they don't like," Gustave said.

"And their cunning perception and excellent aim," Poltro sniffled, but it came out very muddled, as her lips were starting to swell.

"Bah," Toby barked. "Myth and hyperbole. But they do make an excellent mead. And here we are. Morningwood."

As the words left his mouth, the smooth stone road disappeared into the rich forest loam before them, and the wagon bumped onto soft earth as they entered the shadow of the great green forest of Morningwood. The air seemed to dance with magic itself, tiny glittering flecks of dust turning to gold as they spun through sunbeams piercing the verdant canopy. The birds called sweetly, their songs somehow more musical, more intricate, as if these birds had perhaps been sent off to study opera and returned home after having their hearts broken and learning valuable lessons about birdhood. To either side of the path, which was really just two dirt ruts now, soft green fronds of ferns unfurled along with periwinkle carpets of velvety violets. The oxen had to struggle to pull the wagon now, but no one really noticed the beasts' plight because everything that people cared about was extraordinarily pretty. No one could hear Moxie and Doxy snorting and groaning, what with all the sneezing.

"Oh, my," Fia breathed before she fell into another sneezing fit.

Somewhere in the forest, a bright voice giggled.

"Who's there?" Toby shouted, pulling back his sleeve to give his magic fingers more nimbleness. Taming the challenges of stately Morningwood would no doubt require two ready hands.

In response, an arrow zipped past uncomfortably close to his face, taking a patch of his beard with it.

Thwack!

Everyone stopped walking to turn and stare at the arrow quivering in a silvery birch.

Toby went for his chin, checking that it was still in place and that his beard wasn't completely gone, taking his powers with it. Fia soon had her sword in one hand and her pruning shears in the other as she squatted in a fighting stance, her muscles rippling and her chain mail creaking with effort as her cloak fluttered to the ground. Argabella held her lute and shook with nervous anxiety as she continued a series of tiny baby sneezes. Poltro simply struggled to breathe, her face as red and swollen as a baboon's posterior. After assuring himself that he was still in possession of his chin, Toby licked his finger and held it up, turning slowly in a sunbeam until he faced the direction from which the arrow had obviously originated.

"O wise and fair elves of Morningwood, we humble journeymen beg passage through your demesne," he shouted. A confident woman's voice replied, though the owner of said voice remained unseen.

"Take heed, children of men: we fair folk are aware that no one comes upon Morningwood without good reason. It is sprung from your dreams of greatness and magic, a monolith of beauty and strength. But beware that you will also, in passing through, discover the steely strength of our Morningwood, whose limber limbs bend but do not break yet bear succulent fruit with each new stroke of spring."

In the quiet that followed, Fia could hear Poltro not breathing. Argabella dropped her lute, fell to her knees, and tried to find the girl's mouth but failed. Fia stood over them, weapons ready, sneezing.

"I'm not sure what all that means," Gustave called, "but a member of our party is in dire need of the renowned elvish healing. Like, right now, unless your woody magnificence needs fertilizer of the dead and rotting kind."

When no one appeared, Fia added between sneezes, "Please. And might I mention that I assure you of our respect for your proud Morningwood, which is most impressive and eternal."

The air shifted, and everyone stopped sneezing to gasp. An elf stood there among them, quiet and dignified, everything that Fia had dreamed of seeing when she'd heard tales of the fair folk back home. The elf woman was as pale as the heart of a rose, tall and slender and graceful, her snow-white robes fluttering in a breeze that wasn't there. Her eyes were fathomless, glittering green, her ears coming to slender points that peeked out from beneath hair like spun gold. A jewel glittered around her neck as she bowed slightly.

"I am Sylvinadrielle," she said, her voice sweet as chimes kissed by a breeze. "And you guys fell for the oldest trick in the book. It's called sneezing powder. And you just kept breathing it in like absolute morons. Lord, what fools these mortals be, am I right?"

"Gadzooks, yes," a new voice answered, dripping with condescension. "Dumber than a third nipple."

It belonged to another elf who appeared at her side, this one masculine but still refined and suppler than most men in Fia's opinion. He was clad in a hunting costume woven of the colors of the forest, moss green and birch gray with a silver sash from shoulder to waist. His blond hair was long and flowing past his shoulders, and he had a bow in hand and a quiver of arrows on his back.

"Poltro's still not breathing," Gustave noted. "That's bad, right?"

Sylvinadrielle laughed her wind chime laugh and knelt smoothly. Removing a handful of powder from a velvet reticule at her waist, she blew a cloud of glitter into Poltro's face, then tossed the rest in the air. Fia had never been happier to not be sneezing. The glitter settled on Poltro's swollen cheeks, and after a long moment, the huntress jerked with a deep, gasping breath and set to coughing. Fia helped her sit up, and the more Poltro coughed, the more the unhealthy burgundy faded from her face, leaving her ashen and exhausted and positively riddled with glitter.

"It's called a remedy. Ever heard of it?" Sylvinadrielle said. "You're welcome."

"The great healing power of the elves is celebrated in our realm," Toby explained tersely, "but we didn't get the memo about how the elves instigated the sickness they later treated."

"Yeah," said the male elf. "Well, who do you think spreads those rumors? We do. So there. I'm Bargolas, by the way, son of Rodmoore, the king of the elves. And you may not pass through our demesne without the king's leave."

"Wilt thou take us to thy king?" Toby asked.

"Pardon?" Bargolas said, cocking a long ear at the mage.

"Oh, goodness. The poor peasant is trying to speak theatrically," Sylvinadrielle whispered.

"Wherefore art thou, yon kingeth of thine elves?" Bargolas said, and both elves collapsed into giggles that sounded less like crystal chimes and more like weirdly delicate hyenas. "The king does not suffer fools like you, human. Not anymore."

"Oh, how we elves long for yesteryear," Sylvinadrielle began, her voice going misty with sadness and a mysterious blue-green nimbus glowing around her person. Bargolas nodded soulfully, pulled out a reed flute, and began to play a somber tune as she continued. "Once the elves ruled supreme, and the land was rich and wise and kind."

"How can land be wise?" Argabella asked, but Fia gently placed a hand over her mouth and put a finger to her own lips.

"The glories of our ancient days were uncountable, the aching beauty of that long-gone world beyond words. Many a wise and aged yet still surprisingly youthful-looking and limber elf has turned his back—"

"Or her back," Poltro added.

Sylvinadrielle shot her a dark look, the mystical blue-green nimbus turning momentarily indigo and sparking. "Do you not understand how pronouns serve the narrative?" the elf scolded.

"It's called poetic license," Gustave added.

To Fia's surprise, the elf smiled at the goat. "This venerable song of our people will help you better understand our mysterious ways, lest you rouse our wise hearts to elvish anger."

Bargolas's flute disappeared, and a lute materialized in his hands, bone white and carved with esoteric symbols, its strings made of pure gold. He strummed once, and it was a sound so beautiful that a dove flat-out fell to the ground at his feet, dead. He began singing:

"Humans are the worst of things
They show up and they steal our rings
We need to breed so we have flings
Still, humans are the worst!"

Fia, while not liking the way the song was going, admitted that she was enraptured by the complex beauty of the music, as were the rest of her friends. Gustave danced back and forth, agreeing whole-heartedly with the simple truth of the lyrics. For her part, Sylvinadrielle took up a gentle and spiraling harmony, sometimes pointing to one human or another as emphasis. Fia found she couldn't move, so ensorcelled was she by the elvish ballad.

"Humans ruin life, yes they do
They only eat and screw and poo
They are far less magical than you
For humans are the worst!

"Humans destroy all they touch
They fight and grab and steal and clutch
They are not good for very much
Yes, humans are the worst!"

"Okay," Toby said through lips frozen in delight. "We get the point. We can backtrack and go around your rampant Morningwood if only you'll free us from the spell of your . . . rhapsodic disgust?"

"What are you talking about?" Gustave crowed. "This song is amazing!"

"Just one more verse," Sylvinadrielle whispered as Bargolas's lute strings rang in a crescendo.

"But we must let these humans pass
For torturing them is a gas
And we must seduce a human lass
Though humans are the worst!"

"Wait, you must seduce whom?" Gustave said as the others shook themselves awake as if from a dream.

"Alas," Sylvinadrielle began, the nimbus of misty memory yet again coalescing around her silken head in the form of glittering turquoise gas, "so many of our elven lasses have fled the mortal realm to venture west, to the fog-shrouded isles of—"

"Don't tell them!" Bargolas hissed.

"Isles of great mystery and bounty that you're not smart enough to find," she continued. "We elves are not crass beings, procreating willy-nilly. We are creatures of uncommon taste and refinement, and our women are extraordinarily persnickety. Yet we must continue our lineage in our hopes of reclaiming what greatness was once ours."

"So you're not great now?" Gustave asked.

"Quiet, beast!" Bargolas snapped.

"We're still great, but we were once greater, the rulers of all the land, an empire of magic and wisdom," Sylvinadrielle explained. "Once, passage through our realm required gifts of gold and jewels, magical artifacts, or spices from the far dunes. But these days, as destiny looms upon our noble race, we require—"

"Fecund wombs?" Gustave offered.

"Earthy human mothers for our thrice-blessed progeny." Sylvinadrielle eyed their party and shrugged, turning to the elf prince. "Well, the one in all black has mostly healed from her anaphylaxis. She'll do for you, right?"

Bargolas walked around Poltro as if judging a hairless cat at a cat show. "Good general form and physiognomy," he muttered. "For a mortal."

"You're not so bad yourself, boyo," Poltro tried to say with a sexy pouting of her lips. As her swelling had not yet gone down completely, it almost worked.

"She'll do." Bargolas sighed. "Father's orders, and at least there's plenty of glowine in the Crystal Chamber of Allurement and Come-Hithering. Let's go, then."

Fia looked half disgusted and half vexed. "Poltro, you would go with this . . ."

"Hot little elf hunk?" Gustave said.

Poltro shrugged. "He's confident and saucy, he knows his way around a ditty, and he has the prettiest hair I ever saw, plus he doesn't smell like chicken. Morningwood has plenty to recommend it, I'm thinking—I mean apart from the near-fatal sneezing fits."

"Does that mean you'll take us to the elven king that we might bargain for passage?" Toby asked.

The elf's ears drooped a little. "I'll take you to my father so he'll stop nagging me about my duty to sire heirs. Ask him whatever you want, but good luck with it. He's a right jerk. Now stand close, elbows in, no shoving."

The humans clustered together, but it was clear they weren't yet comfortable in close quarters. Toby kept trying to muscle in near Fia, and Fia kept accidentally stomping on his slippered feet and making him screech. The elves just looked bored at this point, as if they'd much rather be enchanting toadstools or riding giant eagles.

"Zounds, how hard is it to follow simple directions?" Bargolas said. "This'll have to do. Hope no one loses a foot. Now hold your breath and try not to vomit."

"Vomit?" Argabella asked, alarmed. Fia put a comforting hand on her back.

The elves raised their arms and spoke a word with approximately a million susurrating syllables, and the world turned itself inside out.

When the world popped back into focus, everything about it was wrong in all the best ways. Fia opened her mouth and sucked in a deep breath. The air smelled like magic, which was something like new roses and ancient seaborne mist. The trees, though in nearly the same position, now seemed to be crafted of silver and gossamer, and the ferns and violets looked soft as silk and moved as if they were having their own conversations. In an affront to all merely nice days everywhere, there were somehow even more sunbeams filled with yet more dancing motes of glittering dust. Bargolas now wore a crown made of pure light and shaped like a tall, nodding mushroom.

Argabella, whose mouth had foolishly remained open, vomited up leftovers from yesterday's feast; Gustave leapt into the air in surprise, fell instantly unconscious, and tumbled to the ground like a puppet with cut strings. Fia didn't know who to help first.

"He's a fainting goat?" Toby asked Fia.

"He is now."

"I call dibs when he dies for real," Poltro said, brazenly laying claim to Gustave's giblets.

The elves bowed and began walking down a path of smooth gray stones laid in artful tessellations along the forest floor. The oxen, clearly being good judges of who might have better grain, followed the elves eagerly, the wagon trundling smoothly behind them as if recently greased by the lubricating magic of Morningwood. Toby followed his potions, and Poltro followed him.

"Are you feeling well?" Fia asked Argabella, helping the rabbit girl stand. It occurred to Fia that she hadn't thought about the heart rose—or her proposed snug but fortified cottage—in quite some time. Right now, all she really cared about was restoring the farm boy to a less dead state and, well, maybe having an adventure with a kind person like Argabella.

Argabella turned away to wipe her mouth. "I'm well, if a bit messy. Always did get a bit motion sick, and I've never been particularly brave about traveling to other dimensions and meeting kings. But I've stopped feeling like a popped bubble, at least. Do you think Gustave will wake up?"

Fia shook her head and squatted, chain-mail bikini creaking, to scoop the goat up under one bulging arm.

"Between the elves' magic and his own stubbornness, I'm sure he won't be quiet for long."

Together, they trailed behind the others, looking around in wonder at the vibrant birds and mist-colored stags gamboling about the forest. At some point, the elves passed out some tiny croutons, urging them to nibble only a corner. Fia almost choked on her small bite, spitting out nearly an entire loaf of bread.

"As mentioned, it expands," Bargolas said with his nearly constant eye rolling.

"How is that helpful now? I almost died!" Fia growled.

"Elves are masters of balance and self-discipline," Sylvinadrielle intoned loftily. "We take only what is needed and leave the world untouched. Human greed is the root of all evil."

"Being a pompous windbag is the root of all evil," Fia grumbled to herself.

When she'd fallen behind a little with Argabella, Fia pinched off the tiniest corner of her elvish crouton and licked it, jerking her head back in surprise as it turned into a muffin, which she bit into and nearly gagged on.

"Pfauggh! Bran, and it's dry. What's the point of Morningwood if it can't even make a muffin moist?"

"I'm sure it will get better," Argabella said, nibbling on her own crouton and blushing through her dandelion-puff fur. "At least it's not meat. And at least I'm out of the castle. It's as if the world didn't change a bit, but—"

"You did?" Fia asked gently.

Argabella nodded. "It's right peculiar. Up until the castle fell asleep, my main goal was to be a good daughter and become a bard to make my dad proud. And then when he was out cold, I had oodles of time to figure out what it was I actually wanted. See, the bard thing wasn't my idea. My dad had a thing for lutes, and my mom ran away with an accountant, so I was left with callused fingers. For the longest time, it was just me with the whole castle, and I tried all sorts of things—archery and sewing and spinning and baking pies. But I never really found out what it was I wanted to do with my life, and now here I am on a real quest, almost like a real bard."

"You *are* a real bard," Fia said.

Argabella looked down and pinged a string on her lute. Up ahead, Bargolas shuddered visibly at the sound. "Maybe," Argabella whispered. "Sorry about that. It's been so long since I've talked to anyone, and even before the whole rabbit thing, I was always shy, and—"

"Come, now." Fia reached out and squeezed her hand. "You don't have anything to apologize for. We're all in new territory. The Morningwood is terribly splendid, isn't it? If a bit inconvenient."

"I'd rather see the gentle slopes of the Honeymelon Hills," Argabella confessed. "All these towers and trees . . . Well, they do insist upon themselves, don't they?"

Fia couldn't help smiling back.

They walked along effortlessly, as if each step bore them miles. Soon Fia heard laughter and music riding the air and smelled herbal smoke wafting through the trees. Normally, in Fia's experience, the road would become a wider road, which would lead into a filthy hamlet or overbuilt city. But in Morningwood, the village grew organically out of and among the trees, doors appearing in huge trunks and the paved walkway splitting off and leading away to buildings that were like nothing Fia had ever seen. Walls of moss and crystal and bark were inset by stately stained glass windows glowing with all the colors of fall. But they kept on along the main road, and soon their destination appeared: the biggest tree of all, wreathed in furry green vines and dripping with soft purple wisteria. Fia had to agree with Argabella: it was a bit ridiculous.

Standing in front of the grandly carved doors were the first elves Fia had encountered besides Bargolas and Sylvinadrielle. It was strange, actually, to have traveled so far through a city without seeing anyone. These new elves were fierce and utterly encrusted in the most beautiful armor Fia had ever seen. Royal guards, she had to assume. If not for the magic she'd already witnessed, she might've challenged them to a fight for their armor. But she was wiser now. The few pertinent bits of her own chain mail were vastly preferable to choking to death on the glimmering effulgence of the Morningwood.

"Prince Bargolas, hasn't your father warned you about bringing home strays?" one of the guards asked.

"No," Bargolas said, sounding very petulant and unelfish indeed. "I mean yes, but that's not what I'm doing, Dribblesprig. This is official business. Really important stuff. Just open the door."

"It would be my pleasure, Your Highness," the guard said, but he was smirking.

Each of the guards took hold of a brass handle and dramatically threw open the double doors.

"Announcing Prince Bargolas and a collection of livestock, Your Highness," the guard shouted, and Fia had to admit it sounded very elegant and royal, aside from the insulting part.

The tree had appeared to have about the same circumference as a small hut, but once opened, its breadth might've rivaled a cathedral. The trunk was hollow and went up forever, so high that birds flittered to and fro, but not any common birds: these had been enchanted so that when they had to air drop a plop, they only rained glitter down upon the elvish court. A carpet of lush grass led up to a throne of darkest ebon, upon which sat King Rodmoore of the elves. He was the most stately, otherworldly, downright smarmy creature Fia had ever seen, robed in ermine with a crown of ice and eyes to match. Seeing the look on his face, Fia pulled her cloak more tightly around herself and sidled slightly behind the wagon, keeping the unconscious and foul-mouthed goat hidden. For all her strength and bravery, she wouldn't cross this king, and she only hoped Gustave wouldn't get the chance.

The king of the elves sighed a mighty sigh.

"Honestly, Bargles, we've talked about this. You're too old to keep bringing home whatever pathetic things you find in the forest," he said, stroking a beard so long and silky that Toby's envy was palpable.

"But Father!" Bargolas whined. "You said I had to sire heirs, and there are three—I think? Yes, three females among them. That's, what? Six heirs? They have two each, is that not so? Or am I thinking of opossums? In any case, I seek only to do my duty." Bargolas knelt and bowed his head.

"My king," Toby cried, stepping forward with his arms raised, and Fia smacked her head at his foolishness. "I am the Dark Lord of Borix, Tobias Fitzherbert, and I wouldst parley with thee."

"What did he just say? Borax? Parsley? I swear, these humans," the king said.

"The Dark Lord of Borix," Toby repeated slowly, as if talking to a moron. "My party and I pray beg thee for passage through yonder fair Morningwood, kissed by dawn's luscious dew."

"It's always afternoon here, if you hadn't noticed," the king said. Then, to Bargolas he added, "I like this one. Had a parrot like this once. Said the darnedest things." Then, louder, to Toby, indulgently: "Pray continue, my good man."

"I . . . I already said it." Toby tried to keep his arms up, but his sleeves kept falling down, as his robes were capacious indeed. "We're on a quest, and we wish only to pass peaceably through your fair demesne."

The king leaned forward, his long ears quivering and his eyebrows drawn down in frustration.

"My old parrot was a better conversationalist. I tire of this. Bargolas, get them out of my sight and do your duty. I want a full report in the morning. Then send them on their way with whatever they need. Can't have humans dying in the forest again. The bones get all tangled up in the ivy, if you recall." He waved a royal hand, and Bargolas stood and motioned the party to follow him out a side door, which they did with much haste.

"Oh, and Bargolas," the king called.

"Yes, Father?"

The king sat back, looking hawkish and shrewd and maybe a little hungry. "Be sure and collect the toll. Humans can't expect a release from the Morningwood without paying it proper homage."

"Begging your pardon, but what is the toll, exactly?" Toby asked.

"All your cheese. We have so few dairy animals in the forest, you know. Tough to find even a chintzy cheddar around these parts. Now, don't fret. You can easily find more on your travels, whereas we cannot. Just leave your cheese, and in return you may expect a swift and satisfying discharge from the Morningwood."

Toby deflated like a melting Brie, but Fia was overcome with relief. At least, unlike Toby, the king of the elves didn't want someone's internal organs. Perhaps they would escape unscathed after all.

10.

Uncomfortably Near a
Giant Uvula

The next morning, the party didn't exit the Morningwood so much as gush from it in a torrent of magical effluvium. This was terribly awkward for a variety of reasons, and they soon found themselves at a fork in the road. Normally, Argabella didn't approve of the phrase "found themselves" because she had obviously never lost track of her own body or mind before. This time, however, it rang true. Whenever the elves did their magic and turned the world inside out, she did in fact lose herself temporarily and generally rediscovered herself in the process of vomiting. Argabella's opinion of magic went down several notches. What was the point if it always made her nauseated and kept spoiling perfectly nice cloaks? At least Fia was there each time it happened, patting her back in a reassuring way and holding back her ears.

Straightening up to wipe her mouth and consider the path ahead, Argabella couldn't help thinking that forks in the road were rather Gloomful things. Since the path diverged, that meant one had to choose, and choosing meant that opportunities were lost forever. In making the choice, one literally murdered possibilities, which didn't seem very fair or nonviolent.

However, forks in the road were also Songful things. Argabella liked to sing about them when she was feeling especially Thinkful because they illustrated how our choices shape our lives rather than some goddess playing at puppets. And perhaps because people were aware of that—perhaps because some people did and others definitely did *not* want to have the sorts of encounters bards sing about—forks in the road were also places where arguments tended to break out, and one broke out soon after they bade farewell to the elves. Argabella had strummed only one chord before her somewhat Gloomful, somewhat Thinkful song about forks was casually destroyed by what began as nonsense and ended up as nearly a brawl.

"Cor," Poltro said. "Elves. Know what I mean?"

"Not really," Argabella answered, wanting to be supportive. "But you seem glad to be gone. I thought you were excited about spending time with Bargolas. Was it not . . . pleasant?"

"Depends on what you consider *it* to be," Poltro muttered. "He just had me brush his hair for a while, and at first I thought that was okay because he seemed to like it; he was moaning and carrying on, and that's pretty good, right? But then he shouted a bit about his father, cried in my lap, expessed a universal fear of crevasses, and fell asleep, and that wasn't any fun for me, was it? Nothing proper to eat in the room either, just some dried fruits, and when I peeked outside to ask for help, they told me to get back in there with Bargolas the Snore Prince. Well, I didn't sign up for a dried peach, no I didn't, and I won't ever have anything nice to say about elves no matter how shiny their hair is, you can be sure."

"That's not so bad comparatively," Toby said. "The rest of us were dumped unceremoniously in a horse stall, locked in with the oxen, and given nothing but a musty bucket of water and a tuft of elvish hay to go around."

"And our own food stores were infected with glitter," Fia added.

"We didn't know if it was the pleasant, friendly sort of glitter, or the bad, actually-bird-droppings glitter, or the oh-maybe-we'll-choke-to-death glitter."

"And those blasted cheese thieves!" Toby howled, arms waggling in the air for emphasis.

"Not this again, I beg you," Fia moaned. "All night, nothing out of this one but whingeing about lost pecorino."

"Oh, and I'm the only whiner?" Toby shot back. "What about your soliloquy about how straw tends to wedge into one's most personal crannies?"

"There wasn't a lot of sleep," Argabella said soothingly. "The night was rather Wakeful. And literally no one brushed anyone else's hair. But perhaps, if we keep moving, we might find some cheese and hairbrushes."

"We need to take the western fork and head south from Humptulips to Malefic Beach." Fia stepped boldly toward the cleft in the road, her form rippling in ways that Argabella couldn't help noticing.

"I agree," Gustave said, pausing as he chewed a strip of elvish leather. "Not because I'm big on maps but because she's the only one who doesn't want to eat me."

But the Crepuscular Lord was having none of it. "South? Are you insane? Our only choice is to take the eastern fork to the city of Groggyn, where we can replenish our cheese stores. And, incidentally, not die! Everyone knows the south is the more dangerous route. I'm for not dying and a nice Groggish Gruyère."

Poltro took his side, saying, "That would be Gouda," and snort-giggled at how successfully she'd delivered one of the oldest cheese puns in history.

"We can't afford the time!" Fia raged. Her chain-mail bikini tinkled a little bit as she jiggled around, and Argabella thought it a winsome sound. "We need to get the sand witch working her magic on the farm boy as soon as possible!"

"We'll have no time left at all if we're dead," Lord Toby pointed out. "That road to the south is almost sure to kill us, and we'll be no better off than your farm boy."

"The south is sure to kill us? What foolishness. You're talking about silly stories!" Fia shouted, advancing on the hedge wizard, but he held his ground.

"*True* stories, silly or not! There's something deadly lurking around the Titan Toothpicks. Very few people ever return from there, as you well know."

"Very few people can fight like me, or, uh . . ." Fia trailed off.

". . . Make almost-crackers like you," Argabella finished.

Toby ignored Fia and turned to Argabella. "You!"

"Eep!" She cringed, ears drooping, eyes watering, nose twitching. She'd been afraid someone would draw her into the argument, but was surprised to discover that someone was herself. Argabella desperately wanted to support Fia, but at the same time, it didn't do to rouse a wizard's anger. It was frustrating how the curse made her even more twitchy and fearful than she'd been before, which was saying a lot. She'd never done well with conflict, but now it made her want to dig holes and dart under bushes, which wasn't considered socially acceptable.

Lord Toby's eyes widened and his scraggly chin hairs waggled to impress her with the import of his next words. "Look, Argy, my dear. You must break the tie because it's two against two. So: Shall we go south and die a horrible shrieking death at the hands of some cruel monster or go east and enjoy some cool Muenster?"

Argabella quivered like a pudding. Everyone was staring at her, waiting for her answer. Everyone except Poltro, who frowned and held up a finger.

"Hang on, m'lord," she said. "I think Cutter told me about questions like these. Isn't that one of those either-or thingies, a fella-you-see or false canary or—"

"A fallacy!" Fia pounced. "A false binary! That's exactly what it is. There are many more possible outcomes than the two he gave you. A horrible shrieking death does not necessarily await us in the south. In fact, I'm sure it doesn't! And I don't think you can even get Muenster cheese in Groggyn."

Argabella's ears perked up, and she straightened her shoulders a bit. "You're right, you can't," she said. "It's too low-fat and therefore banned by the Earl of Grunting, who sure does like his lipids. He had me sing a song about it once—"

Lord Toby growled in frustration. "Gahhh! What is even happening? We are talking about death here, as in the end of your life!" He pointed to the road leading south—first with his hand, then with his almost-beard pointed as well to make sure no one had missed a vital bit of body language. "And our death is that way! So let's not go there, okay? Come on, Argabella."

"Yeah, come on, Argabella," Fia said, her voice uncommonly gentle and a soft smile on her face. "I've heard such wonderful things about the Titan Toothpicks. They're supposed to be beautiful shining pillars of stone with ribbons of color shot through them that sparkle in the sun. It would be the sight of a lifetime and inspire such sublime music. Don't you think?"

Argabella thought she might agree to do most anything—even swim with the man-eating jellyfish of the Awful Salty Sea—if Fia would just keep smiling at her like that.

"That sounds wonderful," she breathed. "Let's all go seek a horrible shrieking death together."

Gustave laughed. "That's perfect. I like you, rabbit girl. Much more sensible about the world than my former pooboy."

Lord Toby spun on his heel, shaking with rage, and after a few steps threw back his head and bellowed, green bolts shooting from his fingers into the sky. He covered his head with both hands, and that was the only warning the others received before a hail of smoking crusts of bread fell down all around them, sizzling hunks thudding onto the turf.

"Now it's raining toast?" Gustave said. "That *never* happened back at the farm. I mean, who's even *heard* of toast showers before—is that what you'd call this? Maybe a bread squall? A loaf storm?" He reached out tenderly with his goat lips and nibbled on some. "Huh. Pumpernickel. It's nothing like a pair of filthy suede shoes, but it's not bad, I guess."

Lord Toby's shoulders slumped, his anger spent, and he flapped one arm toward the south. "Fine. You all go first. I'll follow behind so that when death comes, the last thing you'll hear is me telling you I told you so."

Fia flashed a grin at Argabella. "Thank you," she said.

The bard stood tall and smiled. The fighting was over, and it was easy to speak her mind again. "You're welcome."

While Poltro got Moxie and Doxy headed in the right direction, Argabella hoped there wouldn't be many more of these forks in the road. It almost made her long for her lonely days in the earl's enchanted castle, because sleeping people did not get into arguments or force her to take sides. But, she reflected, sleeping people didn't smile at her either.

The good feeling ebbed away quickly after they swung south from Humptulips, because signs began to appear alongside the road, an entire Worryful series of them. They were Brimful of sage advice, saying things like TURN BACK NOW OR DIE and NO REALLY YOU WILL DIE and CAN YOU EVEN READ I SAID YOU WILL DIE IF YOU DON'T TURN AROUND.

Toby cleared his throat significantly once he saw them. "In light of this new intelligence, can we reconsider this course of action?"

Fia scowled at him. "No, we can't. For all we know you conjured these up to mess with our heads."

The Dark Lord snorted derisively. "I excel at summoning yeasty foodstuffs but have never in my life even attempted to conjure a series of weathered signs planted by the road, overgrown with years of weeds."

Argabella could feel her shoulders hunching in the silence that followed and reached for something positive to say. "Your eldritch crackers remind me of things that are delicious," she said. Toby's eyes narrowed in condemnation.

"I don't think he's *bready* to forgive you," Poltro all but sang.

"But I do so admire his magic! And his snacks!"

Fia grinned. "So you're saying you're his biggest *flan?*"

"Enough!" Toby shouted. "You're all nuts!"

A beat passed before Gustave whispered, "Don't be so *crudité.*"

Toby crossed his arms in a huff, and Fia winked at Argabella, who couldn't help grinning. She'd never had someone stand up for her before, much less have an entire group of friends band together in such a Punful way. Toby's anger with her was now stretched over the entire group, and a warm sort of feeling spread out from her belly. Relief: that's what it was. But it didn't last for long.

Another grouping of three signs appeared later in the day. IT CAME FROM THE TITAN TOOTHPICKS and IT ATE THEM ALL WITH MUS-TARD and OH GODS, WHY? TURN BACK, YOU IDIOTS!

"Now really, this is folly," Lord Toby began. "Don't you believe me yet?"

Fia made a chopping motion with her hand. "No! We are saving time. And these signs are years old. Whatever was there has got to be gone by now."

"I'm intrigued," Gustave said. "You don't typically hear of monsters bothering with condiments. The stories I've heard imply that they adhere to a paleo diet, preferring their foods in a raw, natural state."

"What does it matter?" Lord Toby snarled. "Either way, you're eaten."

"Except for me. I can run faster than all of you," Gustave said. "I'm counting on you to put up a fight and give me a chance to escape in the resulting brouhaha. Fail me not, ye fat 'n' sassy slow-moving monster chow!"

"Unless you get suddenly frightened and faint," Toby said nastily.

"Look, it's all about genes. I got fainting genes, but I also got beard genes, so who's the real winner here?"

With a prissy *"hmph!"* Lord Toby set to brooding silently while making many dramatic gestures to ensure that everyone knew he was brooding. Argabella began to understand that Lord Toby was a

champion brooder and that if there were a Sulky Olympics, he probably would get silver and then brood about it.

They encountered no more signs after that, and the tension slowly
drained away, especially after they had eaten that evening and woke
up again in the morning perfectly safe. It was, in fact, perfectly lovely,
Argabella thought as the days passed perfectly in peace. They had the
road to themselves, and the rich green land qualified as bucolic. Sure,
there were ruins of old villages here and there, but they were so ancient that they looked artful and as if they had been placed there to
improve the scenery. Idyllic scenery that didn't have very many animals in it, even insects. The bard supposed that was a leading indica-
tor of danger but didn't want to bother Fia with her concerns. Time
had passed while she'd been trapped in the castle, and perhaps things
had changed in the land outside, including food chains.

Moxie and Doxy made good time pulling the wagon, and those
with the capacity for speech talked of many things while they traveled, including the coastal delicacies unique to Malefic Beach they
would like to sample, such as poached pepperfish in sea-salted butter
pumpkins and spicy clam biscuits and, for the less Meatful folk, bat-
tered and fried crème-filled spongecake on sticks. Argabella was
grateful to note that as soon as Lord Toby started talking about food,
he stopped brooding and started drooling, which was more relaxing
for everyone.

When they topped the swell of a fetching hill adorned with yellow
buttercups and finally beheld the Titan Toothpicks sparkling on the
western coast, a collective gasp escaped their mouths. Even Toby's
jaw dropped, which was saying a lot when cheese wasn't in evidence.

"Whoa. I didn't expect them to look *that* good," Fia said.

"They're beautiful just like you said," Argabella hastened to reassure her. "Definitely worth singing a song about."

"Resplendent! Spectacularly fetching! Unabashedly stunning!"
Lord Toby said, his face lit with wonder.

"I've not been much of a world traveler till now," Gustave remarked, "but I gotta say, those are some pretty special rocks."

"Now hold the chicken a minute." Poltro lifted a hand to shield her eyes from the sun and squinted at the distant pillars. "Aren't rocks mostly supposed to stay still? I think I remember hearing somewhere that one of their distinguishing characteristics was that they didn't move—yes, I'm sure of it, because during my training I kept tripping on rocks and thought they were sneaking up on me, but Cutter said, 'No, Poltro, rocks don't move, so they can't sneak, ipso facto,' except I think Cutter was wrong about that, and I still don't know what ipso facto means."

"Cutter was right," Lord Toby said. "Rocks don't move."

Poltro pointed at the Titan Toothpicks. "I swear one o' them pillars moved, sir—look! There it is again! It must not've gotten the memo about not moving."

Argabella squinted at the shining pillars of stone, and so did the rest of the party. Something had detached from the mass of the pillars and was taking impossibly long strides in their direction.

"That's no rock," Argabella said.

"What is it?" Fia wondered aloud.

"It's the thing from the sign! The thing that eats people with mustard!" Gustave said. "Flee! But not as fast as me!" He took off down the buttercup hill, heading back the way they had come, leaving a trail of terror poops in his wake.

Lord Toby growled at Fia, "In case I don't get a chance later, I told you so."

Fia drew her sword and her wicked shears. "Fine, you were right. Now shut up and help me fight this thing."

Argabella didn't want to fight—running away seemed to be far more sensible at this point—but she couldn't let Fia fight alone. For the first time, she was able to resist her rabbity urges and stand her ground despite a bone-deep longing to hop into a log. She swung her lute around and strummed a powerful chord, trying to imbue her voice with as much confidence as possible even though she was terrified, and sang an improvised song of obfuscation:

"We are not food
No sir Mister Monster
We taste super bad
Oh gods we are not food
Really really really
You gotta believe me"

Her desperate song appeared to have no effect whatsoever. The colorful thing's long legs covered a vast distance with every second, and the distance it closed was specifically that distance which separated them. As it grew closer, they could tell that the thing from the Titan Toothpicks was indeed not a rock at all, though it had much the same coloring. It was a spindly and severe looking giant with a nose the size of a battleship. Its only hair was a pair of aggressive eyebrows and an enormous white mustache that fell from the upper lip like two foaming tides, which Argabella supposed meant it must be male. His skin was a curious mural of vegetal colors, yellow and green and deep purples mixed with rich reds and browns, no blacks or blues of any kind. And it wasn't smooth by any means but rather bumpy like an angry custard apple except for the tip of its schooner nose, which had greenish-purple layers to it reminiscent of an asparagus floret. His eyes were empty black pits with only a diamond's glow deep in the socket, and he looked angry or hungry or maybe hangry, a hybrid of the two.

As Argabella's song continued, the Dark Lord Toby's wispy beard waved like the tentacles of an irascible squid and his clutching fingers spewed green lightning into the sky, which arced toward the giant and was very impressive for a half second until it turned into a flurry of pointed almost-baguettes that dealt the giant approximately zero damage.

"I was kind of hoping," Fia said, "that you'd hit him with something a bit deadlier than bread!"

"That wasn't what I intended!" Lord Toby protested. "My battle casting is adversely affected by stress!"

"So it's useless in an actual battle is what I hear you saying."

"Well, it's not like our bard is helping! Everybody knows songs only help if they rhyme, and this one doesn't even have a chorus!"

"They didn't teach me that at bard school!" Argabella wailed, forgetting her song altogether. "You'd think they would have mentioned that on the first day!"

And then they had no more time to argue, for the giant arrived and reached out with a six-foot-long hand to scoop up the seven-foot tall Fia, leaving only her head visible in his gnarled and knobby yellow-ochre fist. Argabella stopped playing her lute and cried out as the giant's mouth yawned wide and he brought his hand toward those massive choppers and she could see down his throat, a dank, Moistful cavern into which Fia would go spelunking and never return. The mighty Fia, who had been so sure that she could handle anything, screamed defiance at the giant as she was helpless to do anything else, her arms pinned and her sword useless, and Argabella's heart screeched as her vision dimmed, her rabbit psyche unable to handle the horror of it all as she waited to hear huge teeth chomping down—

Argabella woke staring at the sky with her entire back uncomfortably wet and stinging a bit.

"What?" she said, trying to make her mind and mouth work. "Where? Wet? Why?" She began to panic and thrash as she realized her arms and legs wouldn't move. She was trussed up like a holiday hen.

"Oh, welcome back to the land of consciousness," Gustave said. Argabella turned her head and saw the billy goat lying next to her in a thin layer of pale orange liquid, his legs tied together like a man bun. Beyond him she could see hints of the others—including Fia!—also tied up and lying in an enormous ceramic baking dish. Even the oxen, Moxie and Doxy, were tied up at the far end and mooing dejectedly. "You woke up just in time to be cooked up," he added. Clearly the goat had not run away fast enough.

"Cooked?" she squeaked.

"Grilled, actually," a voice rumbled from above. It was a deep, rolling, scratchy voice, as if three barrels of port had smoked four thousand cigars and wanted to brag about it. "Over an apple wood fire. There are subtleties of flavors smoked into the meat that I find superior to oak. And the orange-lemon marinade in which you currently soak will add a top note of insouciant citrus as I crunch through your bones and slurp out your internal organs."

"Will there be mustard?" Poltro asked, which seemed like a waste of a question to Argabella. She could have asked to be released, for example, or begged for mercy, but had instead inquired about condiments.

"Why would there be mustard?" the deep voice said, a touch of querulousness in its tone.

"We saw a sign on the road that said you ate a lot of people with mustard," the rogue explained.

"Oh, yes, I did do that once, years ago. First I ran them through the meat grinder with spices and made a festive bratwurst out of them, and the only way to enjoy a bratwurst is with some fresh sauerkraut and mustard, yes? But it's foolish to assume I'd eat the same thing every time. When you have been eating as long as I have, you must become a gourmet or perish of boredom."

"Ah, that's wisdom right there," Lord Toby said. "I know what you mean."

"Do you?" A huge hovering triangle of flesh heaved into Argabella's sight, blocking her view of the sky, with two tremendous black, round, hair-lined orifices at the base and, falling from them, a wintry cascade of whiskers that split across an unseen upper lip. The mass of flesh angled down until she could see the horrible pitiless eye sockets regarding them from the boiled corncob head of the giant.

"Well, perhaps I should ask first: How long have you been eating, exactly?" Toby continued, as if it were perfectly ordinary to have a conversation with a monstrous giant while marinating to improve one's tenderness.

"I have been eating for uncounted tens of thousands of years."

"Huh. A smidge longer than me, then," Toby admitted. "Still, I understand the impulse to seek variety in one's diet."

"That's surprisingly empathetic," the giant said. "I don't get much of that from my food. For I must eat you whether I wish to or not. Which is not to say I don't wish to, because I do. It's just that I have no choice. You have seen my brothers and sisters, yes?"

"Uh, I don't think so?"

"The pillars. The stones. What do you humans call them now?"

"The Titan Toothpicks."

The giant sucked his teeth and winced. "Oh, that's a terrible name. And I thought the God Straws was bad! Well, that's what happens to me if I don't eat: I turn to stone like my family before me. A beautiful, sparkly, many-colored stone, but dead and sadly hairless. I used to have a fantastic head of hair, you know, about twenty thousand years ago, but now all I have left are my eyebrows and the mustache."

"I might be able to whip up a handy tonic—" Toby began, but the giant cut him off.

"No, no, never mind that! There's no use trying to bargain or beg for your life. There's nothing you can say that will make me act against the interests of my own survival. Hair today, gone tomorrow, you know. So little food comes this way anymore. Better that we have a nice chat while I prepare side dishes, and then I promise to kill you quickly with a nice pinch to the skull before throwing you on the grill."

"What's your name, sir, if you don't mind me asking?" Poltro asked.

"I am known by many names, some of them intended to be less than kind. Nostrildamus is a favorite of the local assorted cretins, as is Nebuchadnoser, Noseph of Nosareth, Nosy McHonker, Booger McSchnozz, Beaky McSnotlocker, and Lord of the Sneeze. But my given name is Faktri, and the songs and tales about my life that I like best call me Ol' Faktri in that familiar way, you know, wherein one is thought of with affection, but also implying that I have been around a long time, which is a truth. I knew mountains around here when they were but young hills. I smelled the world when it was in diapers and remember well that terrible day when it became ill and shat out humans."

Argabella saw Faktri daintily move a twenty-pound bag of onions between thumb and forefinger across her vision, then heard him dump the lot onto a cutting board next to the dish in which they marinated. An unseen knife began to chop them.

"Wow. If I wasn't already tied up and horizontal, I'd fall over with revelation," Gustave said. "Wow, wow, wow! You know what I wish, Fia? I wish that Pooboy was still alive and with us right now. I would have loved to see his reaction to learning that he was actually poo."

That prompted Poltro to ask, "Are you speaking metaphorically, Ol' Faktri? Because if we humans are the boom-boom of a baby Pell, sir, I'm wondering why you'd want to eat us."

"I'm wondering where the boom-boom came from," Fia said. "I mean, where in the world were you putting these diapers? And who made the diapers, because they had to be pretty big if they're going to fit a planet-sized backside, right? And now that Pell's grown up and not using diapers, where's all the boom-boom going?"

Argabella thought Fia's questions only raised more. "And how'd you clean it all up?" she asked. "You'd need to divert a river at the very least, and then maybe you catapulted some payloads of baby powder in there. You had to do something, right? Because chafing is real."

"Hey, if Pell plooped humans when she was sick," Toby said, struck by inspiration, "there's no telling what she could squeeze out if we just gave her some mayonnaise we left out too long in the sun. A turtlehog, maybe! And if we gave her some dodgy oysters, whoa dang, then stand back, because here come the rhinogators! This could be amazing!"

Ol' Faktri stopped chopping onions, and his mustache drooped, indicating that a frown had formed under the frothy waves of hair, and a deep cleft of worry yawned between his eyes. "I was speaking metaphorically, of course," he said, and a chorus of disappointed groans greeted this news. He slowly shook his massive head and returned to his onions. "I'm disheartened. Really, I was hoping for more elevated discourse than this."

"Elevated—oh, because you're a giant!" Poltro chuckled. "Good one, sir! Ha ha!"

"I'm not really accustomed to high society, but I can try to accommodate you," Toby said.

"That's going to be a tall order for me," Gustave added.

"I'm not much for lofty words," Argabella said, feeling quite liberated by her slyness. "I don't have a towering intellect."

Ol' Faktri sighed and raised a single wild hedge of an eyebrow at Fia. "Well, what about you?"

Fia made gentle sloshing sounds as she shook her head in the marinade. "I got nothing. I hate tall jokes, too."

"Hmmf. Hurr hurr. Aha ha!" Faktri's mustache shook with laughter, and he threw his head back to laugh some more, affording them a spectacular view of his nostrils. It gave Argabella an idea. While the others tittered and giggled along, amused by Ol' Faktri's laugh, the bard quietly sang a song she thought might have a better chance of working than telling him to ignore his hunger, as she'd tried before. Her subtle magic wasn't very effective at changing the fundamental nature of things, but encouraging what was already there? While rhyming? *That* she could do.

> "*Giant nose of Nostrildamus*
> *Be tickled as if by buzzing bees;*
> *Let loose your juicy phlegm*
> *In a most mighty sneeze.*
> *Sneeze, giant, sneeze!*
> *Just like a violent breeze*
> *Give those giant lungs a squeeze*
> *And sneeze, giant, sneeze!*"

The party was all sharing a mad sort of laugh together, and Poltro commented that this was a much more agreeable way to die than the shrieking business Lord Toby had predicted, when something horrific happened in less than a second: Ol' Faktri was seized with the involuntary compulsion to sneeze. And as sometimes happens when a sneeze surprises even the sneezer, there was no time to cover one's mouth. And as sometimes more catastrophically happens, a glob of mucus was ejected with not insignificant speed from the back of the sneezer's throat. And said glob—a giant glob, it hardly needs to be said—first splattered every single occupant of the baking dish, displacing much of the orange-lemon marinade, then settled down upon them like a blanket, warm and moist and a pale green that Argabella would have thought pretty on most anything else but a layer of mucus resting upon her torso.

And then there were many howls and lamentations. Even Moxie and Doxy, the most placid of ruminants, became raucous oxen under the sudden application of Ol' Faktri snot.

Far too late, the giant covered his mouth, and his brow curdled into an expression of deep embarrassment.

"Oh, no! Oh, my!" he said. "My marinade—my luncheon! I'm so sorry! Oh, no! Ew, gross!"

"Oh, really?" Fia shouted. "Gross? Ya think?"

Faktri made a retching noise as his gorge rose. His pimpled, cobbled eyelids closed as he reached out and scooped up the baking dish. The sky whirled in Argabella's vision, the tops of the Titan Toothpicks briefly making an appearance, and then her stomach got left behind as they dropped precipitously before being upended onto warm sand, which immediately made everything worse.

The howls and lamentations grew louder.

"Sorry! So sorry. Here! Take your weapons and free yourselves." Fia's sword and shears fell from the sky, as did Poltro's sword and dagger and Argabella's lute. "I can't eat you like that. You're the opposite of delicious now, ugh! Just . . . go."

Fia wasted no time. She rolled over to her shears and used them to clip through her twine, then freed everyone else as Ol' Faktri continued to apologize.

"You can take your oxen and your wagon, but I'm keeping all your food. I really do need to eat something. I'm just not fond of . . . sandy boogers. It's always a lovely dinner until . . . it's not."

Gargling and gagging, Ol' Faktri shook the wagon upside down, pocketed everything that fell out, and shambled away, opening the distance that he had once closed until he was nothing more than a far-off shimmering stone pillar, quivering a bit more than his fellows and possibly still horking. Argabella, although freed, still sat on the sand, dumbfounded and slimy.

"Need a hand?" Fia asked, her face eclipsing the sun as she leaned over and held out a slime-covered mitt. Argabella gladly took it and stood, her fingers lingering in Fia's strong grip.

"Thanks," she murmured with a smile.

She was about to say something entirely foolish when Poltro shouted, "Cor, enough of this rot! I'm for the ocean, I am!"

Before she could bolt, however, Lord Toby stepped on her long, black cloak. The rogue landed on her face in the sand and shook herself, looking very much like a sugar-dusted doughnut. "If you look clean, you might also look delicious," Toby said. "I'd rather live greasy than die tidy. Let's harness the oxen and hurry to the south while we can."

Poltro stood and tried and failed to dust off her black equipage. "Fair enough, m'lord. Anything's better than being eaten by a moldy squash man. Right lucky that he sneezed when he did, weren't it?"

"Fortunate indeed," Toby sagely intoned. "Fortuna smiles on our happy band."

Argabella held her tongue. If they knew she had saved them, they might expect her to do it again, possibly on command. She shot a glance at Gustave. He flashed a goat-lipped grin and winked a yellow goat eye at her. So he *had* heard her sing that little song but was keeping his mouth shut. What a Sneakful little ungulate.

Argabella winked back at him. She could be Sneakful, too.

11.

ON A BEACH FESTOONED WITH
SPARKLY PINCHY CRABS

They had to travel only half a day before they came to a river in which they could wash off the sand and snot. While the rest of them argued about who should go first, Gustave didn't wait. He leapt into the river and swam back to shore and shook himself off, then repeated the procedure twice more. It was wide and shallow near the banks, deepening to a swift channel in the center, and there was a ferry platform with no visible ferryman or indeed a ferry. There was, however, a sign that said: IF YOU CAN READ THIS, CONGRATULATIONS! OL' FAKTRI DIDN'T EAT YOU. FERRY AT DAWN EVERY DAY, RAIN OR SHINE.

"How much is passage, I wonder," Lord Toby said, and looked at Gustave.

"Hey, don't look at me, man. I don't have a purse full of coins. Wouldn't mind snacking on a purse right now, though. Are you using yours?"

"Purses are for wimps," Toby sniffed. "I use a fanny pack."

After they had all washed and set up camp for the evening, the Crepuscular Lord assaulted the sky with fingers of green lightning and dinner fell out of it, wee pillows of steaming soda bread. There was no butter to be had or anything else; Poltro checked behind at least three trees, and there was simply nothing to be hunted. But at least they wouldn't starve, and Moxie and Doxy had plenty of grass to graze on.

Hunger continued to rankle after they crossed the river as well, for the ferryman turned out to be a rather surly gnome who insisted he had no food to spare. He told them he lived in a fortified burrow with multiple escape routes in case Ol' Faktri ever decided to wade across the river to eat him and his family and their bewildering brood of tiny yapping dogs.

Gustave didn't like them. There were twelve or more lined up on the dock, barking incessantly as if they'd never seen an adventuring party.

"Hey, they aren't waiting around to eat a goat, are they?" Gustave asked.

"They let me know when Nostrildamus is coming," the gnome explained, tugging nervously on a glorious white beard that Toby eyed enviously. He wore a helmet covered in spikes that glistened with something greasy on the tips, and his armor was likewise tricked out. Those were all poisoned, he claimed, to discourage Faktri from picking him up. "Just don't touch me and you'll be fine," he said.

"So if your dogs are barking right now, how do you know when Faktri is coming?" Gustave asked.

"Oh, they sound different when there's real danger around. More growly, lots more teeth showing, that kind of thing. And the little red lights on their collars glow. Just one of my little gnomeric inventions."

"How many people have you ferried across the river this year?" Argabella asked.

"You're the first in three years, actually."

"And nobody has crossed going in the other direction?"

"Nope."

"How do you make a living?"

"I get a stipend from Grinda the Sand Witch down in Malefic Beach. She pays me to work here in case anyone gets past the giant. Says she wants to meet whoever can manage that. So you're doubly lucky, kids: you aren't in Faktri's digestive system right now, and you get to meet Grinda immediately. That's no small thing."

Lord Toby frowned. "And why is that?"

"She throws a heck of a party. She's connected. Loaded. And not just with money. She has some pretty amazing potions. If you want to do anything about those three hairs you have on your chin—" The gnome waved at Toby's beard with a raised eyebrow.

"There are many more than three!" Lord Toby shouted.

"Sure, big guy. However many you have, she can make you grow more. I used to have it rough like you, but I joined her Beard Club for Gnomes a couple years back, and now look at me! It's a veritable thicket! Tough as dragon hide, too. I can let the dogs play tug-o-war with it and not lose a hair. I'll show you."

"That won't be necessary," Fia said, and Gustave made a small sound of disappointment. He would have liked to see that.

The gnome shrugged. "Your loss. Anyway, don't go before I give you a fancy invitation to see the sand witch. You won't want to miss the opportunity."

"We were going to see her anyway."

"You were? Why's that?"

Fia paused before answering, and Gustave saw her face doing things that meant she was still upset about Pooboy. "We need to tell her that her nephew's dead and see if she can do anything about it."

"Like have a funeral?"

"No! Like . . . magic."

"Huh." The gnome's eyebrows tried to rise but were prevented from going far by the spiky poison helmet he wore. "A funeral announcement would definitely get her attention. She loves an excuse to dress up. You might have actually gotten in to see her without an invitation for that. Near impossible to see her otherwise. You have to do something extraordinary, like live through a giant attack."

"There will be no funeral!" Fia shouted. "Because he's only a little dead!"

Argabella put a hand on Fia's arm. "Barely Deadful at all," she assured the mighty and mightily upset fighter. "Definitely much closer to almost being alive."

Gustave shook his head at the mental fragility and psychological gymnastics of humans. Goats were stubborn, but Fia currently was acting downright foolish. Pooboy was one hundred percent dead, the Mayor of Deadsville, the Emperor of Not Getting Back Up Again, a Bowl of Deadamame, the President of the Board of Deaducation, the Deaditor in Chief. Gustave wished the yappy little dogs were somewhat closer to that state, as they insisted on barking and yapping while the party disembarked. Lowering his horns at them in a menacing sort of way, he used his tail to swat pellets in every direction to emphasize his superiority.

For his part, the ferryman shucked his armor and shooed the dogs off, stomping all over Gustave's pellets and grumbling about curry. He might have muttered a terse welcome to the earldom of Burdell, as they had crossed the river that formed the border with Grunting. Once they were all safely standing on land again, the gnome withdrew a stiff envelope from a secret compartment in his helmet and held it out with much ceremonial bowing. Toby began to take it, but Fia snatched it up first.

"I should be the one to tell her," she said, voice husky with gravitas.

Gustave hoped Lord Toby would protest, and he did.

"My dear, where are you going to put it—hkk!"

Fia grabbed him by the throat and squeezed, shaking her head. "I'm not your dear."

"Gahhk. Right," Lord Toby choked out. "Sorry."

Fia let him go, and the letter disappeared inside her cloak. "And I have pockets."

The ferrygnome said that the border town of Petrel wasn't far and they could get some basic supplies there, then assured them that once they arrived in Malefic Beach, they'd have no trouble finding Grinda's place: "You can ask around, but it's the biggest bloody demesne there is." And Malefic Beach would be a better place to restock for a longer journey. "You've got your regular merchants, of course, but I'd recommend a cheesemonger in the Goblin Market by the name of Hornswoggle."

Argabella giggled. "He's really named Hornswoggle?"

"Don't let the name worry you. He's scrupulous to a fault and has an incredible inventory. Anything you could ever want. He even has some of that magic elvish moose cheese."

"Elvish cheese? From the Morningwood?" Toby said.

"Yep. That's the place."

"They said they couldn't get cheese and took all of ours!"

The gnome chuckled. "You passed through and had to pay the toll, eh? Well, they can't get the kinds *we* make. Just squirrel cheese and moose cheese and whatnot, and they don't make a lot of it. Have you ever tried to milk a moose? It's not quite as dangerous as walking near the Titan Toothpicks drenched in raspberry vinaigrette, but it's close."

"Hey," Gustave said. "You said you had kids. They have any old shoes they've outgrown?"

"Yes. Why?" the ferrygnome asked, eyes narrowed in suspicion.

"Well, I'll take them all off your hands and give your wee gnomelets a goatback ride in exchange."

The deal was struck, and Gustave was able to moan in gourmet delight for the remainder of the journey while the rest of the party had to eat whatever sad, dry breads Lord Toby could conjure each night. The only "basic supplies" the border town of Petrel was willing to sell them was water and wine, reserving all else against the day Ol' Faktri came to raid their stores. The goat couldn't help snickering, a greasy gnome bootie tender on his tongue, as he watched the silly humans struggle to swallow the first night's stale pita rounds. Even Argabella's sensitive snoot couldn't find a sunchoke to spare in

Ol' Faktri's vegetable-stripped territory. They were anxious to reach the next province if only to find some sort of roughage besides Toby's almost-bread.

The village of Malefic Beach—or, more properly, the burgeoning hamlet, since it lacked a church—was larger than any the goat had ever seen. There was more than one street, to begin with, and each one of them was in dire need of the attentions of a diligent pooboy like Worstley. Gustave stuck close to Fia so that no one got any ideas about goat stew. He couldn't be sure if the eyes directed at them were lusting after Fia's flesh or his, since it was significantly warmer in the south than in Borix and she had unfastened her cloak.

The ferrygnome had been quite accurate in his description: they really couldn't miss Grinda's place. This was no witch's hovel but a grand palace nestled on a fine stretch of white sand beach, towering over everything else in the hamlet and visible from miles away, an edifice of such brave architectural braggadocio that it caused Poltro to breathe "Cor" in a tone of wonder.

"Yes, well, it's very nice for what it is, but it doesn't have shrubbery like mine, does it?" Lord Toby said, his hands in fists and shedding magical crumbs. "And I think my tower is taller."

"What is it with wizards and the size of their towers?" Fia muttered.

"Right?" Argabella giggled. "What are they overcompensating for?"

The ferrygnome's sealed letter granted them immediate entrance through the gates, and they were ushered through Grinda's castle by an elderly halfling butler who introduced himself as Milieu Goobersnootch of the Caskcooper Goobersnootches. He walked slowly enough to allow them time to gawp at the interior. Both Argabella and Fia pointed to a particular tapestry at the same time and said, "I've seen that before," because they had.

"Where?" Gustave asked. The tapestries depicted unicorns graphically disemboweling young squires, much to the delight of some smiling maidens. Presumably the maidens thought the squires deserved their fates, so they must have been naughty squires indeed. Although he wasn't generally a fan of art, Gustave resolved to delve further into the mysteries of unicorn justice based on this stunning tableau.

The rabbit woman answered, "There's one just like it in the bedchamber of the sleeping Lady Harkovrita."

"It is probably very similar, but not exactly like this one," the butler said with a sniff. "This is an original Pickelangelo from his Blue Period. You have most likely seen another piece from the same series."

"But . . . I don't see any blue," Fia observed.

"Pickelangelo was depressed, for he had prophesied his own death and was plagued by recurring nightmares of being slain by unicorns. He produced these magnificent tapestries during that time and art historians have labeled it his Blue Period."

"Oh, that's very Sadful," Argabella said. "Did he actually die of unicorns?"

"No, he choked to death on an olive in his cocktail glass. Pickelangelo was a fantastic artist, no doubt, but absolute rubbish as a prophet."

The butler paused before a door and coughed politely. Behind the castle, Milieu warned them, shielded from public view, was the Garden of Pellish Delights, famous or infamous depending on one's view of carnality. "We will need to walk through it to get to my Lady Grinda, so avert your eyes if you are scandalized by, er, naughty bits. Ahem."

Gustave wasn't scandalized by such things. He'd seen all manner of creatures doing their business in the barnyard, and thus the moaning and writhing of the assorted beings on the benches and in the baths and acrobatically hanging from tree branches didn't interest him. There weren't any randy she-goats among them anyway. The garden itself was far more interesting. People had left their clothes just lying around, and for a goat like Gustave, it was an all-you-can-eat buffet. He quickly snatched up an abandoned slipper and a nice wide sweaty leather belt, carefully gnawing around the buckle.

"Er, why does she have this garden anyway?" Argabella asked, blushing fiercely.

Milieu looked down his nose at her. "To keep the courtiers out of trouble, obviously."

"Judging by what my father told me regarding the birds and the bees and the bongos, they are getting up to plenty of trouble," she stammered.

"Only the ones who don't keep up with their cardio," Fia said with a smirk.

All too soon for Gustave's taste and appetite for leather, they were through the garden and walking across snowy white sands toward an isolated sling chair that looked out at the ocean. The beach ahead glittered with pinpoints of reflected light, and Gustave quickly realized that they were gems affixed to the shells of countless crustaceans with menacing pincers.

Milieu Goobersnootch spun on his heel and raised a hand to stop them. "Remain here a moment, please. We must take precautions or," he said, hooking a thumb over his shoulder, "you'll get crabs."

Stopping was fine with the billy goat. He still had about a third of a belt to gnaw through. Once the butler was satisfied that they all would stay where they were, he turned, cupped his hands around his wee lips, and drew a wheezing breath to call to the beach.

"Lady Grinda! You have visitors who recently escaped the endless hunger of Ol' Faktri! May we approach?"

An extremely pale white woman hiding underneath a vast bonnet closed a book and swung out of her sling chair to see who'd come to visit. She wore a red swimming costume and oversized sunglasses that gave her the appearance of insect eyes. She threw her arms wide as if overjoyed to welcome long-lost friends.

"Dahhhhlings! I was beginning to despair that no one would ever pass the Titan Toothpicks safely again! Come here, I must meet you—it's perfectly safe." She dropped her hands and flicked long fingers at the crabs. "Shoo now, pets, let them approach." The sparkling guardians sidestepped and cleared a path on the beach, and Grinda looked up, pleased with her trained bodyguards, to grin at the newcomers with brilliant white teeth.

Gustave blinked as he finished his succulent stolen belt. He'd expected someone a bit more haglike in appearance or at least dressed in black and prone to uncontrollable cackling fits. He'd thought there'd be flying monkeys or a long-suffering princess in disguise dressed in rags and singing about her forced servitude with a chorus of forest creatures determined to aid her and provide a winsome descant. Instead there was a loyal and well-dressed Goobersnootch who was proud of his service and a cadre of loving crustaceans. Grinda apparently eschewed all the traditional trappings of diabolical witchcraft. Gustave wondered if this was a conscious decision on her part or an accident. He swung his head around to see how the others were taking it.

Fia looked as surprised and uncertain as he felt; the Dark Lord Toby was trying and failing to conceal his occult arousal; Poltro appeared to be dwelling on the manifest horrors of crabs and possibly running a mental comparison with chickens; and Argabella—whoa. For once, the rabbit woman wasn't afraid. She looked ready to break her lute over Grinda's head.

The sand witch must have spotted that expression shortly after Gustave did, for her smile melted away into something like shock.

"That's ... one of my spells," she said, uncertainty in her voice. "Isn't it? From the sleeping castle? What are you doing here? Shouldn't you be guarding your rose?"

"My name is Argabella, and I thought I'd come south and get some sun," the bard replied, steel in her tone. "Maybe some answers, too. And I wouldn't say no to a little vengeance. I'm not going to be your scapegoat anymore. Darn that stupid rose!"

Grinda's smile was pitying as she clasped her hands and shook her head sadly. "Oh, my dear, I can certainly give you sun and answers, and I can only hope to convince you that vengeance isn't warranted. There's so much you don't know. But come here first and introduce me to your friends."

Argabella didn't soften or relax, but she didn't go directly to vengeance either. Gustave got the idea that for all her brief bluster, she was more terrified of the sand witch than she was of most things. Still, she went through with introductions with a certain stiffness in her bunny back, as if she had to use every bit of politesse she possessed to keep from breaking down.

When he switched his focus from Argabella to the witch, Gustave realized that something was wrong with Grinda's face. It appeared youthful but somehow wasn't, as if a waggish rogue had hastily rubbed out the wrinkles but left everything smeared and just slightly off kilter. When she took off the sunglasses, it was even clearer: those were old, lying eyes. Not because there were crow's feet at the edges of them—there weren't—but there was an utter lack of innocence and wonder like what he used to see in Worstley's eyes. And she also looked vaguely familiar.

When Argabella finished introducing them all, ending with Gustave, the sand witch said, "You know, my sister used to have a billy goat who looked just like you."

"Yeah, that's because it probably was me," Gustave said. "I think I remember seeing you when I was a kid."

"You're the same goat?"

"Yep. Had to leave because your sister had plans to eat me. Hope you're nothing like her in that regard."

Grinda laughed a light sort of laugh that did a poor job of hiding derision and contempt. "I'm about as different from my sister as anyone can be. She married beneath her, of course—girlish rebellion. Thought a farmer with a honey mead habit was a bad boy. And then they lost Bestley, the poor dears. Too handsome for his own good. How's my nephew, Worstley? I worry about him growing up with such backward parents."

"Well, you don't have to worry about him growing up anymore," Gustave said. "So that's good news."

"I beg your pardon?"

"There's no gentle way to say this," Fia interrupted, much to Gustave's relief. Let the one with muscles tell her what happened. "I accidentally fell on Worstley from a great height and broke most of his bones."

"What? There are no great heights at my sister's farm. Mostly mud and putrescence if I remember correctly."

"It wasn't there. I fell from the enchanted tower of the Earl of Borix."

"You know the one," Argabella said icily.

Grinda's eyes flicked back and forth between Fia and Argabella, trying to process the information. "But then what was Worstley doing there? Why would he leave the farm?"

Fia looked down at Gustave, and he understood that it was up to him to explain that bit. "He was under the impression that he was the Chosen One, destined for greatness, but he didn't really know what that meant. He went to the tower because he thought it was the first step of his new destiny. But his second step was getting splattered."

Grinda's eyes bugged out. "Where on Pell did he get the impression that he was a Chosen One?"

"This nasty pixie showed up and told him so. Her name was Steph or Staph or Stump or something."

Grinda startled. "Staph? Staph the pixie? You're sure?"

"Yeah. One blue sock. *Very* suspicious."

The sand witch deflated, returned to her sling chair, and sat down with her face in her hands. A glimmering crab-shaped ring on one bony finger caught the light as her jeweled crustaceans skittered around her feet worriedly. She softly spoke something that sounded like a liquid cough.

"What was that?" Argabella asked.

Grinda moved her hands away and glared back at her. "I said

Løcher. Løcher is behind this." When all she got in response was looks of bewilderment, she explained. "He's the chamberlain to King Benedick and my mortal enemy."

"You mean he's a wizard?" Lord Toby asked, perking up a bit.

"Yes. One who's been after the throne for many years now. I used to spend most of my time at the capital foiling his plans and convincing the king to treat the peasants well. About five years ago, I thought I'd finally checked Løcher for good: I slapped a costly Inhibition on his head to prevent him pursuing any plot against the king. I couldn't afford to perform the same Inhibition regarding plots against myself, however, so I needed to leave after that if I wanted to live, because his rage was boundless. This is obviously how he got around it: convince Staph to anoint a Chosen One to upset the established order. And he gets back at me at the same time by telling her to choose my nephew. What did you do with him, by the way?"

"I laid him in bed next to the sleeping lady in the tower, thinking whatever kept her preserved might work on him, too, until we could find you and perhaps revive him," Fia answered.

"Oh," Grinda said, looking surprised. "That wasn't a bad idea."

"Begging your pardon, Lady Sand Witch," Poltro said, "I'd like to make sure I understand. If you revive your nephew somehow, he's going to wind up killing King Benedick because of being the Chosen One? Do I have that right?"

Grinda blew a raspberry. "I don't think he was the Chosen One at all. Getting crushed by a falling woman is not the sort of thing that enchantment would allow to happen, but it does sound like the sort of thing that would happen to my nephew."

"Well, then, who's the Chosen One if it's not him?" Gustave wondered aloud. "It was only the two of us there." All the human eyes swung around to look at him, and quite a few of the crab eyes on stalks did as well.

"You weren't a talking billy goat before Staph arrived, right?" Grinda said.

Lord Toby chuckled. "Of course! Now it makes sense!"

The truth clicked in Gustave's head: the drunken pixie hadn't used any magic at all on Worstley but had used plenty on him. "Oh, dang," he said, and took a few steps back. "Look, y'all, I don't want to kill any kings or upset any natural orders. I'm not cut out for civics. I can eat the heck out of your ugly old sweaters if you want and turn them into neat little brown pellets a few hours later, but managing a kingdom? No way."

"Well," Fia said, "normally I'd seek a way to hug it out, but it would seem to me that the thing to do is kill this Løcher guy and maybe Staph the pixie for good measure. That way the Chosen One enchantment dies with her and we have no more shenanigans out of Løcher. I mean, that's assuming that the enchantment dies with the caster."

The sand witch nodded. "Yes, darling, that's how it works."

"No, no, wait a second," Gustave said. "If you take me to the capital where Løcher is, that's going to put me in close proximity to the king, right? And this enchantment is trying to get me to kill him. So I'd accidentally poop in his soup or cause his carriage to flip over. This is a bad idea for everybody."

Fia waved away his objections. "It'll be fine, Gustave. We kill Staph first, and it'll all work out."

"Or I'll accidentally step on the king's necklace and strangle him. No thank you. I'll stay right here, and y'all can go have at it."

"Ah, but we need your aura," Grinda explained. "Things just seem to happen around Chosen Ones. Guards turn their heads, torches go out at convenient times, the right key just so happens to fall out of the right pocket. It will be tremendously easier to take out Staph if you're with us. You'll definitely need to come along."

"Gadzooks!" Gustave's goat lips spluttered and spat as he sighed in frustration. "You stupid humans never listen to me."

Once Gustave had wanted only to eat and poo and make Worstley's life miserable. Then he'd wanted to escape the farm boy's mother's stew pot and perhaps see what the world was like outside of his muddy paddock. But now? He wasn't exactly sure what he wanted, but he felt like it included not killing the king and plunging the country into war or whatever happened when people were dying all over the place. When soldiers roamed the land unpaid, the goat figured, lots of innocent four-legged animals ended up roasted over fires. He had a . . . dang it. A responsibility now. Stupid Chosen Oneness.

Grinda stood up. "Well, that's it, then. If we're going to the capital, I have much to do. We'll leave in the morning and stop at the Goblin Market to pick up some necessities. But you must be tired, my darlings. Relax and enjoy yourselves tonight. Have fun in the Garden of Pellish Delights if you wish. Milieu Goobersnootch will see that you are well taken care of and that you have comfortable rooms, won't you, Milieu?"

"Of course, my lady."

"Fantastic. Well, then—"

"Wait." Argabella's voice cut Grinda's jolly farewell short. "You need to tell me why you did this to me. To the sleeping Lady Harkovrita. To the whole castle."

Grinda sighed as if the whole thing was simply exhausting, even for people who had previously been swanning about on a private beach with drink-bearing sparklecrabs. "You see, I had to, my dear. It was Løcher working through Staph again. He had a grudge against the Earl of Borix and assigned Staph to lay an enchantment on the Lady Harkovrita that would have been tremendously embarrassing to the earl while, not coincidentally, inconveniencing me."

Argabella, for one, did not seem to buy it. "What sort of enchantment?"

"An aura of potential similar to the Chosen One's, except with a nautical focus. The Lady Harkovrita was destined to become the world's most feared pirate, the Bosun One. Her father would have lost his earldom, and my shipping interests, which are not insignificant, would have suffered greatly. I tried to dispel the enchantment but failed. So rather than let it work, I set up an itsy-bitsy little plan to put the whole castle to sleep until I could find a solution. That way no one would suffer."

Argabella was quivering with anger instead of fear this time. "Except for me."

"Yes. But I had good reason for that, too, and I'll tell you—if you could just wait one more day." Her old eyes flicked among the rest of the party. "I think it best we keep that matter between ourselves. So let's talk tomorrow in the Goblin Market, shall we?"

Silence fell among them, filled only by the susurrus of the surf, the clicking of crab claws, and palpable tension. Gustave unloaded a pound of pellets on the beach just in case he had to run in the next few seconds.

"Fine," Argabella snapped.

They all exhaled the breaths they'd been holding. Angry rabbits are in fact quite fearsome, and nobody wanted to see one off the chain.

"Sounds like getting rid of Staph will solve a lot of problems," Fia said.

"It will," Grinda said, nodding and smiling.

"Mine, too?" Argabella asked.

The sand witch's face fell. "We'll talk tomorrow, darling."

Gustave was very glad he wasn't an enchanted rabbit lady just then.

12.

At the Goblin Market, Glittering with Magic and Maquillage

The sand witch's hospitality was indeed gracious and boundless, at least according to Toby. He had originally intended to use his time to snoop through the castle, find Grinda's inner sanctum, and plunder her grimoires and potions for a magical object that would allow his full powers to blossom. But the Goobersnootch possessed an aggravating ability to show up any time Toby found himself alone in a promising sort of hall, and there were so many invigorating activities listed on an agenda swirled with the most beautiful calligraphy that he never got around to a proper ransacking. He instead found himself some hours later enjoying a vast banquet that could've filled even Ol' Faktri's capacious gut.

The courtiers at the feast were witty and clever and seemed fascinated with Toby, a lord in his own right. *Borix sounds just precious,* they cooed, *Do tell us about your rampant tower.* In between fragrant nibbles of gourmet cheeses, goblet after goblet of fine wine and mead, and the batted eyelashes of two young duchesses with a dozing chaperone, Toby all but forgot his original plan. When the duchess on the left mentioned that the Garden of Pellish Delights was lit beautifully at night by swans outfitted with softly glowing lantern hats, he couldn't think of a single reason not to join her on the lawn. For research, he told himself. As she led him outside, complimenting the tender down of his beard, he realized he'd forgotten all about his traveling companions and hadn't seen them in hours.

The next morning, Toby woke up nude and halfway tumbled into a topiary shaped like a giraffe. He was missing one sock, and his mouth tasted like he'd licked a swamp ferret. As he looked around, trying to remember the last twelve hours, he saw no sign of the naughty duchesses—or of Gustave, thank goodness. Chosen Ones tended to get in the way of dastardly deeds, even by accident. The Dark Lord hurried inside clutching an irate swan over his frontbum, only to find Milieu, somehow still awake and in perfect form, ready to return him to his well-appointed room. There Toby gladly dumped the swan out the window and availed himself of a wardrobe filled with wizardly garments in just his size and a bureau full of warm woolen socks and pointy hats. The exact moment that he completed his toilette, noting with alarm that several of his beard hairs were missing, a knock sounded on his door.

The Dark Lord smoothed down his eyebrows, checked the mirror, and tried to look urbane should yet another acrobatic duchess be standing in the hall with intriguing promises about swans. Alas, all he found was his party. Fia, for once, looked relaxed and cheerful, possibly owing to the new breastplate and greaves that complemented her chain-mail bikini, although he did find it peculiar that the beautifully molded metal featured a very wide window of cleavage right over her heart, which seemed like a major design flaw for a warrior. Poltro looked sleepy and well fed, and Toby had a vague memory of seeing her in the gardens the previous night, yelling at swans and accusing them of being vanilla geese. Gustave looked about the same as ever, although he had leather shoelaces dangling from his lips and almost seemed to be smiling. Argabella, however, looked like she hadn't slept a bit and had instead paced her room all night without pause, quivering in that way that she had.

"It's good that you've come to me," he began. "As a wise and powerful wizard, I—"

"Time to go," Argabella said, interrupting him. "Er, now. Please."

"I wasn't done."

"We don't care." Gustave slurped down his shoelace. "Grinda's ready to take us to the Goblin Market, and I hear they have some really disgusting edibles there, so let's get on with it."

"Disgusting? No no no!" Toby scoffed. "My dear goat, the Goblin Market is one of those oxymoronic misnomers where you expect it to be revolting but it's actually magical and wonderful. You can't have a horrible name *and* horrible wares and expect anyone to come. The goblins, though a strange people, are marvelous makers."

"Are you sure?" Poltro asked. "Because I met a goblin once, and I still feel like I can't wash my hands enough, because it was a bit sticky, I must say."

"Positive." Toby smiled patronizingly. "My dear children, many wonders await you."

"But have you ever been there?" Fia pressed.

"Well, no," Toby admitted. "But wizards talk."

"What other wizards have you talked to?" This again from Poltro, from whom he would've expected more loyalty. "Because as I grew up in your general farmyard area and watched very few folk come and go from your doorstep, I don't recall seeing anyone properly mysterious or uncanny besides the postman and yourself, of course, m'Dark Lord, sir."

At his wit's end, Toby waggled his fingers at the ceiling and ducked a falling pain au chocolat. "We wizards are an epistolary people!"

"Cor," Poltro said. "Sorry to hear that. Hope the doctor can help."

Toby shook his head sadly. "Let me pack my bags, and soon you will all see." Then, under his breath, "Honestly, the state of education in Pell today."

"But you taught me everything I know, sir."

Toby disappeared into his room, shutting the door in Poltro's face. It wasn't true, of course. He'd been the one responsible for neglecting her education, then later tried to make it right by sending her to Cutter, which had clearly been a mistake. What the lower classes didn't understand about Dark Lords was that their concerns were part of a larger sort of sphere. One couldn't get any magic done or make a mint off hedgehog hybrids if one was thinking about educating the young or healing the old. The nice thing about the top of Toby's tower was that he didn't generally have to see everything happening on the ground, especially if he left off his spectacles. That was the point of being wise and having untold knowledge: you knew well enough when to leave things alone.

And you also knew well enough when to become deeply involved, as was Toby's current role. For all that he didn't like Grinda as a person, he knew that the keys to her power were hidden somewhere in this palace—or on her person. A wand, a secret beard, someone's unbeating heart—it was nearby, and if Grinda would just stay occupied with the journey, he could find it and . . . well, *steal* was such a dirty word. Share? Borrow her powers? Siphon off a little? If he was clever enough, she wouldn't even notice. Although Poltro was correct that Toby had never actually left his tower, he had done quite a bit of reading and was anxious to build his knowledge as he slowly began to consolidate occult power. He knew that several Dark Lords nurtured plans to take over the world, but that sounded like a colossal bother. A turtlehog empire and unfettered access to fine cheeses: that was Toby's dark desire.

When he reemerged in the hall, nothing had changed except that Gustave had begun to nibble on the edge of a tapestry and Argabella was somehow even more anxious. The rabbit woman couldn't stop shaking, and her already buggy eyes were wide and twitching frantically. Toby worried that if she were to see a hawk outside, she'd stamp and start digging a hole. But Grinda had promised to reveal the truth of Argabella's transformation today, hadn't she? Toby needed to stay close in hopes that he might learn some nifty magic.

Not that he wanted to turn anyone into half a rabbit, but it would be nice to know that he *could*. If he needed to.

Milieu appeared in that silent, sneaky, disapproving way that he had and led them down several labyrinthine halls, depositing them in the foyer. "My Lady Grinda will meet you shortly," he said. "Please do refrain from masticating the draperies."

Poltro grimaced. "Oh, gross."

"If you don't want people to eat things, you shouldn't hang them at mouth level," Gustave grumbled.

Apparently, the halfling butler's idea of "shortly" didn't strictly agree with the dictionary's definition. After fifteen very uncomfortable minutes in the elegant but smallish vestibule, Toby could no longer make polite humming noises every time he accidentally made eye contact with someone.

"So, how was everyone's night?" he asked, supposing that if he was going to be uncomfortable, they should very well do the polite thing and join him.

"Lovely," Poltro piped up. "Fine picnic among a stealthy pod of rogues in a shadowy bit of garden. No chickens or crabs, plenty of cloaks and masks and whispering. Played an excellent game of Hide and Goose, although the geese weren't really fond of it."

"Poltro, those were swans."

"A honk is a honk, my lord. And my, what honkers!"

"How about you, Fia? Good night?"

Fia breathed in a sigh of happiness. "Milieu took me to a rough stone hall in the keep where the warriors meet to heft tankards of sturdy ale. They also had a lovely Chenin Blanc, excellent nose with an oaky afterbirth and light tonguing of pear and peach. I played the best game of dice in my life and won this beautiful armor from the blacksmith himself. Feels so good to get some coverage." She exhaled, and Toby had trouble not ogling, as the chestplate was mirror bright with elegant curlicues pointing right at the giant cleft exposed by the armor's unsafe and unnecessary window.

"Finished up with marbled tofu soufflé, fried okra blossoms with debauched guava au jus, and some arm wrestling." She tapped her new greaves. "Which I won."

"And I was led out to a barnyard filled with goats, cows, sheep, and a very arrogant alpaca," Gustave said, "since you were about to ask, I'm sure."

"Could any of them talk?" Toby asked.

Gustave shook his head, and little bits of hay flew out. "No, thank goodness. Can you imagine anything more boring than listening to an alpaca talk? *Oh, I'm just so tall and floofy, and everyone loves me. Look at my long neck and freaky teeth. Alpaca this, alpaca that.* Disgusting."

"So what did you do?"

Gustave gave a caprine shrug. "Ate some trash, peed on things, ejected pellets in areas bereft of pellets. Found a pooboy and harangued him, but he just took the abuse stoically. This Grinda trains her servants well. Oh, and Moxie and Doxy won't want to ever leave here, I don't think. She has dwarvelish cattle masseuses from Åftpümpf, and they gave our old oxen a prod and tickle they won't soon forget."

"That's fine. I don't imagine we'll need them from here on. And how was your night, Argabella?"

In response, the rabbit woman wailed and yanked down a tapestry before kicking it with a fluffy foot. "Wretched! It was wretched! That awful butler dumped me in a room with perfect acoustics and a wide variety of lutes, harpsichords, sousaphones, and bodhrans. There was a lovely lectern with a stack of creamy paper already scored with music staffs and a variety of quills and erasable inks. Magical windows showed scenes of great inspiration, and a giant book called *Ye Olde Rhyme Zone* sat, waiting. And I had bard's block! I couldn't even get one line of a song! So I smashed a few lutes and went outside to get drunk, but all I could find were massive amounts of freshly pressed vegetable juices. It was torture. Torture, I say! That nasty woman wants nothing more than to see me suffer."

This was the most the rabbit girl had ever said as well as the most emotion she'd shown. When she dissolved in hiccupping sobs, spouting tears that matted down her already patchy face fur, Fia gathered her up into an awkward hug and Toby was spared the dangerous responsibility of saying something sympathetic like "Oh?" or "You poor dear" or "How terrible of that monster to give you everything you should require to be happy."

Just then, the front door was opened again by Milieu, and Toby began to wonder if perhaps the Cask-snooper Goober-snitches were a very large clan of identical spy clones. A grand carriage waited outside, and Milieu unfolded a tidy set of steps and held out his hand to help their party aboard. Toby couldn't help noticing that the carriage wasn't shaped like a pumpkin, which was currently all the rage among the witchy elite. No, Grinda's carriage was shaped like an octopus, four of the arms curling to hold the wheels, two arcing toward the team of six dappled gray horses, and two twisting to support the liveried dwarf guards positioned around back and bristling with weapons. Fia was the first to accept Milieu's aid into the carriage, and Toby noted her hand on her shears as she stepped within, giving him a competent nod. Next came Poltro, who somehow managed to trip on a rogue crab, then Gustave, who raised an eyebrow at Milieu and leapt in without help. Argabella looked at Toby, and Toby looked at Argabella, for they were the last two people not inside the wheeled cephalopod.

"Is it foolish that I'm scared?" she asked him.

"Everyone's scared all the time," he responded. "But that's no reason not to keep on."

The rabbit girl gave him a real smile. "Thanks, Toby. I knew I could count on you."

Toby looked down, annoyed. "Don't go counting on me. Dark Lords can't be trusted."

Argabella punched him gently on the shoulder.

"I told you: I always saw you as more crepuscular than dark." With that, she hopped into the carriage, and Toby followed her.

Inside, all was sumptuous and oddly shaped. The carriage was upholstered in aubergine velvet with lilac spots and billowing silky curtains. Grinda the Sand Witch sat on her own cushy bench, smiling and gracious and utterly dressed to the nines in a matching traveling costume of every shade of violet. Her hat, although very wide and chic, held the telltale point that let anyone know she was a witch, and a very wealthy one indeed. Unlike wizards, who boasted of the height and sturdiness of their towers, witches prided themselves on exhibiting only the perkiest cones.

Grinda knocked on the roof of the carriage, which creaked into motion.

"I trust you all had a marvelous night?" she asked, the height of fashion and grace.

"Delightful," Toby said, settling in directly across from her to establish his dominance.

Grinda leaned back and crossed her legs, which Toby immediately mirrored. "I hear you enjoyed yourself in the Garden of Pellish Delights. Did you find my illusions satisfactory?"

Toby swallowed hard. "Illusions?"

"Those twin duchesses." Grinda laughed, throwing back her head gaily. "They were too perfect, were they not?"

"Too perfect," he mumbled, racking his memory. What had their names been? And what exactly had they looked like? Blond, perhaps? Definitely in possession of hair. Also, legs. Maybe? His memory was shifty, shadowy, unclear.

"Not bad for sand golems, I hope. One of my little pet projects."

Toby felt the color drain from his face. At least he understood now why his morning bath had been full of sand. "And the food was a treat."

"Ah, that was real." Grinda's grin gleamed like a tiger's smile. "And now that you've ingested my Bloodhound Blood Pudding Pinwheels, I'll always know where you are. Magic is wonderful, don't you think?"

"Wonderful."

Toby decided to be quiet for a while and immediately stopped aping her behavior, as it appeared to give him no strategic advantage.

"And the rest of you. Were your lodgings satisfactory?"

"Fantastic," Fia said.

"Rather pleasant if I do say so myself, even if a bit sandy, which one must expect at the beach considering the beach is made of sand," Poltro said with a grin.

"Functional," Gustave said. "Could've done with more boots."

"Merely functional? We can't have that." Grinda withdrew a crystal wand from her cleavage, waved it, and shouted, *"Brigan skokhaz!"*

An aged chukka boot appeared in a puff of sand and fell to the floor of the carriage, right in front of Gustave. He nudged it with his nose and cocked his head on the side. "Doeskin, worn for about a year, possibly lost in a swamp considering the slightly peaty odor." He licked it and gave a baa of delight. "I take it back. You are truly the hostess with the mostess on this coastess." For a few moments, the only noises in the carriage were Grinda's teeth creaking in a pleased smile and Gustave nibbling the boot with little moans of caprine ecstasy. To Toby's great disappointment, the wand had disappeared.

He pulled a small notebook from one of the many pockets in his cloak and began scribbling. That shoe spell could come in handy sometime. And he would now train his focus entirely on Grinda's cleavage with the aim of getting his hands on that crystal wand.

"Uh uh," the sand witch said, tapping her face. "Eyes up here, mister."

As the carriage rumbled along and Grinda made flawless small talk and repeatedly reminded him not to stare hungrily at her blouse, Toby let his gaze wander to Argabella. The rabbit woman was sitting as far away from the sand witch as possible and looked terribly uncomfortable, even more twitchy than usual. She tried several times to question Grinda, but the witch inevitably sidestepped the inquiries with her conversational legerdemain, leaving Argabella stuttering on the edge of a faux pas. With each mile, the rabbit girl looked more disgusted and queasy. When the carriage finally jolted to a stop, Argabella lurched forward with a gasp, upchucking a generous amount of carrot juice directly into Grinda's violet-wrapped lap.

"She gets travel sick," Fia said, helping Argabella stand and all but carrying her out of the door Milieu had just thrown open.

"Indeed," Grinda said through gritted teeth. "Destrugerie vamati." One wave of the crystal wand and her lap was again clean. It was at that precise moment, the moment of miraculous vomit banishment, that Toby realized he had never wanted anything as much as he wanted to steal her wand; it was a need, really.

Perhaps he was going about it the wrong way, staring too obviously. But Grinda cut such a dashing figure that it was hard to look away even when one didn't want to reach down her shirt and steal the key to her power. Statuesque and lithe, she was the most radiant thing in the immediate vicinity, which included a scrubby field and a few rotting stumps. Toby straightened his robes and tried to look replete with arcane knowledge. And calculate how much those dwarvelish guards must cost Grinda to keep on staff. Such fighters were not cheap. He was growing insecure about the size of his tower.

"If you need to pass gas, I'd go over there," Gustave whispered. "Near the horses. They don't mind."

"I do not need to do any such thing," Toby snapped.

"Well, then you might want to move the parts of your face around so you don't look pained and constipated. Not a good look for humans, from what I've noticed."

Toby shook his head and put on a wise sort of smirk that wizards used to remind everyone how clever they were.

"Oh, no. It got worse. Tell me what you ate," Gustave said. "So I won't eat it."

On the verge of the sort of rage that incited rain showers of garlic naan, Toby headed over to Argabella and Fia instead. Considering the look of nausea on Argabella's face, no one would ask him about the idiosyncrasies of his own facial expressions.

"What's she doing?" Argabella asked. "And where is this Goblin Market?"

Grinda was walking to and fro, peeking her head around as if she were trying to avoid angry hornets or possibly trying a new dance move that wasn't going to catch on.

Toby didn't actually know what the sand witch was doing. That annoyed him, so he indulged in some self-soothing in the form of sharing his hard-won wisdom.

"Goblin Markets only show up at dusk on a full moon, when their mysteries might remain hidden from the stark light of day," he explained grandly.

"Wrong," Grinda said. "Here it is." She grabbed a bit of air and pulled it back to reveal a completely other place. It was as if she'd found a door in nothing and opened it to reveal . . . something. Toby was painfully reminded of the elves' magic in Morningwood, which had likewise left him feeling unmoored and unmanned.

"Step right in," Grinda urged them. "I can't hold this all day." Over by the carriage, something grunted, causing the dwarvelish guards to bellow bravely and draw their swords. Argabella's foot stamped repeatedly before she could stop herself. Gustave ejected caution pellets, and even Toby felt his beard hairs curl protectively upward.

"Go on, now," Grinda said. "Hurry."

Gustave trotted in, followed by Argabella, still with Fia's arm around her. Poltro slunk in as rogues do, while Toby waited to be last.

"After you," he said.

"Oh, no," Grinda warbled. "After you."

"A gentleman never lets a lady go last."

"Unless you know how to fold time, you'd best hurry in." She chucked her chin toward the commotion behind the carriage. "This clearing is guarded by a troll with very bad anger issues, and my guards can only detain him so long."

Toby had not yet met a troll, and although he had hoped they were jolly people with brightly colored hair, the fact that Grinda didn't want to meet one suggested that Toby *really* didn't want to meet one.

"If you insist," he said, hurrying through the hole in the middle of nothing.

Stepping through was much like stepping through a door in the same way that falling face-first into a tar pit is like swimming. The air was thick with strange smells and raucous noises, none of them good. Toby's party clustered together like scared baby ducks until Grinda urged them on.

"Hurry, hurry," she clucked. "Haven't got all week."

As they walked, Grinda talked with equal briskness. "The Goblin Market is the finest way to shop, provided you touch nothing, talk to no one, and under no circumstances accept gifts from strangers." She slapped Poltro's hand as the rogue attempted to snatch an unrealistically flawless peach from a pile of likewise unrealistically flawless peaches. "Also, no stealing. They'll cut off your pinkie finger."

"S'not so bad," Poltro said.

"But they throw away everything that isn't the finger."

Poltro gulped. "Point taken."

As they walked, Toby was amazed, but mostly at how wrong he'd been about Goblin Markets. It wasn't an outdoor collection of colorful stalls and wagons lit by glowing lanterns and helmed by friendly sprites. No, it was all indoors, two grim and stodgy stories of connected shops helmed by hideous and annoying goblins. The architecture was dull and unimaginative, and the goblins themselves were likewise a disappointment. No wings, no glitter, no smiles. Just twisted creatures like gray, hairless monkeys, most of whom wanted to sell him magical hair curlers and high-priced bedsheets. Several of them followed the group, demanding that they take various surveys.

"No thank you," Argabella kept saying, which only seemed to make the goblins more passionate in their hectoring.

"Just ignore them," Grinda said.

"But that's rude."

"You can't outrude rude people. Now ignore them and keep up before they catch you with those curlers. Your nose hairs will never be the same."

They passed shop after shop, all of which looked fascinating and also slightly predatory. Finally, Grinda led them into a storefront with the words GLAMOR SHOTTES scrawled over the door in what looked like fresh blood. A wizened goblin in a vibrant orange wig met them just inside.

"My Lady Grinda, what a pleasure," the goblin said, although it sounded somewhat like she was gargling. "Are you here for another injection of—"

"No, my dear," Grinda interrupted. "My friends and I are traveling to Songlen, capital city of Pell, and they must look the part. Hair, makeup, wardrobe, toenails. And whatever a goat needs. Put it on my tab."

The goblin bowed low, her wig falling off and forgotten. "As you wish, my lady." Rising back up, the goblin clapped her hands, and out ran at least thirty more goblins, all clad in aprons and carrying pincushions and yet more of the dastardly hair curlers. Soon Toby found himself sitting in a chair, being attended to by five goblins. One buffed his nails, one trimmed his eyebrows and nose hairs, and one styled his hair into the tangled, curly mass that was currently so au courant for the wizardly set. He was most pleased with the beard extensions, and as a goblin painstakingly attached artificial hairs to his chin, he looked around for his friends.

Fia barely fit in the chair and seemed deeply uncomfortable with the way the goblins were waxing off her excess hair and oiling her muscles. Poltro was rocking a smoky eye and looked deeply suspicious in the all-black costume the goblins had practically sewn her into; her last outfit, once Toby's pride and joy, had been rendered filthy by repeated tussles with farm animals and tussocks of grass, not to mention a marination in lemon juice and giant mucus. Gustave had been unceremoniously dumped into a large copper tub and scrubbed within an inch of his life, and he was now standing on a small pedestal surrounded by rage pellets while a trio of goblins curled his silky black fur. He was hating every minute of it, and it was all Toby could do not to burst out laughing.

Poor Argabella, however, looked sodden and miserable. Her fur had been washed and fluffed, but no matter what the frantic goblins did, it fell right back down, limp and scraggly. Her ears flopped down to frame her face, and her watery eyes rejected every attempt at cosmetics as if the manufacturers had simply not bothered to test their products on animals. Sitting in the chair, quaking, she looked like she was in her own personal rainstorm. And perhaps she was, emotionally. Her eyes couldn't rest on one spot, and Toby had to assume she was hunting for Grinda, who had disappeared in all the hubbub.

"Crunch break!" the head goblin called. "Best get out before the store closes!"

"Or what?" Poltro asked.

"Or you get crunched."

Thanking them profusely and spraying them with clouds of putrid perfume, the goblins finally bowed the group out of their shop. As soon as they stepped back into the dreary stone of the market, Grinda appeared, eating a large pretzel. The lines on her face, if possible, were even more blurry. When she chewed, it looked like melting taffy smeared with lipstick. There were limits, Toby realized, to what magic could do.

"You all look fabulous," she enthused. "Now, supplies. We'll be going to Nardstromp's, one of the biggest shops in the entire market. As such, it's of vast importance that you stay close to me."

"But Grinda—"

The witch kept talking, ignoring Argabella completely. "As I'm a longtime customer, the goblins wouldn't dare defy me, but as mere visitors, your treatment may be more . . ."

"Disappointing?"

"Transformative, if you're not careful. So, again: Touch nothing. Take nothing. And most especially, lick nothing." She pointed at Gustave with a perfect purple nail. The goat slurped down the last of the silk ribbon the goblins had tied around his neck.

"Who, me?" he said, then burped.

"Now come along."

Before Argabella could push her with further questioning, Grinda swept majestically down the thoroughfare, leaving the party jogging to keep up with her expansive stride. Toby was the last of them, hanging back to take a closer look at the shops along the way, many of which he longed to enter. He saw a shop of nothing but candles, then one of hats, then one of candles poured into hats. And then came Master Hornswoggle's Cheese Emporium, which passed by all too quickly.

But every now and then something would make him do a double take, and he felt certain his eyes were playing tricks on him. In one shop, the mannequins were momentarily screaming human children, and the next moment they were simply forms of carved wood sporting brightly colored lederhosen. In another shop, a selection of shirts were scrawled with phrases like DEATH TO ALL HUMANS and MY OTHER CARRIAGE IS A HEARSE FULL OF YOUR BONES and I DARE YOU TO LICK ME. Yet another shop blared horrible music, and as Toby glanced inside, he briefly saw an exhausted woman in a ragged red dress and broken shoes dancing like a puppet on strings. He blinked once, and he recognized it as a billowing red curtain behind a display of crystal slippers.

"Toby!"

A hand on his shoulder pulled him backward. He'd nearly stepped into the store with the crystal slippers, but Fia had yanked him back out. "You're into women's shoes?" she asked.

"I . . . I thought that curtain might go nicely in my banquet hall," he offered blithely.

"What curtain?"

Because, oddly, the red curtain was gone. Three goblins stared at him with too-bright eyes among the horrible T-shirts and racks of terrible mugs as he backed out of the doorway and hurried with Fia to catch up with their party. Nardstromp's loomed ahead, looking about as inviting as a cemetery at midnight. The rusted metal gate slowly creaked up as a goblin in a spiked helmet awaited them.

"Who goes there?" Grinda held out a card, which the goblin inspected. "And these . . . people . . . are your guests, my lady?"

"They are."

"They know the rules?"

Grinda glared a warning at them, hands on hips. "They do."

"Then welcome to Nardstromp's. Might I add we're having a splendid sale on sultan's pillows, main floor. Just take the stairs on your right."

Once inside, Toby was taken aback by the hugeness of the shop. It seemed to go on forever in all directions, a sea of clothes ranging from tiny sprite sizes up to robes for giants roughly the size of Ol' Faktri. A pair of men's underpants big enough to use as a shelter for their entire group hung from a clothes hanger like a trapeze, promising exciting new Y-front technology.

Something caught Toby's eye, and he stopped in place.

WIZARDS ONLY, a sign read, right over an enticing sort of heavy curtain festooned with silver moons and stars. Toby watched his group following Grinda toward a display of rucksacks before turning to investigate. He had always considered himself to have the potential of a powerful wizard, and he had never before had the opportunity to shop a selection of items curated just for his needs. Perhaps he could procure a crystal wand like Grinda's or secure a beard spell that would make his extensions permanent and thereby boost his powers. In any case, there was no harm in perusing the goods. With a smirk, he ducked through the curtains, appreciating the wizardly scent of sage and patchouli indelibly drenching the fabric.

Once inside, he waited for his eyes to adjust . . . but they didn't. The room was pitch black. Toby fumbled against the wall for a light switch, then, finding none, fumbled for the curtains. They were gone. The wall was, too. Goblin laughter echoed through the chamber. When Toby tried to take a step, he found heavy manacles around both of his feet.

"What is this farce?" he cried.

"Touched the velvet curtain, didn't you?" a sullen voice said in the dark.

"I had to touch it in order to pass through it."

"That's how they get you," the voice replied. "When they say not to touch anything, they mean it."

"But the sign said this part of the shop was for wizards only."

"Well, that's true. It's an oubliette for wizards. Anybody you have out there has already forgotten about you."

"That's foolishness. Who are you? What kind of a joke is this?"

The voice snorted a laugh and murmured a spell: "Leukhtam."

Toby had to squint at the sudden brightness. After a few moments, he was able to tolerate the light enough to see that beside him sat an aged, spindly man in long blue robes. The wizard, for he had to be a wizard, as he was holding a ball of pure light in one hand, had a most magnificent beard down to his navel and long hair the color of spiderwebs. And he looked exactly like a doll—no, an *action figure*—Toby had adored as a child.

"It can't be. Are you . . . Merlin?"

The old man rolled his eyes. "Oh, yes, well, very fine. They've forgotten me out there, but I suppose people in here can remember me all day. Yes, I am he. And this is Glandalf." He pointed at a gray-robed skeleton manacled to the floor on his other side.

Toby's heart just about fell out of his butt.

"Then we're trapped here? Together? Forever?" he asked.

Merlin kicked Glandalf's skeleton. "Something like that."

"Well, then. Considering we have nothing but time here, perhaps you could teach me that light spell."

Merlin looked bored beyond belief. "Sure. Trade you for a spell that magically releases goblin manacles."

"Er," Toby said. "My main skills involve making it rain bread." Overcome with anxiety, he waggled his fingers at the air just above Merlin's tall blue hat. Raisin buns hailed down, pelting the old man and making him grunt.

"I hate raisins," Merlin said.

For several moments they just sat there, Toby staring at Merlin, his hero, as Merlin picked apart a piece of his raisin bread and sulkily threw the raisins at Glandalf's corpse.

"Toby!"

"Did you call me, Merlin?"

"It was not I."

"Toby? Dark Lord! Here, Dark Lord!"

"He likes to be called crepuscular."

"I don't care what you call him; I just want him found before I have to speak to your manager."

"I am a manager—"

"Find him, or you'll be a manager-colored stain."

"I'm here!" Toby screamed. "By the skeleton! Behind the curtain that says WIZARDS ONLY, but don't touch it or you'll get stuck here and die."

"Very optimistic of you," Merlin noted.

"Ah, there you are." A powerful hand bit into Toby's shoulder, lifted him off the ground, and swung him through space. The next thing he knew, he was standing in the middle of Nardstromp's, staring at a display of harpy brassieres. A large, buff goblin stood before him wearing nothing but a small pin reading STORE MANAGER.

"My lady Grinda, on behalf of Nardstromp's, I thank you for your continued business, but I am forced to request that you keep a better eye on your charges. Perhaps next time you'd like to borrow one of our complimentary strollers."

"Of course. It won't happen again." Grinda gave Toby what could only be termed a stare of doom. "Will it, Dark Lord Toby?"

Toby looked down at his feet, now free of manacles. "I shall try to restrain myself," he said through gritted teeth.

The manager backed away, bowing, and disappeared into the rows of goblin-sized tap pants.

"While you were amusing yourself, we were able to purchase all that is necessary for our trip to Songlen," Grinda said, sounding annoyingly magnanimous. "Waterproof rucksacks, food, silken tents, lotions and potions. The works. Now we just need to visit Ye Olde Mappe Shoppe to plot our course."

"Grand."

Grinda stepped close and put a finger under Toby's chin. "Loosen up, wizard. Adventure expands the mind and—"

"And traps me in a dungeon with some old crazy stranger and a bunch of bones. How were you able to remember me, anyway? Oubliettes make you forget people."

Grinda's face collapsed like a flying buttress made of putty. "I . . ."

"It wasn't her. It was me," Gustave said. "I remembered you. Not these guys! They were all, *Who's Toby? What Dark Lord? With what sad excuse for a beard? What kind of ding dong would use magic to make rye bread?* That's all I heard until we were right next to that freaky curtain. And I was like, you guys are under some kind of crazy goblin magic. Grinda wanted to leave, but I found the manager."

"You mean you pooped on a carefully crafted pyramid of brandy snifters," Fia said.

"Yes. That's how I summoned the manager."

Grinda cleared her throat and pasted on her smile. "Everything worked out for the best then, yes? Let us continue."

But Toby stopped where he was. A strange feeling slunk into his heart, and he felt as if he were a thousand million miles away from home and comfort and as if all his goals were immeasurably far away. He'd wanted to leave his tower, sure, but only because he'd been so sure that he'd be the ruler of any realm he entered. Smart, moneyed, a little bit magic and hungry for more, the Dark Lord had nowhere to go but up. Or so he'd thought. As it turned out, the real world was a terrifying and ridiculous place where people with little sense made foolish rules that could ruin one's life with the flick of a curtain.

"I want to go home," he said very quietly.

"Don't say that." Fia bumped him with her elbow, nearly knocking him to the floor. "I felt that way right after I left my village. When I lost my armor and got bitten by a zebra and dropped all my food in the mud. But I kept going. Sometimes that's what you have to do: just keep going until everything makes sense." Her gaze flicked to Argabella, and she smiled a secret smile. "Keep moving, and good things will start to happen again."

"But I was chained next to a pile of human bones!"

"Did you not hear me? I got bitten. *By a zebra.* Now come on."

Grinda had reached the gate out of Nardstromp's, followed by a fleet of goblins pulling and pushing bits of luggage and picnic baskets and a small sled of tent parts pulled by a grimy pegasus, which was more like a Shetland pony mixed with an angry goose. The metal cage was raised, and the guards saluted, and the winged pony snapped at everyone on her way out, and then they were finally alone in the middle of the market with their wares.

The moment he stepped out of Nardstromp's, Toby immediately forgot why he'd been so angry and sad and terrified. "This beard is doing me some favors," he said, stroking the extensions sprouting from his chin. "Everything's coming up Toby!"

"Take your bags and don't let go, darlings," Grinda warned. "There are always cutpurses about."

Poltro pulled out her knife and jumped around a bit to discourage any other thieves in the area, and Gustave sighed and wiggled into the harness of the travois that pulled the tent poles along. Fia shoved an indigo velvet rucksack into Toby's arms, and he accepted it, staring down at the gift.

"Do I smell . . . cheese?" he asked hopefully as he flipped back the flap.

Fia gave him a rare smile. "From Hornswoggle himself. The ol' witch is easily talked into deluxe baskets that come with free goblets."

Moved by this kindness, Toby struggled to pay it forward by caring about someone else. "Is Argabella okay?" he asked.

At that, Fia's smile grew wider. "She will be. She's been asking Grinda constantly to reveal that big secret, but the sand witch is slippery. She'll have a hard time avoiding the question on the road."

"The sand witch is certainly no *hero*," Toby mused, and arched an eyebrow by way of challenge.

"But neither is she a *sub*-human," Fia replied.

"Ha! Excellent," Toby said, and stroked his fake beard, pleased to have punned at Grinda's expense.

"She ain't fun on a bun," Gustave muttered. When they both turned to gape at the interrupting goat, he shrugged his narrow shoulders. "What? I like to be part of whispery conversations, too. We're here, by the way."

The party had stopped in front of one of the numerous kiosks generally blocking and disturbing the Goblin Market's customers. But this one wasn't sprouting a dozen goblins with clipboards and curling irons; no, it held merely one aged goblin, his face a topography of lines and bumps and strange archipelagoes of skin tags. Before this ancient creature sat a globe that finally satisfied Toby's yearning to see real magic. The sphere was forged of seamlessly pieced together crystals and stones, with oceans ranging from light blue to an indigo so dark that Toby imagined he could see giant monsters smoothly undulating under the surface and fluffy otters cavorting atop it. The part of the globe facing him showed the western earldoms of Pell, from the verdant pastures of Borix to the mighty swell of Morningwood to the southern shores of Teabring. The Coxcomb of the Korpås Range towered above all, and there might have been some tiny gryphons circling it. Toby longed to set the globe twirling and see what might lay across the entire sphere, but the goblin looked grouchy and implacable, his gnarled fingers protectively splayed across the glittering stone.

"Ah, Grinda. Come to yet again attempt to steal my map?"

The witch clutched her hand over her heart. "Of course not. You're so silly. I would never!"

"You always."

"We merely seek news of the way to Songlen. Best route for the current weather and giant feeding grounds, if you please."

The goblin grunted and held out his lined palm, and Grinda dropped in several jewels that instantly made Toby drool, as he could see the magic throbbing in their depths. The goblin merely opened his cratered maw and tossed the stones in, swallowing audibly.

"Hmm," he said, running wizened fingers over the globe. "No use taking the southern route to Songlen at Nockney. The giant laborers are striking, calling all travelers union-busting scabs, twisting them into meat pretzels, and eating them with a rather regrettable ketchup made in the Several Macks. You'll want to circle around far to the east and take the ferry at Pikestaff. Or risk traveling under the mountains through the Catacombs of Yore if you're feeling brave and didn't have a particularly horrid childhood."

"Oh, not again," Grinda said, crossing her arms and pouting. "Every time we let them out of Yglyk, the giants cause trouble. Why must they continue with this nonsense?"

"Because they deserve to get paid like everybody else?" Fia growled.

Grinda skewered her with a stare. "I do appreciate their right to fair compensation for their labor. You will never understand how much I support that principle. But they are not demanding to be paid like everyone else. They are demanding they get paid in human bones, which they grind into bread."

Mighty Fia blanched. "Ah. Catacombs it is, then."

Grinda looked her up and down, which took longer than usual. "You had a good childhood?"

"I meant to say that going east sounds great."

"East it is, then. Let's be on our way, shall we?"

"Pleasure doing business with you," the old goblin said. "Unless anyone would care to trade their first memory or second-born son for a magical gift."

Toby started to raise his hand, and Grinda shoved it back down.

"He'll just give you an enchanted hair shirt or a sloth that slowly belches the alphabet," she warned. "Never trust a goblin."

"But you're trusting him! You just let him plan our entire route!"

She looked down her long, slightly melty nose at him. "Yes, but I know what I'm doing. Or would you like to go back to wizard jail and play with your little friends?"

Toby's shoulders slumped, but he wasn't sure why. He didn't know what wizard jail was, but he liked the idea of having friends.

"Catacombs it is," he said.

The witch smiled a pedantic smile. "Well, actually, we decided to go east."

Toby decided he never wanted to go to the Goblin Market again.

13.

NEAR THE BUSHY CLEFT
OF MORTAL PERIL

They stood on a very impressive promontory, laden with junk and more than ready to get on with it in Gustave's opinion. Grinda had opened yet another door into nothing, and now here they were in the great outdoors, which the goat found deeply comforting. The Goblin Market had been a bit of a disappointment to Gustave, but then again, what did a goat really want in life? Boots and the company of many other herbivores who looked to be fatter, slower, and more delicious than he did, mostly. As he'd passed the shop windows, Gustave had seen room after room of succulent trash, subdivided into specialties: belts, harnesses, aprons, and of course shoes. After a while, he got bored and watched his friends' reactions. Which made him curious.

As they set off marching after Grinda, who now wore a very expensive pair of delectable hiking boots and a puffy sort of vest, Gustave asked, "Hey, so what did you guys see in the Goblin Market that looked good?"

Poltro sighed. "Cor, what didn't look good? The sneaky black cape store, the shop full of boots with silence charms on 'em, the boutique absolutely dripping with chicken guillotines. I would've gone into that one for sure if not for . . ." She kind of trailed off, sounding sad.

"Got your purse cut, did you?"

"Them goblin thieves must have the market cornered on silent boots and sneaky capes. Didn't even feel the weight of it gone. So now it's chickens, crabs, and goblins, that being the list of things I don't like, and can you imagine if you combined it all? A goblin riding a crab riding a chicken? Boggles the mind, that does. In bad taste, it is."

Fia caught up with Poltro, looking concerned. "What? I didn't see any of that. I simply saw endless armorers, chain-mail craftsmen, swordmasters, martial artists, and shops that sold badly made throwing stars and lots of camouflage."

"What?" Toby said. "I saw lots of . . . er, magic stuff. Nothing weird. Just magic stuff. It seemed to change when I confronted it directly, though."

"What about you, Argabella?" Fia asked.

The rabbit girl kept stomping along, her eyes pinned to Grinda's well-clothed back. "There was one music shop filled with lutes that filled in the missing words in songs, but most of them were just . . . forget it."

"No, what?"

It took a few moments of marching, falling in behind Grinda's lead, for Argabella to say, "I kept seeing abacuses and ledgers and mirrors that showed me what I looked like before I was a beast. When I was just a normal girl. I'm not saying I was much to look at then, but . . . I don't know. I kept feeling like if I just went in the right shop and promised my best memory to the right smirking goblin, I could be me again and possibly earn an associate's degree in accounting."

"But this is you," Fia said gently. "For now. And there's nothing wrong with you. Your heart is the same either way."

Argabella shook her head so hard that her ears flapped. "No, I don't think that's right. I was different then. I'm not sure what changed, but I feel like I lost something. I want to be all me."

Fia stood in front of her, stopping her, and Gustave lingered to watch the show. If only he had some old laces to munch.

"Then let's get answers," Fia said. "Come on. I'm sick of this."

Looping her arm through Argabella's, Fia stomped ahead as fast as her boat feet could carry her and planted herself in the path in front of Grinda. Gustave capered behind them, considering this the most interesting escapade currently on offer. At best, he'd find out how the rabbit girl had become half rabbit. At worst, he'd see Fia turned into something half animal, and maybe it would be an okapi or a narwhal or something really interesting.

"Listen, lady. You owe this girl some answers. So get talking."

Grinda drew back, one eyebrow up—the usual display of Chronic Resting Witch Face. Her fingers waggled like she was considering reaching into her puffy vest for her wand but wasn't yet ready to go to such trouble.

"I don't owe her anything."

"Er, well, but you do," Argabella said, spreading her rabbit feet in a powerful sort of stance. "You said you'd tell me today, and it's today, so get on with it."

"Time is relative," Grinda said, fluttering a hand in the air. "And the time is not yet ripe."

"Oh, it's ripe," Fia said, standing slightly to Argabella's other side. "It's practically brown and spotty. Fruit flies are interested."

They were all now in a rough circle around the sand witch, although Gustave had his doubts that Toby and Poltro had really meant to lend their personal placement to such an aggressive arrangement. Just a little farther on, the path led under a stand of tall trees, not quite as impressive and lofty as Morningwood but still thick and sturdy in their own right. Gustave vaguely recognized them as pines, notable for their needlyness and sappiness and the sharp scent they lent the air, not to mention the fact that they were utterly inedible. The path Grinda was following disappeared into this pine forest, lined by blocky orange mushrooms and inhabited by birds that pooped normal poop instead of glitter if Gustave was any judge of that sort of thing, which he was. He was also getting to be a good judge of character, and the bunny girl had it. She deserved answers. For his part, at that point, he planted his four hooves and lowered his horns. It's not often one gets the chance to ram a sand witch right in the buns.

But Grinda, being the sort of person who wasn't easily cowed, put her chin up and kept walking. One foot in front of the other, she strode forward. Soon Fia and Argabella were in real danger of collision, and they both began stepping backward, neither giving way or backing down.

"Why did you do this to me?" Argabella asked, half begging. "What did I ever do to you?"

"Nothing," Grinda said, wiping a hand through the air as if erasing blame. "You were just in the wrong place at the wrong time. You were the catalyst of someone else's destiny. Trust me on this, darling: never give a rose to a pretty princess."

"She was a lady."

"Whatever."

Gustave was watching Argabella as that line was delivered, Grinda's tone dripping with dismissiveness. The rabbit girl fluffed up as if struck by lightning and screamed, well, like a rabbit, and a terrible sort of noise it was. Grinda reared back in confusion before shoving Argabella aside with one hand and barging past her along the trail, calling back, "Be as dramatic as you like; it won't change the cost of caviar."

But that was the wrong thing to say, and Gustave knew it immediately even if the spoiled witch did not. Argabella howled in anger this time and launched herself after Grinda, who took up running as soon as she heard fluffy feet pounding the trail behind her. They were all running now, even Toby, who was panting and holding his potbelly with one hand. For a woman past her prime, Grinda could sprint like a kid after an ice-cream wagon, and if Argabella hadn't been half rabbit and Fia hadn't been in spectacular shape, the witch might've escaped. Instead, the rabbit girl tackled the witch to the ground, and they skidded painfully in the dirt with Fia right behind them. Gustave pulled up short, followed by Toby and Poltro, who was actually quite swift when not encumbered by chickens or waylaid by stealthy pebbles.

Argabella straddled the sand witch, one furry hand in the older woman's coiffure, grinding Grinda's face into the dirt.

"You like that, Sand Witch? That taste good?" Argabella growled.

"She's going for her wand," Gustave hinted, as he'd noted the witch sliding a hand inside her vest. "Which is what I would call a bad thing."

"Can't have that," Toby said, edging in from the side. "Just hold her wrists."

Fia dutifully grabbed the witch's wrists, wrenching them behind her back.

"You're going to regret this," Grinda growled.

"Yeah, well, I regret a lot of things," Argabella said. "For one, BEING HALF RABBIT."

"Ah! There we go." Toby slid the crystal wand from the witch's vest. "I'll just keep this safe for you, shall I? Yes? Good." He stood, cradling the wand as if he'd finally found his sweetheart. Waving it experimentally, he said, "Brigan skokhaz!"

He must've said something vaguely incorrectly, as the thing that appeared on the ground wasn't quite a shoe, but it was big and leathery and close enough for Gustave's needs. The goat immediately set to nibbling just in case the faulty magic should waver.

"Now," Argabella said, holding a small, dull dagger to Grinda's throat, "tell me why I'm a monster."

Gustave backed off the shoe. "Whoa, now," he said, edging closer. "Is this really the way you want this to go? Whatever she did to you, you're basically saying you're willing to let her make you into a killer. But that's not who you are. You're a bard. You love roses and lettuce and cheese. You don't need to go killing uppity witches just to hear excuses for why they did selfish things that messed you up. Wouldn't you rather be a great person who's half rabbit and has some unanswered questions than a human being with blood on her hands?"

Argabella's mouth dropped open as the knife fell from her hand.

"Er, wow. Gustave. That's . . . gosh, you're right. I don't want—"

Argabella didn't get to finish her sentence, as Grinda flung her off and leapt to her feet, shouting, "Ah ha! You fool! You will never know true power until—"

Grinda didn't get to finish her sentence either, which Gustave considered fair. She'd started backing up, and she tripped over something and fell on her kettle with a witchy shriek. In one fell swoop, Gustave found himself yanked into the air, upside down and with his face shoved into Toby's butt. His trotters kept connecting with something soft that was apparently Argabella's stomach.

They were caught in a net.

The entire party had been swept up in it and now dangled, all tangled together, from a giant bag woven of vines that perfectly matched the forest floor. Even Grinda hadn't escaped the indignity of capture and had one leg flopping out of the net, her expensive hiking boot having fallen to the ground, revealing orthopedic socks and an ankle with so many varicose veins that it could've been its own map.

"Some rogue you are," Gustave grunted at Poltro, who was poking him from underneath. "How could you miss a trap like that? Isn't it kind of your entire job to check for that sort of thing?"

"I don't think I'm a very good rogue," Poltro said. "Cutter only gave me my Sneaking Certificate because Lord Toby paid him extra."

"I'm stuck, and my armor really is uncomfortable, and Argabella smells, like, really good," Fia said, followed by a more confused, "Wait, what?"

"I don't really mind this, as I still have the wand and Poltro has a stunningly cushy posterior," Toby said before stopping suddenly.

"Keep touching it like that, my lord, and I'm going to blackmail you when I get home, as I don't think my brother will approve of your handsiness," Poltro said. "Cor, maybe I'll finally be rich! Then I won't need to be a rogue at all!"

"Er, I think this net is somehow ensorcelled to reveal hidden truths," Argabella said. "Which is fine by me, as I was already saying exactly what I wanted to say, which is that you owe me answers, Grinda. And now that we're stuck together, you're going to start talking, by Borix."

"I don't have to tell you anything . . . except actually I do," Grinda said, all snappy. She tried to close her lips, Gustave noticed, but they wouldn't stay shut. "The thing is, I needed someone to guard the castle, keep out any troublemakers who might wake up the sleeping lady. The curse was supposed to attract someone who would fall deeply in love with Lady Harkovrita and give her a rose despite Staph's edict. It was supposed to be a rather strapping lordling— I had a nice one picked out from Retchedde, more brawn than brains, really, and I'd sent him on his way to court. But you got there first, and I suppose you gave her the rose, which meant that instead of a lordling turning into an overprotective, angry half-lion beast, I got a lovesick bard who became half rabbit. So there. Like I said—just bad luck."

As they were all crushed together, it was impossible not to feel Argabella quivering with unhappiness like a live mouse fallen into a gelatin salad.

"Then change me back!" Argabella moaned. "You did this, you can undo it!"

"It's not that simple," Grinda said quietly. "And you know that's not a lie. Curses are complicated, tangled things. I can magic the hair off your face or turn you into a half newt instead, but I can't pull the curse out of your blood. You won't be back to normal until I personally destroy the heart rose, and even then, the damage is done. You can never go back to being what you were. Circumstance changes people. Nothing is ever the same. If I sent you back to the castle now, you'd never be happy with what you had before because you've seen too much of the world beyond. Beast or no, better or worse, you are changed."

"I like you as you are," Fia said, "and I don't think you need to change."

"That makes me really happy, and I don't mind being tangled up here as long as I'm tangled up with you." Argabella cleared her throat. "All of you. I like all of you. I've been pretty lonely for the last five years, and it's nice to have friends again."

"I've never had friends before in my life, and I don't think I'm very good at it," Toby added.

"You're not, m'lord," said Poltro.

A profound silence descended, and Fia broke it by casually mentioning that lots of people she knew died in freak accidents, and so they were all probably going to die, too, and she hoped they'd all been sensible about their mortality and made some end-of-life decisions. Gustave found his mouth opening of its own volition.

"I would eat almost every one of you, given the chance," he said. "Over fifty percent of you are really annoying, and I don't even think you see me as a person."

Another profound silence began but was interrupted by Poltro. "Couldn't agree more. You're just meat on feet. Goat curry is pretty easy to make, provided you can cook the meat over a low flame for a long time, preferably in a large pot with some sort of acid and some sort of fat and quite a bit of spices to get rid of that unpleasant goaty flavor."

"Let's be quiet now," Gustave whispered. "If you're really quiet, you'll be able to hear me peeing on your backpack, Poltro. Also, I have some friends who are chickens, and they really are plotting against you. You're basically a national joke to them."

"Enough!"

Argabella's yell was so loud that all the birds in the forest went quiet.

"This has been terribly useful from a standpoint of personal growth, but I'm kind of ready to get down now. Can anyone with a knife pull it out and hack at the net without hurting anyone else?"

"Hmm." The net shifted and creaked where it touched Fia's huge shoulders. "I would only stab Toby a little, and I think he can take it."

"I can't! I'm an excessive bleeder!" Toby yelped.

"Gustave, can you gnaw it?" Fia asked.

"The only thing I can currently gnaw is, I think, Lord Toby's sweaty haunches. Let me see. Mrrph."

"Ouch!"

"Yeah. I'm facing the wrong direction. Sorry."

"Well, then. Here we go. What's the point in having rabbit teeth if you can't use 'em, am I right?"

"You might be good at opening bottles," Poltro said. "Or, say, gnawing carrots into interesting sorts of shapes. Oh! Or sharpening pencils."

He couldn't see anything but butt, but Gustave could hear Argabella gnawing on the thick vines that formed the net. And it was a good thing, too, as he could smell something heading toward them, something with a trollish odor, something that was probably hungry. It was far off still, but prey animals with a fondness for stink could smell such things, and Gustave, for one, didn't like it.

"Faster would be better," he whispered. "And quieter would be better than louder, seeing as how loud would attract the wrong sort of attention."

"But then someone could get us down!" Poltro said altogether too loudly for Gustave's taste.

Just like a predator who had forgotten how to predate. Being all loud and stupid.

"That someone will get us down, prod us a bit with spears, and put us in a stew pot," he whispered. "So shut up."

"You'd be good in a stew pot," Poltro noted. "Bit of spear prodding will help with the tenderizing, and goat can be a bit chewy, especially if it's overcooked. Nobody likes that."

"Nobody likes you," the goat grumbled.

"Almost got it," Argabella said, and then she must've gotten an important bit chewed through, as the whole net lurched sideways and Poltro, who was under Gustave and rather damp now, started to fall out.

"Keep chewing!" Gustave ordered. "If Poltro falls first and we all fall on her, no loss."

The sound of gnawing doubled down, and soon the vines snapped again. The solid body beneath him disappeared, and Gustave barely had the time to mutter, "Hope I don't land horns down" before he, too, was experiencing the unique and unpleasant sensation of tumbling through space. He did indeed land on Poltro, but feet down, which probably wasn't better from her point of view.

"Oof," Poltro grunted, and shouldered the goat off her before standing up. "Think I took a hoof in the giblets or possibly the kidney. Whatever it was, I do believe it's time to go pee behind a tree, and if there's blood, I'm going to be very upset and also a little concerned."

"Don't worry," Gustave said, standing on shaking knees. "That's just tenderizer."

Another creak overhead was his only warning before the rest of the party tumbled down like very awkward hail. The goat darted off the trail right before they landed in an ungainly heap. Argabella, he was glad to note, landed on top, which was the least of the good turns she deserved.

Everyone stood in various ways, all of them dizzy and inspecting themselves for damage. They seemed whole to Gustave, who didn't have a fantastic grasp of human anatomy and considered them awkward, gawky things at best. Poltro already had disappeared into the trees, and it was a good thing, as Gustave felt very much like kicking something.

"Well, now that we've all revealed our darkest secrets, we'd best get on the road," Grinda said, sounding older and sicker of life than she generally tried to pretend she was. "Gustave, get back in your harness."

"Oops. It's all broken," he said as innocently as possible now that nothing and no one could force him to tell the truth about anything that wasn't in his best interest.

Sure enough, the travois of tent poles had gotten bashed about in the fall from the net as well as by his stamping around on it and gnawing through some of the less noticeable bits, because it was bad enough being a beast of distinct edibleness without also being a beast of burden.

"I can fix that easily," Grinda said, doing her best to look elegant in her hiking gear, which was all mussed from falling out of a tree. "Toby, the wand?"

"Er," Toby said, holding out a handful of crystaline shards. "I fell on it."

"Drat and blast!" Grinda shouted, stomping a foot. "This is the most incompetent band of fools I've ever traveled with, and that in-cludes the Fellowship of the String."

"You saw the famous elven ring?" Toby asked, his heart dark with jealousy.

"No, the string. It wasn't very remarkable. And I was more of a groupie than an actual member of the fellowship. But be that as it may, we must get on the road and out of this cursed wood."

"It's cursed?" Argabella asked, looking up at the silvery towering pines.

"Considering the net, I think that's obvious. Can we move now?"

Gustave poked at the tent poles with his nose in a way that sug-gested he was incapable of feeling regret, and she sighed.

"Fine. We'll sleep on the ground like, I don't know. Who sleeps on the ground? Chipmunks? Lost princesses being chased by their step-mothers? We'll rough it. But I'd really rather not argue with whoever set that net. Deal?"

"Deal," everyone said at the same time, for footsteps could now be heard, along with branches breaking in their path.

They took off at a fast clip with only their rucksacks, and Gustave felt deliciously unencumbered at first before he realized he was the only member of the party without his own sack. He had no belongings, which wasn't much of a bother, except that he really did prefer a nice strip of leather to grass, and he also felt a bit left out. Maybe a goat would like a rucksack. A rugged brown thing made of leather and filled with old tin cans full of yet more leather. Was he not the equal of anyone here in valor and brains? Maybe not in meat yield if they were put on a scale, but he was definitely the one most in danger of becoming dinner. For the first time in his life, Gustave felt like he might not be as much of a person as those around him, and it brought him much consternation. Just in case things went south, he stayed close to Fia, as their earliest discussion had hinged on her sympathy toward the plight of creatures who tasted good with sauce.

As Fia had begun of late to travel rather close to Argabella, Gustave was able to watch the women as they stole glances at each other and smiled secret smiles. They were a cute couple, he thought, even if it was taking them quite a while to figure that out themselves. They stayed right behind Grinda as if expecting her to suddenly betray them. Which, Gustave thought, was the kind of thing that was likely to happen.

"Your teeth saved us back there," Fia said softly at one point.

"Er," Argabella said, looking down. "I guess it's nice to have a use."

"You have lots of uses. Your songs have saved us before. Hey, that's it! You could sing a song about how very swift and silent we are and how we get out of these woods unscathed."

Argabella considered it, then pulled out her lute. They were walking so fast that she could barely strum it once without falling behind Grinda's fast pace, so she strung it over her back and hummed a few bars.

> *"Well she's a real tough witch with a long history*
> *Of turning people into beasts just like me*
> *But she can lead quite a march when she gets down to it*
> *Left, right, left, there's nothing to it*

Hurry to the next spot
Come on let's hurry to the next spot
Hurry to the next spot
Let's all run away."

It took Gustave a few moments to realize that the forest was fly-ing by far faster than a forest had any right to. His trotters barely touched the path as he wound around aged pines and zipped past slightly confused stags. The pines gave way to maples, and the forest went from greens to yellows, golds, and fire-bright orange. With each repetition of her song, Argabella magically propelled them miles. When she stopped singing, it was like suddenly being mired in sand, and Gustave nearly fell over.

The reason they'd stopped was obvious: they'd reached another fork in the road.

The road split evenly in two directions around a bushy copse, and Gustave couldn't discern a visible difference in either path. They looked the same, and neither one was hung with a helpful sign em-blazoned with THE CAKE IS THIS WAY or SO MANY TEETH NOPE NOPE NOPE. The road to the Titan Toothpicks had at least been up front about such things. As far as Gustave recalled, the wizened map gob-lin had said nothing about annoyingly signless forks.

"We're going to step off the path to powder our noses," Fia said delicately. With her arm around Argabella, she disappeared among the golden trees. Everyone else continued to stare at the bristly cleft.

"Well, Grinda. You know everything. Which way do we go?" Toby asked, enjoying himself far too much.

Grinda glanced left and right and reached for a wand that no longer existed. "I don't know, Dark Lord. My wand is sand. Do you perhaps know any navigation spells?"

"I know eeny meeny miney moe," Poltro added, stepping into the circle. "Although you'll have to indicate which side is eeny in this case."

"Did your map goblin not tell you which path to take?" Toby pressed. "Or did you skimp on the magical jewels you tumbled into his paunch like they were cheap bars of nougat?"

"You know nothing of goblins, or maps, or nougat, you insignificant hedge wizard!" Grinda howled.

"How dare you," Toby said, drawing his cloak around himself and using his magic to drop a half dozen day-old bagels on her head.

"Wizards, witches, and various friends," Gustave said, daring to step between them. "This should be fairly easy to solve. We simply need to find the nearest river and follow it into the mountains because cities tend to be located along rivers by mountains or along the coasts. My highly refined snoot indicates we'll want to take the path on the left."

"Goats can smell water?" Toby asked.

"Of course. Do you know nothing of goats? Or, for that matter, how water works?"

"I KNOW MANY THINGS ABOUT MANY ANIMALS," Toby shouted. "AND ALSO HOW DARE YOU?"

Poltro stepped up, her dagger in hand. "You know, my lord," she said with a grin, "I know a way we can kill two goats with one stone. I mean one goat with two stones. Basically, you and I each take a stone, and we sneak up on the little freak, and—"

"You know I can hear you, right?" Gustave said, backing up, his rump coming increasingly close to the cleft between the paths.

Poltro looked at him, and he could see visions of goat curry bubbling in her eyes. Toby glared at him, and in the wizard's eyes Gustave could see visions of victory dances and ads taken out in the local paper avowing that the Dark Lord had killed the Chosen One. Which Gustave personally didn't believe he was and didn't particularly want to be, but his current issues were a bit more pressing than whether he'd been formally anointed by a pixie wearing one blue sock.

"Whoa now," he said, backing up until his rump hit a tree and then angling it so that he was pointed down the path he firmly believed to be the right one in that it was on his right and also correct. "I'm a contributing member of this traveling party."

"What do you contribute," Toby said slowly, "besides excrement?"

"And possible future deliciousness, provided I can find the right spices," Poltro added.

It was at that moment that Gustave noticed the dagger rising in her hand and the rock held in Toby's.

"I thought we were friends," the goat said.

"Dark Lords don't have friends."

"Cor, but that hits me where it hurts!" Poltro whined. "We might not be bosoms, my lord, but many's the evening we've dined together and discussed items of general interest, including chickens, animal husbandry, the dangers and delights of nougat, bread, and your plans to one day kill a Chosen One." Gustave couldn't help noticing that her current stalking behavior was the first thing he hadn't seen her botch up.

"Grinda," Gustave called. "A little help."

"Honestly, goat, I just brought you along to pull the travois, and you see how that went."

He was affronted to note that she was casually buffing her nails as she said it.

"Fia? Argabella?" he called. "Surely you two have something to say about the attempted murder occurring in your vicinity?"

But whatever they were doing, they didn't respond.

"But I'm the Chosen One!" Gustave bleated.

The Dark Lord grinned.

"That's kind of the point."

As if on cue, Toby and Poltro lunged for Gustave's throat.

14.

IN THE DANK NECROPOLIS OF HONEYCOMB AND DREAD

Grinda reflected that it had been many years since her patience had been pushed to the brink, but this crew of misfits from Borix had done the job. Profoundly unprofessional, the lot of them. How they'd ever managed to survive meeting Ol' Faktri was beyond her, and she'd never asked because she'd been so distracted by the news of her nephew's death.

Their escape certainly couldn't be thanks to this so-called Dark Lord and his fantastically clumsy rogue. When confronted with the simple task of slaughtering a goat—a talking one and a Chosen One, true, but still a mere goat—what did they do? The rogue stumbled on absolutely nothing and fell in the middle of the road, thereby tripping the Dark Lord and leaving the goat stunned for an entire second that he was still alive. But he recovered and took the opportunity afforded him, smartly ramming the hedge wizard in the head, knocking him unconscious and causing a few surprisingly soft dinner rolls to rain down by reflex. The rogue was trapped under her employer, and the goat backed up, said, "Nighty-night," and rammed her in the head, too. Then the cheeky beast looked up at Grinda. "You want some?"

"No thanks," Grinda said, flashing him a quick if fake smile. "I try to avoid attacking Chosen Ones. The odds are never in one's favor."

"That's right—hey, yeah! I didn't even need to be afraid there, did I?"

"Oh, no, you were right to be afraid. These powerful auras are a finicky business. They excel at keeping you alive until you turn everything upside down, but they're notoriously bad at making sure you get to that point unharmed. They tend to lead your quest into ridiculously dangerous situations, like this turning fork, where your party inexplicably turns on you."

"Say what now?"

Grinda motioned to the unconscious hedge wizard and his rogue snoring peacefully in the path. "When people act so strangely that you start to hate them, it's worth looking to see what might be controlling them. In this case, it's an enchanted path that craves blood. See how red the dirt is?"

"Gross."

"All part of your aura. It led you here. And once you fulfill the aura's intended purpose, it dissipates entirely, leaving you quite vulnerable. Most Chosen Ones die within a month of becoming king or waking the princess or whatever, so you have that to look forward to." Her grin this time was much more genuine.

The goat cocked his head and glared at her with one yellow slitted eye. "You keep smiling, but it's at all the wrong things."

"We have different senses of humor, I expect."

"We sure do. Look, I was grateful that you summoned some delicious chukka boots before—the doeskin was fantastic—but that's done, and I kind of think you just did it to put me in your debt. Well, I'm not in your debt, and I'm going to be keeping a close watch on you."

"Watch away, billy goat. Just help us get to Songlen so we can deal with Staph the pixie and Løcher, and then we can all lead blissful lives unencumbered by each other or troublesome enchantments or the machinations of power-mad men."

"Oh. But the machinations of power-mad women are okay?"

That accusation caused Grinda to abrade a cuticle rather painfully. The goat's gall was simply goading her giddy. But she kept her tone civil as she replied, "I don't seek power. You'll note that I live very far away from the seat of local government. What I generally pursue is independence, the freedom to spend my time in peace and quiet on my beach with my crabs, reading grimoires and romances and the occasional recipe for tarts. But now I seek revenge for Worstley."

She failed to mention that she also sought to end Løcher's foul maneuvering against her by killing him once and for all. And she'd like the poor folk of the kingdom to be treated better, as she'd been poor growing up and had benefited greatly from a hand up. Now she employed hundreds of people and paid them well. Helping folks when they needed it was a good policy, and it would be one she pursued if she could. No point in mentioning any of that to a goat.

"Well, I suppose we can agree on revenge for Worstley. He was a good pooboy, I must admit, except near the end there, when he said he was going to eat me. And all the times when he came to take my barnyard friends away and I never saw them again. You know. Like my parents."

A rustling of the shrubbery announced the return of Fia and Argabella, both of them smiling and slightly out of breath.

"Sorry!" Argabella practically sang. "Couldn't be helped. So, what did we miss—oh. What happened?"

"They tried to kill me because Fia left me all alone with them," Gustave said, bobbing his head at the two unconscious forms.

"What? But you had Grinda—" Fia began, but the goat interrupted her.

"Who was no help at all! We had a deal, and you shirked!"

The mighty Fia crossed her arms. "I don't think we ever had a formal deal. I said you could travel with me, not that I would protect you. And you said you'd be some kind of superspy, but I haven't heard a word of intelligence so far."

"Fine! Grinda likes tarts!" Gustave yelled, rolling his eyes.

Argabella gasped in delight and clapped her hands. "Oh, do you? I love tarts, too!"

"Never mind dessert," the goat said. "Let's get back to the main course here. Poltro wants to turn me into curry!"

The rogue grunted and moaned underneath her employer's weight. "Curry? Yes, please."

"See?"

"I already told you," Grinda said in that singsong voice people use to feel superior, "that it's not her fault. Enchantments!"

"There is literally nothing enchanting about me becoming curry."

Fia sighed and scratched the goat between his bony shoulders. "Gustave, I'm sorry," she said soothingly. "I'll try to keep an eye on them from now on as long as it seems they're serious about doing you harm, okay?" She stomped over to the pair and lifted both up by the material bunched up at the backs of their necks. There was much groaning and wincing and rubbing of the head.

"Oh, I'm going to have a welt," Lord Toby said.

Grinda felt no sympathy whatsoever and sought to steer the conversation productively. As long as they stood there, the others would continue arguing. But if she brought it up again, they'd just argue about that instead.

"So. Now that we're all in one place and conscious, can we decide which way to go and leave the influence of this annoying enchantment? It doesn't impact me, of course, as I'm attuned to the higher spheres, but action is the best course. We agreed we were going to head around to the east, so—"

"Mmf, I don't remember agreeing to that," Poltro interrupted. "I don't think I was asked."

"I didn't agree either!" Toby added, though of course he would disagree with anything Grinda said at that point, the jealous little weasel.

"Aaaand while I don't ever really want to be on *their* side again," Gustave said, "add me to that list. Aren't the giants eating people in that direction? No thanks. Had enough of that already. I don't think we can count on them all to sneeze on us and then let us go because they're embarrassed and grossed out. I'd rather take my chances on the danger I don't know."

"Wait," Grinda said. "*That's* why Faktri let you go? Because he sneezed on you?" She threw up her hands, helpless. "We're doomed. We can't handle anything serious. We need to go east from here."

"We need to get this over with quickly," Fia replied. "And that means taking the other fork."

"You'd rather face the Catacombs of Yore?" Grinda challenged. She widened her eyes and tried to sound incredulous.

"Well, er," Argabella said, "what's in there, exactly?"

"Yore. So much yore."

"That doesn't sound . . . that bad?"

"Oh, sure," Grinda said, waving her hand in the air, "everybody likes to make light of 'days of yore' because it's in the past, right, and the past is *perfectly* safe because it's in the past. But it's not so safe when your childhood fears come to life. That's what's waiting for you in the Catacombs of Yore."

"Moths?" Lord Toby whispered in the voice of a tiny little boy, his eyes unfocused in the distance. "Moths diving and swooping for the lights in my eyes, intent on sucking out my soul?"

Fia broke the long uncomfortable silence that followed. "Wow. Most people just have some kind of shapeless thing under the bed or something hairy in the closet. Extra credit for originality, Lord Toby."

"I understand where he's coming from, though," Argabella said. "You know those little tiny bugs that live in your pantry and get in your oats and flour? Well, one morning a swarm of them flew at me and got in my ears and up my nose, and ever since I've been terrified of breakfast."

"I *know*," Poltro said. "Eggs, right? Eggs is horrifying, they is. Sinister future chickens. Never eat anything that comes from a cloaca."

"Okay, I empathize with you all," Fia said, "but I'd also like to point out that moths and gnats and eggs will not eat us and giants will. We're better off going through the catacombs."

"No, we'd be better off circling all the way around to the east and taking the ferry across the lake from Pikestaff, like the goblin said," Grinda insisted grouchily. "That way there's no giants, no catacombs, none of it." If only she'd had her wand, she could've broken this enchantment and possibly reenchanted everyone to agree with her. It had been so long since she'd been cut off from magic, and feeling helpless put her in an uncommonly bad mood. Back home, she had several spare wands stashed about, but she'd assumed that this trip would be far easier, that these fools would be easier to control. Without her magic, she could already feel the various spells wearing off her joints and causing her spine to warp and her skin to sag.

"No matter which way we go, there will always be something," Fia said. "Better we don't waste any more time. I have some armor to pick up in Songlen, better than these half measures I'm wearing now. Besides, Groggyn is on the way to the catacombs. Maybe you can find something there to replace your wand."

"I would have to make it," Grinda said, shaking her head. And if she didn't hurry, her body would grow too weak, her eyesight too blurry.

"So what do you need?"

Grinda deflated. "Sand. Soda ash. The use of a forge for a day."

"Great! We can get all that in Groggyn."

Grinda marveled that she had been outmaneuvered and isolated so completely in the group. Clearly she was out of practice and needed to pay more attention. Years of lounging on the beach with crabs had dulled her sharp edges. She considered striking out on her own but dismissed the notion almost immediately. She had no wand and therefore very little in the way of defense, so traveling with them at least to Groggyn made sense. Soon enough, she'd merely be a wizened old woman shouting about taxes. And the goat's aura, she supposed, might see them all through the catacombs safely. And after that, he'd almost surely lead them to Løcher and Staph the pixie.

Resigned, she followed as they took the left fork and saw that it did follow the river that formed the border between Burdell and

Grunting. With Argabella using her song of speed to quicken their pace, they traveled upriver, far from Ol' Faktri, to the river crossing at Fapsworth. They were able to sleep in comfortable rooms and reach Groggyn the next morning, though Argabella said she'd probably need to rest her voice after two straight days of singing. She took a nap while Grinda sweated over a glassmaker's furnace all day, crafting a new wand that was the equal to the first if not its superior. Toby watched her in a creepy, hungry sort of way that suggested he had a longtime case of scepter envy. She would have to make sure he never got his hands on this new wand. The damage the hedge wizard might do when in possession of any real magical apparatus was stunning and terrifying. Challahs the size of cities might plummet from the sky should his steak be cooked incorrectly. He was simply one of the most dangerous creatures in the world: a person of small talent and large purse who was thoroughly certain that he deserved more.

Back in her room at the inn, Grinda carefully recast all her spells. Joints, bones, skin, hair, eyes, memory. She went from bent to statuesque again, grouchy to lively. With great relief, she realized that she no longer wanted to read newspapers to see who'd died and complain about what the weather might be. Finally, she was herself again, and she did feel most herself when she looked half her age. That night, free from the enchantments and worries that had nearly torn the group apart the day before, they dined on pasta and red wine, acting as if nothing horrible had ever been revealed in the magic net. Even Poltro didn't mention the word *curry* a single time.

Leaving Groggyn, they skirted the Quchii Hills that formed the border between several earldoms, and almost as soon as they left Grunting, the land began to dry out underneath their feet and springy turf gave way to brown, thirsty earth with only occasional sad shrubs longing for a tall drink of water. And then even that meager substrate began to slip and break down until they were cruising across the rippling dunes of the Qul Desert, and Grinda exulted in the feeling of sand between her toes again. If she didn't like the beach so much, she would've enjoyed living among these dunes and all the

Qul people. Their penchant for gauzy, flowing fabrics and vibrant head coverings maximized her beauty, which was even further accentuated by the sultry gait of a leggy camel undulating over the dunes. Carriages were lovely, but there was something to be said for the poetry of a lolloping dromedary. And also for good old poetry: a single verse from a Qul poet could titillate or tantalize like no other, and their chapbooks made fantastic beach reads. For someone like Grinda, it was a win-win-win situation, with an extra win tacked on after a camel spat on Lord Toby.

When they finally reached the entrance to the catacombs, a heavy wooden door reinforced with bars of rusted metal confronted them. Grinda wondered if the handle would even work. There were no footprints in front of the entrance but plenty of weathered warning signs.

RATS AND BATS! one sign said.

BEWARE THE ACID LEECHES! another cautioned.

WATCH OUT FOR THE TONGUES! FOR REALS, but it included an illustration that didn't look like any real tongue Grinda had ever seen.

THE HORRORS OF YORE! yet another sign warned.

AND BEES!!!!! the last one cried out, its lettering drawn in an unsteady mad hand, the excess of exclamation points obviously placed there to inspire fear.

"I have so many questions," Poltro said. "It all starts out just fine, rats and bats being the sort of thing you'd expect in the catacombs, but then it all goes a bit wobbly, doesn't it? Are the acid leeches made of acid, or injecting their victims with acid, or are they actually leeching acid from your blood and tissue? The adjective is ambiguous. And these tongues, now: Are they hanging out by themselves, so to speak, or hiding inside something's mouth? If they *are* in something's mouth, how are we supposed to watch for them? And aren't catacombs at least partially defined by a complete lack of sunshine, which would not be an ideal growing environment for flowers, and without flowers you're probably not going to have bees at all, right? Much less BEES!!!!! with surplus punctuation."

"There's an easy way to find out," Fia said, twisting the creaky handle until the mechanism slid open with a screech and clunk. She hauled the door open, and an unholy fusty funk of death and black licorice assailed their nostrils.

"Interesting," Gustave commented. "Y'all go first."

"Specifically Lord Toby and Poltro," Fia amended, "for your crimes against goatkind."

"There are no such crimes," the Dark Lord huffed. "I was enchanted. And you can't be mad at someone for being enchanted. That's double jeopardy."

"Hold on," Grinda said, peering into the entrance. Light penetrated only so far into the yawning orifice, and she doubted there would be handy torch sconces around. Time to try out the new wand. She withdrew it, traced a circle in the air as it pointed downward, and chanted, "Krogla svetloba." A small tempest of topsoil whipped up from the ground, formed a sphere of dust, and began to glow from within. It dropped into her outstretched hand, and she presented it to Poltro. "It's fragile," she explained, "but at least you'll be able to see where you're going in the dark."

The so-called Dark Lord snorted contemptuously. "There's no need for such cumbersome trinkets," he said, fishing a small vial from his pack, the contents of which glowed green. "I have a much better solution."

He unscrewed the lid, shook out a tiny bit of the green stuff onto his fingertips, and placed his hand flat against the wall on the right-hand side.

"What's that, m'lord?" Poltro asked.

Toby's voice glided into pomposity like hairless arms into the sweeping sleeves of a comfortable robe. "A curious kind of algae that thrives in darkness and emits its own light. I can spur its miraculous growth and spare us the need for these dirt balls." He turned to the wall and intoned in a more respectful voice, "Gleep na globin sobol." The algae bloomed and spread underneath his fingers and then rapidly raced down the rock of the hallway, providing a faint eldritch glow to which their eyes would soon adjust.

"That's so much more useful than bread," Fia murmured, and when everyone looked at her, remembering that his almost-crackers had once been their only source of nutrition, she hastened to add, "I mean right now, anyway."

"It's quite useful, I'm thinking," Poltro said, tossing Grinda's globe back to her; the sphere promptly crumbled when the sand witch tried to catch it. "We can walk in there and have both hands free, which will be terribly handy if one might need a dagger in one hand and a turkey legge in the other or if, say, one must swat away some bees."

The Dark Lord looked supremely smug as he sauntered to the other side of the corridor and repeated the process with the algae. With the glow coming from both sides and even the beginnings of the ceiling lighting up, nothing would surprise them in the dark.

In fact, a skulking rat intent on skullduggery squeaked its dismay at the sudden illumination and scampered off into the cavernous depths, trying to find someplace appropriately dark in which to skulldig.

"Yes, this is good," Argabella said. "I need both hands to play my lute."

Grinda ground her teeth while Lord Toby preened and fondled his beard extensions as if they had made him infinitely wiser than she. Some of the glowing algae got in his beard, she noted, and nobody said anything. He was an occasionally useful fool, and she would need to remind herself of his usefulness when his foolishness tested her patience.

Like now, when she needed to protect them. "Hold still, please," she said, waving her wand to encompass the entire group. "I'm going to cast a seeming on us before we enter. We are all just grains of sand, something that looks exactly like whatever the denizens of these catacombs are used to seeing. Do nothing to disturb them or their environment and they shouldn't even notice us."

Lord Toby snorted derisively. "Seemings," he said with disdain. "Illusions can't match the practical arts."

Grinda quietly reminded herself not to turn him into a crab. He might prove to be practical later in human form; the glowing algae trick, much as she hated to admit it, was a good one. "It is not a question of matching. It is merely pooling our talents to maximize our chances of survival."

"Hey, are you talking about talent pools?" Poltro asked. "I've heard of those but haven't ever seen one. Cutter said I probably never will, so I'd like to prove him wrong. I'm not much for swimming, though. Think they have one in Songlen? And do they allow swimmy wings?"

No one knew quite how to answer that, so she received a visual chorus of shrugs, and then they entered the Catacombs of Yore, two by two. Toby and Poltro took the front, Fia and Argabella walked behind them, and Gustave took up a spot in the rear with Grinda, keeping suspicious yellow eyes on her at all times. The goat went up in Grinda's estimation; he was the only one clever enough to recognize how dangerous she was.

For a good half hour there was only the single hallway and no terrors to speak of. Few rats or bats either, and those they saw took no interest in them. But the smell of rot grew stronger as they probed more deeply into the wide tunnel, and soon enough passages opened up to either side. The main hall also changed its nature, adding scalloped hollows set into the walls in which muslin-wrapped bodies of expired Pellions had been deposited, only to be chewed and gnawed on by the creatures living there.

Something loud and large buzzed by Poltro's head, startling her. "Cor! What was that?" She squinted after it. "Was that one o' them bees the sign warned us about? Didn't seem beeish. Looked gray to me."

"Hmm. That could be interesting," Toby said, but refused to elaborate.

"I can't help but notice," Argabella said, "that some of the bodies don't appear to be stored properly in the little recessed shelving unit thingie doodads. Like, maybe they weren't already dead? Like, maybe they died here?"

Grinda noticed that, too. A couple of bodies were sprawled on the ground and did not appear to have ever been wrapped up. And there were more of the strange gray bees now.

The sand witch craned her head to peer between Fia and Argabella. There were more bodies ahead on the catacomb floor, some of them just scattered bones and skulls at this point. And Toby was accelerating, obviously excited, and in the wrong sort of way for a journey through a cave full of corpses and bees.

"This could be truly remarkable," his voice floated back to them. The words were furry around the edges because of all the buzzing. He was walking straight into a veritable swarm of the things. "Yes. Yes," he said, growing more excited. "Oh, yes!"

"What is it, Lord Toby?" Fia asked.

"Come see!" He was practically dancing, and they could see him pointing at one side of the hallway, presumably where a body was stored. When they reached him, they were surrounded by hundreds of the gray furry insects looping through the air, each one slow and fat like a bumblebee except somehow not appearing very friendly. And what he was pointing to, Grinda saw, was a skeleton's rib cage that had become the framework for a hive.

"They're necrobees! Real necrobees!"

"Don't you mean zom-bees?" Gustave quipped, but everyone ignored him.

"Beg your pardon, sir?" the rogue asked.

The Dark Lord sighed. "They don't collect pollen, Poltro. They have been mutated. They eat the dead—mostly the skin—and turn it into one of the most prized substances in the world: flesh honey."

Argabella gagged and covered her mouth. "Auggh! That is nasty!"

"No, no—well, yes. But a single spoonful is supposed to add ten years to your life!"

Grinda had to interrupt. "I'm sorry, Lord Toby, but this mutation can't be natural. Someone had to do this to them."

"Absolutely correct! A diabolical piece of magic, but so powerful one cannot help but be in awe. And I think you know only one mage could have accomplished this: the infamous eastern scalawag—that rascal!—the Dread Necromancer, Steve."

Fia's fists clenched, and her muscles bunched and rippled. "Gah! Not Steve! I *hate* that guy!"

"You *know* him?" Lord Toby said, his estimation of Fia visibly creeping upward.

"Let's just say he's one of the reasons I came to the west."

"I don't suppose," Poltro said, nervously eyeing the swarm around her, "the Dread Necromancer Steve thought to make his mutated bees harmless?"

"Oh, no! They're lethal in the extreme," Toby said cheerfully. "A single sting means certain death."

The buzzing around them got ominously louder.

"So, uh . . . shall we move on?"

"Yes. As soon as I admit to Grinda that seemings do have their uses. We should all be dead by now and adding our bones to the fabulous charnel house you already see here." He sounded way too delighted for someone standing ankle deep in bones and bees, but the sand witch had never expected to hear him act even the tiniest bit humble.

"Oh." Grinda felt genuinely surprised. "Thank you, Lord Toby."

"Might you also have a way for us to get some flesh honey without dying?" he asked.

Argabella made a horking noise. "Auggh. No, please don't say that, Lord Toby. It just gets worse in my head every time I hear it. I just threw up a little bit in my mouth."

"I don't have a way to do that, sorry," Grinda replied, annoyed that he knew so much more about this newfangled flesh honey than she did. "If they're anything like regular bees, the moment you invade their hive, they will notice you despite my seeming. Let's move on and not tempt fate any longer." She took great pains to hide how very much she wanted a spoonful—or, actually, jarful—of the honey for herself. At the end of each day, the youthfulness spells hung about her like layers of frayed, broken spiderwebs, and she was well enough aware that the wrinkle treatments were making her more and more smeary every year. Still, many an old witch had died in pursuit of a bit of age magic like this flesh honey, and their corpses looked just magnificent. Until something worse than necrobees ate them.

"I'll have to come back later better prepared," Lord Toby said with the sort of foolish bravado that got men killed while spelunking. "Now that I know they're here, I can return anytime."

They carefully tiptoed through the bones of others who had obviously been even worse prepared, and once safely out of range of the buzzing, Argabella whispered to Fia in a perfectly audible voice, "So you dated a dread necromancer?"

"Very briefly," Fia admitted. "A huge mistake. I don't want to judge him on what he was into because everybody has their thing that works for them, but it didn't work for me; that's all I'm saying."

"What was he into?"

Fia gestured to the bodies lying still all around them. "Death."

Poltro pointed to the shelves, which now had slight rectangular bulges in the middle of them. "Those are new," she said. "Okay if I take a closer look, m'lord?"

"Of course."

Lord Toby touched his hand to either wall to keep the glowing algae growing in front of them and to shine light on the new architecture. Poltro brushed the dust from one of the rectangles and uncovered an inscription. "Oh. It's a name and some dates. Very fancy. This must be where all the swell folks are stashed."

Argabella pointed down the hall. "If that's the case, whoever's entombed there must have been very swell indeed."

Grinda followed her direction and spied a collection of candles and a couple sticks of incense burning several niches down. As they drew closer, a hooded figure detached from the gloom and greeted them. Apparently, he was not fooled by the seeming. Grinda felt a thrill of fear twang up her magically fortified spine.

"Blessings to you, travelers. Welcome." He put his hands up to show he was unarmed, perhaps in reaction to something Fia did involving creaking armor and unspoken threats of bodily harm. "I am a man of peace."

Grinda thought that he was more a man of illness once they got closer. His skin tone and lack of a chin were very similar to Lord Toby's, except his upper lip glistened with sweat that may have been the result of a fever. It couldn't be from recent exercise; he seemed to be barely breathing at all. Dark circles under his eyes testified to a lack of sleep, however, and the eyes themselves hinted at a touch of madness—or perhaps that was just the greenish tint given off by the algal illumination. Grinda subtly readied her wand in case he proved to be hostile in spite of his protestations to the contrary. In her experience, people rarely pointed out how peaceful they were unless they were preparing to threaten violence and wanted you to be a bit more relaxed.

"And what is your purpose, my good sir?" Toby asked.

"I tend the final resting place of my master, the Most Glorious and Puissant Hirudo Brønsted, who illuminated the world with his knowledge. May I tell you how he conquered death very briefly? It is my duty and will allow me to rest."

"Isn't that him?" Toby pointed to the body resting behind the candles.

"Yes."

"So . . . he's dead."

"Yes."

"That would appear to belie the premise of your argument."

"No, no, I promise, the truth is fascinating and instructive. Only a moment of your time." The man gestured at them to come closer. "Behold his face. Is it not miraculously preserved? He has been dead for three hundred years, yet it appears he could wake from a nap at any moment!"

As curious as the others, Grinda drew closer to examine the person lying in repose, hands folded across his chest. A distinguished

figure of dark brown skin and fine embroidered robes, Hirudo Brønsted indeed looked to be merely sleeping and not long dead.

"It truly is a marvel," Lord Toby admitted. "How did he do this?"

"Leeches."

Poltro flinched. "What?"

Grinda also registered that something was terribly wrong with
that answer, but before she could process exactly why, the hooded
man extended a finger toward the corpse and said, "Look there,"
while audibly pulling a lever with his other hand, which was hidden
by the bulk of his body. The floor dropped out from underneath them,
and they succumbed to the merciless clutches of gravity.

Howls and lamentations and panicked bleats erupted from their
throats as they fell, and these met the mad cackling of the man who'd
gulled them into danger.

Grinda splashed into shallow water a couple of body lengths
below, crumpling to her recently remagicked knees before standing
quickly. It was only deep enough to reach her calves, but it was utterly dark, and getting out of the pit would be problematic. Magic
could do many things, but the liquid in this cave seemed to have
some sort of dampener that leeched away power, which was bad
news for Grinda and Gustave in particular. Even Fia couldn't jump
high enough to escape the pit, and the maniac wasn't going to keep
the door open long anyway. It closed even as Grinda considered
giving Fia as much of a boost as the wand could squeak out. She
checked her wand to make sure it hadn't broken in the fall—it
hadn't—but it felt light in her hand, the sensation reminding her of
the disappointment of an empty pitcher of margaritas. In the last
remaining seconds of light, she pulled some of Lord Toby's algae
off the walls and brought it down into the pit, where she redistrib-
uted it to the nearest wall, frowning as she did so. No wonder the
algae worked—it wasn't particularly magical, which meant Toby
just liked carrying around tubs of parasitic goo. Her ankles didn't
feel right; she must have strained them or maybe even sprained
them in the fall.

"Lord Toby, could you please spread your wonderful fungus around this room so we can see what we're dealing with?"

"It's *algae*," he said. "And I'd be delighted to be able to see. I think I might have done something to my shins when we landed. I skipped leg day."

"And arms day," Fia muttered under her breath. Toby splashed toward the wall, and the others commented that they weren't quite feeling a hundred percent either, though they stayed still in the darkness.

"That wasn't such a terrible fall," Fia said, "but I kind of hurt everywhere. Not like an oncoming bruise, either, or a cracked rib."

"I cracked a rib once," Poltro reminisced. "I got ambushed by a henhouse. Lucky to escape with my life. But this feels different for sure."

"It's getting worse, too," Fia said, "not better."

Grinda noticed that as well. Her knees were shaking with effort. Without her spells, she'd soon be both in pain and swiftly succumbing to her age. "Toby? Please hurry. Something is awry."

"Hey, I could use a shot of rye," Poltro said, a hopeful note in her voice. "Might you pour me some?"

"This is really hurty, and I don't like it," Argabella said. "It feels like . . . hey. Hey! There's something on me! What is it? Get it off! Gah, get it off!"

Thus began much splashing and yelling.

And soon, thanks to the rapid spreading of glowing algae, there was light, and they saw that they were in a somewhat sizable cavernous space with a couple feet of water at the bottom and that the water was full of leeches because the leeches were now all over them. The things were a peculiar rotten yellow-green and resembled nothing so much as mucusy boogers come to life and equipped with teeth.

"Cor, it's the acid leeches!" Poltro shouted. "They're gonna dissolve our giblets!" The splashing and yelling intensified.

Grinda thought it was much worse than that. She was fairly sure the water itself must be a low-grade acid, for she wasn't covered all over in leeches yet but her skin was beginning to burn all over, and that was from falling in the pool to begin with. She scanned the walls and pointed. "There! A ramp up and out on the other side! Let's get over there and then remove them!"

As they discovered the ramp, the rest of the group ran for it. In her haste, Fia knocked Grinda with an elbow, and Grinda gasped as she rocked off balance and fell into the acid. Her hands burned in earnest now, her arms trembling, and she groaned as her very bones went frail and full of fire within withered arms. She felt her every year in that moment, every past ache and every hint of osteoporosis she'd magicked from her limbs.

"Help!" she cried. "I've fallen, and I can't get up."

But the others were already ahead of her, even Gustave bounding out of the acid, his belly leeched of hair and glowing a painful red.

"You didn't stop them from wanting to eat me; I'm not stopping them from running," the goat called over his bony shoulder.

Grinda struggled to her feet, veiny hands on shaky thighs, wand still clutched desperately in her fingers. Her back was hunched, her hair falling out in clumps. One of her teeth went loose in its socket, and the world went blurry with myopia. She was old, by gods, truly old, and with this knowledge came utter helplessness. She couldn't even cross a street by herself, and she longed for a cane, even an ugly and twisted one like lesser witches carried for smacking cutpurses. Her knees wobbled, and she began to fall again, visions of broken hips dancing in what was left of her mind.

"Worstley?" she called, seeing a shadowy figure gambol up ahead. "Is that you, boy?"

"Gah!" someone who was definitely not her nephew shouted, and then Grinda felt strong arms like oak branches catch her and swing her up to carry her like a baby, thankfully away from the burning pool.

"You're a good boy, Worstley," she said, and a distinctly feminine voice answered, "You owe me for this, witch."

Soon Grinda felt stone under her crabbed feet. She could barely stand; her balance wasn't what it used to be. Someone held her up-right, and someone else began tugging at her here and there, and it hurt but also felt lovely.

"You stop that right now, whippersnapper," she hissed. "I'll turn you into a newt."

"That might be preferable," a peevish woman said. "Damaged newts can regrow limbs, but damaged rabbits just look patchy and furious."

The blur around Grinda's eyes suddenly went clear, and she saw Argabella and Fia on either side of her, annoyed as they pulled long acid-green leeches off her withered arms. Each beast left a hideous burn behind, some showing muscle and a thin layer of fat. But as they were removed, she found her magicked strength returning, and she was soon able to pull out her wand and shout, "Ruddi laece!"

All the leeches in the general area tore from their bodies and splattered the walls with yellow-green slime, causing a collective sigh of relief from Grinda's compatriots.

"Well, that was useful, I suppose," Toby said, "but do you have any healing spells?"

Grinda patted at her swiftly regrowing hair. "That wasn't my con-centration. Major in illusions, minor in manipulation. You?"

Toby turned a deep shade of puce. "I went with a more hands-on approach."

"Then we'll just have to get out quickly and find a healer." Grinda looked around grimly, noting that they would have to hurry if they wanted to survive long enough to do so. Their skin bubbled and hissed and oozed in the many places they'd acquired leeches, and it was irritated everywhere else from the acid bath, and she wished for the first time that she'd at least considered healing as an elective.

"That's it," Fia said, standing tall. "Forget magic. We can do this. Toby, don't you have some milk in your pack? That neutralizes acid. So pass it around."

"But it's goblin yak milk! A rare—"

"My fist in your teeth won't be rare. Hand over the yak milk."

Soon they were dabbing their wounds with Toby's milk as Fia meted out her NyeQuell and Argabella sang a new and improved version of "The Ouchie Song" that featured many fine rhymes and a repeating chorus of, "So let good healing reign! Not today, pain!" Grinda was surprised to find her wounds going from red to pink to her usual pasty white as the wounds and pain simply melted away. She had never before considered that there might be a decent answer to anything other than magic, and she began to consider a trip to the Seven Toes, where there were supposed to be skin chirurgeons capable of altering one's appearance and even reversing the effects of aging. Soon they had a lovely collection of scars that would impress any future romantic prospects but were no longer in agony as their flesh dissolved away.

This curious quilt of healing worked, but it left them exhausted and with no remedy for future injuries. They shuffled up the ramp until they reached a door, and after confirming that it would open and they weren't actually trapped in the hateful leech pit, Grinda suggested that they rest in the chamber beyond, since it seemed a place of relative safety. "With rotating watches, of course."

Not that she would ever admit how very close she'd come to dying, old and blind, in the vat of leech acid.

"That guy took us for suckers," Fia groused.

"Bloody awful," Argabella agreed.

Poltro nodded along. "Cor, what a slimeball. We totally fell for it."

They grabbed a few hours of sleep each and ate some provisions— Lord Toby shared a wheel of cheese to go with some almost-crackers, although they were forced to listen to him whine about his lost yak milk—before they deemed their entire party rested, wary, and determined to press on. As the others slept and Grinda took her watch, she carefully, quietly replaced all her magical spells, tightening up her body and mind for what was to come. She never again wanted to feel as hopeless and alone as she'd felt in the leech pit even if her cold heart was warmed just the tiniest bit to know that her compatriots— maybe one day her friends—had waded in to save her. Witches didn't give credit where credit was due, but she laid some enchantments over them while they slept to strengthen them for the journey ahead. When they woke and prepared to venture forth, the best way forward seemed to be a twisting stone stair that led them ever upward in tight circles that left Poltro quite dizzy. Fia took stock of where they were, tested several hallways, and then beckoned to the group to join her. "This is the main passage," she said, pointing to the left, where Toby's algae marked the walls. To the right, the algae hadn't spread so far. "So we're ahead of where we got dropped into the pit."

Only Fia felt like going left and getting revenge; that sickly madman had been too confident, and Grinda argued that the Hirudo Brønsted character might not have been dead at all.

"I think he might waken if we attacked, and we don't know his abilities. Surviving was victory enough, I think. Let's not make the same mistake twice." She glared at Fia. "We should press on."

This time the party agreed with the sand witch, and the giant fighter was left to fume. Argabella was kind enough to sing a small ditty called "You Can Get Revenge Later, I Promise, and It's Not Like That Guy Is Going Anywhere," and Fia was at least entertained if not completely mollified. They followed the main passage for a long stretch without interruption, and in the first hour the fancy inscriptions disappeared and they were again passing the anonymous, less swell dead, ranks and ranks of them trussed up like particularly unappetizing hams and shoved clumsily into niches. But then the receptacles for the dead also ceased and they were back to a single, featureless corridor that closed in on them as they went.

"I've got a bad feeling about this," Poltro said as the path seemed to dead-end ahead.

"If it turns out that this is a maze, we're going to get that monk and make him show us the way out," Fia said. "Maybe use him as a battering ram."

But the dead end was merely a sharp turn. They rounded the corner, and the narrow passage abruptly opened before them into a large chamber lit by warm candles and torches on the walls. There were richly woven rugs on the floor. Upholstered chaise lounges. Tapestries between the sconces. Sculptures of graceful pixies and fairies and centaurs and what looked like a bust of the king of the Morningwood oddly juxtaposed with a frolicsome oil painting of the lethal llamataurs of the northern Teabring savanna tearing into some hapless travelers and playing tug-o-war with their entrails. The aesthetic was one of charming menace. On the far side of the room, on a raised dais, rested what could only be considered a throne. And behind it was a carved wooden door that certainly qualified as fancy and quite possibly as schmancy.

"What is this place?" Poltro wondered aloud.

"And who lit the candles and torches?" Grinda responded, which she thought was a much more pertinent question. As if in answer, the door behind the throne opened and a singular being emerged, bringing with him a distinct whiff of black licorice.

He was mostly human, Grinda thought, but he was simply covered in an awful lot of gray hair. He looked borderline fluffy, but in an entirely different way than Argabella. Bare chested and barefoot, he wore a green and blue kilt and carried a brushed copper goblet in one lightly furred hand. He had an impressive white mustache and beard that fell down to his sternum. His eyes were smeary shadows underneath a deep brow. Where the gray hair didn't cover it, his skin was bright white—not white in the way she was, like the pale-skinned people of Borix or parts of Burdell, but white like powdered sugar. He stopped when he saw them.

"Oh! Hello!" he called, his mouth splitting into a pleasant smile. His voice rumbled and tumbled like the joyful growls of a puppy tugging on a sock. "How nice to have visitors today."

"Good morning, sir. Or is it afternoon? I don't know what time it is," Fia said. "Who might you be?"

"I'm the steward of these catacombs, known in the world as Yör."

"Oh, so that's why they call these the Catacombs of Yore."

The smile disappeared, though the voice remained friendly and patient. "No, it's Yör."

"Isn't that what I just said? Yore."

"Yör with an umlaut over the *o* and no *e*."

Fia stole a glance at Grinda, perhaps seeking guidance, but she had nothing to offer but a helpless shrug. If this was the namesake of the catacombs, he had to be hundreds of years old, and such people often developed eccentric behaviors.

"I'm sorry, I'm not hearing a difference," Fia said.

"There's a tremendous difference," the man said, placing his goblet down on a small table next to the throne and taking a few steps closer before folding his thin hands together. "Try again. Yör."

"Yore," Fia said.

The man's expression darkened, and his voice lost much of its initial warmth.

"You know, it's quite rude not to make the effort to say someone's name correctly. It's a basic courtesy that should be extended to everyone."

"I'm trying, sir, honestly. Please forgive me. I've never been able to roll my tongue or swallow my *r*s. I just don't know what I'm doing wrong."

"You're not pronouncing the umlaut. You *must* respect the umlaut." He pointed a bony white finger at Argabella. "You! Rabbit of unusual size. You try."

"Umlaut?" she said at first, then gulped, her entire body shaking. "I mean . . . Yore?"

"*Nnnno!*" he roared, all civility gone, and the avuncular grumble turned to unnatural rage. "You disrespect the umlaut! I can *hear* you not saying it!"

"I tried, I swear. I'm so sorry!" Argabella cried. "We don't have umlauts where I come from! I don't even know why we have semicolons. Please don't be Shoutful!"

The catacomb steward demanded that each of them try to say his name and grew increasingly angry as they all failed, in his judgment, to respect the umlaut. Poor Gustave, when it was his turn, dropped a steamy bevy of fright pellets and wailed, "I don't have a uvula! I don't even know how I can talk! Goats weren't made for umlauts!"

"You." The enraged man pointed at Grinda. "You've got some miles on you. Surely you've traveled and studied among other cultures. Show these youngsters how it's done."

Grinda cleared her throat and drew herself up tall. "Yore."

He flinched as if from a blow, then raised his chin in a fit of intense pique. "I'm afraid," he said, "that it is time for you to feel afraid."

"But I'm already there," Argabella wailed, and then the gray-furred man clutched his hands into fists, threw back his head, and bellowed at the ceiling, "*Yöööööööööööööööör!*"

His shadowed eye sockets focused on Toby, and his right hand shot toward the Dark Lord's head, a black vapor snaking out and wreathing Toby's skull for a brief moment before dissipating. For a second it seemed as if absolutely nothing had been accomplished, but then a swarm of fluttering paper-winged moths manifested in the room and flew at Toby's face.

"Moths! No! Augggh!" he screamed, green bolts issuing from each fingertip and incinerating a few of his attackers as they traveled to the ceiling, where a doughy cloud formed. The Dark Lord fell under a hail of moths and a panicked summoning of delectable buttery croutons, and his cries of terror eventually ceased, leaving only a mound of fried bread chunks and moth bodies atop a sobbing man-child.

"That was pretty weird," Yör said into the silence that followed, his voice flat. "Let's try the dashing rogue next."

His hand shot black oily smoke at Poltro, and she jerked, grunted, and found herself confronted by a ravenous llamataur. A horrific, crazed llama head with carnivorous teeth grimaced at her and spat as it loomed above a thickly muscled human male's body dressed in ill-fitting clothes taken from past victims. These brainless, spitting monsters no doubt had been created by some witch or wizard long ago for a cause he or she thought noble, but now their reproducing population in the northern savanna of Teabring made the entire area a death trap. The creature made a noise somewhere between a yodel and a gargle before the head whipped down at Poltro's face and snapped its teeth where her nose had been a second earlier. Said snoot was no longer there only because the rogue had fallen back with a cry of fear, and Grinda wondered why Yör's spell hadn't summoned a chicken.

"Better! And probably fatal," Yör commented. "But I've seen it before. Come on, rabbit girl. Give me something fun."

Argabella rocked back under the black mist but steadied herself just in time to confront a slender and somewhat familiar-looking man wearing a Swords n' Daisies concert shirt. He smiled placatingly and brandished a pair of bongos in one hand and a maraca in the other.

"Accountants never account for anything," he said. "The arts! That's the way to go! Music is the only steady career for a girl like you. If you'd just make some effort to look like you have loose morals and a song in your heart. C'mon. Shake the maraca."

"Dad?" Argabella's jaw hung open in horror.

"If you keep clacking those abacus beads all night, your palms are going to grow hair. Keep wearing those sweater vests and parting your hair down the middle and no one will ever love you!" Grinda had seen enough. Argabella's dad looked withering and damaging but not immediately lethal unless one was allergic to percussion instruments. The llamataur was something else, for it had taken a step forward and was zeroing in on the cowering Poltro.

The witch employed her wand to blow dust into the llamataur's eyes just as it lunged forward again. It flinched and missed, its teeth clacking on air, and bugled its frustration. Knowing what was coming next, Grinda faced an enraged Yör, who shot a geyser of thick smoke at her head. She twitched the tip of her wand to dissipate it and grew mildly alarmed when that didn't work. The smoke did not behave as smoke should. She applied more mental force, slashing the wand's tip through the air, yet still the smoke came for her, and she realized that there was no avoiding it. Her eyes widened, now fully alarmed, and then her vision dimmed as the smoke shrouded her sight and the spell invaded her psyche. Her vision cleared a second later, but Grinda did not move. She did not move because she could not. Her fear was no tangible thing but rather the inability to act, to control her environment, to feel anything but utterly helpless; the spell had paralyzed her in place instead of manifesting anything with teeth.

She was able to perceive, however, that Fia wasn't standing still for her secondhand smoke. She grunted and charged Yör with an implacable expression on her face, sword ready to strike. Yör hit her with the spell before she could get in range, and her charge abruptly ended as a small boy with dark brown skin like hers filled the space between her and the white-furred wizard, dead eyes staring at her and a hatchet buried in his left temple. Grinda couldn't be sure because Argabella's dad was loudly haranguing her about getting a real job as a wench down at the bar, but she was fairly certain she heard the mighty Fia say "Beef?" or something similar in a tiny voice. Grinda focused on the warrior. The small boy calmly wrested the hatchet out of his skull, switched it to his right hand, and threw it at Fia, who flinched away at the last possible second. The axe sank into her unprotected left shoulder instead of her face. Any hope Grinda had cherished that Yör's magic was limited to illusions shattered—that axe was very, very real. Fia cried out and dropped her sword as the boy advanced on her with slow, plodding steps.

"Yes! Now that's what I'm talking about!" Yör said, his voice triumphant. He grinned nastily and said, "Might as well," shooting another stream of black mist past Grinda. She wondered for a moment who he was targeting until she heard a despairing bleat and realized she'd forgotten the goat. No—the Chosen Goat! Perhaps his aura would deny Yör's magic, and even if it didn't, she reasoned, what possible fear could a kid goat have that would do them any damage? Grinda felt a spark of hope for an entire second before it was utterly crushed.

Gustave did have a kid fear, and when it manifested, Grinda would have screamed if she hadn't been frozen in place. For it was her nephew Worstley, alive and unharmed and smiling a merciless smile at the goat as he brandished a knife in his hand and said, "Sorry, Gus, but my mom's ready to try out some new recipes, and you're the main ingredient." Unlike Fia's adversary, this Worstley didn't maintain his focus on his target: he looked about him, utterly confused by his surroundings, realizing that he was not on his farm in Borix. His eyes fell first on a sobbing Poltro, trying to escape the llamataur that had latched on to her cape and was trying to reel her in, but then they slid past, and he said, "Aunt Grinda?" an instant before the llamataur gave up on Poltro and lashed out its long neck to take a mortal bite out of the innocent and somewhat stupid boy staring at her, dumbfounded. The razor teeth scissored into Worstley's flesh and pulled away, blood fountaining out of the boy's throat as strands of muscle clung to the sides of the beast's mouth. Grinda's nephew gurgled and fell backward in a shower of his own blood, and Grinda felt the strangest sensation, something she hadn't known in many years: grief.

"That was a surprising resurrection," Gustave said, almost as if nothing had happened. Grinda could hear him trotting up beside her on the stone floor as the llamataur hunched over its kill and took another bite of her nephew's raw flesh. "I mean obviously more so for Pooboy than for me, but wow, you know?"

Grinda was an old witch, and she had seen many things, and she knew that this version of Worstley wasn't real. It was some sort of golem or seeming called to life by Yör's magic. Yet deep within her frozen form, her heart felt heavy and cold.

The others, however, seemed to feel nothing.

"Cor, that was a close one!" Poltro said, scrambling over to them with tears in her eyes. "Thank you, Miss Grinda, for what you did, or else that would've been me getting all chewed on."

"I don't think she can talk right now," Gustave said.

"Well, we should help her, then! We'll get out of this together!"

The goat snorted. "Help? When have any of you ever helped me?"

"Just now! My llamataur ate your farm boy."

"But that wasn't you. Or him either, because his body is in Borix. None of this is real."

"The llamataur wouldn't be here if it wasn't for me, so I reckon I did help, and I reckon it is real, as I'm covered in blood and viscera and whatnot."

The billy goat spat directly at the rogue's face, but he then turned his head to assess the remaining threats. "Fine. The llamataur is busy eating my pooboy, so I'll take down the mean dad and you take care of the boy with the gaping head wound. Grinda, you stand there and do absolutely nothing, as per usual."

"That's a solid plan, that is," Poltro agreed, and slunk off to the left, where Grinda could just make out Fia backing away at the advance of the smallish boy she should have had no trouble cutting down. Or she would have had no trouble if she were armed at this point with anything beyond pruning shears, though Grinda supposed Fia could at least remove the hatchet from her own shoulder. Perhaps, like her, the mighty warrior was fighting a bigger battle on the inside.

Argabella was likewise backing away from her father, who was loudly explaining that if Argabella would have *just listened* and practiced more with her lute, then maybe her mother wouldn't have left her father for a slimy CPA and they could all make tie-dyed shirts and go on tour with a band called Phische. The bard screamed at him to shut up, and the father's grip on the maraca became a bit more serious and, as Argabella would've said, Smackful. Gustave lowered his head and charged, thudding his head into Argabella's father's flanks and sending the man staggering to the left, where he stumbled and hit his head against the base of a marble statue, lapsing into unconsciousness and mumbling about royalties.

Argabella shouted for joy and praised Gustave as the goatiest goat who ever goated, leaving Grinda to wonder at what tender age Argabella must have run away from home or started hiding who she really was from her father. But that celebration roused the attention of the llamataur, who looked up from its meal and realized that there was even fresher meat walking around than the farm boy it had just killed. It rose with a bloody muzzle, bugled a yodel-gargle, and lunged after Gustave. By that point, Grinda was actually rooting for the llamataur.

A glow from the back of the chamber drew her attention for a brief moment: Yör had closed his eyes, and his lips rippled in an ecstatic curl at the edges. He was taking delight—even nourishment—from their fear, and his skin radiated a soft light that hadn't been there before, his sagging flesh a bit filled out and his wrinkled features smoothed to the chiseled planes of youth.

Movement drew Grinda's eyes to the left; her eyeballs were beginning to ache and dry out. Poltro leapt onto the back of the shambling boy plaguing Fia, reached around, and plunged her dagger repeatedly into his chest, all to no avail except to affect the boy's posture somewhat. He did not even jerk in response to the stabbings but kept on moving toward Fia, who continued to back away. Poltro eventually gave up, slipped off the boy's back, and looked curiously at her knife, which was bloodless.

"Cor," she said. "Cutter led me to believe knives would work a whole lot better than that. Maybe I should have paid the smith for that Extended Warranty of Functionality and Efficaciousness. People say their knives always stop working and go bad right after the two-year Limited Warranty you get with the blade, but I didn't believe them until now."

But Gustave didn't have time for warranties; he was running for his life.

"Fia!" he bleated as he galloped around the cavern, the slobbery llamataur giving chase. They were behind Grinda now, and she couldn't see them, though she could hear the goat's trotters clopping and the heavy footfalls of the llamataur punctuating its demented bugling. "A little help?"

It occurred to Grinda that the goat could lead the llamataur to her and she'd be devoured easily, unable to dodge or even flinch as the teeth closed around her throat. She felt panic rising and interpreted every new sound as potentially the last she'd hear, and she had never known such perfect helplessness. Not even in the leech acid, not since she was a little girl, long before she'd mastered magic, and—

"Fia, help Gustave!" Argabella said, rushing over to where Poltro stood, bemused by her knife. "We'll take care of the boy."

It sounded so simple. But the boy, who'd been content to shamble forward slowly, became quite animated once Argabella tackled him to the ground. Any interruption of his progress toward Fia aroused a spirited defense. Argabella's inexpert attempts to subdue him only resulted in her getting punched in the nose and throat until she rolled off with a cry. Poltro fell upon him again, having decided to give her malfunctioning knife one more try. She stabbed him in the throat, and that produced no blood or even wasted breath, for Fia's fear was not anything alive but rather something dead. Grinda guessed the boy was something conjured by the power of the Dread Necromancer Steve, though Fia's meeting with him hadn't been during her childhood. That was what you got for confiding in someone on a third date, she supposed.

"Go for the brain!" Argabella cried. "Mess with its brain!" A flying fist punched her again, and she gave a tiny yip before falling still.

"Oh! Right!" Poltro said, and plunged her knife down through the boy's eye even as he clocked her upside the temple. His struggles ceased, and he lay still while Poltro moaned and clutched her head. Argabella didn't move at all.

Fia inched forward into Grinda's view as the warrior pivoted to face the llamataur. She finally wrenched the hatchet out of her shoulder with her right hand, grunting in pain but looking determined and murderous. Blood poured from the wound, but her eyes blazed as she found her target. She threw the axe at the llamataur, and it at least hit him, though it wasn't with any part of the blade. The haft thunked off its chest, and the creature grunted and roared, fully aware of what the intent was. Or maybe, Grinda thought, it was roaring in response to Fia lunging to retrieve her dropped sword. Whatever the impulse, the llamataur was already running full speed while Fia was starting from a dead stop. Gustave rocketed past and looped back to where Grinda was frozen, and Fia and the llamataur crashed together to the ground, fighting over her sword. She hammered a fist into its jaw, and the fuzzy head slid away from her on the long neck like a yo-yo on a string, its body rolling over slightly so that its front was exposed. Fia took advantage and levered up a knee into its groin. It ceased grasping for the sword and instead rolled over completely onto its back and grasped at its bruised nads. That allowed Fia to retrieve her sword, regain her feet, and plunge the blade into the llamataur's chest.

It died with ululations and a torrent of diarrhea.

Yör clapped three times and grinned in appreciation. Grinda thought he looked a bit taller and had filled out to the point where his kilt strained to contain him. "After a slow start, those were some fantastic fears. And delicious, by the way. That meal will last me a while. And congratulations on surviving your fears, because most people perish by them. You are free to go." He waved at the wall nearest the mound of moths and bread under which Toby had fallen and under which he remained, inert. A door that had not been there before appeared between two sconces and opened, revealing a hallway bereft of corpses and well lit by torches. "That will lead you out. Belladonna the healer is just outside the catacombs should you make it past the tongues." He cast a doubtful gaze at them, ending with a look at the mound of moths and bread chunks burying Lord Toby. "I don't think you'll make it. But maybe you could pay her with some of those golden croutons if you do."

Yör chuckled at his own joke as he scooped up his copper goblet and sauntered toward the door behind the throne from which he'd originally emerged. "Respect the umlaut, kids," he said.

Fia yanked her sword out of the llamataur's chest and bloody goo fountained out of the wound, splashing noisily onto the floor. She roared and charged after the emotional vampire, but Yör shut the door in her face, and its outline immediately disappeared as if it had been a solid wall all along. She hurled some choice eastern slang terms for anatomy at the wall, hoping he'd be able to hear them.

"Oooh, what's that last one mean?" Gustave asked, his trotters shifting next to Grinda. When the sand witch didn't answer, he cocked his head at her. "Still can't move or speak? Guess he exaggerated about your freedom to go." Gustave clopped around until he was standing uncomfortably close to Grinda's flashy new hiking boots, with his tail facing her knees. He swung his head to look at her over his bony shoulder. "I just nearly got eaten by a llamataur. Not really different from any other day, though. Being a goat among humans means I could be on the menu whenever you guys get hungry. Every time your nephew appeared in the barnyard, I wondered whether it was to feed me or to feed his family. Remember when Lord Toby and Poltro were trying to turn me into curry and you did absolutely nothing to help me? Well, I've whipped up a little something to pay you back for that."

The billy goat's tail lifted, and Grinda felt hot little plops landing on the tops of her feet and the bottoms of her shins. "I call those cocoa pebbles. Or chocolate soil. Gourmet butt dumplings, if you prefer. Cooked to order just for you at my body temperature. That's what I feel like all the time living in your world. Helpless and crapped upon. You get to feel it for a few minutes. Please enjoy this tiny serving of justice."

Grinda's first instinct was to internally rage and swear vengeance on the goat, but she just couldn't get up the energy. Something about being defenseless for the first time since her youth made her realize that for all her haughtiness, she couldn't survive alone. Whether it was Milieu Goobersnootch's loving care, the adoration of her sparklecrabs, the aid of the goblin beauticians, or Fia and Argabella bravely storming through acid to help her, she couldn't get by without a little help from her friends. And now she knew: Gustave's greatest fear was being betrayed and eaten by his so-called compatriots. No wonder he pooped on everyone—he expected that everyone, sooner or later, would poop on him.

Ignoring the warmth on her feet, Grinda watched events unfold, still out of her control. Fia turned from the wall and surveyed the room, and her broad shoulders slumped for a few seconds. Then she sniffed, flicked her sword to sling away the gore adhering to it, and stomped over to where Argabella lay curled up next to the twice-dead corpse of that stubbornly undead kid. Poltro moaned and rubbed at her temples but otherwise didn't move.

"Honey bunny," Fia whispered tenderly, kneeling down and stroking long fingers through soft fur. "Are you okay?"

Grinda noted that Fia was not okay despite walking around as if she were. That hatchet wound looked nasty, and it was still bleeding. Fia shook the bard's shoulder. "Hey. Wake up, girl. We have to go."

The bard did not respond.

"Argabella?"

Even Grinda's cold heart ached.

The rabbit girl wasn't moving.

15.

NEXT TO A NEWLY CREATED ORIFICE
AND MUCH SCREAMING

Fia could feel the tears welling in her eyes and didn't care. She was just about to shout Argabella's name when the rabbit woman coughed, wheezed, spat blood, and made a tiny mewling noise.

"Everything hurts. My nose especially. Is my lute broken? I need to sing 'The Ouchie Song.'"

Fia laugh-cried in relief. Suddenly everything was fine again. "Your lute's okay, I think. And you'll be fine, too. But we've got to get you to the healer."

Argabella's eyes went wide, and she almost touched Fia's shoulder. "You, too, though."

Gustave pranced over to Lord Toby's moth mound and festively kicked him in the ribs.

"Oof!"

"Good news! You're not dead yet!" the goat told the hedge wizard. "Get up so we can get out of here."

"Pfaughh!" A spray of crispy bread and insects at one end revealed where Toby's mouth was, and soon the entire pile shifted as Toby struggled to his feet, flailing and squeaking a tiny bit when he realized there were moth corpses on him. "What! No! Get off! Bah! This is an outrage! No one treats the Dark Lord like this!"

Fia noticed that he had a dead moth stuck in his beard extensions and failed to mention the fact. Added to the glowing algae and crouton muck, it looked rather hardcore.

"Pasty dude treated you pretty well, considering," Gustave said. "Most everyone else wound up getting zapped somehow. All you got were ineffectual butterflies."

"That was my fault," Fia said, because she felt it to be true even if it wasn't. It was why she wanted nothing but to tend roses and hide from all the trouble the world kept bringing to her door. Even here, trying simply to pass through, she'd endangered everyone with that horrible reminder of her past—and with the way she'd been so busy dealing with it that she'd neglected the llamataur. At least she hadn't gotten Worstley killed again. Or had that really been him? "Hey, Grinda, was that really your nephew, or some kind of weird copy, or . . . ?"

"She's frozen. Can't talk or even avoid being pooped on," Gustave explained as he trotted over to commiserate. "And I don't think this was your fault. I mean, that umlaut guy came after everyone. Speaking of which, who or what was that kid?"

Poltro groaned and sat up, holding her head. "Cor, I'd like to know that, too, because he rung my bell good, he did."

Fia shook her head and clutched at her wound, putting pressure on it. "I really don't want to talk about that. I mean, obviously that was a traumatic thing from my childhood, but . . . I don't think I can share it with you. I'm sorry."

"Oh. Well, I can share mine. I'm sorry about the llamataur, everybody," Poltro said. "When I was young, they ate my parents when we were trying to cross the Llama Drama. Me and my brother, Morvin, watched them do it, too. Still have nightmares. They were going to eat us for dessert, they was, but we got saved by a nice caravan of Qul people, and we got sent to Borix for adoption, where we were lucky enough to have Lord Toby take us in."

Toby sniffed and turned red. "You never told me about the lla-mataurs," he mumbled, then turned his gaze sharply to the uncon-scious man slumped nearby. He pointed at the sleeping form in the concert T-shirt. "Who," he demanded, "is *that?*"

"Oh, bother," Argabella murmured, then spoke up louder. "That's my da. We should probably go before he wakes up. Especially since he's still got bongos. He used to be okay, but after my mom left, he went a little barmy. He was yelling at me in the earl's castle when everyone fell asleep, and it's like I've been waiting all these years for him to wake up and continue the castigation. He can be quite . . . Nagful."

"I think you mean emotionally abusive," Gustave said.

"Now that I think about it . . ."

Before she could get too deep into the past, Fia pressed on. "What about your mom?"

"She's dead. Maybe."

"Maybe?" Fia asked.

"We haven't been in touch for quite some time. On account of her leaving my da to run away with a halfling CPA and getting awards for being great at doing taxes. But I received a small sum in the mail a few years back, along with a receipt for a frugal but tasteful funeral, so I think she might actually be dead."

Hearing this, the mighty Fia frowned down at Argabella, whose head rested on her lap, and then she felt her expression soften be-cause everything inside her went gooey. She realized that even more than roses, even more than a proper set of armor, she wanted to be kind and generous and the whole range of happy adjectives to this truly unique woman for a long, long time. She felt luminous and certain about this but equally afraid that perhaps that moment, when she was light-headed from blood loss and Argabella was probably concussed, was not the right moment to say everything out loud. So she confined herself to saying, "You know your da was wrong about everything, don't you?"

"I don't know. Maybe he was right about some things."

"Oh, no. Like what?"

Argabella grinned through a bloody mouth. "I'm never going to find a decent man. Not the way I am."

Fia laughed, delighted. "Okay, okay. He was right about that one thing."

"Not to rush anyone," Gustave said, "but why don't we rush along now?"

"How is Grinda going to rush along," Poltro wondered, "if she can't move?"

"Hmm." Fia gently helped Argabella stand and then clambered to her feet, feeling somewhat dizzy. She needed NyeQuell and fumbled about for it before remembering that they had used it all to heal themselves from the acid leeches. "Well, perhaps the healer that Yör spoke of can help with that. And with everything. I'll carry her."

"What about those tongue things he talked about?" Gustave asked.

"That's right. We need to watch out for them."

"What's all this?" Lord Toby asked. He'd missed much of it since he'd been the first to fall. "Something about a nice tonguing?"

Fia pointed to the open door. "That's the way out, and supposedly there's a healer near the exit if we can live long enough to get there. Yör seemed to doubt we'd survive the tongues, whatever they are."

This comment finally tore Poltro's attention away from her headache. "Cor, there was a sign warning us about them, remember? All the other signs have been true so far, so I guess we'd better watch out."

"What are they going to do, lick us to death?" the Dark Lord sneered.

Fia nodded at him. "We're all messed up, Lord Toby, except for you and Gustave. So I think it's up to you two now to save us from a licking."

"What? I gotta work with him? He wants to kill me," Gustave protested.

"If he does, he'll answer to me," Fia said. She pointed at her eyes with two fingers and then pointed them at Lord Toby. "I'll be watching, although I wish you two would make peace. We've fought together against an impossible enemy and won, and that means we are a legitimate dungeon party. We can join the union and everything."

"Hmmpf." The Dark Lord had no retort to make, so he straightened his robe and inspected himself, brushed some clingy croutons away, but still missed the moth in his beard. Argabella checked on her lute, strummed an experimental chord, fiddled with the tuning, then sang the new, improved version of "The Ouchie Song" for them all. It helped ease their pains somewhat, and Fia's wound clotted. Encouraged by that, the mighty Fia picked up Grinda and draped the witch over her injured left shoulder like a sack of barley, keeping her sword arm free.

"If we get in a fight, I might have to drop you," Fia said, "but I'll do my best to protect you. And your glass wand. I'll just slip that gently into my scabbard. I keep it oiled and ready. Ah, look at that! A perfect fit. Now I'll just keep my sword handy should we need to rub out any obstacles as we venture down the tunnel."

"Um. So we're just leaving those bodies there and you're all cool with that?" Gustave said.

"Yeah. They're not real," Argabella said.

"They bled real blood and behaved like real bodies," he pointed out. "Worstley and the llamataur did, anyway."

Fia shrugged. "So? Wizards can do some amazing stuff. Right, Lord Toby?"

The Dark Lord swelled with pride. "That is correct."

"Then please proceed to be amazing and get us out of these catacombs."

Gustave and Toby led the party this time, both of them going slowly, alert for an ambush. Argabella and Poltro backed them up, albeit with woozy steps as they still felt unsteady from the beatings they'd received. Fia brought up the rear with the sand witch over her shoulder, and from that position no one could see her face as she struggled to deal with the facts: She had been the one who insisted they take the fork that led to Ol' Faktri, where they'd almost died; she'd been the one who'd insisted on coming through the catacombs, where they'd almost died. Only a sneeze and disorganized teamwork from at least some of the party had saved them from certain death. She wondered if she had been cursed in the past, unawares, to be a mortal danger to her companions. The opposite of a Chosen One, maybe—an Unchosen One. That would almost be a relief, because then she wouldn't be responsible for bringing those closest to her to such harm. Or bringing accidental murder to literal innocent by-standers. Or—now her worst fear—causing harm to Argabella. She longed for the day when she would be a mortal danger only to the aphids on her roses. Fighting no longer held such an appeal, for all that the sword felt hungry in her hand. She shook her head, willing that feeling away. Before, she'd been running away from something. Now, perhaps, she was running toward something even better.

Fia dwelled in a prison of regret for an untold while, her thoughts weighing her down far more than the dead weight of the sand witch on her shoulder. But when the dimensions of the hallway changed and she saw skeletons on the floor, she knew yet more danger was ahead.

"So . . . these bones?" she said, but she didn't actually have to say anything. Everyone was already tense and on the lookout.

The width of the corridor instantly doubled, always a sign that something particularly horrid was about to appear. The rock walls were stained with dried blood, which Lord Toby's algae covered but did not hide, making everything glow brown. And the ceiling had doubled in height.

"A bit of extra illumination might be wise, I think," the hedge wizard said, touching his hand to either wall and encouraging his algae to grow up and spread down the length of this new space. Scattered bones will make a person cautious that way.

"I don't see any tongues," Gustave said. "Just an awful lot of dead folks."

"They didn't all die of natural causes right here, though," Toby said. "Let us proceed, but keep looking around, including above. The height of this chamber makes me suspect that an attack may come from overhead."

Twelve whole steps into the expanded chamber and the Dark Lord was proven right. A wet slithering noise was the only warning before something slimy and pink bungeed down from the ceiling and plunged into a soft bit behind Gustave's right shoulder. He screamed an outraged goat scream, and the thing retracted, tearing out a chunk of his flesh as it did so.

Everyone followed the trail of the muscular weapon and saw that it was indeed a tongue being retracted into the greedy maw of a toothsome red thing crouching on a hidden shelf near the ceiling. Possessed of cruel yellow eyes and a huge mouth that must've largely served as tongue storage, it could safely take bites out of them from a distance and seemed, in fact, perfectly designed to do so. And it was not alone. There were many more of them appearing all along the tops of the walls, drawn by Gustave's scream, and some were even approaching down the hall on the floor, gurgling in their hunger for fresh meat. They were utterly like frogs in all the ways that are terrible—and weaponized.

Fia realized she had heard tell of these creatures before. The Dread Necromancer Steve had mentioned them once during a particularly bad attempt at seduction. "These are hooktongues!" she cried. "The only way out is through! The longer we wait, the more concentrated they'll become! Go! We have to charge and hope they don't eat us to death one lick at a time!"

The goat, at least, knew what it meant to charge. He lowered his head and ran straight at the hooktongues coming for him. Not to be outdone, Lord Toby was only a step or two behind, throwing up his hands and shouting "Leet na logah!" as fast as he could, and with each repetition of the chant a loaf of incredibly dense ciabatta shot forth from each of his fingers, which he waggled around to make them arc through the air in as many directions as possible. And thus, while every member of the party suffered unwelcome tongues creating new bloody orifices in their flesh and then ripping out succulent bites of it, at least they were spared far worse by the random protection of loaves of bread flying through the air. The hooktongues speared through the dough and retracted, giving the creatures an unexpected carb load instead of a bloody protein snack and completely destroying any ongoing ketogenesis.

Fia knew that poor Grinda was suffering an inordinate amount of tonguing, but since the witch was still frozen, at least she couldn't complain. The best thing Fia could do for them both was to get the heck out, and if the sand witch lost massive chunks of buttock, at least she knew how to dress to hide her flaws.

Gustave's horns proved impregnable to the hooktongues, and several squishy bodies deflected off his head as he charged into the hideous monsters that were foolish enough to stand in his way. When he plowed through them and trampled their bodies, they stayed down, unable to recover in time to do any more damage. Fia was able to slice through a few of the tongues coming for her by sheer luck, but she still felt them stab into her and steal away her vitality every few steps. Poltro was in much the same situation, hacking away as she ran, confidence restored in her knife, but poor Argabella had only her butter knife, no defense against the creatures at all, and she simply ran as best she could while chunks of her neck, shoulders, and chest were sheared away and gobbled up by hungry mouths.

Were it not for the goat plowing the path ahead and the bread wizard protecting them from above, they never would have lived to bleed to death on the other side.

But after some distance that seemed interminable but truly wasn't, Gustave had no more hooktongues to ram and the ceiling went back to being a normal height that didn't promise hidden monstrosities. Poltro barely made it out, crawling the last few steps, but Argabella fell down before she could get there, bleeding from so many wounds.

"Toby!" Fia shouted. "Help me!"

The Dark Lord turned, bloodied and frenzied, his fingers extended, forming a veritable ciabatta umbrella over them as Fia carefully picked up Argabella under an arm while still clutching her sword; she couldn't use her scabbard because Grinda's wand was still in there. She carried two women now as her strength waned and she could barely move. Every step was an eternity, and her muscles quivered with exhaustion.

Behind them, hooktongues plunged into breads with thaps and fwaps and retracted without penetrating the party. But Fia had lost so much blood. They all had. Groaning and growling, she staggered forward, past Lord Toby, past the wounded rogue and goat, who stared at her all forlorn as if she were stepping into the grave, and then her knees would no longer bear all the weight she carried and they buckled, sending her crashing to the ground with her burdens forgotten. Her eyelids were so heavy, heavy as the world. At last, even they fluttered closed.

16.

In the Spectacular (If Tentacular) Hut of Belladonna the Healer

Something soft and cool caressed Argabella's forehead, and she sighed in comfort. Or, more accurately, she attempted to sigh in comfort and ended up throwing up in her mouth a little, as sighing requires that one breathe in deeply, which forces one to smell anything in one's particular vicinity. In this case, with her eyes still shut, Argabella had to assume she was being licked across the face by a troll with gingivitis who'd recently partaken of fresh garlic and sardines and possibly eaten another, even sicker troll for breakfast.

Her eyes burst open, but everything was dark and fuzzy. She soon realized that this was because she was staring directly into someone's extremely furry armpit. She gasped, and that only made it worse, as some of the long hairs sort of wafted toward her open mouth.

"Help?" she said, almost in a whisper.

"Ah, darling, you're finally awake!"

The voice was nearly a purr, sensuous and womanly and the sort of voice one generally hears only when drinking reddish liquors in the darker corners of the more sultry sort of halfling bar. The tuft of black hair disappeared, replaced by the face of a beautiful woman whose thick eyebrows and rippling hair were of the same dark black. She was in her early thirties, maybe, and she had the sort of smile that suggested you were somehow already sharing a delicious secret with her. Despite the fact that her entire body hurt and her nostril hairs were singed, Argabella had no choice but to smile back.

"I'm Belladonna, and this is my love shack. Welcome. You've been through quite an ordeal."

"A . . . love shack?"

"Yes. Just outside the Grange."

"But where are my friends? We were looking for a healer—"

Belladonna smooshed a finger to Argabella's lips, the long, red nail pressing in. "Shh. So many questions. You're still weak." The finger left Argabella's lips, leaving behind the flavor of dirt and vanilla. "Your friends are here and safe. I am the healer you sought, and my apprentice and I have been lovingly tending to you all. You've been sleeping for some time, and you are the first one awake." Belladonna stood, her white healer's robe slithering around her ample curves. The garment had holes cut out in the shoulders and a deep, drooping neckline, but the red cross Argabella was looking for was right there, stretched across the woman's voluptuous chest.

"You're the healer? But I thought healers were . . ." Argabella couldn't quite find the right word. *Clean* seemed insulting, but *prudish and nerdy and yes also clean* seemed a bit too on the nose.

Belladonna smiled from beside the table where she pounded herbs with a grimy mortar and pestle. "Sensual? Yes, the Order of Erotonia is a rather unique branch of the healing arts, but our goddess is just as powerful and goddessy as any other goddess."

Argabella sat up a little to get her bearings. She'd expected the usual sort of healer's hut, spotless and spare, painted white and well swept with plenty of sunlight and scented with growing green things that looked healthful if bitter-tasting. What she found was a crowded, jumbled room edged in dead plants and stacked dishes buzzing with flies. Buckets were everywhere on the ground, full of dark liquid that gave off a briny sort of smell. The beds weren't in neat rows at all, just haphazardly placed and tangled with sheets of burgundy silk. That seemed rather convenient, as bloodstains would totally disappear as they dried. As Belladonna ground her herbs, moving her arm up and down and heaving her bosoms, her body odor billowed into the room as if driven by a bellows. Yet despite having little faith in the healer's outer appearance, Argabella knew that she had been very near death and now was well enough to mentally complain about a lack of deodorant on the part of her savior. The chunks taken out by the hooktongues appeared to again be smooth, slightly furry skin with nary a dimple to poke.

"Where's Fia?" she asked.

"The tall, curvy one with the muscles? Still out cold. Carried you and the frozen glamour granny out of that cave like a hero. She'll look a bit rough just now, but I promise, my cures work."

Belladonna pointed to a red-swathed cot in a dusty sunbeam by a dirty window, and Argabella nearly screamed. She was accustomed to seeing Fia's body, or at least the parts of it not concealed by her chain-mail bikini or the more recent partial armor, and so it wasn't the massive topography of flesh that threw her off. She rather liked that bit. No, it was the dozens of purple octopuses spread over Fia, their tentacles curling this way and that in ways that made Argabella feel like she should cover her eyes.

"What is happening to her?" Argabella wailed, struggling to untangle her legs from red silk sheets that smelled of roses and funk.

Belladonna hurried to Argabella's side with a kind smile and gently pressed her back down onto the pillows. "I told you—my medicine is unusual. Some healers use leeches."

"Ugh! No." Because Argabella remembered the acid leeches and wasn't anxious to revisit that cure. "I'm allergic to leeches."

"And some healers use powdered mouse ears or dried wood lice or special mushrooms or maggots. But the healers of Erotonia are taught to use the healing powers of the sextopus." Belladonna reached into one of the many buckets on the floor and pulled out an aubergine octopus—or sextopus, really, as it had only six legs—and squashed it against her cheek, stroking it. For its part, the creature stared with intelligent, almost bedroomy black eyes and wrapped a tentacle around the woman's neck in a friendly sort of way.

"The sextopus secretes a healing slime. As their suckers pull out any toxins or infection, their slime reinvigorates the skin and organs. And, in your case, regrows acid-burned flesh and fur. Don't you feel better?"

Argabella held up her arm, and it was true. She wasn't Bleedful or even Scabful, and her fur was silky and seemed to have new highlights. "I . . . I guess. Yeah."

As she looked around the room, she saw all of her friends in various stages of undress, covered with an indeterminate number of sextopuses. There was Fia, swirled in purple cartwheels of tentacles. Toby was flat on his belly, showing a lower back tattoo written in elvish script. Poltro was curled into a fetal position and sucking her thumb. Grinda was still frozen in place, although the sextopuses seemed to be trying to stretch her limbs into movement by using the bedposts. Even Gustave, flat on his side, had not escaped the cephalopod treatment. One sextopus straddled the goat's face, its tentacles curling about Gustave's horns and its eyes blinking black where Gustave's creepy, yellow, sort of judgmental eyes usually were.

"See?" Belladonna said. "You've spent three days lying there butt naked and covered in sextopuses. So you have Fabio here to thank for the fact that you won't live the rest of your life with tongue-shaped chunks taken out of your soft bits."

Belladonna held the sextopus—Fabio—out toward Argabella.

After a strange silence in which Belladonna's sensual smile grew bigger and her eyelashes batted fiercely and forcefully, Argabella stuttered, "Th-thank you, Fabio?" uncertain whether sextopuses expected verbal gratitude but at least half sure that Belladonna did.

"Excellent!" Belladonna cried, dropping Fabio back in the bucket with a plop. "Now, you'll be hungry. My assistant, Bigolo, is fetching lunch as we speak. Just try to relax. You can't truly heal if you're anxious or twitchy."

"But I'm always anxious and twitchy. It's kind of my thing."

Belladonna rummaged about in a rusty tackle box and withdrew a crusty brown bottle. She sat on the edge of Argabella's small bed, just a little too close, her plush hip nudging Argabella's arm. Dipping her long-nailed finger into the bottle, she withdrew a substance that looked like old bacon grease mixed with curdled cheese.

"This should do the trick."

Argabella reared her head back. "That doesn't look, er, sanitary."

Throwing back her head to laugh, Belladonna cried, "Sanitary? What has sanitation to do with healing?"

When Argabella opened her mouth to explain that the answer to that question was basically EVERYTHING, Belladonna slipped her finger in, depositing the paste on Argabella's tongue. The taste of, yes, old bacon grease and curdled cheese exploded in Argabella's mouth.

"Grck! What? Why? Oh. Ohhhh."

Argabella licked her lips and slid down a little, nestling into the lovely pillows. Everything suddenly felt very soft and squishy and pleasant, very blurry around the edges.

"Whazzis?" she asked. "Z'nice."

Belladonna patted her on the head. "It's opium, mixed up with old bacon grease and curdled cheese. That should help you relax. And hey, if you go back to sleep, all the better. Just don't act weird if you feel someone tenderly stroking you while you're unconscious."

A tremor of anxiousness fought for control of Argabella's body but was only able to exert any force over her left eye, which bulged a bit. "Who's gonner stroke me?!"

"The sextopuses. You're not healed all the way yet. And we must get you well."

"Yezwemust."

"Good bunny."

"I'm a goooood bunny."

With that, Argabella closed her eyes and dreamed of writing hit love songs and then doing her own taxes.

When next she woke, Argabella was prepared for the stench and strangeness but not for all the shouting.

"Who are you? What is that smell? Where's Argabella? Why is there an octopus on me? And why, in the name of all that's holy, am I naked?"

It was Fia, and she was past annoyed and moving firmly into murderous.

"It's okay!" Argabella shouted. "It's all pretty weird, honestly, but it's fine. We're at the healer's hut."

Argabella rubbed her eyes until the crust gluing them shut crumbled out, then sat up to find Fia. The warrior was at maximum pump as she fought a sextuple of sextopuses, all of which were using their sticky tentacles to hold her down on the bed. Fia's face was flushed with fury, but her skin was almost completely healed and even glowing a little. On seeing Argabella, she went limp and smiled back.

"Oh. Hi. This is really awkward."

"Belladonna?" Argabella called. "Bigolo? Anybody?"

They appeared to be the only conscious people in the hut, and the smell was definitely less apparent than it had been the previous day. It was dawn, and the glow of orange lanterns lit the hut's interior, turning the mounds of dishes and junk into a mysterious nightmare topography for those not currently in the know and still recovering from the relaxing effects of yesterday's opium. Poor Fia, waking up like this, in the dark, alone, and covered in tentacles and slime!

Argabella figured out where her feet were, remembered how to stand, stepped over Gustave, and wobbled over to Fia, all while ignoring the fact that she was wearing a hideous gown covered in faded ducklings that was open all down the back, showing her fuzzy little tail to anyone with eyes. Sitting on the edge of Fia's bed, she was careful not to touch the sextopuses, which were cautiously spreading back out across Fia's curves to complete their work. But she did put an experimental hand on Fia's arm in a comforting sort of way.

"Everything is fine," Argabella repeated, her voice low. "I've never heard of this healing order before, and it definitely has its quirks, but from what I can tell, we're all going to be okay. I woke up yesterday and met the healer, and she's . . ."

"Trustworthy?"

"I was going to go with 'a bit of a hippie lunatic with a raging libido,' but sure." Argabella held out her arm, showing the lustrous new fur. "Remember what this looked like in the caves? Raw, abraded with acid, bleeding, and missing a few chunks?"

Fia stroked a finger down Argabella's arm, raising goose bumps that made the rabbit girl shiver. "Wow. Yeah. I guess that's good work. You look amazing. When you passed out, I wasn't sure you were going to make it. I was terrified."

Argabella looked down, blushing under her fur and feeling warmth bloom in her chest. She remembered a little of that time—what it felt like to be cradled in strong arms and carried out of danger. Her whole life, she'd longed to feel safe and cherished, and she'd felt that with Fia even as the hooktongues tore them to pieces. But the Catacombs of Yore hadn't claimed them, had they? It was a new dawn, and Argabella felt somehow more whole than she ever had. When she looked into Fia's eyes, her heart just about exploded with joy. The warrior made her feel strong and capable, too, which was saying quite a lot.

"You saved my life, Fia. I don't know how you did it or where you found the strength, but you got me out of there. So thank you. For that. My hero."

Returning the smile, Fia reached for Argabella's hand, twining their fingers together. "Well, it's kind of crazy what a girl can do when she's in—"

"Loaves! Fresh loaves! Gnomeric flour with ancient grains! Hot sticky buns! Robust eggs, ready to pop!"

The shrill voice from a vendor outside the grimy windows caused them to break away shyly, which was just as well, since Belladonna burst in the door seconds later in a cloud of funk. She had a basket over one arm and mud all over her bare feet. A handsome youth wearing nothing but a flimsy linen kilt came in behind her, slamming the door in a way that would've gotten him kicked out of most healing huts and nicer restaurants.

"Ah, my little bun, you're awake again!" Belladonna crossed to where Argabella sat, took her face in both hands, and air kissed her cheeks. "And our fine fighter, you're conscious just in time for breakfast. How do you feel?"

"Whah?" was all Fia could manage.

Belladonna was, even for those accustomed to strangeness, a lot to take in. She seemed to take up the entire healing hut as she bustled around, singing to herself and shimmying her hips as she danced and muttering "Chickaboom" to herself. Soon she brought a platter to place on the bed beside Argabella. The piping hot loaf, probably from the noisy vendor outside, had the sort of artisanal feeling that Lord Toby couldn't quite conjure even on his best days. There were also chocolate-covered strawberries, figs, grapes, bananas, and oysters that smelled like they might be a day too late.

"Eat, eat!" Belladonna urged. "These are healing foods!"

Argabella ripped off a hunk of bread and nibbled on a strawberry just so the healer would stop staring at her so keenly. As she and Fia ate, Belladonna gave Fia another hideous robe, this one covered in capering bears, and removed the sextopuses one by one, remarking on their fine job and thanking them personally as she dropped them back into their dank, smelly buckets.

"Do I smell bread?"

Lord Toby popped awake one bed over, a tiny sextopus perched on his chin with tentacles curling up either side of his jaw in a rather fetching sort of violet beard. Argabella handed him a chunk of the loaf, hoping that they could skip the Shoutful terror and outrage bit this time.

"Where—"

"This is the hut of Belladonna the healer. She does weird stuff, but it works. The octopuses are harmless and helpful."

Toby considered the sextopus attached to his chin, chewed his bread, and nodded conspiratorially, making the cephalopod waggle about like a purple tumor. He winked at Argabella to indicate that he totally knew what was going on. "Gotcha. Animal code phrases." He changed his voice to an absurdly loud stage whisper. *"The eagles are fond of moose milk,"* he rasped. "And, uh . . . oh! *The otters are giddy regarding tomorrow's gopher races."*

"I think Bigolo overdid his opium allotment," Belladonna said, moving closer to pluck the tiny sextopus off Toby's chin, revealing an entirely bald patch of skin that they were obviously going to hear a lot about later. Lord Toby's eyes darted down to the healer's cleavage and stayed there, enraptured and almost entirely without pupils.

"Hello, nurse," the hedge wizard said. "What's a filthy hut like you doing in a bosom like this? No, wait. What's a filthy girl like this hut doing in a . . . No, that's not it, either. Hello. I'm the Dark Lord."

Belladonna smiled at him like he was five. "Well, hello, Dark Lord. I'm the healer, and I'm going to fix all your nasty boo-boos."

"Yeah," Toby muttered. "Fix 'em good."

"Bigolo? A little help? Maybe bring the Dark Lord some coffee to help him focus?"

The attractive youth, who was mostly muscles and cleft chin, stumbled over a sextopus bucket and hurried to the pile of dishes.

"Yes, ma'am. Of course, ma'am. Coffee it is. Right away. Yes, indeedy. Coffee."

"Bigolo?"

"Ma'am?"

"Remember how we talked about how you were better seen and not heard?"

Bigolo gave a despicably sexy smile and winked a sparkling blue eye while tipping an invisible hat with one hand and pointing at his boss with the other. Argabella was fascinated to find that this gesture was both utterly ridiculous and pretty appealing in a weird sort of way. Soon the boy had bumbled over with a brown clay jug on a tray, which he placed carefully by Toby's side.

"Why, we could be twins," Toby noted, which made everyone laugh uproariously.

"Bigolo will be admitted to the Sacred Order of Erotonia next year," Belladonna said. "He's been training under me for three years, and I work him hard. Night and day, I pound him with fresh challenges, and he always rises to the occasion."

"I have a very spacious tower," Toby told her. "Surrounded with well-trimmed hedges."

Belladonna smiled at him. "I bet you have a lovely tower."

"I do. And hedgehogs. But that lady? You know the sandy magic lady? She has crabs."

"Mmm-hmm."

"I can make crackers out of nothing."

"Bigolo," Belladonna urged. "The coffee?"

Nodding energetically, Bigolo put the jug to Toby's lips and whispered, "Down the hatch, sir!"

Toby being Toby, even when deeply drugged, he obligingly gulped the coffee down as rivulets trickled over his hairless chin. But Argabella was surprised to note that the coffee wasn't the dark brown of good, dark coffee or the light brown of coffee mixed with cream and sugar. It was, apparently, a bright sort of green.

A very poisonous-looking green.

A green that she didn't feel so confident about.

"Belladonna?" she asked, beginning to stand. "Is your coffee a different sort of coffee?"

"Is it what?"

"Ah! Piquant," Toby commented as he smacked his lips, "with an unusual fungal bouquet you don't find in many coffees, yet it possesses rare viscosity. Ah—urp!—this is. Ugh. Ew. Unpleasant aftertaste. And burning?"

Argabella pointed. "Is your coffee supposed to be . . . green and bubbly?"

"No! Bigolo, you fool!"

Belladonna leapt to her feet and swept across the room in a swirl of fabric and black hair. Reaching for the jug, she wrenched it out of Toby's hands and threw it against the dingy wall, where it smashed to paint a swath of bright, violent green across the stained tan. As it dripped, the green liquid briefly formed a skull and crossbones shape just in case anyone was unsure of its level of unsafeness.

Argabella ran to the Dark Lord's side but didn't get too close, as he was starting to foam a bit. "Toby?"

"Tastes ... like ... frogs and dire shrooms in a sherry reduction ..." Toby sputtered.

"That's because it *is* frogs and dire shrooms! Toxic bog frogs from the Figgish Fen in the Skyr! I was whipping up a mortal smoothie to kill a troll hereabouts and clearly marked the jug with a sign that said NOT COFFEE!" Belladonna practically shouted that last at Bigolo, who cringed.

"Oh," he said. "Sorry, mistress. I must have misunderstood the part where it said 'not,' but I can fix that right away and fetch the real coffee."

"I don't think that's going to fix anything," Argabella said, pointing a trembling claw at their patient, whose unblinking eyes and stillness indicated that he was quite beyond all refreshment. "I'm pretty sure the Dark Lord Toby is dead."

17.

Under the Lone Lamppost
Where Lurks the Squeaky Marmoset
of Side Quests

Poltro had woken up in some pretty strange situations. There was that time Cutter had taken her hunting in the Pruneshute Forest, for example, and they'd woken up surrounded by blitzed boars that had broken open their cask of Puissant Porter while they slept and gotten bombed out of their piggy minds. But she'd never woken up with sextopuses all over her bits and Lord Toby being dead. That was a page in her life's book she'd never read before.

She remembered her parents like faded vignettes, except for the super clear memory of that time they died screaming. All her more pleasant memories centered on Lord Toby. He'd been a bit peculiar and forgetful, but he'd never beaten her or allowed himself to get eaten by anything with a llama's face. She remembered the pride in his eyes the day she'd headed off to Cutter's academy riding the wrong way on Snowflake—well, maybe that wasn't pride so much as concern, but she'd soon learned to ride a horse facing the head instead of the rump. Lord Toby had always brought her a nice wheel of cheese on her birthday and forgave her for fighting his chickens. And now he was gone, just like that? Her brain wasn't always a mighty thing, and it had quite a bit of trouble wrapping around a definitive lack of Lord Toby. She felt quite empty inside, but not the sort of empty that could be soon filled by food.

"She's in mourning," Belladonna kept reminding everyone, but Poltro didn't care enough to explain that it was clearly the afternoon.

All things considered, though, Poltro supposed she should be grateful that she'd woken up at all. She'd dropped down into unconsciousness outside the healer's hut after helping drag Fia and Argabella there and thought that was it: she'd been licked for good. But despite her being fully restored to health by Belladonna's purple squids, people kept asking if she was okay after she learned Lord Toby had died from chugging a bog frog smoothie. Fia sympathized and said she understood that frogs were just the worst, far more perilous than chickens, even when they were dead and blended into a nice foamy beverage. She hated frogs, and Poltro managed to nod along and grunt as Fia talked about their many amphibious dangers. But even the talking goat looked worried. He nudged her with his horns and looked up at her with those goggly yellow eyes.

"Hey, uh. You still want to eat me someday, right? A nice curry? Very roguish of you?"

"What? Oh. Yeah. That'd be . . . hmm? What were you saying?"

"Nope," the goat said to Fia. "She's lost it."

"I did? What did I lose? Not the potions he gave me? My stuff— where's my cloak? I need my cloak!"

Belladonna fetched it—yanked it, really, out from underneath a pile of bloodstained clothing—and gave it to her. Those potions had suddenly become the most important thing the rogue could think of, and she didn't know what she'd do if they, too, were gone. Poltro twisted the black cloak around frantically, looking for that inside pocket where she'd put the potions for safekeeping, realizing as she did so that she hadn't checked on their safety until now. They could have been smashed when she fell into the pit of acid leeches or shattered when she tussled with the llamataur in Yör's cavern. They might have been tongued into shardy oblivion. She hadn't even thought to use them when she was bleeding to death. She should have paid more attention, because if they were smashed—but no. Her fingers closed around them, and they were intact.

Poltro pulled out the vials in victory, holding them up in the lurid light of Belladonna's hut. "Yes! I still have them!"

"What are they?" Argabella asked.

"They are not to be taken rectally! But I've kind of forgotten otherwise. They're labeled, though, even if the instructions are kind of smeared like sad clown makeup. I think I can still make out the names. Let's see. Invisibility. Sleeping. Healing. Oh! That might have come in handy earlier . . . if I'd been awake, maybe I could have saved him."

She could have saved him.

But she hadn't been quick enough.

Or tough enough.

Now she'd never get a chance to make Lord Toby proud. If only she'd been able to get that farm boy's heart, beating or not. If only she'd been a slippery enough rogue to steal Grinda's magic wand. If only she'd been able to smash Staph the pixie like a flying roach. The whole quest just seemed so silly now. What was the point of questing if everyone was going to die anyway?

If only. If only. If only.

Poltro had difficulty remembering much after that. Time slipped through her thoughts like lubra eels, and happenings were like blurry paintings ruined by splotches of someone's yakked-up lunch. There was some rain outside the hut, a rolling sort of meadow under gloomy skies with a lonesome red barn that reminded her of the farms in Borix, and they kept calling it the Grange. She was pretty sure they buried something there. Someone got paid some coins for helping them. And then they walked for a long time. Going to the lake. No—to the capital. To Songlen, capital on the lake!

"Enough of this," someone said, and Poltro gasped as someone threw water in her face. It was the older lady who looked younger and was moving a great deal more than she had previously. The sand witch, unfrozen! And very annoyed, judging by the smeary lines of her face.

"Hey!" Poltro protested. "That was . . . wet." Perhaps, she thought, that wasn't the brightest thing she'd ever said.

"You've been in shock for a long time now. We need you to be present before we go into town."

"Shock?"

"Over the Dark Lord's death, yes. Let's talk about it. What are you going to miss about him?"

"Miss about the Dark Lord?" Poltro felt tears welling in her eyes. "Cor. His stupid scraggly wanna-be beard. His obsession with arti-sanal crackers and cheese. Those grand luncheons with the invigo-rated ham jam!"

There was more, much more, both good and bad, but as she listed those things and wept, she let them go. The others listened, sniffling a bit themselves. Whenever Poltro faltered, Grinda grimly urged her on. Poltro felt as if her heart were a particularly infected wound and the older woman was squeezing it to get all the pus out. It hurt, but something about it felt good, too.

"And his peculiar compulsion to be a Dark Lord. Cor, what a thought! Lord Toby was good at organizing a dinner party for two, but he was terrible at bringing people together. Especially hedgehogs and turtles, but I imagine taxpayers and unions would've been a bit beyond his ken. D'you think he just woke up one day and said, 'I want to be a Dark Lord'? Such folly!" She laughed until she cried again, then cried until she laughed. At last, there was nothing left but a few chuckling hiccups.

When she was finished, she looked up and saw the world with new eyes. Tiny details stood out: the leaves drifting to the ground, birds pecking at peckish things, and Gustave munching disconso-lately on some grass nearby, supremely bored.

"That's right, Curry Kid," Poltro said, licking her lips. "Fatten up for me."

Gustave's head jerked up and around to regard her, and he spat out a mouthful of grass. "Hey! You're back to your old murderous hungry self! That's great. Now stay away from me."

Poltro would see to him later. Time would only serve to make him more succulent. Time stewing in the pot, that is. "What are we doing now?" she asked.

"We're after Løcher and Staph the pixie," Grinda reminded her. "Løcher is quite an accomplished wizard, mind you, and the grounds of his estate are protected. There's someone who knows how to get through the security, but she'll want something in return. And to find out where she is, we have to visit a rather unsavory halfling."

"Does that mean he's sweet? Isn't sweet the opposite of savory?"

"No, it means that he's a rogue and smells bad."

"So he's kind of like me at this point."

"No. Well, yes. Look, Poltro, just let me do the talking. After we all clean up and get something good to eat."

The prospect of comfort plus comfort food cheered Poltro considerable much as they approached the gate to Songlen. She would comfortably revel in comfort like a fluffy white kitten rolling around in comfy marshmallows.

The guards, having seen it all—for most everything comes to the capital—waved them through without even making obvious comments about Fia's stature or Argabella's rabbit ears.

"That goat looks like he would cook up pretty nice," one remarked, and Poltro grinned at him.

"I know, right?"

Gustave bleated in dismay and edged closer to Fia.

Grinda led them to a fine inn in the Highwaist District, where she apparently had favors owed her. The sign proclaimed it the Grand Balzac, and the wrinkled Balzac himself hastened to show them to fine rooms and have baths drawn for them and inquired what they would like from the kitchen.

An hour later, clean and refreshed, Poltro joined the party downstairs for an exquisite supper replete with a generous appetizer of candied nuts, the house specialty. Lord Toby's influence had informed her gourmet palate, and she indulged it in his honor. She had blistered pheasant cheeks on bourbon waffles with assorted bison bits and a light arugula medley on the side. Argabella enjoyed a homespun roasted artichoke pizza on gluten supernova dough. Fia wolfed down an entire cornucopia of heirloom squashes and mung bean sprouts in a rustic soy butter reduction and quaffed a tankard of elderberry mead. Grinda had a flash-seared monkfish filet in a scraped hazelnut roux topped with a tart lime sea sponge, and Gustave ordered Balzac's sweaty shoes flash-fried in beer batter and sprinkled with cinnamon and sugar.

Fortified and feeling saucy, the cobbled streets of Songlen lit by whale oil lamps, they set out to rendezvous with Grinda's contact, one Humbert Beadlebone of the Cheapmeat Beadlebones, a halfling who made his living in the Sadbra District by knowing more than anyone else about things he shouldn't know. As expected, Beadlebone sat alone on the back stoop of a liquor merchant, a single duck-fat lantern on a round table providing illumination. A pipe and pint also sat on the table, ready to be enjoyed later. Everything, of course, was halfling size, made to fit the fingers and lips of a creep about the size of an eight-year-old child.

No, Poltro didn't trust this halfling at all. His friendly grin sandwiched between two mutton chops engulfing the sides of his face was surely a ruse to draw them in. He had olive skin like hers, carried an artisan-crafted leather bag, and appeared to be completely unconcerned that he was flaunting his wealth in a district known for pickpockets and footpads. A gold medallion gleamed on his hairy chest, spied through a loosely tied poet's shirt and an unbuttoned paisley waistcoat. The medallion testified to his membership in the Dastardly Rogues Under Bigly-Wicke, the infamous and widely feared halfling criminal organization that had its chubby fingers in most everyone's pies. It was probably all the protection he needed. There were two kinds of halflings in Poltro's experience: the kind that would trick you to rob you and the kind that would trick you to kill you and then rob you, and all of them either wore that medallion or owed favors to someone who did.

Grinda had no obvious reservations, however. She slapped a fake smile on her face to match Humbert's and greeted him like an old friend you've secretly hated for a long time. He held out his palm and she pressed a single coin into it. He frowned at the profound lack of jingling.

"That's it?" he said, his voice an aggrieved tenor with a pronounced northern accent.

"Simple question gets a simple coin, Humbert. I need to know where I can find Mathilde tonight."

"Mathilde?" His eyes flicked among the party before him with frank curiosity. "Hmm. A fighter, a bard, and a rogue. Going questing, are we? What's the goat for? Dinner?"

"I'm for witty banter," Gustave said. "Now answer the question. We're on a schedule."

The halfling chuckled and rolled the coin along the top of his knuckles.

"You don't see a talking goat every day. Tell me about your friends," he said to Grinda.

"Give me the coin back if we're going to barter."

The halfling looked pained. "It's just an introduction. You know I can find out who they are anyway."

"Then go ahead and find out, Humbert. I've paid you, and generously, too, for what is probably common knowledge in town, so tell me where to find Mathilde tonight."

He grimaced. "I've heard she's in Fraidhem this week, in the alley behind Testy Tom's Blue Orb Room."

"Thanks."

"Need anything else? Magic rings? A thing that does stuff? Hey. I don't suppose any of you folks could use some flesh honey?"

In response, Argabella abruptly vomited on him. Loudly. Violently. Chunks of roasted artichoke and pizza dough soaked in stomach acid sprayed him down in a high-pressure geyser, and he recoiled, howling in horror.

"Sorry, sir," Argabella quavered, wiping off her twitching whiskers with a furred hand. "I have a bad reaction whenever anybody says that."

"What's your name?" he demanded, all his friendly demeanor dissolved as a sodden artichoke chunk slipped off his nose and splatted on his lap. "Tell me your name!"

"No. Don't," Grinda said, warning Argabella. "Let's just go. She apologized, Humbert, and it wasn't on purpose. Just an accident."

"Oh, no," Humbert said, shaking his head and sending bits of dough flying from his hair. "One does not simply vomit on a halfling and walk away. That would set a disgusting precedent." He rose to his feet and pointed a stubby finger at the bard, her stomach contents dripping off him as he moved. "You're going to pay one way or another. Pay quite a lot or be made an example of."

He was so focused on Argabella and everyone else was so focused on him that they were all quite surprised when Fia swept her sword diagonally down from the point where his head met his neck and continued to the opposite side, underneath his arm, causing his head and shoulder to slide off from the rest of his body. His heart squeezed once more in surprise, showering them all with blood, and then Humbert Beadlebone's bones fell over dead.

"Cor, I just took a bath," Poltro complained. But the sand witch didn't think that was very significant.

"Are you mad?" she yelled at Fia. "You practically halved a halfling!"

"He threatened our bunny," Fia explained. "And don't worry; nobody saw us."

"That doesn't matter! They'll find out. They always do."

"So what?" Fia wiped off her sword on Beadlebone's trousers and sheathed it. "I don't get it. Why is everybody in the west so afraid of halflings? They're easier to chop up than most."

"Ugh, I forgot you're from the far east," Grinda said. "He was a drub—a Dastardly Rogue Under Bigly-Wicke."

"What?"

"A member of the halfling mob. You can always tell by the medallions they wear."

"Oh! *That's* what they mean? That's what that one creep must have meant by a *consortium*."

"What creep?"

"Probably a friend of Beadlebone's here. I owe him forty percent of whatever I got out of the tower. But he can't have even one percent of Argabella."

"We'll have to worry about it later. Let's just get to Fraidhem. And let me take care of this." Grinda took out her wand, said "Klainoz emetikos!" and wicked away the blood from their clothes and skin.

They tried to hurry away without precisely looking like they were hurrying, all the while worrying. Or at least Poltro was worried. She knew very well that it was not wise to cross the halflings, and she fretted about the possible consequences all the way from Sadbra through Skidmark and St. Codpiece to an alley behind Testy Tom's.

It smelled of repressed desire and unwanted potatoes. A single lamppost burned the midnight whale oil, a nimbus of yellow-orange light settling over wooden crates and piles of refuse. Their footsteps clacked and echoed off the stone walls of the buildings on either side.

"Mathilde?" Grinda called, but Poltro didn't see anyone in the alley at all. "Mathilde? It's your old friend, Grinda the Sand Witch."

"Grinda?" a tiny voice squeaked, and the stacks of crates underneath the lamppost wobbled and made a peculiar scratching sound. Poltro drew her dagger, expecting some sort of vile, terrible-clawed, chicken-based monster. The boxes shuddered, and that monster proved to be a tiny adorable primate that topped the crates and perched there under the lamplight.

"Oh, look! It's a monkey!" Poltro said, her face splitting into an unreserved grin. She loved monkeys.

"I am not a monkey!" Mathilde bristled. On either side of a white face, she had two tufts of black hair that were practically made to bristle. Her high-pitched voice dripped with wounded dignity. "I'm a white-headed marmoset. At least for now. I hope to be human again soon." Her tone warmed as she addressed the sand witch. "I don't suppose you've come to help me, dearest Grinda?"

"I think we can help each other, Mathilde. Løcher's time has come. I'd like to know how to get to him."

The marmoset's eyes blazed with blue fire. "Yes!" Then her fur flattened all around, and she drew back. "I mean no. I want to get him. Personally. Vengeance shall be mine." And a very squeaky vengeance it would be, Poltro couldn't help noticing.

"But Mathilde, you know very well that you can't in this condition. And if we get him *for* you, then the enchantment's broken and you'll be free."

"What's going on?" Gustave asked. "Did she get zapped by Staph the pixie, too?"

Mathilde's marmoset mouth formed an adorable *o* of surprise as she turned to Gustave, then her eyes burned blue again as her tiny head made minuscule movements, checking him out. "Is that the aura of a Chosen One I see on him?"

"It is," Grinda confirmed.

"Staph laid it on him?"

"At Løcher's instruction. He's still after King Benedick, and this is how he's going to get it done. Unless we get to him and Staph first."

"Auughh!" Mathilde squeaked, shaking her tiny marmoset fist at the sky. "I hate Løcher!"

"Still don't know what's going on," Gustave reminded them.

Mathilde composed herself and explained. "I used to date Løcher, even though Grinda warned me not to. I should have listened, but I have a thing for bad boys, whoa dang. I mean, let me tell you, I used to hang out with the Dread Necromancer Steve, okay?"

"Augggh!" Fia cried out, shaking her massive fist at the sky. "I hate Steve!"

"Gadzooks! You dated him, too?" Mathilde asked.

"Briefly."

"Oh, no!" The marmoset's face scrunched up in disgust. "Did he want you to do that one thing with the—"

"Yes!" Fia's anguish was plain.

"Ew! Gross!"

"I know! Totally!"

"Anyway!" Gustave interrupted. "You were saying."

"Right. Well, Løcher found out about Steve, and even though it was a long time ago, I guess he's jealous of necromancers or something. Pitched a fit and said I'd betrayed him somehow, even though that business was all before I met him and I didn't even *like* Steve! So Løcher turned me into a marmoset with my own wand and scattered all my other magic doodads around, transforming them into this and that and guarding them with horrible monsters. I've managed to get most of them back thanks to other people questing for them, but unfortunately, I can't turn them or myself back to normal without my wand. I still need it. And if you want me to help you, Grinda, I'll need you to get it for me. Only then will I tell you how to get through Løcher's defenses, because he is vulnerable there, though he doesn't realize it."

"Wait, wait, sorry. Just trying to make sense of this," Poltro said. "Why didn't he just destroy all your stuff once he had you beat? Wouldn't that have been the ultimate victory? Seems like a right waste of his energy and everybody's time, hiding objects that will restore your power."

Mathilde leveled a blank stare at the rogue. "He did it for the sake of sadism, I imagine. He would never think it a waste of his time or energy to be cruel to me. Dangling the possibility of a return to my powers is exquisite torture, I assure you."

"But if you're successful, then he'd just have to defeat you again. Though now that I think of it, I suppose I've done stuff twice lots of times too. Thing is, I usually apply some special creams and lotions afterward or else I get an awful rash."

"Fine," Grinda said with a resigned sigh. "Where's your wand?"

"It's being used as an unbreakable toothpick by a troll in—"

"Nope!" Fia said, shaking her head and cutting Mathilde off.

"I'm sorry, but I really need to clean my ears," Argabella said, attempting to be more polite.

"Infinite nopes," Gustave added. "Goats are a troll's favorite snack food."

"I adore you, Mathilde darling, I really do," Grinda said, "but no way."

"No problem," Poltro said, and everyone stopped to make sure they'd heard that right. "Don't get me wrong, Ms. Marmoset: if your wand was being guarded by a henhouse, then I'd be saying 'no way!' too, because chickens are nightmares and I'm out the door at the first sign of a cluck or a cloaca. But trolls, now: trolls is easy."

Everyone glared at her, and Poltro smiled back at them, confident that for once she was on sure ground with no tricksy pebbles lying about. "Trust me. I got this."

18.

DOWN AN ALLEY ECHOING WITH A
TROLL'S PATHETIC ANGST

As she stared at Poltro and Gustave ejected a platoon of be-fuddlement pellets, Fia couldn't help wishing for momentary omniscience. Was the rogue in fact the most stupid sentient being alive? As Poltro went to stick a finger in her ear and nearly poked herself in her eye, Fia had to assume that she was. Still, perhaps Poltro's instincts could prove useful in more ways than one.

"Great. You've got this. So where's the troll?" Fia asked nervously, anxious to leave.

Her sword jerked in her hand, and she was overcome with the obscene need to swirl it through another hotheaded halfling. She quickly slipped it into her scabbard, knowing that its song wouldn't cease and hoping no one had noticed her smiling as she sliced the blasted Beadlebone. She really didn't like violence.

Although she hadn't mentioned it to anyone, her sword was en-chanted to crave blood, and she could feel it singing for more, calling to her hand to just swish the blade a little somewhere near a bit of exposed flesh or goat flank. The halfling's half-liquored splashing of the ol' red stuff only made the warrior and her blade both crave more wanton destruction. Or wonton destruction, as her high metabolism had made quick use of that delicious cornucopia of gourdly delight at Balzac's. That was why she'd become a vegetarian in the first place: the less meat she ate, the less she longed to drink a river of blood. Because she truly yearned for that dream of peaceful existence to be hers someday. Killing a troll, though, did seem like it could be construed as a public service, a manner of keeping the peace, should Poltro require backup.

"I'll lead you there," Mathilde said, her fur all fluffed out like a frightened cat. "But I'm not getting close personally. That troll looks at me like the last piece of popcorn, and his breath is bad enough to make me pass out."

"I do that, too, sometimes," Gustave said helpfully. "It's easier to deal with great horror when you're unconscious and being speedily carried away by your companions."

"Speaking of which, if you don't mind?" Mathilde was looking up at Fia, and Fia felt like she had missed something.

"Uh? No, I guess not."

With a squeak of victory, the tiny marmoset scampered up Fia's legs, swung from her precariously positioned breastpiece, and hurtled onto her shoulder, where she wrapped one tiny claw around the metal bra strap and wound the other one into Fia's hair.

"Did I just agree to be your steed?" Fia said, gritting her teeth against the creepy feeling of claws tangled in her scalp.

"You're the tallest," Mathilde agreed. "And the least likely to be eaten, judging by your . . ."

"Muscles?"

"I was going to say your enchanted blade that calls for blood. Gurrrl, I bet that thing has cleaved many a meanie! Go that way, by the way."

As Mathilde steered Fia's head like a horse and Fia began walking in that direction, she realized that she'd rather face a troll than have this exact conversation. She glanced at Argabella and found the bunny looking at her in the worst possible way, doubt and fear scribbled on her fuzzy features.

"Enchanted blade?" Argabella asked.

"Cor, that sounds cool!" Poltro practically yodeled. She was pumped up over this troll hunt.

"Well, kind of." Fia sighed and felt her shoulders slump in a very unwarriorlike way that reminded her all too well of the year she'd turned fourteen and grown three feet, dwarfing all the other girls in her class at school. "My sword is a gift from Steve, and it's kinda enchanted to sorta want to murder everyone constantly. It really likes blood. Like, a lot. And when I don't use it for a while, it sleeps. But that halfling halving really—"

"Woke it up?" Argabella asked.

"More like rang a bell in its ear and reminded it what bacon smells like."

"But you wouldn't hurt us?" Gustave asked. "I mean, any of us? Especially those of us who are particularly edible and unable to defend themselves because all they have are hooves and horns?"

"No! Of course not. You guys have traveled with me for weeks now and never been scared of me. Don't start now. I can control it. And maybe, if the troll gives us trouble—"

"Addiction is a slippery slope, my dear," Grinda said, gliding along with the sort of frown older people reserve for rock music and new ways to smoke things that they smoked differently when they were younger.

"It's not an addiction. It's not me. I can control it. I've been going to AA meetings, and—"

"AA meetings?" Argabella asked. Gods, how Fia hated the worried way Argabella was looking at her, as if she'd uncovered every horrible secret all at once.

"Assassins Anonymous. They teach you how to follow the One Step for Not Murdering Someone."

"What's the one step?" Gustave asked.

"You don't murder them."

"Huh. Sounds like a solid program with a refreshing lack of nuance."

"Yes. I've been going, and it helps. Turns out it's not my fault if I want to murder everyone, but it is my fault if I actually do it. The only sword I can control is my own, and then, sometimes not—like when a halfling threatens us. But you don't have to be scared of me. I'm fine."

Argabella reached for her hand—not her sword hand—and gave it a squeeze.

"I support you," she said softly, and Fia finally exhaled and squeezed back.

That was all she needed, really.

"Good. Then let's go get this troll."

"I support you, too," Gustave added. "For the troll-killing part. Not the general murdering part. Think about vegetables. A tasty lentil stew. Roasted cauliflower. If you're feeling particularly violent, contemplate tearing the tender leaves from a charbroiled artichoke."

"That just makes me think about tearing legs off a goat," Fia muttered darkly.

Gustave bleated and ran behind Poltro, which showed just how afraid of Fia he was at that moment.

All along, Mathilde had been turning Fia down this street or that by using her hair like reins. As they passed a particularly dank alley, the marmoset yanked back hard, and Fia skidded to a stop.

"Ow! Careful!"

"Shh. We're here. Good steed." Mathilde released Fia's hair and scampered down her body and back to the slick cobbles. "So the troll lives at the end of Rotbritches Alley here. He's of normal troll size and stature and level of stench, but there's one thing you should know about him."

"He's particularly fond of sand witches?" Grinda asked.

"His mother was kicked in the head by a goat?" Gustave pressed.

"He has a fondness for chicken farming?" This from Poltro, who looked far less confident regarding the troll than she had previously.

"None of that," Mathilde said, shaking her furry little noggin and trying to look serious but failing, because she was an adorably tiny monkey. "The thing is, he's not dumb at all. He's quite clever and will debate you to death. A devil's advocate. So it would be best if you didn't attempt to talk him out of the wand but rather charge right in and kill him before he can get a word out."

Fia was already shaking her head. "Nope. That would violate the One Step. We have to talk to him. I feel certain we can get the wand without any violence. Especially considering Poltro's potions."

They all stared at Poltro. "Poltro's potions?" she muttered. "Ah, yes. I am Poltro, and I have these potions. *Not* rectal ones." She held up three vials, and one slipped out of her hand, smashing on the ground. Everyone drew back from it, but it looked like nothing more than a small puddle of water.

"Cor, who could've guessed that might happen?" Poltro said, holding up the two remaining vials. "And now the barely legible labels have all gotten mucked up with my nervous sweat. I have no idea which one broke or which ones these are that ain't yet broke. Lord Toby, what—" She looked around, sweat forming on her nose. "Oh, yeah. That's not good, is it? Ha ha! Mystery potions. Oh, yes. I'm sure these will do . . . something."

"Invisibility, sleeping, and healing," Grinda reminded her. "Let me see them. Perhaps I can figure out what you have left."

"Wait!" Poltro fell to the ground on her hands and knees. "Just let me lick up whatever this is, and then we'll know one out of three."

"Poltro, no!" everyone shouted, but it was too late.

The rogue was lapping the clear liquid off the filthy cobbles.

"Tastes a bit like if velvet and vomit had a baby," she noted, eyes going round as she sat up. "Also, a bit like sharp shards of glass. Oh!"

"Is that a good *oh* or a bad *oh*?" Gustave asked.

"If she goes to sleep, it won't be the worst thing that ever happened," Argabella murmured, and Fia was gratified to note that the bunny girl was standing rather close, indicating that maybe she wasn't so frightened of Fia's potential for violence anymore.

Grinda was studying the potion vials, but she shrugged and pocketed them. "The Dark Lord apparently never learned the trick of color coding potions. They're all clear and odorless. Not even a tang of scent."

"Cor, I feel . . ." Poltro stood and flexed her arms. "I feel rather stronger, I do say! And goodness, what a failure of basic motor skills, dropping that invaluable potion! I warrant my neuromuscular system is not precisely tuned for roguish feats of stealth and skill—a poignant irony considering my professed métier."

"Poltro," Grinda said slowly, "were you ever . . . dropped on your head?"

"Many times, sadly. Lord Toby felt rather guilty about it, but he could never figure out which end was up when I was a child. Dandled me upside down all the time. It's a wonder I never became addlepated, is it not? Ah, my friend and benefactor! May your bones feed the worm that feeds the fish that feeds the savior of the world someday!" Poltro sniffled once, wiped a nascent tear from the corner of her eye, then crossed her arms in front of her and squinted into the darkness. "Enough of my rhapsody. Now, yon troll. What is our strategy, my boon companions?"

Grinda leaned over to Fia and Argabella and whispered, "It was a healing potion, and it's healed something in her brain. Knowing Toby's powers, it won't last long, but we should use it while we can." Then, louder, to Poltro, "We thought you might best lead us in this venture, fair rogue."

"Ah, yes, I have it!" Poltro spun around and held up a finger. "These potions are vital to our mission. If we give one drop of each to our two animal companions, we can see which creature grows sleepy and which one grows ever so slightly invisible. Then I can use the invisibility potion to sneak up and give the troll the sleeping potion."

"That's . . . kind of genius," Argabella admitted.

"I don't know how I feel about that," Mathilde said. "Now is not the best time to be ever so slightly sleepy."

"Fia can carry whoever feels sleepy," Poltro pointed out. "And you can all wait right here while I do my rogue whoosiwhatsit down in the alley."

At the word *whoosiwhatsit*, everyone else traded concerned looks.

"Let's hurry," Grinda said, handing over the vials.

Poltro opened each of the remaining vials and dipped a single drop onto each index finger. She held her hands out to Mathilde and Gustave, who both grimaced but recognized that there was no way out except licking the rogue's besmirched fingers.

Gustave immediately let out a jaw-cracking yawn, and Mathilde faded just a tiny bit.

"Eureka!" Poltro cried before swilling the invisibility potion.

Grinning as she vanished, she said, "Fear not, my friends. I will soon return with that whatchamacallit, that, uh, that . . . wand."

As the rogue's footsteps announced her invisible progress down the alley, Argabella and Fia traded looks.

Fia frowned sadly. "I have to go, too, don't I?"

"You're the only one among us who could best a troll," Argabella said. Her hand reached up to Fia's cheek and pulled back uncertainly, then returned, fingers trailing softly down the side of her face. "I believe in you."

"You do?" Fia's heart thumped hard against her armor from the inside, threatening to burst through it. A nameless fear had been building within her that Argabella didn't feel as strongly as she did, that she was reevaluating, reconsidering, perhaps even regretting their closeness. And feeling was so blasted easy. Putting those feelings into words—the right words at the right time—was much more difficult than climbing a tower covered in deadly thorns.

Argabella left her hand on Fia's cheek, met her eyes, and spoke in low tones. "I do. You are safety and warmth and comfort in front of a fire until you need to be the fire itself. I understand that. I trust that."

Fia smiled in relief and gratitude. Bards were so much better at the parts where words were necessary. "You have no idea how much I needed to hear that." Argabella stood on tiptoe and kissed her, and Fia marveled at how such an intoxicating draught of courage could be so soft. She let that kiss take its lingering time, for the next moments would not be so fulsome or fine, but she would meet them better for knowing Argabella felt so about her. Their lips parted reluctantly, and they looked away, embarrassed that the others had been watching. But Fia decided quickly that she did not care, for the moment of joy was more important, and she sprinted into the dark alley, fearless of what horrors it might hold. If they could watch her halve a halfling, they could by gosh watch her rub noses with a bunny.

As she ran, she noted that it was funny how the alleys in Songlen seemed to go from rather nice streets to dark, dank, smelly dead ends. Along the way, Fia couldn't help noticing occasional parchments tacked to the bricks, several of which showed a highly optimistic portrait of Worstley—when he was alive, looking very uncrushed. She slowed down to read one. "Hast thou seen this foine ladde?" they asked.

"I have," Fia murmured to herself. But she didn't take a frayed paper tab with Worstley's mother's address on it. She still had hope that she could make amends for that mistake.

Like the other alleys they'd encountered in the city, this one featured a single whale oil lantern at the end, casting terrifying shadows over the blood-splattered brick and filth-strewn ground. Under this light sat the first troll Fia had ever seen close up. He was bloody huge, at least twice her height and five times her mass. He looked like an elephant crossed with a poison mushroom, thick and rubbery with weird gills and spots. Although Fia would've expected a troll to be rending a corpse to fritters or stomping puppies, this troll lazed on a too-small office chair, murmuring to a book. A tiny pair of pince-nez were perched on his nose, which must have been an affectation since his wide-set eyes could not possibly focus through them, and he wore a black vest and a felt hat, the brim pulled down rakishly. The book in his hand looked new and expensive, and he licked his bulbous thumb before turning each page.

It was peculiar, Fia thought, that a troll could afford so many books, considering they were generally paid very little for their services as bouncers and muscle. Then she noticed a stack of bones off to the side, muddled up with green bags, piles of cloth, and pairs of spectacles. The top piece of cloth read BARNS AND GIBLETS BOOK SHOPPE, and Fia realized she was looking at a long string of delivery persons who had not been tipped appropriately. Her distaste for the troll grew.

Fia stopped while she was still hidden by shadow and hadn't yet attracted the troll's attention. Trolls, she knew, rarely began any interaction; they preferred to let their victim make the first move so they could control how to react in the most egregious way possible. For most trolls, this consisted of bashing in one's brains with a large mallet, but Fia didn't see any mallets lying about. Although the troll appeared entirely absorbed in his book, she could hear evidence of Poltro climbing a towering stack of old crates filled with yet more books and leather journals. The rogue must've been attempting to pour the potion directly into the troll's mouth, which seemed utterly ridiculous considering that he was drinking a growler of local beer, which sat on the ground by his feet. The healing potion must've been wearing off if Poltro thought it was a better idea to climb twelve feet into the air and dribble a potion into the yawning troll's gaping maw of rotten teeth than to just pour the liquid into his ale.

"Mm. Yes. Two sides to every issue," the troll rumbled. "The man in the middle is a knave. A tasty knave."

The stack of crates wobbled, and a lone call of "Cor!" was the only sign that something terrible was about to happen. As Fia watched in horror, the entire tower of boxes and books and bobblehead dolls came tumbling down around the troll. As the dust cleared, a lone figure was seen flopped on top of the crashed pile: a half-invisible Poltro.

"What's this?" the troll thundered, rising to his feet. "My reading time is sacrosanct!"

The sword in Fia's sheath shivered like a grumbling stomach, but she didn't reach for it. There was still time for the rogue to follow through and be the hero.

"The potions," Poltro mumbled. "Got to . . . drink the potions? Yeah, that's good. Drink 'em."

"Poltro, no!"

The troll's bulging eyes flicked from Poltro to Fia at the sound of her voice, which was just as well, as Poltro made quick work of the sleeping potion and recollapsed bonelessly on top of a stack of books.

"And what are you doing in my private demesne?" the troll asked Fia as he pulled a heavy wooden club from where it rested against the wall and rose from his long-suffering chair. He, too, pronounced it "deh-mez-nee," but Fia knew that those who learned from books frequently mispronounced words that weren't spoken often. She herself had thought picturesque was pronounced "picture-squee" until she was sixteen.

"Do you mean domain?" she asked, trying to buy time, worried about the sword twitching in the sheath strapped to her back, demanding a meal. At least the troll was concentrating on her instead of the insensate Poltro, but that wasn't the strongest "at least" Fia had ever considered. As he approached her, step by ground-shaking step, her eyes darted all over the troll's figure, hunting for Mathilde's wand. Ah! There! In his front vest pocket beside a carved pipe and a selection of quills.

"Well, actually," the troll began, "since its etymology originated in the late thirteenth century in another part of the continent, it can be pronounced in a variety of ways, and HOW DARE YOU COME INTO MY SPACE AND CORRECT MY SPEECH!"

The troll swung his club straight down, and Fia leapt nimbly aside, feeling a whoosh of air as the wood thundered into the cobbles, cracking them to pebbly shrapnel.

"My mistake!" she shouted, her quivering sword calling for trollish blood. "What an interesting custom of social behavior you have. My name is Fia. What's yours?"

The troll paused, clearly trying to regain control. His breathing slowed down, and he straightened up and fiddled with his hat.

"Well, m'lady, you can call me Holden."

"I thought troll names were all about . . ."

"Murdering people? I know. So obvious. I like to think I'm a different kind of troll, a gentleman troll. Sure, my surname is McBonecrunch, but I'm nothing like my father. I'm more worldly— cosmopolitan, if you will. Tell me, Fia," he said as he picked up a book and rubbed a splotch of dried blood off the cover. "Are you a reader?"

"Um." She heard feet pattering up the alley, and a half-invisible marmoset waved from the shadows, pointed at Poltro, and made a "keep going" motion with her teeny little marmoset hands. "Sure. I love books. Especially romances."

"Paugh!" the troll scoffed. "Romance. Kissing and folly. Where's the story, where's the philosophy? I'm a troll, and even I can't rip a bodice. You should read real literature. The classics." He held up a book called *Ye Olde Clubbe of Fisticuffs*. "This is one of my favorites. It's all about, like, rejecting capitalism." He held up another, the spine as yet uncracked, called *Alliance of Nincompoops*. "Or this one, about a misunderstood genius. You should read it. I'd love to chat about what the true meaning of success is when we're living in a world that values looks instead of substance."

Fia wanted to point out that the world generally valued trolls only as paid muscle because they were giant, terrifying man-eaters with questionable hygiene and terrible fashion sense, but she figured this would merely incense him further. Arguing with trolls only ever served to make them more horrid. As much as it pained her to consider it, she would have to use something other than her intellect or brute strength to get that wand. Stepping into the light, she held out her hands.

"Gosh, that book looks fascinating. Intelligence is so much better than whatever you just said."

Holden nodded eagerly and stepped toward her, right past the unconscious and half-visible Poltro, and a thin rope of drool escaped from the corner of his mouth in his excitement to talk about his own brilliance.

"I had this girlfriend up by Mudskip Ferry. We were pen pals, but she just didn't seem to understand that the male is naturally superior to the female. I kept trying to explain my genius to her, and I told her my IQ several times, but in the end, it didn't work out. I couldn't get her to read anything good."

He put the book in her hands, and as it was a giant-sized book, it took everything the muscular warrior had not to fall over. "Oh, yeah. This looks great. What's your favorite part?"

The troll loomed down over her, taking back the book and flipping through it. "Oh. Um. My favorite part. Where is it?"

While his attention was entirely focused on the book that he clearly hadn't read, Argabella darted in from the shadows, grabbed Poltro by the shoulders, and dragged her back out of the alley. Holden startled as if he might look up at one point, but Fia leaned over, giving him a fantastic glance at her cleavage, and he completely forgot everything else.

"This book, whatever," he finally said, tossing it onto the pile. "There's much better stuff. I'm writing my own book, you know. It's about the struggles of an intelligent but misunderstood young troll fighting the kleptocracy as he stumbles through failed relationships on his quest to become a best-selling author. Let me read you the first chapter. Hang on."

As he bent over to paw through the pile of fallen books, Fia sidled close and snatched Mathilde's wand from his pocket. Her heart beating in her throat, she kept waiting for him to notice, but he was too busy hunting for his book. A flicker of motion behind her suggested that Mathilde was ready, and Fia held the wand behind her back, sighing with relief as tiny fingers plucked it from her grasp and the sound of scampering faded up the alley. With the wand safely recovered and Poltro out of danger, all Fia had to do was extricate herself from the troll and get out of the alley without dying.

Holden McBonecrunch found his manuscript, attempted to flourish it gracefully but rather flailed it about instead, and cleared his throat thunderously before beginning to read: "Alisdair von Murderknuckles sat on a stump, pondering the many colorful facets of his life. It was a normal day, and his mother had already urged him to follow his dreams . . ."

As the troll read, infusing every sentence with nuances of wounded angst, Fia winced. It was terrible. Truly terrible. Alisdair thought about the proletariat, then mused on how foolish and flighty women were, then had a dream about conquering the world as a renowned barbarian despite his poor social skills and lack of actual fighting experience. And then, of course, he became a Chosen One, but not by Staph the pixie, of course. By winning a downhill skiing race. As the moments of her life ticked by and her sword again began to whisper to her and beg for succor and/or silence, Fia felt the rage of battle fall down on her shoulders like a holy mantle from heaven.

This troll had to be stopped.

She didn't mind fighting. She understood that larger creatures had to eat. She was even, on some level, understanding of Ol' Faktri's tender taste buds.

But listening to a troll read his narcissistic screed cut right through the metaphorical twine holding together her patience.

"So what do you think so far?" Holden asked, a thick and greasy finger marking his page in the leather journal. "I feel that it hearkens back to the great—"

"No!" Fia shouted, drawing her sword and pointing it at his book. "Anyone who told you that book is good was trying not to get eaten, but I'm not scared of you, so here's what I really think. It's terrible, it's derivative, the prose is more purple than an eggplant at sunset, and there is literally no story. It's just a dude sitting around, thinking about being great instead of doing anything about it, and I have no respect for it. If you understood anything about greatness, nobility, or altruism, you would eat that and crap it out where it belongs: in the sewers."

Holden tenderly put his book on a crate. He removed his hat and placed it carefully on a ragged nail on the brick wall. Unbuttoning his vest, he folded it and gently draped it over a book. He turned to Fia, his shoulders hunched and his mouth curled into a ferocious snarl, all pretensions of courtesy gone.

"YOU'RE JUST A JEALOUS HAG!" he howled. "A FAT, UGLY WITCH WHO DOESN'T UNDERSTAND HOW THE WORLD WORKS!"

Holden made a lumbering, troll-like swipe for her, but Fia danced back.

"No, I've got a pretty good handle on how the world works, having lived in it," she said. He grabbed for her again, but he was easy to dodge, telegraphing every clumsy move. "And insulting my personal appearance is simply a waste of your bad breath, because why would I care what a troll thinks about my looks? Trolls always attack that way, though, and honestly, it's pathetic. There's nothing for me to be jealous about. If I wanted to sit in a dank corner of nowhere and write books about how hard I'm struggling to do nothing, I could."

"OH, AND OF COURSE YOU'RE GOING TO TROLL-ZONE ME," he howled, fists swinging impotently. The predictable pattern of troll attacks would be sad if they weren't so often destructive.

"If by 'trollzone' you mean 'avoid,' then yes. Everyone does that. The only people who could possibly stand you would be trolls with similar views who were similarly trapped by their own inability to accomplish anything of value. The thing is—"

He grabbed for her with both hands, and she finally gave in to the bloodlust singing in the sword, slashing the troll right across the chest, a deep cut through the muscle layered over his rib cage. Black blood welled and sheeted down his torso.

"The thing is that there's a reason nobody likes you, and it's that you suck."

The troll grunted, staggered back, and pinched at his pecs like he could press them whole again, trying in vain to staunch the flow of blood. "Well, actually . . ."

"Will you just shut up and die?" Fia thrust her sword beneath his hands, found a gap in the ribs, and punctured his liver or perhaps even a lung.

Holden gasped and toppled over among his books.

"Magic . . . wand . . ." he wheezed, reaching for his vest.

"Yeah, magic can't fix dead. Ask me how I know."

As the troll coughed up bubbles of blood and shuddered his final breath, Fia yanked out her sword and cleaned it off on his velvet vest. Normally after such an affair, she felt guilty for having given in to her sword's yen for gore. This time, however, she felt satisfied. "You won't be eating any more innocent delivery people," Fia said to Holden's corpse. "And thank goodness you'll never finish writing that book. Not that you ever would have, probably."

Fia walked back up the alley feeling almost as if she'd leveled up as a person. Instead of immediately solving the problem with violence, she'd worked to reach an understanding, then faced off with a bully. She'd spoken her truth, even though it made her feel vulnerable. And in the end, after exhausting every other option, she'd slaked her sword's thirst for destruction while ridding the world of a creature that delivered nothing but negativity and strife. And think of the countless literary agents and editors who would never have to suffer that prose.

For a monster fight, it had truly been an enlightening interpersonal experience.

"You're alive!"

Argabella ran for her, and Fia barely had time to hold out her arms before she was being hugged within an inch of her life.

"Yeah, I guess I am."

Fia melted into the hug, feeling pretty darn good about herself. A few moments later, they broke apart, and Fia blushed to find everyone staring again.

"Is Poltro okay?" she asked.

"If you mean, is Poltro asleep and probably as stupid as ever, then I would say definitely yes." Gustave nudged the rogue with his horn, and she snorted and rolled over on the garbage-strewn cobbles, snuggling a confused rat.

"S'nasty chicken," she mumbled. "An' that troll. Cor, what a big-gun! Roast him up good. Stuff the goat inside. Maybe stuff a duck in the goat. Trollgoaduck. Mmm."

Gustave turned his back to her and let a volley of pellets fly to surround her like tiny chocolate chicken eggs.

"Hey, did you see the missing person posters, Fia?" he asked.

"I did. Where'd the rest of them go? Weren't they all around this alley?"

If a goat could smile, Gustave did. "I just decorated Poltro with their remains. That farm boy wanted to eat me, but I guess I ate him! Or at least ten copies of his ugly mug. Now the pooboy really is poo. I wish he was alive again so I could tell him about that."

Before Gustave could talk about the dead farm boy any more, Fia looked around for the other missing part of the troll puzzle. She found Mathilde squatting on the ground by Grinda's feet, furiously polishing the wand against her fur and occasionally spitting on it.

"Uh, how's that wand polishing working for you?" she asked. "Or is this, like, a private thing?"

"It has to be clean to work," Mathilde explained, annoyed. "Do you know how hard it is to get troll tooth glob off a wand? It won't work if it's sticky."

"It's true," Grinda added. "Nobody likes a scabby wand."

"Ah, there we go." Mathilde held up the stone wand, an equal in beauty to the glass one Grinda had lost and then remade. The sand witch, in fact, had a covetous and almost Toby-esque glow about the eyes that made the marmoset skitter a little closer to Fia and Argabella.

"Perhaps I could be of service, Mathilde?" Grinda sidled a little closer. "Help you tidy it up?"

"Torner guman!" Mathilde shouted, and a bilious white vapor spurted from the wand to coat her in a sickly glaze. As they watched, the marmoset expanded up and out, and then the white mist popped like a bubble, revealing a feisty looking middle-aged woman with brown skin, bulging biceps, and ... well, nothing to hide them.

"Bit cold without fur," she noted. Fia blinked, because even though Mathilde was now fully human, her voice was still as tiny and squeaky as it had been before.

"Wait here!" Fia called. She jogged back down the alley, grabbed an armful of clothes from the troll's discards, shook out the bones and discount cards, and returned.

She needn't have bothered. Mathilde tapped her bare shoulder with her wand and said, "Gunna mec!" and a dress appeared on her figure, simple but well fitting in a charming indigo.

"Show-off," Grinda muttered, feigning interest in a snail on the brick wall. "But now that you're back to normal, perhaps you'd care to hold up your end of the deal."

"We had a deal?" Mathilde's innocent face was as bad as Grinda's.

"Tell us how to kill Løcher," Argabella said.

"Ah. Yes. That. Well, if you want a chance, you'll need a billy goat and a jar of pickled herring."

"And?"

"And what? That's it."

Fia stepped forward, her sword beginning to whisper about how lovely blood was on a summer morn. "You said you'd tell us how to kill Løcher, not name two unrelated objects that are generally ignored during political assassinations."

Mathilde shook her head, and her stomach audibly grumbled. "You're misremembering. I said I could get you through his outer defenses, not that I knew how to kill him. A goat and some herring will get you inside, where you'll have a shot at Løcher. I can walk you through that much. Killing him is up to you, and I frankly don't know how you're going to manage. You'll probably all be dead by morning. But at least you already have the goat! All you need is a jar of pickled herring. And I know where to get one, along with a nice growler of beer and some seriously tasty toasted fairy wings. There's this dwarvelish inn just a bit out of town, and I suggest we go there to talk it over. Like, now."

"Why now in particular?"

Mathilde sighed and began walking, the wand disappearing into her pocket. "Now, because I'm hungry, and marmosets mainly eat small fruits and insects, which I'm desperately sick of and also can still taste from breakfast. And now because if you didn't notice it, my return to human form set off the itty-bittiest magical alarm."

Fia looked to Grinda, who was patting her hair and straightening her own costume.

"The thing about magical alarms," she said, "is that much like bells, they cannot be unrung. We might as well go where Mathilde suggests and do whatever it is she wants to do." When the sand witch's eyes roved to the pocket containing Mathilde's wand, Fia realized that magic wielders were all terrible people obsessed with wands and towers, and she wanted nothing more to do with any of them.

Fia shrugged. "To the dwarvelish inn, then."

"Just one more thing," Gustave said, trotting past her. He pawed at a bit of paper on the ground, finally managing to uncrumple it with his cloven hooves. There was Worstley, yet again looking all innocent and pure, his mother begging for news of the foine ladde. Gustave began nibbling the corner, and the entire flyer disappeared into his weirdly small mouth.

"Ah," he murmured happily. "It's the little victories. I never dreamed I'd get to crap on him even after he was dead. But you know what's weird? Pooboy had himself a billy goat and a jar of pickled herring at the beginning, before Fia crushed him. Quite a coincidence, don't you think? Makes you wonder if Staph the pixie wanted us to take out Løcher from the start."

"What are you on about?" Grinda said.

"Well, people always want more stuff, right? It's a bit of a pattern I've noticed. Like wizards and wands, say. Y'all are just driven to possess and consume. This Løcher guy is next to the king, has himself a nice spread, lots of power, and hot ex-marmoset ex-girlfriends, and he *still* wants more. Not surprising, then, if Staph wants to get a little bit for herself. She's got one blue sock, for crying out loud, and if I remember her breath correctly, a taste for cheap halfling spirits. Maybe that suits her fine, but I suspect she wouldn't mind an upgrade, and if Løcher's calling the shots and using her to get around others, she probably took a page from his book and decided to try the same thing on him."

Fia noticed Grinda and Mathilde exchanging a look of surprise.

"Goat's got a point," Mathilde squeaked. "But we should go."

As the smell of the dead troll wafted up the alleyway, Fia picked up Poltro's limp body, slung it over her left shoulder, and followed the witches up the street. Argabella fell in step with her to the right, and Fia smiled. The whole troll quest had gone pear-shaped, but so long as the bunny girl looked at her like that, it didn't matter. Her sword, for now, was quiet. The troll could troll no more. A light rain began to fall, and Fia welcomed it. Soon the troll's book would be nothing more than pulp and ink, his words lost forever.

"How does it feel to be a hero?" Argabella reached for Fia's open hand and squeezed.

"Well, actually, it feels pretty darn good," Fia said, squeezing back. "M'lady."

19.

Over a Board of Charcuterie Floats the Word *Murder*

Now that her honey had bravely vanquished the troll, Argabella looked forward to visiting the dwarvelish inn outside the city gates. They were usually Loudful and Cheerful places that offered a selection of extraordinarily messy foods along with magic napkins that cleaned up all your skin and/or fur afterward. They were also reputed to be places of occasionally intense violence, in which case the magic napkins were helpful in soaking up the blood, but those occasions were rare, Mathilde assured them. The inn she had suggested was called the Braided Beard, and the ex-marmoset said she knew the proprietors, who originally hailed from Håpipøle.

"Why is it so far out of the city?" Argabella asked. They'd been walking almost an hour westward out of Songlen and already were heading uphill into the great mountains there. They'd passed all the outlying homesteads and farms, and Argabella's sensitive nose could smell the swamp to the north, which meant they were also close to the Harrowing Hills at the base of the Korpås Range, and the infamous Perilous Poplars. Such places were considered Scareful, but Argabella found she wasn't as prone to anxiety when Fia was around.

Perhaps there was something Songful about the area that would in-spire her to twiddle the lute.

"This inn in particular is close to the mountains because that's where dwarves want to be," Mathilde said with a shrug. "I like it because it's a bit far from the more unsavory elements of the city, like my ex."

"And because they put uncut pixie pepper in the beer," Grinda said out the side of her mouth.

Argabella's bunny ears heard the Braided Beard before she saw it. There was some raucous merrymaking going on inside, a bawdy sing-along about the legendary Nåtålø Kaer and the Hair Down There. She'd heard that one before and hummed along with a shy grin. This would be a warm and pleasant change from scary halflings and trolls. Dwarves were generally a friendly and welcoming people. Hopefully, no one would give Fia a reason to be scary either.

The Braided Beard turned out to be a long, low-ceilinged lodge with orange light glowing from the many windows and stout silhou-ettes inside. Six chimneys—two from the kitchen, two from the common area, and two from an attached wing—testified that it would be warm.

Argabella prepared herself for the assault of smells once they opened the door and was surprised to find them pleasant. Normally, food warred with body odor in such places, but in this case the food battled for dominance against notes of cedar, lemon, and lavender.

"Whoa. Whoa. Why doesn't it stink?" she said. "What sorcery is this?"

"No sorcery," Mathilde said. "Just fanatical devotion to personal hygiene. The proprietors and their employees wash and oil their beards before every shift and won't serve guests until they bathe as well."

"You mean we have to get a room?" Grinda asked.

"No, just visit the attached bathhouse." That must account for the extra two chimneys, Argabella thought. They were heating water in there.

"What about me?" Gustave asked. "Like, what's their stance on indoor goats? Pro? Con? Are diapers involved?"

"I'm sure we can arrange it. The dwarves don't have anything against hair and fur, obviously, so long as it's clean. And it would help if you didn't poop in there."

Gustave promptly unleashed a landslide. "All cleaned out. Because I'm thoughtful."

Conversation quieted somewhat as they entered, curious eyes sizing them up—especially since Fia still had a sleeping Poltro draped over her expansive shoulder—but the chatter resumed soon enough as one of the proprietors, who introduced herself as Yåløndå Køpkümp, recognized Mathilde and ululated in joy as she embraced the witch.

"You're free of the curse! How wonderful!" she cried, her long silken blond beard braided in seven tails and festooned with decorative pansies.

Argabella thought Yåløndå was sweet but didn't pay attention to her reunion with Mathilde. She swept her eyes across the room to see if anyone was looking Hurtful. There were dwarves, of course, the beards of both the men and the women shining with health and scented oils, but there were also humans from most every earldom, halflings, gnomes, and even a pair of elves seated among the long tables and benches. All were very well scrubbed and did not look Troubleful whatsoever. A tall man with skin the same dark brown as Fia's nodded at her and raised a flagon in greeting, and Argabella turned to see if Fia responded. She merely nodded back at him, her expression neutral.

"Do you know that guy?" Argabella asked, recognizing the tiniest twinge of jealousy.

But Fia's attention was entirely focused on her. "No. But it's rare to see people from the east out here, so we always say hello to each other when we meet."

The party moved to the bathhouse after that, and Argabella had to admit that it was an outstanding idea. They all got their own rooms with scented candles and hot water and a selection of soaps and exfoliating scrubs. The solitude was relaxing and safe, and she realized that although she had always been very shy about her body, she would not have been shy about watching Fia, especially when she wasn't covered in purple sextopuses. A small alarm chimed, letting her know that bathtime was over and she was in danger of turning pruney. Rising from the bath, she wrapped herself in a plush robe and selected a spritz of rose, thinking of Fia all the while. Opening the door to the antechamber, she felt so much better, reflecting that this was the most civilized inn she'd ever visited and betting that the bathing custom here reduced the incidence of fighting considerably. Who would want to engage in bloodletting so soon after bathing, when they were still feeling soft and Cleanful? And, pursuant to that, how many deaths could be prevented in less hygienic inns by posting signs outlining the steps for a rigorous beard washing?

Someone managed to wake up Poltro in the bathhouse, and the partially ensorcelled rogue joined them at a fine square of space between the lodge's two fireplaces, far from the front door's draft. Argabella appreciated the privacy afforded by their quiet corner, which had a designated spot for "extraordinary customers" where Gustave was allowed to stand. Poltro was mostly visible now and looked triumphant and dashing and completely unaware that she'd utterly bungled the business with the troll. She also suggested that they have Gustave for dinner, which earned her an angry bleat.

"No need for that," Mathilde squeaked, looking past them all at a pair of approaching dwarves. "I ordered us the World of Cheese Board while we were in the bath, and here it comes—along with the pickled herring you need. But I beg you, don't open the jar."

The pickled herring looked pretty nasty, Argabella thought, but the cheese board was a work of art. Cheese wedges from eight different earldoms made from various milks got her whiskers twitching and her mouth watering. There were assorted crackers and breads, the toasted fairy wings Mathilde had promised, and mustards and charcuterie as well, shaved thin and ready to eat, along with a bunch of local grapes.

The dwarf server took their drink orders and promised to return speedily as everyone reached for something delicious. Argabella opted to begin with a rye cracker and a soft gnomeric sheep cheese from the western side of the Honeymelon Hills.

Poltro layered a shaved slice of dry-cured Teabring thunder yak on top of a rare Grunting beaver cheese and commented that Lord Toby would have loved such fare had he still been alive. "Kind of sad, really, that he survived Ol' Faktri and the necrobees and the hooktongues that tried to lick him to death only to die in a tragic smoothie acci-dent. I bet if he had to choose death by necrobees or death by a healer's apprentice named Bigolo, he'd pick necrobees every time. It just sounds cool. Cor, I hope I don't die a stupid death."

"Let's try to avoid that, shall we?" Mathilde said, munching on a veined log of Pyckåbøg Styffy cheese, a hard dwarvelish variety with a nutty flavor. She moaned in delight, but the high pitch of her voice made it sound more like a squeal, and several heads turned in her di-rection. "Sorry," she said. "I'll try to keep it down. Marmosets are trag-ically lactose-intolerant, and I missed the mouthfeel of a nice Styffy."

Once the strangers had looked away and Argabella had given Gustave a hunk of Drabbe ox cheese to nibble, Mathilde leaned over conspiratorially and tried to squeak quietly. "Now, look, the pickled herring is for the goatherd Løcher has watching over his goats. He can't control himself around herring, but he's allergic. Puts him right to sleep. And the billy goat there," she said, pointing at Gustave, "is for all the she-goats."

Gustave nodded and waggled his ears. "I like this plan already."

"I don't understand," Fia said. "Why do we have to worry about a bunch of goats and a goatherd?"

"Because they're not normal," Mathilde explained. "They're his early warning system."

They were interrupted by the arrival of their drinks and took a moment to slake their thirst before the witch continued.

"The she-goats are like Gustave over there. They all talk, and they can sense magic spells. If they get worried about anything, they can trigger the rest of Løcher's defenses, a dense web of traps impossible to pass through safely. He keeps the magic on standby because it's draining to maintain and has killed a couple of innocent visitors in the past. But take care of the goats and the goatherd and you can just walk in. Once you're in, you'll still have Løcher to murder, but you'll never get close to him otherwise."

"Why don't we just approach him while he's at the king's court?" Poltro asked. "Seems like that would be easier."

"We don't want the Chosen One there to get too close to the king," Grinda answered. "Or put anyone at court at risk besides Løcher. He's the problem, so we have to go after him alone."

"Ah. Got it."

"So what am I supposed to do to the lady goats to prevent them from getting nervous?" Gustave asked, panting a little.

"Charm them. Keep their attention. That shouldn't be difficult since they haven't seen a talking billy goat in years. Be friendly and keep them distracted while everyone else sneaks past."

"Oh, I'll be friendly, all right."

"As long as we don't have to watch you—"

Before Grinda could finish demanding the impossible, the door to the inn burst open abruptly and armed soldiers poured in with a familiar filthy figure hovering above them in midair.

"They've found us!" Mathilde squeaked.

"Who?" Poltro said.

"Staph the pixie! Remember that magical alarm? Løcher must've sent her here to deal with me."

As if summoned by her name, the pixie rotated toward their cozy corner and pointed a filthy finger in their direction. "There they are!" She hiccupped, then added, "Kill them all!"

The problem with such a vague command was that everyone on the crowded eastern side of the inn thought the pixie meant them. As one and in a puff of lavender, the patrons rose or staggered from their benches and drew weapons, all conviviality gone, and Argabella knew the peaceful inn was about to get Deathful. Beside her, Fia drew her Bloodful sword, and her pretty face twisted into a snarl. Songlen's soldiers rushed in, weapons swinging, and the collection of rogues and travelers gladly joined them in a good old-fashioned melee, the clash of swords and shields and armor deafening in the enclosed space.

"Meet back here later!" Grinda shouted, which indicated to Argabella that they should leave. That sounded like a fine idea to her, and several others felt the same way. Behind her, on the north wall, the tall man from the east rammed the hilt of his sword through the window and then cleared away the shards clinging to the frame with the blade until he could safely exit through it, giving his unfinished beer a brief look of longing before he went.

"I'm not prepared for a good skewering by acrobatic armored lads," Poltro said, and Argabella agreed. Lutes were famously ineffective against steel plate.

"We should exit out the window," she said, already scurrying in that direction.

"I'll be right behind you!" Gustave shouted, but he was immediately not behind them, much to Argabella's confusion.

"Be safe," Fia whispered fiercely, her sword shivering in her hand and her eyes full of apology as she cupped Argabella's cheek with one callused hand.

"You, too," Argabella whispered, then added, "Have fun murdering!" because she wanted to seem supportive.

Additional windows got broken as others thought a quick exit might work out better than facing a throng of professional killers. Argabella politely waited her turn as the pair of elves somersaulted out the window.

"Better alive and clean than pretty much anything in that room," one said snidely.

Fia and her Bloodful sword weren't thinking along those lines, Argabella noticed. Neither were Grinda or Mathilde, who had drawn their wands to engage Staph, casting visible curses at the pixie that she deflected and returned with her own. Argabella's ears and shoulders both drooped in fear. How skilled that dirty single-socked pixie was to be able to withstand attacks from two powerful witches and still launch a counterattack!

She was so skilled, in fact, that one of her curses landed on Mathilde and turned her back into a marmoset, causing Mathilde's wand to clatter onto the table, suddenly too cumbersome for her tiny monkey hands.

"Auggh! Not again!" she squeaked.

Argabella saw Poltro dive out the window and took one last look at her mighty Fia, who deflected a lunge from a soldier and now had him out of position and vulnerable to a counterstrike. The bard turned away so that she wouldn't have to see the killing blow and hoped that Fia would be all right and she'd see her again soon and enjoy her gentle smile, hopefully once all the blood had been washed off.

With a last air kiss in Fia's direction, Argabella dived out the window, landing in some soft mud, and scrambled away to avoid the hooves of Gustave, who followed after her as promised. A torch swooshed at them threateningly, and the soldier holding it said "Halt!" but no one was in the mood to do any halting. There were two of them, Argabella saw, dimly lit by the torch, and Poltro was already scampering away from the grasping hand of the smaller soldier while the bigger one came for Argabella. Gustave bleated and charged him and planted his horns beneath the man's ribs, knocking him aside and extinguishing his torch in the mud. That allowed them all to escape, though Argabella quickly lost her companions in the darkness. No one wanted to make any noise for fear of attracting soldiers, and so she let her inner bunny take over and ran away, hunched down with her lute strapped to her back, tears running down her furry cheeks as all sense of safety and comfort faded. She could only hope to see her friends again when and if she could find the inn during the light of day.

The world suddenly felt very big and Doomful, and Argabella knew no song could fix that.

20.

Inside the Perilous Poplar of Personal Problems

The patrons of the Braided Beard who chose to fight rather than run were all very accomplished in the skills of wanton slaying and disregard for personal safety. Fia was the best of them when she allowed herself to forget all about her One-Step Program. This wasn't that kind of situation anyway: it was self-defense since the armed brutes had declared their intention to kill her already. She cut down six soldiers and saw that more already lay dead. Her sword practically hummed with ecstatic pleasure as she paused to look around for the rest of her party. They were all gone except for Mathilde, who was grappling over her wand with Staph the pixie. Staph was a target for sure, and Fia took a step in their direction. But Staph landed a kick to Mathilde's face, wrenched the wand out of her grasp, and flew out the window before Fia could render any assistance. Mathilde screeched in anguish, and Fia stopped, unable to do anything for her. She could do nothing now except run for it.

More soldiers were coming, too many to handle. She could hear the rhythmic pounding crunch of armor approaching the inn. It was time for her to leave as well. Her sword had to sing out once more to clear the doorway, and then she turned west because it was the least heinous of her options. To the south was the Grange and Belladonna's hut, and she had no wish to place herself at the questionable mercy of the healer and her apprentice. To the north nothing awaited but the supposedly haunted Harrowing Hills and a fetid swamp that no doubt teemed with malevolent frogs, and she'd had more than enough of them ever since a Yilduran shockfrog had eaten her mother.

The soldiers were coming from the east. So west it was, into a stand of poplar trees that had somehow earned a bad reputation. People just said "Don't go in there" and expected you to believe there was a good reason, the way parents said "Ugh. Llamas. So much drama" without explaining how deadly llamataurs could be. Fia was sure these trees had some sordid history from which those rumors had sprung, but in the moment, they were vastly preferable to facing frogs or overwhelming numbers of soldiers.

Not that she could see any trees or much of anything once the soft glow of the Braided Beard failed against the night.

The soldiers pursuing her quickly gave up, figuring that there were targets with shorter legs and less bloody swords waiting for them back at the inn.

As silence settled about her and she could hear nothing but her own ragged breaths and clunky footsteps, Fia slowed and turned to check her trail. Dim pinpoints of light winked at her in the darkness, the windows of the Braided Beard interrupted by the silhouettes of more soldiers moving in. There was nothing else to see but the hint of lights farther back toward the city of Songlen and the stars in the sky. Towering poplars surrounded her, beckoning her deeper into the forest.

But where was the rest of her party? Had no one else run west? Never mind the rest of them: Where was her honey bunny?

Fia flicked the blood away from her thirsty sword but did not sheathe it. She was still on high alert. She took one step back and then another before turning uphill to seek some shelter in which to hide until dawn. But she never got to turn around. Something tripped her up, and she toppled backward, sword in hand. She fell farther than she thought should be possible even for a tall person with a long way to go. Much to her surprise, she wasn't just falling backward, she was falling down an incline, which meant she must have topped a hill without realizing it. She tumbled once in a backward somersault and then slammed her spine and the back of her head against something that wasn't stone but wasn't a pillow, either. Wood, maybe. A sharp intake of breath carried the tang of bark and leaf litter. One of those poplars, probably, and not perilous at all.

Fia struggled to clear her mind. Something had happened. Was happening. She blinked and couldn't tell if her eyes were working. The light from the Braided Beard was gone, but she could simply be in the dark and not actually be blind. Except that the stars were gone, too. Which way was up?

Something creaked in the darkness, and Fia tried to raise her sword. Her elbow banged painfully against something unseen, and she stifled a cry of surprise.

There was a loud snap, and something groaned and shifted over the ground. Fia brought her sword up, more carefully this time, and realized that her arm had less space to move than before. She tried to get to her feet, but her head objected; it was much too dizzy, too wobbly up in there. She had really cracked it good. She needed to stay here, where things were more certain.

Gooood, someone said in a deep, rumbly whisper.

"What? Who's there?" She couldn't see anything. She jabbed her sword forward almost by reflex, and it traveled mere inches before it thunked into something solid. Not flesh. But not anything she'd ever stabbed before, either.

Stop that and think, the voice said. *Is this not the root of all your problems? This unthinking violence? This impulsive need to strike first?*

"Right now I'm thinking you should tell me who you are."

You can call me . . . Pop. I'm here to help.

"Then help me up, Pop."

That would be unwise. You're injured, but you're safe. Let's just rest and think. Wouldn't it be nice if all the people you cared about didn't keep dying?

"What? That's not helping. Maybe you should just go away. That would be helpful."

But you came to me. How can I go anywhere?

Fia blinked to try to clear her vision and again failed. Still nothing to see. "Where am I again?"

With me. I sense some guilt in you, and we must work through that. You keep making choices, don't you? And every time you choose a direction, something terrible happens. That could make a person suffer intense self-blame.

"I disagree. I think we need to talk less about me and find out what's making that creaking and groaning noise I keep hearing. Is that you?"

Yesss.

"Well, cut it out. And stop being creepy while you're at it."

Perhaps my "being creepy" is really you experiencing shame. You would feel better if you addressed your issues. Who was it that died first? Your mother, perhaps?

"Hey, shut up now."

And after her, who was it? A mentor or another family member?

Fia's chin dipped and her shoulders slumped as she remembered what had happened in the catacombs. "Bief."

Beef? You're hungry now?

"No. I mean I killed Bief with an *i*."

You killed beef with an eye as in you just looked at a cow and it died, or you threw an actual eyeball at it and this proved fatal?

"No, I mean my friend Bief, who spelled his name with an *i*. He always introduced himself that way. 'Hello, I'm Bief with an *i*, nice to meet you.' Such a sweet kid."

I understand now. And how did you kill him?

"We were twelve years old. I was practicing my axe throwing with a hatchet, and he walked in front of my target just as I let go. Caught him right on the temple. Lodged in his skull, and he just fell over, already dead. Now I don't throw axes anymore. I use the sword only. Or pruning shears."

Violence again. And more recently? Who have you killed accidentally?

"Some farm boy named Worstley. He died twice."

You killed him twice?

"Well, no. Just the once. A llamataur ate him the second time. But we might still be able to revive him, because I don't know if the second time was really him or not, and his body—the first one—is being preserved by magic. Probably."

I'm not sure I understand how someone can suffer multiple deaths, but I hope you can see that this pattern is destructive. You should let it all go.

Fia blinked, this time in surprise. That didn't make sense. "Wait, what pattern? I didn't mean to fall down on the kid or kill Bief with an *i*. They were just in the wrong place at the wrong time. They were accidents."

You're blaming the victim. They may have been accidents, but it's your life of violence that makes such accidents possible. To bring peace to yourself and those around you, wouldn't it be best to let the violence go? You could atone.

"How?"

Renounce violence and live in peace and bring peace to others.

"I'm trying. All I want is a rose garden where people will leave me alone."

You don't need a rose garden to be at peace. True peace can be achieved anywhere. If you do not try, who else will you hurt? Someone you love? A new love, perhaps, who trusts you?

The creaking and groaning resumed, and the air changed subtly. Something wasn't right about Pop, Fia thought. But not just the noises he made or that she couldn't see him. Argabella did seem to fear her at times and Fia worried that she would scare the bard away eventually, but she would never, ever hurt her, and Argabella had told her that in spite of her moments of ferocity, she understood and trusted her. And it was her so-called life of violence that had brought them together in the first place. Perhaps she'd not always chosen the wisest path, but she'd become the product of her choices, and she really liked her current trajectory.

Which meant Pop's counseling was worth less than week-old tuna left on the docks.

Time to get away from Pop, whoever he was. He might mean well, but he really didn't know what he was talking about. Walking the world as a pacifist sounded great, honestly, but some people tended to take one look at Fia and start a fight simply because she dared to be taller. Living a peaceful life wasn't a luxury she'd ever be able to enjoy.

She thrust her sword forward again and immediately met resistance. A twist of the wrist to test the sides and the blade met something there, too. Scratchy solidity at her back as well, which she realized now must be tree bark.

"I'm boxed in?" Fia said, slowly processing what that meant. "How? I was on the hill in open air."

You were. But now you're with me and you're safe. You can relax. It's for your own good.

That didn't sound safe or relaxing to Fia at all. She struggled to get up again, fighting through the dizziness, and realized something had snaked around her right foot at the ankle, keeping her from shifting her weight properly. An actual snake? No. She brought her sword down on it and the sound and feel of it was just like the wooden thunks she'd heard before. It was a tree root. She was somehow inside a tree, and that tree was trying to get inside her head, fill it with doubt, and then kill her while she flailed in self-recrimination, all the while telling her it was here to help.

Pop was slowly killing her while urging her not to kill.

So much for preaching nonviolence.

Hey there, settle down, Pop said. *You're sabotaging yourself already.*

"I think you're the saboteur here."

She chopped down more forcefully on the root a couple of times and succeeded in freeing her ankle. Metaphorically swollen on blood, the blade kept a sharp edge. Or perhaps on some level, if it had any sentience, it realized that if Fia was trapped in here, it would be, too, and there was definitely nothing juicy to hack at inside a tree. Sensing the sword's willingness to do damage, Fia laid into the obstacle in front of her with everything she had, again and again. It was like chopping an unripe squash that wouldn't shut up.

There's no need for that. This is counterproductive, Pop said with increased urgency, but Fia ignored him and kept up the attack despite a growing sense of nausea and a pounding headache.

You can't accomplish anything like this, Pop said. *You're going to hurt yourself.*

She'd already hurt herself by waiting so long to get started. Pop had surrounded her and strengthened his defenses against the inevitable moment when she tried to escape, but he'd delayed her alarm as long as possible with his mind games. It was doubtless a strategy that worked most of the time. But Fia was beyond most humans. She didn't just have muscles. She had those supermuscles, those things, those doodads, what were they called again . . . ?

"Thews!" she cried, suddenly remembering. "I have mighty thews!"

Though she wondered if there were, in a practical sense, any other kind. People never spoke of their weak or mediocre thews, which implied that one simply did not possess thews that were anything less than mighty. The phrase itself gave her a boost, and Fia set her mighty thews to work, hacking and kicking at Pop as she ignored his pleas to calm down and discuss this like civilized beings and focus on her breathing. She worked up a sweat as she toiled, thinking that in the daylight she'd be able to admire her glistening thews as they strained, maybe see if Argabella was into thews. No point in having mighty thews if you didn't strain them and make them glisten along the way when a thew admirer was nearby.

It was impossible to see her progress in the dark, but she knew she must be making some headway because she heard splintering after a while instead of dull thuds, and a cold blast of fresh air proved she had punched through to the outside.

You're only hurting yourself, Pop shouted in her head, *by carrying on like this. It's not healthy! You'll never find love if your only answer is violence.*

"I think I know when the answer is love," Fia grunted. "And you're no honey bunny."

If you keep fighting, you'll have to be restrained, Pop said. *Stop that this instant!*

But Fia could tell that she was winning by the fact that his cloying kindness had turned to demands and threats.

Pop's powerless whining filled her with triumph, and she kept hacking away and widening the gap in front of her. Eventually Pop stopped talking altogether, and she saw the stars again. That renewed her vigor, and she was able to kick at the edges of the cleft she'd created until it was wide enough for her to squeeze through into open air.

Her eyes, hypersensitive to light now, were able to see by starlight that Pop was the first of an entire stand of noble trees that had to be the aforementioned Perilous Poplars. Their trunks and branches were perfectly normal, but their roots were swollen and twisted, stuck through with graying bones. Fia understood why no one came here now. Not only did they have some aggressive ideas about self-care, they also wrapped you up in their hollows, got into your head, and talked you into resting until your body fed their roots. Someone should come out here with a torch and set the whole lot of it on fire—before the poplars could talk them out of it.

"I'd very much like to be at peace, Pop," she said. "But until that day arrives—until I can hack my way there, I guess—violence works for me."

Turning back to face the lights at the bottom of the hill, she ran.

21.

WITHIN THE AMBULATORY DWELLING
OF A MOST FEARSOME PERSONAGE

Poltro flew through the night in much the same way that time flies: unwillingly and without really thinking about it and maybe with some future regrets. She tripped and fell on top of what felt like approximately half a dwarf, which was better than landing on most other things, especially pointy ones. As it actually was the bottom half of a dwarf, it wasn't even able to complain. She stood quickly and skulked into the bushes before whoever enjoyed cutting people in half realized she was still whole.

"What to do, what to do?" she muttered. "Cor, Lord Toby would suggest I think first, but I'm betting that's a mistake. What good did thinking do him, anyway? He was a thinking man, and now he's big frog-flavored worm food. It's obviously better not to think. I'll just follow me instincts."

Thus, when she heard the sound of yet more soldiers thumpity-thumping toward the inn, she took off to put more distance between herself and that noise. She had no idea what direction it was or what might've lain in wait for her, but she was pretty sure that as long as no one was brandishing something slicey toward her midsection, she was doing rather well, considering. Doing better than all these dwarf bits, anyway. The farther she skulked, the fewer gutted dwarves she encountered, which also seemed like a good sign for those who wanted to remain ungutted. The bushes gave way to scrawny trees, buxom copses, and the sorts of hills that would've seemed wavy and rolling and picturesque had the rogue not been running up them as quickly as her still-somewhat-asleep legs could take her in the middle of the night.

About halfway up the hill, she remembered two things: for one, that she had left all her friends behind, and for two, that without her three nonrectal potions and the guidance of Lord Toby, she was screwed. She stopped and looked down the hill, hoping for a sign of some sort. In Poltro's life, signs were usually obvious things. They ranged from Lord Toby sending her on a faraway quest right after she'd broken her brother's very favorite chamber pot to people with swords threatening violence and therefore giving her a direction in which not to go. When she looked down the hill toward the Braided Beard, she hoped for such a sign. Her friends calling for her, perhaps, or someone conveniently shouting, "Well, that nasty fight is over. Let's partake of fine cheeses!"

What she got was the flash of moonlight on armor and the twinkle of a torch as well as a man calling out, "You, there. Stop running!"

"You're not the Dark Lord, and I don't have to do what you say or pay back my student loans to you!" Poltro shouted before doubling her hustle up the hill. Judging by the grunting in her wake, the soldier wasn't going to catch up. In addition to her stealth, which she'd always considered healthfully stealthy if not exemplary, Poltro could be very quick when it came to not getting chopped in half.

The lights of the Braided Beard faded behind her, and she stopped hearing the soldier shout further requests that she stand and be slain, so she had to assume that whichever direction she'd chosen was a fine one. Licking her thumb, she held it up and slowly spun in a circle. She didn't know what said gesture did, but she'd watched Cutter perform that action multiple times, and he seemed rather adept at avoiding being chopped in half, so she figured it was worth a go.

The only real information the action brought her was that the cheese she'd eaten had been very garlicky, and that her thumb still smelled of troll even after the bath, and also that the night was a shifty and windy thing that, much like chickens, could not be trusted.

"The marmoset said she would meet us, but where?" Poltro asked the wind. "Or maybe she was talking about edible meat? So squeaky, it's hard to understand what she meant."

The wind, wisely, said nothing.

"Well, people do say onward and upward, so it sounds like those two things are related. Upward it is."

The wind yet again refrained from comment. Poltro took this as acquiescence and retuned to climbing the hill. There were rocks here and there, poking out of the scrubby grass like goose eggs on a rather large scalp. When the hill got too steep, she used the rocks and the twiggy trees growing around them to pull herself along. All this time, she didn't encounter any people or animals, which also seemed like a good omen. There were no animals to tell the people that Poltro was here, which meant she could remain unhalved by sharp blades.

"I do miss the goat, though," she told the wind. "He gives me focus. I focus on wanting to eat him, and that's invigorating. Not as invigorating as ham jam or running for your life, but it's better than hanging around someone else's tower with no goals. Or goats."

When at last she crested the hill, she tripped and unceremoniously sat down, which didn't feel like sitting down should. There were mushrooms everywhere, bright red ones with white spots. When she hopped up and felt of her fundament, she found it covered in maroon goo, probably from the mushrooms. In revenge, she ate a few of the dratted things. Which meant that Poltro had won.

Her stomach slightly more satisfied and her lips oddly numb, Poltro meandered about the hillside, wobbling around trees and patting boulders, telling them to sit and stay. The stars were more unruly than usual, swirling about and playing hide-and-seek with the moons, of which there were two. When had Pell acquired a bonus moon? Considering this to be a rather odd thing, Poltro found a well-behaved boulder and squatted on it.

"Meat here?" she asked. "Must be overcooked, if you ask me."

"Oh, Poltro," Lord Toby said, appearing in solemn, unbedazzled robes that didn't suit him at all and made him look oddly wise. His beard had grown in thickly, and he was more see-through than usual and also sort of glowy blue. "You've done it again, haven't you?"

"Done what?" she asked, pointing at her middle. "Not get cut in half? You're right, I did that again! And I think not getting cut in half is a good policy."

"No, Poltro. You've used up your potions, lost your group, and eaten something very dangerous."

"But in my defense," Poltro said, holding up an admonitory finger, "I didn't do any of that *rectally*, so I was following your orders. And I'm planning to meet the group over some meat to mete out some justice, if I can just remember where 'here' is and when 'later' is. Everything gets muddled when it's squeaky."

Lord Toby looked a bit sad, and Poltro wanted to ask if it was because he was dead, but that seemed a little rude, so she just smiled at him and said, "Had any good smoothies lately?"

At that, his brows drew down in the way they tended to do when he was out of crackers and could summon only bricks of rye crisp-bread. "Poltro, this is serious. You need help."

"Oh, you always say that."

"No, I don't mean in a therapy sort of way, although I stand behind that. You need to vomit up those mushrooms and find your friends before something truly irreversible and dire occurs. You're very far from—"

"Home?"

"I was going to say sane, but yes. Head back down the hill. Follow the bisected dwarf corpses until you're at the inn again. I do believe the fighting has died down. Use the—"

"Some sort of mystical force?"

"No, child. *Your knife.* Use your knife if anyone comes at you."

Poltro drew her dagger from its sheath at her hip. "Oh, cor. Forgot about that. Not much use against a sword, though, is it? Or squeaking?"

Lord Toby's smile somehow managed to get sadder. "Some things can't be fought."

"Like smoothies?"

"Yes. Like smoothies. And hubris and ego and wand envy. I didn't realize it until I was dead, you see, but I was nearly as daffy as you. I spent all my days in that tower, longing to be a proper Dark Lord like my father, but even he told me I was totally unsuited to the task. I craved power and magic and money and cheese and never really enjoyed what I already had. I made lovely crackers, but to me they only ever tasted of failure."

"And sometimes garlic and other flavors."

"Sometimes. But life is what happens when you're making other plans to steal someone's still-beating heart for magical reasons. And I didn't value my own heart. Remember that rose garden at the base of my tower? I think it must be the loveliest in Pell. And I never went down there and smelled the flowers. Just stood on top of my tower, felt superior, and wished for more."

"But sir, there were chickens down there, too."

"Ah, but one must be willing to encounter a few chickens if one wants to smell the roses."

Poltro burped softly and tasted her own liquefying kidneys. "I could skip both."

"You might feel differently if you still have an olfactory system tomorrow. Go down the hill, Poltro."

Poltro stood, feeling very loose in all seven limbs. Something about that wasn't quite right, but she was so glad to have Lord Toby around again to tell her what to do that she didn't stop smiling. He was a comforting sort, Lord Toby, always able to fix whatever she'd bungled. He could fix this, too.

As she began walking, she turned to speak, but Lord Toby wasn't ambling along behind her. He still stood at the top of the hill, in the shadows near the trees, looking bluish and sad and serious.

"Come along, my lord Dark Lord, sir. They'll be glad to see you, the others will. Missed your crackers, we have. Got all my words mixed around, haven't I?"

"No, Poltro. You must go on alone."

Poltro looked down the scary dark hill, knowing full well that the bottom of it was thick with dwarf corpses and slicey soldiers and squeaking. She looked up at the top of the hill, seeing only a pleasant grove of trees and a glowy sort of Dark Lord, plus some large building behind him, snuggled down in the forest. It was instantly apparent to her which was the right way.

"Got you, Dark Lord. Stay with you here." She walked back to where Toby stood, or rather floated, and tried to put a hand on his shoulder. Her fingers slipped through him in an embarrassing sort of way that recalled a certain uncomfortable moment back at the tower in which she'd gone to the kitchen for a sandwich at just the wrong time and found Lord Toby doing something she couldn't explain. Ever since the Pudding Incident, she'd refrained from eating at night and had lost her second chin.

"Sorry about that, sir. Didn't mean to . . . er . . . put a hand through your torso."

"POLTRO, I AM A GHOST. I AM A SPIRIT SENT TO GUIDE YOU. PLEASE DO STOP MUCKING UP MY GUIDANCE AND JUST DO WHAT I SAY AND GO BACK TO THE INN."

Poltro's eyes grew wide, and she backed away, wishing she hadn't dropped her dagger down the hill a few moments ago.

"A guh-guh-ghost?"

"HOW COULD YOU POSSIBLY FAIL TO NOTICE?"

Poltro relaxed and exhaled. "All good, then. You told me yourself that ghosts aren't real. So there it is."

Lord Toby gave a comforting sort of exasperated sigh and rubbed his glowy ghost eyebrows. "Poltro, I was wrong. I know, I know—I'm never wrong. I was surprised, too. But ghosts are real, I am one, and if you don't go back down that hill and find a healer—no. A wizard. I don't trust healers anymore. If you don't get help, you're going to be a ghost, too."

She cocked her head on the side, considering. "That doesn't sound so bad, m'lord. You're a ghost, and you're about the same as before, except you've got a bigger beard and nicer clothes and can just pop around as you wish without mucking about with horses. I could do okay like that."

Toby hung his ghost head and sighed sadly, another comforting sound. "I didn't want to do this, but it's for your own good."

That struck fear into Poltro's heart. This was not the first time Lord Toby had said those words, and it had never, to Poltro's recollection, been good. As she watched, fingers fumbling for her lost dagger and used-up potions, Toby knelt and then seemed to sort of . . . bubble up. His ghostly shape grew into a terrifying cloud of swirling vapor. The vapor coalesced into . . . a chicken.

"GO DOWN THE HILL OR I WILL . . . GOODNESS . . . I DON'T KNOW. CLUCK AT YOU. CLUCK CLUCK. EGGS WILL RAIN DOWN," Toby boomed.

And because Poltro was Poltro, she let rip with a fearful, high-pitched ululation, dodged around the giant ghost chicken, and tore into the woods, heading for a promising sort of shadow that spoke of people and stairs and locking doors, albeit in the opposite direction Ghost Toby had indicated.

"NO CHICKENS!" she screamed.

Branches tore at her jerkin and snagged in her hair. Her hat got knocked off, and something smacked her across the face, leaving a burning welt. She looked behind, but as she'd predicted, the giant chicken couldn't navigate the dense woods. Because chickens were stupid, of course.

Dangerous but stupid.

She slowed down, stepping more carefully. Woods like these contained other horrors—adders and harpies and face-eating spiders—

and she had to keep her wits about her to ensure that her lucky streak kept on. She could see the building's outline clearly now, and it had the look of a beloved grandmother's snug cottage, all round with tufty bits of thatching poking out. On the keen lookout for a gate or a fence or stone steps or some other way to properly approach a kindly matriarch, Poltro realized she must've been headed toward the back door like a stealthy creeping person. She circled the house but still found no clear entrance path.

"Gardener around here is a right goof," she muttered, not at all bothered by the fact that her legs had grown three feet and were bendy like rope and the trees had noses. "Might want to talk to Lord Toby's hedge man. Get you a proper bit of hedge for your snug bungalow. Bug snungle." She sniffed and waved her hand in front of her numb face, watching the blue-green vapor trails they left in the air. "Snugalow."

Garden path or not, she'd found a narrow porch and a door that looked frontish enough. She didn't see any chickens in evidence, and she didn't want to face any large and angry dogs, which meant she had to announce herself. Clearing her throat, Poltro called, "O kindly grandmother, are you at home? And will you shelter a poor starveling stranger?"

That was what she meant to say. What came out was more like "Oi, gram! You gots any biscuits? Polty's hongy!"

No warm lantern lit the window, nor did the door open to release the scent of baking cookies. But then again, no dogs began barking, either. Poltro's eyes got that crafty, stealthy look, and she grinned.

"Rogue's gotta rogue," she said, sneaking up to the front door and gently wiggling the knob. Much to her surprise, the door opened easily, creaking inward.

"Gram gram? Rover? Biscuits?" she tried again.

Nothing.

Well, something. A faint rustle of straw in the thatching. But that was normal enough. Heaven knew, oodles of animals had lived happily in the thatch of her room in the barn on Lord Toby's estate. Pigeons and mice and badgers and one very surly tortoise named Roy, as Pell in general had a problem with pestilential thatch-tortoises.

That didn't stop her. She rootled about the kitchen, finding none of the tasty evidence of grandmothers she'd hoped to see. No basket brimming with muffins or cookies, no cauldron full of stew. The cauldron, in fact, was full of something foul that smelled about how her stomach was beginning to feel, so she took that as a sign that it was a good place to yark and felt a lot better afterward. The floor was swept wood, and there were bits of herbs and sticks tied together, dangling creepily from the ceiling. Brooms leaned in every corner, suggesting an unhealthy hoarding problem. A black cat glared at her from under a chair, and a hand-painted sign suggested that WITCHES GET SHITE DONE.

Far too slowly, it dawned on the tripping rogue.

"Wait. You're not a grandma. You're another dratted witch!"

The thatch overhead rustled in a way that seemed impudent and set Poltro's guard up. She knew from her rogue training that thatches shouldn't have thoughts regarding witches, especially not in reply to her voice.

"Wait. Is the . . . witch . . . here?"

Silence. No rustling.

Poltro picked up the broom and jabbed it in the thatch, hollering, "Then don't bloody rustle at me!"

In response, the strangest thing happened. The house lurched upward unexpectedly, knocking her to the wooden floor. And then the house began to move. It was a hurried, ungainly lollop that caused Poltro to crash around, knocking into a table and the hearth and several brooms, which honestly seemed like the only things in the house that weren't nailed down.

And then the house did the most terrifying thing that a house could do.

Even more terrifying than standing up and running with her inside it.

It clucked.

"Ahhh!" Poltro shrieked, scrambled to her feet, ran for the door, and leapt out of it into the aether. Her legs danced for purchase, finding only air, and she fell ten feet and finally hit the ground, rolling in a roguish manner that didn't break anything but made her look pretty cool.

It took her a moment to find her feet, and when she did, she looked up to find . . . more feet.

Because the house had feet.

Not just any feet.

Chicken feet.

Giant, scaly, talon-tipped chicken feet topped by bony orange chicken legs.

"Buckaw?" the house asked, listing slightly to the side in an interrogative fashion.

"AAAAAAHHHHH!" she screamed.

"Poltro, no!" The ghost of Toby appeared suddenly, robes askew and still half chicken. He threw a glowing arm over his half beak. "Ignore the . . . the thing you see before you. Return to the inn. This is your last chance."

"LIKE I'M GOING TO TRUST ONE AND A HALF CHICKENS," Poltro shrieked, running in the opposite direction from the inn and Lord Toby's ghost.

As if sensing her weakness, the chicken house gave chase, clucking and stomping behind her. So Poltro did the only thing she could do. She ran for her life.

She didn't know where she was running, except that it was away; it was senseless flight, driven by fear. Every thought, every tiny bit of sense Cutter had implanted in her, fled with her. Trees, boulders, clouds—the world spun together, trails and phantom chickens everywhere. Screaming, clawing at her own face, promising to never eat eggs or mushrooms again, even in a tasty omelet, Poltro flailed through the forest and straight off a cliff.

Her last thought as she plummeted to the swamp far below was a peaceful one.

"No more chickens," she thought. "Never again."

Lord Toby's ghost watched her final moments with a grim frown. He had definitely wasted his money sending her to Cutter.

"That's a right mess," she said, appearing by his side in a glowing rogue costume with a fine hat and staring over the edge of the cliff.

"You were tripping balls," Toby noted. "It wasn't your fault." But Poltro's ghost could kind of feel that he *did* think it was her fault, because he'd always had that way of saying one thing while obviously meaning the other, more unpleasant thing.

"My house can be very territorial," a witch said, and she seemed as if she'd always been there, standing beside the two ghosts, her arms crossed in her black dress and her eyes narrowed under her peaky black hat.

Poltro looked down at her hands. They were glowing, just like Lord Toby.

"Huh," she said. "You're right. Being a ghost is pretty cool."

"I never said that," Toby muttered.

"The clothes are good. I didn't get a beard, though."

Toby rubbed his ghost beard. "No, Poltro, you did not."

"Hey, does this mean I get to haunt stuff?" Poltro asked, sounding hopeful.

"Only very particular things. It would appear that ghosts form irrational attachments to the last moments of their lives. As I can only haunt you, Poltro, you can probably only haunt this house."

The witch put her head in her hands. "Boff that. I'm putting it up for rent tomorrow." She walked away purposefully, chasing her house as it pecked among the trees.

"I don't know why you kept telling me to run the other way, Lord Toby," Poltro said. "This is great."

Toby's ghost looked at her like she was a raging idiot, which she still was.

"Great? YOU ARE DEAD. *Forever.* IT IS NOT GREAT."

Poltro's ghost smiled and cracked her knuckles. "I get to haunt that giant chicken, m'lord. And that means that in the ongoing fight between myself and chickens in general . . . I win. And I don't think that I should settle for the rules here regarding who I haunt. If there's any time to go rogue, m'lord, it's when you're a glowing blue ghost."

22.

Atop a Roof of Questionable Structural Integrity

All was chaos back in the Braided Beard. In the half second of triumph Staph experienced after turning poor Mathilde back into a marmoset, Grinda was able to get part of a curse through the blasted pixie's defenses and knock her one blue sock off, setting it aflame. That came with a certain measure of satisfaction but also inspired a rare case of Pixie Rage.

"You heinous witch!" Staph shrieked, her hair standing out like she was about to get struck by lightning. "That was a gift from my Aunt Strep! It was all I had left of her!"

In retaliation, she assaulted Grinda with a furious barrage of curses that the sand witch was hard pressed to absorb and redirect. Grinda could feel her face melting a bit to one side, the cold caress of old age seeping into her skin and bringing with it a desire to eat at a buffet before 4 p.m. The air around her glowed with eldritch fire. And without Mathilde joining in, Grinda realized that the raw power of this pixie far exceeded her own not insignificant talents. Løcher's did, too, of course. She had always beaten him by being a bit smarter rather than by burning through his defenses. She had studied magic to impose order upon unchained power; Løcher had sought power sufficient to disrupt order, and Staph's arsenal was a significant part of that.

The dying flail of a soldier slain by Fia sent Staph tumbling, causing her next blast to strike the ceiling near a supporting column. It punched right through the thatched roof and left a smoldering hole in it, an object lesson in why Grinda needed to keep her defenses up.

The pixie dipped briefly out of sight, and Grinda saw her chance to escape. Directing her wand at herself, she intoned, "Canza oposs," and then struggled to hold on to her wand with both hands as they shrank into tiny possum front feet that still had fingerlike toes and nails painted in a flamboyant pink. The rest of her shrank, too, of course, her perspective of the battle shifting significantly, her vision blurring and the sounds of combat altering into tinny echoes that reminded her of digging through a trash can. But she could smell fear and sweat now, dwarvelish beard oil, Fia's rage, and so very much coppery blood mixed with the tang of iron. She poked her tail through the loop of her crab ring, then scampered underneath the table with her wand clutched awkwardly in one tiny hand. As soon as she was out of sight and smelling all the crumbs of food people had dropped onto the floor, she transferred the wand to the grip of her handy-dandy twisty tail, over which she had full control. That had taken some practice the first time she'd shifted into this form, and even though it had been years, it was still as natural to her as ordering Milieu Goobersnootch to take care of the estate in her absence. It was much harder to return to human shape and remember that she had no such useful tail. Milieu had told her in an unguarded moment that her post-opossum recovery included embarrassingly obvious butt clenching that was visible even through the most robust pantsuits.

The nearby column leading to the ceiling was more of a post beam, she supposed, stout milled lumber supporting the roof but not slick or lacquered. Stained, perhaps, to seal it, but there was plenty of texture to allow her nails to dig in and climb. She paused and sniffed the air more carefully. Mathilde was above her on the table, swearing in her squeaky voice that she was going to turn Staph into a newt and use her eyes in a potion recipe once she was human again. The marmoset was having a bit of trouble with the human-sized wand, though, which she'd dropped onto the table in her transformation. Still in shock and trembling with rage, Mathilde found it difficult to pick it up with her tiny hands and get it pointed in the right direction. Why Mathilde didn't simply craft a marmoset-sized wand was beyond Grinda; if one was going to get oneself turned into a small monkey with such frequency, one should at least have a plan B.

Grinda smelled the lingering scents of Poltro, Argabella, and Gustave but knew they were already gone. Only she and Fia and Mathilde remained of their party.

Moving fast, wand wrapped up in her tail, Grinda scampered behind the post and began to shimmy up the side of it that would be hidden from the far side of the room.

"Where'd she go?" Staph demanded, obviously searching for her. "Oh, no you don't!"

Grinda felt a spike of fear and adrenaline course through her, certain she'd been spotted in a moment of vulnerability, but Staph had been talking to Mathilde. An outraged squeak alerted her, and she looked down, seeing the blurred shapes of the pixie and the marmoset locked in physical combat over Mathilde's wand. She took the opportunity to scrabble to the top of the pillar, circle around to the opposite side, and leap up through the hole Staph had blasted in the roof, sinking her nails into the thatch and then carefully drawing her wand and ring up through the hole after her. A furtive thatch-tortoise glared at her, unamused by her arrival and obviously blaming her for the new hole in the roof, since she had crawled through it.

Things were better, up high. The sounds of men dying under the thirsty sword of Fia and a despairing squeak from Mathilde reached her ears, from which she could infer that Staph had jerked the wand free of the marmoset's grip and flown away with it.

She waited a few moments for some of the clamor to die down

before risking a peek down into the inn. Mathilde was still there on the table, looking forlorn and heartbroken but adorable. Staph was nowhere to be seen. Grinda risked a soft call to Mathilde, though her high-pitched possum vocals garbled it somewhat. She'd have to work on that.

"Mathilde. Mathilde!" The marmoset cocked her head, trying to focus on the sound, then turned her face up to Grinda. "It's Grinda! Come up here!"

Her old friend didn't need to be told twice. She leapt directly off the table to the post beam and climbed up to the roof far faster than Grinda had. Marmosets had mad skills.

"I'm back where I started," Mathilde whimpered, her wee black eyes watery in the starlight. "She brought all those soldiers with her, and a bunch of people died just to get my wand. I really hate that pixie."

"Why did she want it so badly?"

"To keep me stuck like this. It's what Løcher wants. It's that sadism I was talking about. That pig isn't happy unless I'm playing second fiddle in the magic department."

"Then we'll get her, my pretty," Grinda said. "And that fiddle hog, too."

Mathilde glanced down through the hole in the roof. The Braided Beard was mostly cleared out now. All that remained were the dwarvelish proprietors, a few of the staff who hadn't run off screaming, and the bodies of the slain. But more soldiers were coming in and even more were surrounding the building.

"Why are they staying?" Grinda asked. "They got what they wanted, didn't they?"

"Cleanup, to begin with," Mathilde explained, "but they're going to occupy the space for a while just to deny it to us. It's the only safe place around here. And once the bodies are out and the floors mopped, those soldiers are going to want a drink. Way they figure, they've earned it."

"Are they the City Watch?"

"No, this is Løcher's private force. Did you see the blue circles on their shoulders?"

"I didn't, but I'm sure you're right. He keeps his own private army these days?"

"Yes. It's not huge, but it's muscle at his command separate from the king."

"That's new. The king is okay with it?"

"Not really. They're not allowed in the palace for any reason."

Grinda snorted. "At least Benedick has that much caution. Good."

Mathilde shook her head. "Less and less these days, though."

"What do you mean?"

"He's drinking even more than he used to."

Grinda tooted a note of marsupial dismay. "He already drank spirits like water when I left."

"He's almost constantly pickled now. He's developed a taste for red wines. From Corraden, of course, but more and more from Kolon."

"Oh, no!" Grinda winced and put a paw up to her eye, peeking at Mathilde through her possum pinkies. "Don't tell me he's turned into one of those guys who says he needs a Kolonic every day."

"He has. He loves his Kolonics."

"And still no heir, I presume?"

"The lack of one may have driven him to drink more. Which of course reduces the chances of there ever being an heir to almost nil."

A silence fell about them, cold and damp like a used bath towel, bereft of joy or fluffiness or contentment or anything good. It was the grim silence of the self-aware adult, contemplating mortality and the mathematical certainty that things would get worse before they would get better, if at all, and even if they *did* get better in the short term, there was still the dismal prospect of arthritis and incontinence ahead. Few people can bear such silences for long, but Grinda and Mathilde had iron constitutions, and they bore it until the dead had been cleared away and the soldiers occupied the tables below, talking of past battles and current scars and trading their mothers' recipes for the best yak casserole they'd ever had, as men were wont to do.

The paid fighters eventually began to compare what they were currently drinking with almost anything else they weren't drinking.

"This ale is pretty good," Grinda heard one soldier announce, "but it's no halfling peach elixir."

"It's no Kolonic, either," a companion agreed. "Speaking of which, I hear our illustrious leader has acquired a full cask of the good stuff, the latest vintage of the master, Amon Tiyado."

Cries of disbelief greeted this news.

"No way!" the first man said. "A cask of Amon Tiyado? Why'd he go to the trouble?"

"He wants to have the king over, so, you know, only the best for Benedick."

As conversation swirled in the wake of this revelation, Mathilde's high-pitched whisper broke their silence.

"That's probably your best way in, Grinda," Mathilde said.

"Eh? What's that?"

"Once you're past Løcher's outer defenses, tunnel underneath his estate with that earth magic of yours and come up in his wine cellar. You'll avoid all the guards that way. Easier to fight your way out than in."

"You know where it is?"

"Sure. The wine cellar is beneath the kitchen, which is on the west side. You'll see the chimneys of the cooking fires. They have three of them—very fancy."

"That's good to know. Thank you."

"You're welcome. I hope you get him. And Staph, too, somehow. I'm going to go back to Songlen, try to figure out where she's hiding my wand this time."

"Would you like me to try to change you back?"

The marmoset sighed squeakily. "No, it won't work. I've had others try, and the transformation rebounds coming from any other wand but mine."

"Rebounds how?"

"The casters all turned into what I look like as a human, but with a marmoset's face."

"Oh."

"Yeah." Mathilde huffed and rubbed at her eyes. "Well. Good luck, Grinda. And thanks to everyone for giving me at least a little while to be human again."

"You'll have a long while soon! We'll get them, Mathilde. Now be safe, dear."

Mathilde hugged Grinda awkwardly—there was no graceful way for a marmoset to hug a possum—but Grinda cherished it nonetheless. Sand witches had few real friends, after all, and who knew if her traveling party would ever reconnect, considering that everyone had scattered to the winds.

Mathilde bounded away and disappeared in an acrobatic dive off the roof, and Grinda felt countably sad, as opposed to unaccountably. She wished for a world in which she and Mathilde could be girlfriends as they used to be. The impossibility of that tender simplicity was one of the great sorrows of her life, a life of many such great sorrows for all that she pretended now that she had none. And she knew that if she truly wanted such a world to happen, she'd have to work for it. Mathilde was doing her part for it by finding her wand and restoring her old self. And Grinda would have to work for it by defeating Staph and Løcher. She'd been fighting them—or the ideals they represented—all her life.

Growing up poor in Cape Gannet, the southernmost city of Burdell, she'd learned that the earls and the king not only didn't care about her family's personal struggles, but they were not even aware of what struggle really meant. The higher classes were completely unaware of the peasants' daily bewilderment at how to afford sharply increasing rent or where to find the next meal. Sharks did not concern themselves with the worries of chum. And Grinda saw, when her father died on the spear of a city guard bent on quashing a protest of the earl's policies, that those with power never gave it up willingly. According to those in power, there was no acceptable way to resist their rules. Peacefully, violently, with words or actions—the peasantry were supposed to know their place. The ruling classes expected everyone to play by their rules, which were designed to keep them in power and benefit no one else except by accident—and those who tried to break those rules ended up run through with a pike. That was what propelled a younger Grinda into libraries and then into the Seven Toes in search of ways around the system. That was what made her seek a power outside the control of the government. She apprenticed to a sand witch and eventually built a shipping company and rose to the level of an adviser in the capital . . . at least until tensions with Løcher forced her out.

With a thought, she brought her diamond crab ring up to her face, balanced on the tip of her possum tail. It was time to remember why she'd fought and scrabbled to get where she was. It was time once again to be uncomfortable, to be challenged. Because although she'd improved things for many people while she'd had influence at the court and was almost solely responsible for the recent prosperity of Malefic Beach, Løcher was doing all he could to erase whatever progress she'd made. She couldn't let him win.

Those crabs on her beach—people thought she simply used them for protection, a warning and a threat. That was fine. But it was not that simple. That was not why she wore a ring of remembrance in their image. Those crabs lived an extraordinarily difficult life and had to fight for their very existence in a world that didn't care whether they lived or died, unless they died and were served en croquette with tartar sauce. Yet they were all beautiful individuals. Like her family. And yes, that included her sister and her nephew. That also included these ludicrous people traveling in company with the Chosen One.

Perhaps, Grinda mused, she had spent a bit too long enjoying the luxuries she'd earned, basking in the comforts of wealth, and shrugging off the sting of exile from the capital. She'd played the chessmaster for a while, but now it was time to get back on the board herself. The goat's arrival was a clear sign that it was time to work again on behalf of everyone who was playing a game rigged against them. Grinda backed away from the hole and climbed to the very top along the beam, stretching herself out but making sure her wand and ring were tightly curled against her and safe. She glared at the thatch tortoises in warning: she was not to be disturbed. Might as well catch some sleep and recover what strength she could. The soldiers were probably going to stay until dawn at least, so there was little chance the others would return until then.

If they returned at all.

With some surprise, Grinda realized that ... she hoped they would.

23.

ATHWART A CORPSE AND QUAKING WITH UNACCOUNTABLE MIRTH

Being part rabbit was terribly useful when one had to leap through a window and run away in a zigzaggy fashion. Argabella's brain went from normal anxious human thoughts to a sort of hyperactive whirl of instincts driving her to safety while also reminding her that she should eat more carrots. The end result was that instead of being cut in half like a grapefruit, her bits all pink and juicy and leaking out, she went right into rabbit mode and returned to conscious thought sometime later, her instincts having delivered her alive and well to a boggy sort of place quickly turning into a Stenchful swamp.

At least she hadn't gone full Gustave and dropped a load of pellets as she bolted. Or had that been Gustave that rammed into a soldier outside the inn and gave her room enough to zoom past? She couldn't rightly remember.

"Well, where are we now?" she muttered, hands on her hips as she looked around.

Behind her, in the direction of the Braided Beard, she could still hear the thunk of metal and the slick swish of swords meeting flesh. Quite Bloodful back there. But before her it was super Bogful. Mud and algae and potential bacterial infections all vied for her attention. A little stream wobbled out into the darkness, moonlight gleaming wanly on its surface. On the left side, boulders rolled up comfortably against a rock wall that was unclimbable for anyone of rabbitesque physique.

"Too cold for alligators and crocodiles," she murmured to herself. "Never too cold for snapping turtles. Rather a lot of frogs, but as Fia's not around, that shouldn't be an issue."

At the thought of Fia, Argabella spun suddenly to look back at the melee she'd left behind. Fia had sent her on, certain that they would be reunited. Grinda had promised they would meet again later, and later probably meant when soldiers stopped killing people willy-nilly. Later was certainly not now. Even if Argabella had wanted to return to the Braided Beard, her nervous system wouldn't allow it. Because wow, was her system ever nervous just now. Her ears twitched back and forth, searching for noises that might indicate friend or foe, but mostly she just heard the soft swirl of water nearby and the pleasant plop as slimy things flopped around in said water. Every now and then, the scrape and clank of metal suggested that the soldiers might be fanning out in her direction, hunting for yet more potential victims.

"Better forward than backward, I suppose."

As she stepped gingerly into the quaggy mud, Argabella decided to keep close to the boulders on the left. That way, should something Toothful decide it could use a little appetizer of bunny hocks, she could attempt to scramble upward and perhaps pelt it with rocks from above. The swamp felt a bit too endless and flat in the other direction, and she was certain she'd soon be lost. Rabbits were not swamp things. Rocks firmly on the left, she spread the cattails with her hands and bravely squelched forward.

Since becoming a rabbit, Argabella had given some thought to the new instincts and thoughts that overlay her old consciousness like a soft blanket. She still liked most of the same things, except meat and cats, but she was also more easily frightened. And yet Fia didn't frighten her at all—not in the fear way. More in the *if you don't look at me, I'll die* way. Fia, who could cleave a halfling in half like cutting butter. Fia, who sent Argabella out the window and remained inside to fight without a second thought. Fia of the too-small bikini and mighty thews and soft lips and . . .

Well, it was time for Argabella to acknowledge that perhaps she now shared some of that famed lapine passion.

She had to get back, which meant she had to stay safe. But she didn't actually have to keep going, did she? It wasn't as if her only choices were plow through swamp or sit down and wait for death. She could just clamber up behind some of these boulders and hide for a while. The soldiers most likely wouldn't wade into the water and poke about. Of course, she didn't need to gambol dangerously around the rocks the way Gustave the goat would, either.

"Silly rabbit. Such acrobatic tricks are for kids," she thought, finding a foothold among the rocks, scrambling up, and carefully hefting herself over a large boulder.

Argabella expected her foot to land on rock on the other side, possibly of the wet and slimy sort. She'd given some thought to the fact that she might encounter dirt, mud, water, or a rogue axolotl. But what she did not expect to feel under her furry toes was something soft and clammy and firm.

A person.

She immediately backed off, perching on the boulder in case this person, too, possessed a sword.

"Oh, gosh. Sorry!"

The person—for surely it was a person, she knew that much—did not respond.

"Hello?"

Still nothing.

Her nose wiggled, but she could only smell swamp. Her ears twitched, but there was no sound other than the wind rushing through cattails. Definitely no sounds of a person shouting at her or threatening her. Although, far off, she detected the splash of a boot landing in mud. Still, that wasn't nearly as important as the person in front of her, who'd found the hiding place first and was definitely winning in the realm of silence and stillness. They had to be a champion at hide-and-go-seek.

"Didn't mean to intrude," she said, but she was now becoming aware that bodies generally objected to being trod upon by rabbit people. They most certainly didn't just lie there, stiller than still, being strangely clammy, even when playing hide-and-go-seek.

"Um. I don't mean to be rude, but you're dead, aren't you?"

The body neither confirmed nor denied this question. It merely lay there, as bodies tended to do when no longer animated. In the low light, Argabella couldn't tell much about it other than that it seemed quite fresh and not cut in half or riddled with necrobees. It was head down, and she'd trod upon its back in a shadow behind a black rock. Its hair and cloak were also black, which didn't help.

"I'm going to turn you over now, so please don't be a zombie," she said.

Clutching its black-clad shoulder with her hands, she gently pried the body up and discovered the last possible thing she'd expected, which was Poltro, the rogue.

Poltro, for all her faults, had never been dead before, and Argabella had never seen Poltro be dead before, either, so it was very awkward for both of them. The only thing that seemed right was for Argabella to scream, so she did that.

In her befuddled state, she was almost sure she imagined Lord Toby's voice muttering, "Honestly, it was bound to happen sooner or later, so shut up."

Argabella ignored her imagination and focused on the present. This was her friend Poltro, and Poltro was Deadful. And if Argabella hadn't run exactly this way and chosen exactly this boulder to hide behind, she never would've known what had happened to Poltro.

But still, dead bodies tended to make one Screamful, and that was exactly how Argabella felt for a long horrifying while. Then her scream fell off to sobs. Her sobs turned into coughs. Her coughs turned into very choppy giggles. And then she was quaking with mirth, one hand over her mouth, trying not to burst out laughing.

"Madam, are you in travails?" a deep, manly voice asked.

Argabella looked up, cheeks puffed out with unspent laughter, to find the dark brown–skinned man from the inn staring at her. Even in the low light, his soulful eyes gleamed with kindness and under-standing, and he had his hands out as if to calm her rather than reaching for his sword. He was almost like a masculine version of Fia, possessing the same fine cheekbones and lush lips, the same volume of muscles, and the same lack of proper costuming. He wore only a metal loincloth and a scrap of leather tied around his head. Almost Nudeful. Argabella's eyes shot back up, and she swallowed down her laughter and cleared her throat.

"Well, it's just that I've stumbled across a corpse," she said. The giggle that followed her words might've been a hiccup.

The man's eyes looked soulful and sad, like a particularly emotive pit bull. "Aye, 'tis a grave day at the Braided Beard. Løcher's men are as unkind and vicious as their master, and many lives were lost this eventide. I followed your scream, assuming one of yon varlets had cornered a lady." His eyes softened and shone, his mouth curling into a smile as he held out a hand as if to help her down. "Let me take you from here, rescue you from the dark deeds spreading in this land. I'm a prince in the east, searching for adventure and a wife. They call me Konnan. What's your name?"

Argabella's whiskers twitched. She didn't take his hand.

"My name is Argabella, and I'm taken."

"As am I. With your beauty and sangfroid in facing so horrid a scene. But why did you laugh?"

Argabella stood her ground and shrugged. "She was my friend. The corpse, I mean. I don't know how she got here, although evi-dence suggests she fell off the cliff. But that's the thing." Another hiccupy giggle found liberation. "My friend was a rogue, and this is literally the first time she ever successfully snuck up on anyone. Ever. The irony is . . . oh, Pell!" Doubling over, she cackled, her mad guffaws echoing over the swamp.

Konnan reached for her, his eyes nearly incandescent with concern. "My lady Argabella, are you well? Methinks you're in shock."

Argabella stopped laughing, cleared her throat, crossed her arms, and looked down, stepping out of Konnan's reach.

"I'm not in shock. This is just my life now. And if you'd like to be useful, you can escort me back to the Braided Beard, so long as you think the fighting is over."

"If it is not, I will fight for you. I'd die for you."

"Whoa, slow down your speedy horse there. You just met me."

"True. But some moments arrive with such clarity that their significance is plain."

"All right, I'm happy for your clarity. But I'm not seeing things that clearly, so give me some time and space, all right?"

"Of course," Konnan replied, smooth as polished marble.

Argabella wasn't sure what to do about Poltro, though. She was fairly certain some etiquette book somewhere had something to say about leaving dead friends behind to rot in swamps, and that something was probably "Don't." But she couldn't ask this stranger to carry a corpse for her, could she?

She looked down at Poltro and let her gaze follow the rock wall up to the cliff where her friend must've suffered a nasty fall. Probably while being chased by a chicken or something that vaguely resembled one. It was a very Poltro-ish way to die. Something at the top of the cliff seemed to glow ever so gently.

Two words floated along in her imagination, sounding very much like Lord Toby: "Don't bother."

But she had to bother. If Fia thought Worstley could be revived, then surely the same spell could help Poltro.

"How strong are you?" she asked Konnan.

He grinned. "I can carry a boulder."

"What about . . . stuff behind boulders?"

Soon she was following Konnan's exposed buttocks out of the swamp, through the forest, and back toward the warm lights of the Braided Beard. Poltro flopped over his shoulder very much like a corpse, because she was one, but he didn't seem to mind. He told Argabella that in his lands, it was no big deal to carry a corpse around, and Argabella realized she had a lot of questions for Fia about where she'd come from.

The route seemed longer than it had been under the influence of bunny brain, when she had been sprinting to safety, and Argabella spent her time playing around with various healing songs that might work for Poltro. Unfortunately, she couldn't think of any useful words that rhymed with *corpse, carcass,* or *cadaver.* She did manage to work *hen* and *fen* into a chorus that also rhymed "You won't get any older" with "Because you hit the boulder." None of her tunes did Poltro any good, though. As they'd learned with Lord Toby and as she wished she could help Fia understand, magic was magic but dead was dead. Unless maybe a necromancer got involved, and from what Argabella understood, nobody wanted that. Especially not if it was Steve.

Still, she held on to hope. There was always hope.

It was dawn when they finally saw the Braided Beard. Although all the soldiers seemed to be gone from the area of the inn, aside from the dead ones being looted by enterprising rogues with better skills than Poltro, Argabella could tell that the fight was over. Living dwarves were everywhere, showing their usual enterprise by tidying things and removing the separate halves of their friends. They all seemed a little forlorn, whether because they were grieving or because everything was filthy now and nothing smelled like lavender, Argabella couldn't guess. The two elves she'd noticed earlier sauntered back in through the front door, their clothes miraculously bloodless and their hair suspiciously spotless, muttering about cold soup and whether one was expected to tip when one's meal had been interrupted by a bunch of state-sanctioned axe murders.

Konnan went inside first, but then again, in this short time, she'd learned that Konnan went everywhere first just to make sure it was safe. Argabella wanted to argue that if the whiny elves were going in, it had to be safe, but she just let him do his thing, his eyes darting to every corner as if looking for hidden assassins. Argabella didn't care about assassins. She just wanted to find Fia. And the rest of her party, too, especially the witches and their magic wands. Unfortunately, it appeared that she was the first one back.

Konnan looked like he was going to start being annoyingly chivalrous, so Argabella chose a table that had already been wiped off and sprayed with bleach. She could barely see the bloodstains, and the hatchet marks only served to give everything a rustic feel. She sat down, and Konnan carefully placed Poltro on a bench, crossing her arms over her chest—or trying to. Just like when she'd been alive, Poltro's arms flopped everywhere.

"Shall I dig a grave?" Konnan asked, his tone . . . grave.

Argabella was trying to flag down a waitress and didn't look to see if his eyes were wobbling with unshed tears. "Not yet. There's this witch. Maybe she can do something."

Konnan tried to look sympathetic, but it was clear he thought nothing further could be done for Poltro. When the waitress appeared, Argabella requested two cups of tea, and Konnan put in his order for half a suckling pig and a tankard of mead.

"Carrying corpses makes a man hungry," he said, rubbing his nine-pack to demonstrate.

"Uh huh," Argabella said, eyes pinned to the door.

"In my land, there is no aphrodisiac like a hirsute woman," he said, casually eyeing the soft fur of her arm.

"Great."

"My friend Steve said—"

But Argabella only squealed in excitement.

Someone had just walked through the door.

24.

Uncomfortably Smooshed in a Throng of Normal Goats, Forced into Bleatful Complaint

If there's one thing goats are good at, it's evading capture while loosing droves of slippery pellets and screaming their fool heads off. In this way, Gustave was indeed an exemplary goat. As soon as the fighting broke out in the Braided Beard, he nimbly leapt onto a bench, catapulted himself off a dwarf's beer belly, ricocheted off a bulbous nose, and sprang out the window with a bleat of victory behind the rabbit woman. He did ram into a soldier and knock him over, but that helped Gustave as much as it helped Argabella, because he had some room to run around in circles and bleat some more.

But his thinking brain thought that maybe he shouldn't make any more noise that might draw attention, and he noticed the herd of tightly packed goats milling around in their pen—regular, nonspeaking, nonquesting goats—and he scrambled through the fence and head butted his way into the throng. The ground was knobby-knee-deep in emergency pellets. Gustave began to understand why others might not value his own contributions.

"Bleat," he said. "I mean, for real, BLEAT."

The other goats looked at him in confusion, tongues hanging out and mad eyes jangling every which way.

"Oh, yeah. I can't bleat when I'm thinking in words. Um. BAAAA."

"BAAAA?" another goat asked.

"Yes, I clearly said BAAAA. Don't patronize me, Deirdre."

But he had the good sense to say it quite softly just in case any of the soldiers could hear a whispering goat among the other fifty screaming goats and the thirty people loudly dying on the ground around the inn.

"So this isn't fun," he said to another goat, a rather attractive white nanny.

"BAAA."

"I know, right? You try to have a nice meal, and there are suddenly soldiers everywhere. Like we live in a police state. And they didn't politely ask us to disperse or read us our rights or anything. They just waded in with swords and started stabbing people. And don't think I didn't notice that they went for my friend Fia first. They obviously have something against vegetarians who protect goats like us. This happen a lot around here?"

"BAAA."

"That's fascinating, Cynthia. What a unique perspective." He wiggled around a bit until he was facing a different goat, this one a lovely tawny brown that reminded him of a delicious belt he'd once eaten. "How about you? Any thoughts on the rise of fascism?"

"BAAA."

Gustave nodded thoughtfully. "Excellent point, Meredith. It's all about the shadowy plots of halflings who have infiltrated the postal system to cause chaos in the kingdom. If you want to destabilize a country, everyone knows all you have to do is mess with their water supply or their mail."

Heaving a deep sigh, he squeezed through the crowd, hunting for some sign of intelligence in the fellows of his species. He found none. He tried to remember what it was like just being a goat, but everything in his memory went sort of muddy, like looking into a fast-flowing stream. He'd always enjoyed leather and pooping, but honestly, who didn't? It was a lifestyle unto itself. Yet when he tried to think back to the first spark of genius, his first intelligent thought, all that came to mind was staring at Worstley's sodden boots and thinking, "Man, I want to eat that and excrete that, the ol' one-two, the number two following some hours later."

On the upside, no one had threatened to kill him in at least twenty minutes, and outside the fence no such deal had been struck. But staying inside the fence, as he'd done most of his life, meant he'd just be killed at a later date for a hearty supper served with soda bread and a refreshing tankard of ale. Self-awareness had its downside, for he had lost the bliss of ignorance.

Butting his way around the throng, he muttered, "Excuse me. Pardon me. Hey, pretty mama, how you doin'? Your friend seems like she's into me. Oh, that's not an udder."

The billy goat in question nudged the nannies apart to step closer to Gustave. The herd had been tightly packed, but now it spread a little, the nanny goats softly bleating to one another as if whispering, "Fight! Fight! Fight!"

As for the billy, he was a beastly specimen, probably one of those more expensive goats that looked very fine up until the day they went in the stew pot and their horns appeared on some feisty warrior's helmet. He was filthy white, his eyes a lurid gold, but all goats had lurid gold eyes as far as Gustave knew. Worst of all, the billy looked furious.

"BAAAAA," he growled, and Gustave noted the extra *A* for emphasis.

"Who, me?" he said, stepping backward and finding his path blocked by yet more goats. "Look, I was just passing through and making conversation. Have you met Deirdre and Cynthia and Meredith? I have so much respect for . . ."

The billy lowered his not inconsiderable horns.

"Ooookay, now. Let's be reasonable. You're maybe three times my size, and your horns have got to be hormonally enhanced. Nobody gets muscles like that from standing around in a pen. Let's talk this out, bro. I'm not threatening your herd or leadership abilities—which, by the way, great job at spending your entire life inside this tiny fence without going insane. I'm just looking for an exit here. There's no need to . . ."

The billy reared back a little, and Gustave's goat brain took over. Screaming a bleat of his own, he lowered his head and ran for the billy. But instead of crashing his skull against the other goat's skull, he veered around him, picked up speed, and bounded into the air. Hopping off a stump, he sprang right over the fence and into another pen, landing in thick, cold mud.

The mud sucked at his hooves as he struggled toward firmer ground. Enraged bleating from the other pen suggested that the billy was still looking for a fight when no one was interested, a condition he'd noticed many dudes often suffered. The wooden boards creaked dangerously as the goat rammed his substantial horns against the fence.

"Like that's going to work," Gustave muttered, heroically clambering out of the muck. "Just like a goat, bashing your head against whatever gets in your way. Hey, billy! You don't have to be what they tell you to be!"

Gustave immediately realized his error as a soldier outside called, "Oi, Petyr. Did you hear somethin' from the goat pen?"

"Baaa," Gustave muttered out the side of his mouth. "Dicks."

As the soldiers approached the fence, the billy was kind enough to transfer his rage to them, ramming the post nearest the new interlopers with his horns.

"Barmy little nutter," one soldier said.

"Right?" Gustave muttered.

"Did you say something?" the other soldier said.

Gustave finally hit higher ground and swore he would be better about pretending to fit in around the farmyard, at least so long as there were stupid people standing about with swords. Navigating a huge pile of moldy hay, he ran afoul of a bloated pig splayed out pornographically in the mud.

"Oh, gross," he muttered.

"What, and you're a prince?"

Gustave had to do a double take. The sow's eyes were closed, her belly and bits exposed to the moonlight.

"Did you just talk?" he whispered.

"An idiot says what?" she whispered back.

"What?"

"That's what I thought."

Carefully traversing the mud that he now recognized as being at least half pig excrement, he maneuvered his way around to behold the sow's enormous jowly face. Her eyes blinked open, looking annoyed and yet also like tiny raisins in a very large pudding.

"It's rude to stare," she said.

"Yeah, well, you take up most of my vision field, so it's kind of hard not to."

"You smell like goat."

"There's a really good reason for that."

"Why are you in my pen?"

"Why are you talking?"

The sow grunted and wiggled, rolling this way and that until she was able to gain her feet. She had to weigh as much as fifty Gustaves and had a solid if pungent sort of power about her.

"I'm Gustave."

"I'm a pig."

"Okay, but what's your name?"

The sow shrugged and waddled to a vat of slop. She daintily nibbled at an apple core before addressing him. "Look, son. Pigs don't have names. They call me things like Piggy and Bacon and Porker and Sooey, but that's more like calling you Curry or Glue."

"Who enchanted you?"

The sow huffed a laugh. "Nobody. All pigs can talk. We're one of the five most intelligent animal species in the world. And that means we're smart enough not to let the humans know our little secret. Unlike you, who almost blew it out there."

As she snorted around in her trough, Gustave struggled with this concept. "So let me get this straight. You're smart. You can talk. Your entire species can. But you're all content to sit in this pen or that, wallowing in your own filth, and wait for the day they come for you with an axe?"

The sow swallowed something and turned to face him. He was startled by the intelligence in her eyes—and the anger.

"What are we going to do, then? Take over the world? Do I look like I can heft a sword or load a boulder into a catapult? This way, they do all the work and we live lives of leisure. I like to think of them as a team of really incompetent butlers."

"But you get that they're going to kill you and eat you one day, right?"

The sow shrugged massive shoulders that would one day be slow roasted and pulled apart into delicious sandwiches, served with a side of slaw. "Us and the cows and the sheep and the goats. The ducks and the geese and the chickens, too. That's what usually happens."

"And you're not even going to run away or fight back?"

She loomed over him now, the bristles standing out around her head. "Oh, sure, I'm quite handy in a sprint. I run marathons in my spare time. Didn't you see the '26.2' tattooed on my arse? Don't be foolish. Things are what they are. They have thumbs and weapons, and we don't. Every pig knows from suckling that one day we'll be nothing more than an invigorated ham jam on some pompous lordling's artisanal crackers."

Gustave stammered for a moment before blurting, "But that's insane."

The sow laboriously turned her back on him and flopped back into the mud.

"That's life in the pigpen, kid. Hedonism and mud packs and birdsong in the mornings until they knock you out and you go to hog heaven."

Gustave looked at her broad back, then at the pen of goats, then back to the sow. It was one thing to accept a fence when you had no proper sense of what it meant, but the sow's suicidal worldview was incomprehensible.

"What if you just ate a little less, got some exercise, built up your muscles, and masterminded your own escape?"

"Too much work."

At that moment, Gustave realized that intelligence was only one part of the equation and the rest was predicated on rebellion, hard work, and tenacity. He also realized that no matter how intelligent the pig claimed to be, she was an utter moron.

"What's on the other side of your pen?" he asked.

"Chickens. Then a milch cow. Then a magical boot. Then sheep."

"Wait. A magical boot?"

"Did I stutter?"

"What's it do?"

The sow leaned her head back to look at him, her ears flopping over. "How should I know? I can't get over there."

"Then how do you know it's magical?"

"Well, it's got a golden, sparkly sort of aura around it."

"Would you mind if I wandered over there to check it out?"

The sow flopped back down on her side and closed her eyes.

"I rather hope you will. Get lost and take your judgment with you."

Gustave was more than glad to squeeze into the next pen. He did not say goodbye. He had decided that he did not like pigs. This realization was cemented when he heard her muttering, "I thought regular goats were bad, but jeez. What a jerk."

None of the chickens sought conversation, and neither did the milch cow. Only when he was two fences over did he turn around and shout, "You're a prisoner of your own choices!" at the pig.

"And for all your self-righteous blather, your gamy flesh will still be slurped up in a broth of carrots and potatoes someday!"

"Moo," the cow lowed.

"Right?" Gustave said. "She was about as pleasant as a peck of hot chili peppers setting my arse on fire on the way out. I don't recommend hot chili peppers, by the way. Just a friendly grazing tip." The cow appeared more interested in chewing her cud than in anything he had to say, however, so he turned his attention to the next pen.

The sow had not lied to him about this, at least. There sat a perfectly normal stump, and on that stump sat a perfectly abnormal boot. It was as if a sunbeam had pierced the night to shine like a spotlight, and little glints of gold gently floated through the glow as if they'd just escaped the Morningwood and left a magical stain behind. The boot itself was a cobbler's masterpiece to a goat's eyes: old seasoned leather, cracked and greasy with age, the tongue poking out like a welcome mat and the laces delectably slurpable.

"What's the magic boot do?" he yelled into the night.

"If it makes you shut up, that's magic enough for me!"

He was really coming to hate that pig.

Gingerly, he nudged the boot with his nose, and nothing happened.

More aggressively, he butted the boot with his horns, and it toppled off the stump, taking the beam of golden light with it. Even lying on its side, a ragged sock half slithering out, it looked like Gustave's fondest daydream. With a frisson of joy, he gave it a lick, and his eyes rolled back in his head.

"This is it," he whispered to the night. "The Boot, capital *B*. The paragon of boots, peerless in Pell. Everything I ever wanted in a piece of footwear. Aged to perfection, slick with wear, redolent of foot sweat." He nibbled a lace, bit off the tip, and swallowed it, moaning with pleasure.

"Do you need some privacy?" the pig called.

"Don't listen to her," he murmured to the boot. "She doesn't understand what we have. It's just you and me, baby."

Bit by delicious bit, he ate the boot. The tongue was a revelation, the laces were dreamy, and the actual leather was so good that he had to force himself to slow down and taste each bite. Time seemed to stop as Gustave consumed the boot of his dreams. As he chewed the last chunk of sole, the sunbeam gently faded away, and then he was just another goat in the darkness. The night seemed still all of a sudden, the fighting over and the soldiers gone, or at least drinking more quietly in the inn. The normal goats bleated, the pig muttered about predestination, the cow mooed, and Gustave hovered for once on the edge of fullness. For at least a solid minute, he didn't think about eating anything. And that was a sort of magic in itself.

As he swallowed the very last bite, he thought, "I wish I was anything but a goat. Except a pig. Neither of those things, please."

Gulp.

The boot was gone. The stump was just a stump. The magic had disappeared.

But something rumbled in his tummy, and he looked down to find a faint golden glow suffusing his midsection.

"What's this all aboot?" he asked, giggling a little.

And then the magic glow winked out, and he was still a goat.

But at least he wasn't a pig.

"I am so done with animals," he said. Which, he realized, meant he was going to be pretty lonely from now on.

When Staph had been talking to Worstley, she'd said something about him being cursed as much as blessed by this aura of the Chosen One. Probably because of the "one" part. There was no one else who could understand how isolated he felt, for he was not truly part of the herd anymore, nor was he accepted as an equal among the bipeds.

Squeezing through the next fence, Gustave emerged in a clearing beyond the inn. He'd managed to clamber over or through all the animal pens, and dawn was just beginning to break. It had been a long night, and he was feeling the effects of flight, fight, intellectual debate, painful epiphany, and unrepentant gluttony. He realized that in all his years on Worstley's farm, he'd never noticed a sunrise, never paid attention to the gentle aroma of blood and metal bedazzled with dew. His life had once been as simple as that of the goats still huddled in their pen, bleating stupidly and pooping on one another's hooves. It was, he thought, quite a different world outside the fence.

The sun rose pink in the east, and a rooster crowed, breaking the tender silence of the sleepy world.

"Or a rooster," Gustave said to his belly. "I don't want to be a rooster, either. Everybody hates a rooster."

Leaping onto the stump that the inn used for chopping firewood, he surveyed the yard for trouble. No soldiers could be seen, and the only humans still able to exert themselves were looting the bodies of their less exertable colleagues. There was no sign of Gustave's party, but then again, they'd be inside the inn, recovering their strength with food, as he had. He leapt down from the stump and stopped to sip cool water from a trough outside the pens. It tasted of insouciance and freedom, and he savored it before he trotted toward the front door, ever ready for some clumsy lout to threaten him with axes, swords, or threats of future curry. Fortunately, no one attempted to goathandle him, and Gustave clattered into the inn anxious to get the heck back out again, but with company.

The first thing he saw was Argabella, mainly because she was staring directly at the door, her face showing clearly that he was not what she'd been expecting. Her whiskers and ears drooped.

"Oh. Gustave."

"Glad to see you, too, Argy."

"It's not that I'm disappointed to see you; it's just that . . ."

"You were waiting for someone else."

The bunny blushed through her fur. "I'm just glad you're okay. Did you happen to see Fia outside?"

Gustave scrambled up onto the bench across from her and nodded at the tall man sitting next to Argabella.

"Did you ask her brother?"

Argabella shook her head and frowned. "That's Konnan. It's a long story. Although . . . Poltro . . ."

"Let me guess. Outside fighting chickens?"

"The opposite."

"Inside and loving chickens?"

Tears filled Argabella's eyes, and she held up a human hand from under the table that looked even to Gustave's eye rather too bluish and clammy.

"I don't know. I found her in the swamp. Already dead. I think she fell off a cliff."

"She chickened out, eh?"

"Gustave!"

"Well, she did want to eat me," he huffed indignantly.

Before Argabella could lecture him—his lecture sense was tingling—something fell from the ceiling with a clatter, slamming onto an empty plate and smashing it to bits. The tall man beside Argabella leapt to his feet, his sword out and held before him menacingly, its tip pointed at the interloper.

"Is that a giant rat?" Argabella asked, but not like she was disgusted, because clearly, she had no room to talk in the furry and weird area.

"It's a possum," Gustave said.

"I think you mean an opossum," the man said from behind his sword.

The creature opened its beady eyes and muttered, "Don't even start with that pedantic tripe after the night I've had. Possumsplaining a possum."

Gustave sighed and raised an eyebrow. "What is it about this dwarf joint? Everything can talk. Do they make magic kibble? What next—the spoons are going to start complaining about dental hygiene?"

Rising to her legs, the possum stretched and yawned, showing pointy teeth and a long pink tongue. "No, but they do make a pretty poor roof, at least if one wishes to sleep past breakfast. Darling, do you not recognize me? It is I, Grinda the Sand Witch." As if to press the point, she waved a long pink tail in which was clutched Grinda's glass wand, and her sparkly crab ring was looped around the tip.

"Oh, Grinda!" Argabella said, hopping up like she wanted to hug the witch but fairly certain it would be awkward. She settled for waving, which was no less awkward but felt much safer, considering the possum's teeth and temper. "I'm so glad to see you. Have you seen Fia?"

Grinda gestured with a pink paw at the exit. "She fought valiantly through the door last night. That dratted Staph got the better of Mathilde, sadly, and turned her back into a marmoset."

"And she got you, too?"

The possum hissed, and Argabella drew back. "No, she did not overpower me, thank you very much. I chose this form to escape her, and now I've . . . forgotten how to change back. But I still have my wand and ring. I merely need to speak to another wizard or witch, or perhaps get my paws on some grimoires. But never fear: I am in my right mind and still capable of my previous powers." She licked her chops. "And I could use some cat food. Or garbage, perhaps. But fancy garbage."

"I like you in this form," Gustave said. "We have a lot in common."

Grinda was about to say something nasty to him, according to the way her adorable pink nose wrinkled up, but then she stopped and canted her head. "You. Goat. There's something different about you. Have you been poking your nose into the foul demesne of the magical arts?"

Gustave felt his shoulders go up as he ejected a volley of shame pellets onto the newly cleaned floor. "I ate a boot," he admitted.

"And?"

"And it was sort of glowing in a magical kind of way, if you know what I mean."

The possum puffed up, seeming nearly twice her previous size. "HAVE YOU LEARNED *nothing* FROM THIS JOURNEY?

Magic is powerful. You can't just go around eating everything that sparkles!"

Gustave cleared his throat and stepped back on the bench. "I'm a goat. That's what I do."

It occurred to him, briefly and uncomfortably, that the pig had said something quite similar to him earlier and that he was gently dipping a trotter into the realm of hypocrisy. He was now a thinking creature, but he hadn't even considered *not* eating the boot. Was that because he was a prisoner of his animalistic nature, or was he, as a magical being, merely drawn to magic? Was eating that boot part of his destiny? Would something horrible have happened if he *hadn't* eaten the boot? Which part of his nature was goat, and which part was becoming all too human? Speaking of human nature: If Poltro was dead, why was her body just sitting on the bench while people ate breakfast? Weren't humans pretty creeped out by death in general? Why would they sit companionably next to a corpse, especially while eating other dead animals with butter, which was itself made from fermented animal milk? Conscious thought was really starting to get his goat.

And then his attention was drawn to the door, which had just slammed open and bounced off the wall.

There, mighty thews and all, was Fia.

25.

In the Room Where the Disposal of a Persistent Suitor Is Effected

Fia returned the huge grin Argabella flashed at her when she walked through the door of the Braided Beard. Her honey bunny was alive! And so was everyone else—whoops! Maybe not Poltro. She didn't look well. And, uh, that one guy, her countryman she'd seen briefly before the fighting broke out, was hovering awfully close to Argabella. She didn't see Grinda anywhere, nor Mathilde the marmoset. There was, however, a possum on the table with Grinda's glass wand wrapped up in its tail and a sparkly crab winking on the tip of it, and Gustave the goat had managed to avoid being turned into curry somehow. The jar of pickled herring they'd bought hadn't survived the evening, though. Sad fish eyes stared unblinking among the shattered remnants of a jar sitting in a puddle of brine and onions that everyone was trying to ignore.

The bodies and the bloodstains from the fight had been cleaned up, however, and you'd never know that anything amiss had happened except that everyone looked uncommonly dirty for the Braided Beard. Fia's entrance was apparently too much for the proprietor,

Yåløndå Køpkümp, who watched her clomp in all muddy and shouted for everyone's attention.

"All right! We're mostly back to normal, and we do have standing rules for being served here. We let that slide a little bit while we were disposing of corpses, but it's time to reassert our civilization. Everybody to the baths, now!"

Fia had no problem with that. Argabella practically leapt out of her seat, leaving Poltro there with the easterner and the animals, and the two of them ducked into the bathhouse before the rest could catch up. They'd have time to talk later.

Argabella hugged her tightly, mud and all, then delicately picked out a piece of bark that had somehow become lodged in her cleavage.

"What's this?" her bunny asked.

"That's a piece of Pop."

Argabella regarded the bark for a moment before turning limpid, worried eyes back to Fia. "As in . . . your father?"

"No, as in a poplar tree that tried to eat me. It's been quite a night. For both of us, I imagine. We have catching up to do."

"Yes! Lots of catching up."

They caught up in copper tubs placed side by side, where Fia learned about the tragic demise of Poltro. Her fate and Toby's, at least, did not weigh on her conscience, though Worstley's still did and she remained determined to make that right if she could.

Argabella also informed her that the man who'd been sitting so close to her at the table was named Konnan, a prince who found hirsute women attractive and had not been subtle in broadcasting his desire for Argabella.

"What a duck dork," Fia said.

Argabella giggled and then gasped, remembering something. "Also—I don't know if it's the same one you knew—he said he had a friend named Steve."

Fia gripped the sides of the bathtub and pressed her lips together over a scream of frustration. When she could manage, she said through gritted teeth, "It has to be. Steve was well connected with princes and such."

"What are we going to do about Konnan?"

"Nothing. We're just going to leave. And not tell him my name. The last thing I need is for Steve to hear that I'm hanging around Songlen these days. He has people in town. This Konnan may well be one of them."

"Does Steve want you dead or something?"

"I don't know what he wants. I do know that I like having no contact with him whatsoever. Come on. I want to get out of here. We need to get more pickled herring and do something daring."

They did not, unfortunately, escape the Braided Beard without confronting Konnan. He accosted them near the door while they were waiting for Yåløndå to bring them another jar of salty fish.

"My lady Argabella," he said, his dark brown skin newly oiled and scented with cinnamon and cloves, fully aware of how handsome he was. "May I inquire whither you are bound? I would like to offer my services."

Argabella raised one ear along with an eyebrow. "What kind of services?"

"Many things. I have a bag of holding, a windwalker's cloak, a torch, and many bonuses to my strengths provided by various potions and spells. But the main thing I'm known for is offering protection. I am an excellent fighter."

"Is that so?" Fia asked. "Then why were you the first one out the window when the soldiers came last night? I fought my way out the door."

Konnan scoffed and rolled his eyes at her. "There was no need to fight. You could have done the same. Instead, you chose to put your life in danger for no good reason."

"My sword was thirsty. And the point you're missing is that she already has more than competent protection. She doesn't need you."

"Who do you think you are, to speak to me like that?" Konnan demanded, amusement gone, his brows meeting in the middle as he scowled at Fia.

"I'm the woman who will gut you if you don't leave us alone right now," Fia said, aware that she didn't sound like the peaceful person she wished to be. But this Konnan guy, friend of Steve, wasn't taking the hint.

Argabella cleared her throat significantly as the two tall people drew closer, staring each other down. "Actually, Konnan, you could provide a valuable service to me for which I would be very grateful."

Both Fia and Konnan looked down at the bard and spoke as one: "He can?" and "I can?"

"Yes. I need you to take the body of our friend down to the Grange, where you'll find the hut of Belladonna the healer." They followed Argabella's furry finger to where she pointed and saw that Poltro was slumped over the table like she was passed out drunk instead of dead.

"Why? Can she bring your friend back to life?"

"No, not quite. But our friend's former employer and guardian is buried near there, and we think she should rest beside him. We have urgent business in town or we would see to it ourselves. Would you do this tremendous favor for me? I will wait each night at Testy Tom's Blue Orb Room so that I can thank you properly. Look for me there." The bard smiled as winsomely as she could, that furry finger now tracking down his arm, which Fia observed with a flash of hot jealousy.

Konnan saw Fia's expression, gave a smug grunt of satisfaction, and then leered down at Argabella. "It would be an honor, my lady. It will take me a few days, but I look forward to seeing you at the Blue Ball—"

"Blue *Orb*," Argabella reminded him. "Tom gets testy if you get it wrong."

"The Blue Orb Room. Right. I will see you soon, my lady. I depart forthwith."

Konnan moved to take Argabella's hand to kiss it, but the bard clasped her hands together near her cheeks, beaming up at the prince with a breathy sigh. "Thank you *ever* so much, Konnan. It is such a tremendous gift of your time! We must also depart forthwith, so if you'll excuse us for now, we'll see you soon!"

"Of course." He backed up and bowed, and Fia bowed back once Argabella nudged her. Yåløndå arrived at that point with their new jar of pickled herring.

"Here ye are," she said, extending it to Argabella. "A little something for the road. Do visit us again when ye can, dear. We generally offer less death and dismemberment, and here's a coupon for ten percent off."

They had no choice but to exit after that since they had already said they really needed to. They bade farewell to both Yåløndå and Konnan once more and walked right out, Fia keeping a tight rein on everything she wanted to say until it was safe to do so. She pulled Argabella to the right once they were outside, and they circled the building, heading back to the rear entrance of the baths. Fia stopped them before the door, figuring it was a safe place to talk.

"What was that all about?" Fia asked in an urgent whisper.

Argabella shrugged. "I got rid of him."

"With a ridiculous promise! I can't believe you'd do that!"

"Do what? Make a promise or keep it?"

"Make a—wait. What do you mean?"

"I mean I'm never setting foot in Testy Tom's Blue Orb Room." Argabella squatted down on her haunches and placed her hands on top of her knees, making herself as small as possible while peering up at Fia, looking very much like a wild hare. "What? Cute li'l ol' me can't ever tell a lie? Of course not! That's why he believed me. Put down the herring for a second."

Fia complied, and as soon as she stood up, Argabella launched herself into her arms, wrapped her legs around her midsection, and held on to her shoulders. She put her soft forehead against Fia's and said, "I rather thought that was a situation where we didn't have to kill anybody, so I used my tricksy rabbity wiles. Hope I didn't foil your plans."

"I had no plans except to be with you."

"You sure? Looked like maybe you were planning to start a fight."

"Well—" Fia thought back and recalled clearly that yes, she really had wanted to fight him. "Maybe just a friendly kick to the groin," she admitted.

"And if he escalated?"

"I might have been forced to kill him."

"Yet here we are, all alive and unstained. Will you try to always make that happen first, before you resort to violence? Just try?"

Fia could not even begin to argue. She didn't want to. "I will try."

"Thank you. Let's get this done and go grow some leggy roses together."

"Yes, let's."

They entered the baths and called to the rest of the party to meet up in the back when they were ready. No need to risk any of them running into Konnan and alerting him that they were, in fact, still on the premises.

"I think we'll finish this one way or another today," she told Argabella.

"Those are the two most common options," her bunny agreed. "Though sometimes there is yet another way to finish things, or a way we had not even thought of, or this really weird way you'd only consider if you had ingested some dodgy gnomeric mushrooms first."

There were, Fia supposed, many ways the evening could go, not just one way or another, and she hoped she'd get to experience one of the ways in which she was alive and happy at the end of it.

"Let's begin the end, then," Fia said, and put Argabella down as Grinda and Gustave emerged from the bathhouse in a lavender cloud.

"All right, stop stalling now," Gustave said. "Y'all said there would be a bunch of nanny goats without any other billies around. Take me there to meet my destiny."

26.

ABROAD IN A FULSOME FIELD
OF GOATLY PARADISE

The nanny goats were not heavy with kid, for which Argabella was profoundly grateful. That was still a couple months away, most likely, as was the act of animal husbandry that would get them there. Grand nannies could be grouchy, but just now, Gustave would be like a slice of pie sitting on the windowsill.

When they approached the fencing that surrounded Løcher's estate, a few of the enchanted nanny goats were having a nice scratch against the wooden posts, and they started talking about him, assuming he was the normal sort of goat and wouldn't be able to understand.

"Mmm-mm, looky what's coming our way, girls. A fine-looking billy on the hoof. Got himself a righteous beard," one said.

"Oh, my, cut me off a slice of that."

"Only a slice, girl?"

"Well I *was* going to share, but if you're going to make comments about my appetite, I can just keep him all to myself."

"Ladies, ladies. There's enough for everybody," Gustave assured them. "You can all have a slice of the Gustave."

The nanny goats froze for a few seconds, trying to decide whether to scream or run or faint away. Argabella could sympathize, because she'd frozen in exactly the same way many times when addressed by erstwhile suitors.

"Am I hearing things, or did that billy just say we could all have a slice?" the first one said.

"That's right. I'm a free-range, organic talking billy," Gustave replied. "Tastefully accessorized with a very tall human, an irascible possum, and a singing bunny woman."

Argabella's ears drooped at her description, but apparently she was a point of interest to the other goats. "Where'd you get the singing bunny?" one of the nannies asked.

"Up in Borix," Gustave replied. "They're everywhere you go. Head up there and you can have one for free."

"I don't know if I even want one yet. What does she sing?"

"She croons tunes you haven't heard in many moons. Say, what's your name? I'm Gustave."

"I'm Beatrix," the nanny said. She was mostly milk-white except for a single black patch on her back and black tips to her ears.

"Shh! Don't disclose your personal info!" another said. She was a salt-and-pepper gray. "We ought to tell Blurt about this."

"Sure, have Blurt come over," Gustave said. "Who's Blurt, by the way?"

"He's our keeper. He gives us little snacks," Beatrix said.

"Kind of like a pooboy?"

"No, he's not a pooboy. We have so much room on the grounds that we don't need a pooboy. He just jokes around with us and feeds us, gives our coats a nice brush once in a while."

"You're living the high life, Beatrix. What are the snacks like? Little rolled-up pieces of leather?"

"No, they're mostly oats and dirt stuck together with some syrup and bugs, I think."

"Ah! Trail mix, then."

"Right. So where are you headed, Gustave?" Beatrix asked.

"Here, actually. I heard in town you nannies were talkers, and I wanted to come over and have a chat. How'd you get the gift of gab, anyway?"

"Some filthy pixie did it to us. She has only one blue sock."

"Hey, me, too! Meaning I'm a victim of Staph, not that I have a blue sock. We're on the same team. Any idea why she has only one?"

Beatrix bleated in amusement. "I ate the other one. She nearly blasted me to bits, but Løcher stopped her."

Gustave bleated back, and the other nannies joined in. And then they just kept going for the count of a hundred, at which point Argabella couldn't stand it anymore.

"Are you talking in some kind of goat language now?" she asked, and the ungulates all stopped and stared at her.

"No, we were just laughing," Gustave explained. "When you can eat a sock with so much sentimental value to the owner that they want to kill you for eating it, you've had a rare victory. Beatrix here is a legend."

The nanny goat preened and blinked her yellow eyes a few times, then whispered audibly to the other nanny goat, "He gets it. We gotta get this guy inside the fence."

"All right, I'll go get Blurt," the salt-and-pepper nanny groused, and she gamboled away, hooves tearing up turf and udders swinging pendulously as she headed for a larger collection of goats milling about in the distance and a lean silhouette standing among them.

Beatrix took a couple steps closer to the fence and peered through the slats up at Fia. "Where'd you find the big one?"

"Oh, she fell out of the sky and crushed my pooboy," Gustave explained, and Argabella saw Fia wince a little at that stark reminder. Her warrior was fierce and merciless when in battle but had a soft spot for the innocent. "Now she protects me from meat eaters. You'd be surprised how many people look at me and think of dinner."

"Wouldn't be surprised at all. Does she sing, too?"

"Not that I've noticed."

Argabella thought the goat's version of small talk was infuriating

and didn't think Fia liked it either, but she kept her mouth shut because it was all part of the plan. A plan that was going spectacularly
well so far in that they had not yet set off any magical alarms. Was
this, she wondered, what it was like to be an adorable little dog that
people talked about all the time but that got punished if it made any
noise?

The tall, rangy goatherd ambled over soon enough, his herd of
nanny goats accompanying him, all excited to see this talking billy
goat who was outside the fence. As soon as he turned in their direction, Fia threw back her cloak. She'd taken off her slightly more sub-
stantive armor and was wearing only her chain-mail bikini again.
And she brought out the jar of pickled herring and rested the base of
it on the top strut of the fence. Her sword was hidden behind her
back.

Blurt squinted as he drew near, uncertain that he could believe his
eyes. He looked, Argabella thought, as if he squinted quite a lot. His
face was tanned and cracked from a life spent out in the sun, with
wrinkles spreading out from his eyes like dry riverbeds cutting
through desert sand. As he neared the fence, those squinting eyes
widened to ogle Fia properly and Argabella had to clamp down on
something Shoutful she wanted to say.

"Hel-looooo," Blurt said in a wheezy sort of voice that broke into
a whistle whenever he had to pronounce an *s*. "It's a good day to get
some sun."

Fia beamed at him. "Indeed it is. Are you the Blurt we've heard so
much about from Beatrix?"

"Indeed I am, miss. Who might you be?" He flashed a yellow-
brown grin at her that sported several black columns that had once
been teeth.

"I'm Fia. My goat wanted to meet your goats. But now that you're
here, maybe you can help me with this jar."

"Jar? You mean jugs?"

"No, this jar. Right here. Look here, Blurt. At the jar. The jar of
pickled herring. Over here."

"Hm? What, pickled herring? Oh, there it is! Right in front of me."

"Precisely. This is a jar of top-shelf fish from the Braided Beard, and I've had the worst trouble trying to get it open."

"What, a strong woman like you having trouble with that? I bet you have more muscles in your hand than I have in my whole body!"

"I'm strong, but this is tough for some reason. Maybe my technique is lacking. I don't suppose you could give it a try? I promise to share if you get it open."

Salt-and-pepper nanny goat spoke up: "You can't eat those, Blurt. You know that."

Fia blinked. "What? You can't handle a few fish?"

Blurt scoffed. "Aw, sure I can."

"You ca-a-a-an't," the nanny goat insisted.

Argabella saw that there was a possible panic building. She nudged Gustave to signal that he should say something.

"Hey, ladies, what's the wildest thing you've ever eaten?" he said. "I ate a kumquat once with a snail on top. Not a combination I'd recommend, but at least it was different!"

The goats immediately shifted off to one side to discuss gustatory adventures while Blurt did his best to open the jar of pickled herring. Fia had given it an extra twist closed to make opening it a challenge, and he grunted and sweated for a while as he tried to get the top to budge. He succeeded eventually and Fia clapped, which made jingling chain-mail sounds that so distracted Blurt that he nearly dropped the whole jar. Argabella was close enough to reach out and save it from ruin. Her nose twitched at the powerful fishy funk wafting from within.

"Oh, those smell good," Fia said. "You first."

"No, no, it's your jar, you go first," Blurt said, smiling his gap-toothed grin.

This was not part of the plan. Fia was a vegetarian. She wouldn't want any of the fish, but she had already said how delicious they must be and had indicated how much she wanted the jar open.

"Thing is, I'm not hungry right now," Fia said. "Just ate, in fact. But I figured if I couldn't get this open I'd never eat again. Please, Blurt. You try. It would be rude of me to take one when you worked so hard to open the jar." She thrust the jar toward him. "Go on. Tell me if they're any good."

"Well, all right, if you really want my opinion."

"I do."

Argabella tried not to show any of her revulsion as Blurt dipped his dirty fingers into the jar and plucked out a shining, stinking herring. He made slurping and smacking noises as he closed his eyes and chewed it, interspersing those sounds with running commentary on the bursts of salty revelation traveling across his tongue.

"Moh," he said, smacking away. "Muh. Whoo! Unh. Oh."

"They're that good, huh?" Blurt nodded enthusiastically. "Well, have another." Fia extended the jar to him, and he fished out another fish, cramming it awkwardly into his mouth.

"Wow. Nuh. Mmm."

"Tell me, Blurt," Fia said as his jaw worked. "What makes them so special?" Argabella noticed that the goatherd's eyes were already beginning to droop.

"Deesh?" He swallowed with effort. "Jesh, omah gawwwd, yinnow. Hnngh."

"I see. Well, you'd better have another, then." Fia slipped another slick fish out of the jar and handed it to Blurt.

"Dangoo."

"You're welcome."

Blurt did not bring the herring to his mouth so much as smash it inside, swaying a little as his fingers lingered in his maw. He did remember to remove them before he started to chew, but just barely.

"Ohhhh," he moaned, and his eyes rolled up in his head as his knees buckled and he fell squarely upon his buttocks. His mouth cranked up and down twice more, then he flopped on his back and ceased to move.

Argabella checked on the goats. They were all gabbling away about some disgusting thing they'd eaten that one time and hadn't noticed that Blurt was unconscious.

"Let's go," Grinda whispered to Argabella, breaking her silence. "You keep them happy and distracted," she added to Fia.

Argabella didn't want to leave Fia, but that was part of the plan they'd made on the way over from the Braided Beard. She ducked down a bit and followed the possum counterclockwise around the fence, circling to where they could get a better view of Løcher's villa, which had ambitions of castledom. Mostly they saw the walls and four thin towers capped by domes painted a soft lavender with a darker purple stripe along the bottom.

Grinda skidded to a halt once they were a goodly distance away from the goats but still the same distance away from the walls. There was no getting closer, since the fence appeared to form a perfect circle with the villa in the center.

"Time to see if this mad caper will work or not," the sand witch announced. "Bust out the lute and wax poetic with the tunes, bunny girl."

Argabella sighed and swung her lute around, strumming an experimental chord or two and tuning the strings with her sharp ears. Then she took a breath, told herself she could do this, and strummed more confidently as she softly sang:

> *"There's nothing of note that's happening here;*
> *There's nothing to see or smell or hear.*
> *There's nothing of note and we're doing no harm,*
> *So there's really no reason to raise an alarm.*
> *Just enjoy yourself with that billy goat,*
> *Because over here there's nothing of note."*

"Good," Grinda said, aiming her wand at the ground over her head using her uncanny tail. "Keep that going on repeat."

Argabella only nodded and continued, trying to keep her mind in a soft unthreatening space full of fluffy harmless snuggly things where there was no plot to literally undermine Løcher's villa and be totally Sneakful about it. They were operating on the theory that Løcher hadn't prepared properly for bardic magic, and thus Argabella's subtle song would not trigger the nanny goats' rumored ability to detect magic, and if so, they'd be prevented by her song from detecting the much stronger magic wielded by Grinda.

For the sand witch was going to shift some serious sand. "Kuchimba handaki," she intoned, and Argabella heard the soft rumble of earth sliding behind her as she faced the distant cluster of goats. She didn't look, however: her role was to sing of innocence and think of nothing threatening. So she repeated her song of nothing to see here over and over until the sun was nearing the horizon and her throat cried out for water. The only thing that kept her going was the fact that the nanny goats made no move in the distance: Gustave and Fia were keeping them wholly occupied, and Blurt remained knocked out by three whole pickled herrings. The plan was working. Except for the part where Argabella had nothing to drink and had to keep playing and singing for hours in the sun.

There were many times in those hours of soft and progressively hoarse singing when her fingers ached and indeed when they eventually started bleeding that she thought she wasn't up to such a chore. That she wasn't good enough. That she wasn't of the bardic quality required.

But then she remembered that Fia was counting on her.

And she remembered that she had survived years of isolation in the cursed thorny tower of the Earl of Borix. Cursed by the very same witch she was now helping! But still.

She had endured. She had persisted. And so the blood running from her fingers onto the neck of her lute after an hour meant nothing. That blood, that pain, was only one more trial she had to pass, for her life was an unending series of trials that frightened her. Still she fought and sang and loved because that was why she lived. And eventually, as the sun sank down to the horizon, sweet and red and kissable like a lover long missed, a scratch at her leg caused her to look down.

"It's done," Grinda said. "You can stop now. We can go get them."

And Argabella found that she had nothing left after all those hours, her fingers shredded like holiday yak meat. She collapsed on her back, lute lying on her belly, ears spread out on the ground like clover drinking up springtime sun.

"You'll go get the others, I hope," she said. "I know we're both tired now, but I'm the one that's bleeding."

"Fair enough," Grinda said. "We'll be inside before nightfall."

Argabella made no comment. She had no strength left to muster one. Only a brief thought, there and gone again, that perhaps her father would stop haunting her now. She had done some serious bard duty today and proved to herself that she possessed the will and strength to continue her studies and possibly do some graduate-level work. And perhaps for the first time, she felt the desire to seek true creative greatness instead of wishing for the boring safety of accounting.

After an uncountable time, the sky, edging from blue to purple and thinking about settling into a deep indigo, became occluded by a beautiful face.

It was Fia's, looking down at her.

"Honey bunny?"

"Yeah?"

"It's time to kick some arse."

"Oh, good. I thought that that time would be coming along soon."

"The time is now."

"Like right now? Or are we going to travel a tiny bit before the kicking begins?"

"Oh. I see your point. Yes. Come on." Fia extended her huge hand, and Argabella raised her tiny, bloody one and braced herself for the coming pain. But Fia saw the blood, gasped, and rummaged in her cloak for a new bottle of NyeQuell.

"Where'd you get that?" Argabella asked before taking a swallow. The pain subsided, and the skin, though still tender, at least closed up.

"I got it from Yǻløndǻ at the Braided Beard. Now, let's try that again." Fia took Argabella's hand and hauled her to her feet as if she weighed no more than a throw pillow. "We just need to run down that rather low-ceilinged tunnel the sand witch made, and I'm sure everything will work out fine, unless it doesn't."

"That is typically how everything goes," Argabella agreed. "Fine until it isn't."

She hadn't taken time to look at Grinda's progress, but the sand witch had excavated and shored up a tunnel accessed through steep stairs cut out of the packed earth. Along with Gustave and Grinda, Argabella and Fia padded quickly down the passage, lit by fragile luminous sand globes like the one Grinda had made outside the catacombs of, of . . . that umlaut guy. Grinda scurried bravely onward until they were all short of breath and wondering when it might end. They emerged into the light of a single wan candle before ranks of shadowy circles arranged in rows and stacked on top of one another. A sour, sweet scent rode the heavy air.

"Whaaaat is even going on here?" Gustave asked. "I gotta say, I miss Beatrix already."

"Those are casks of wine," Grinda said, "because this is Løcher's wine cellar."

"Oh. Um. That means we're still operating according to plan, doesn't it?" Fia said.

"Definitely," Argabella replied.

"Except we didn't really have a plan for this part," Fia pointed out. "We just followed the instructions Mathilde gave us to get past Løcher's defenses."

"Those were good instructions," Gustave said. "I'm going to party with those nanny goats later."

"The plan," Grinda ground out, "has always been to rid the kingdom of Løcher and Staph the pixie. They turned Mathilde into a marmoset. They're responsible for that mess at the castle of Borix.

They turned Gustave into a Chosen One and made my nephew run off to get himself killed. They're the reason Toby and Poltro are buried in the Grange. And I'm pretty sure they want the king to drink himself to death. Getting that cask of Amon Tiyado would be a clever way around my inhibition because it would count as an innocent gift."

"Speaking of that cask, where is it, do you think?" Argabella asked. "I could use a good drink. For courage." She had never heard of a story in which a mediocre bard overcame a powerful wizard, so some courage would be good to have.

"Drink from any other cask but that one," Grinda said. "We'll want to use that Kolonic as leverage."

They found the Amon Tiyado with little trouble; it was sealed with fancy waxes and painted garishly. Save for Gustave, they each took a gulp or five from some other Kolonic that was the best wine Argabella had ever tasted. Fortified for the unknown, she hitched the small cask of Amon Tiyado on top of her shoulder and gathered with the others at the steps leading up to the kitchen. Fia was going to go first with her weapons waving threateningly, and she looked back at them all to make sure they were ready.

"I don't think it's smart for me to walk into a kitchen," Gustave said, but no one wanted to take that moment to unpack whether they were being smart or not.

"I'm ready," Argabella said.

"Ready," Grinda affirmed.

Fia nodded. "Then let's go end this once and for all."

27.

IN THE GRIP OF A SINISTER MIND

When she burst from the wine cellar into the kitchen, Fia's sword practically wiggled in delight, light in her hand and eager to slay something. But there was only the kitchen staff present, and they were not interested in fighting or being slain. They had a gourmet dinner to serve soon to Løcher and his guests. The saucier was tending an oxtail gravy; the sous-chef was flash searing a medley of Qul succulent cactus pads in olive oil and Sixth Toe spices that Fia thought looked delicious; and the chef was applying finishing touches to a roast Corraden megapheasant. They didn't even notice her at first, and it was only the others making noise behind her that drew their attention.

"What? Hey. Whoa. Wait," the sous-chef said, her eyes on Fia's sword.

Argabella had the small cask of Amon Tiyado wine in her arms and spun a bardic tall tale. "We were sent to fetch this for the chamberlain. Is he in the dining room yet?"

"No. Are you the entertainment or something? A sword swallower and a bunny woman and a goat and a . . . ew, what is that thing?"

"I'm a possum sand witch," Grinda snarled.

The sous-chef nodded, her eyes wide. "Of course you are. Sorry."

"I am *not* a sword swallower. Where is Løcher?" Fia asked.

"Beyond the dining room in the entrance hall, I think. He's waiting."

Fia didn't ask who or what he was waiting for. He was waiting for vengeance as far as she was concerned. She pointed to a door spied through the maze of countertops and hanging pots and pans. "Through there?"

"Yes."

"Thanks. We'll let you carry on, then. Looks delectable, by the way." Argabella, Gustave, and Grinda followed Fia as they passed many delicious smells on their way to the exit. The dining room was a sumptuous affair, and there were stewards setting the table with dwarvelish silver, fine gnomeric crystal, and exquisite porcelain fired and painted by Qul artisans.

They tiptoed into the entry hall to discover that the person Løcher was waiting for was none other than King Benedick himself. The two men were at the other end of the long room, doing that weird half-hug that bros do while shaking hands. Fia had seen sketches in eastern broadsides and thus could easily identify both men. Løcher could have been a father to Poltro with his dusky-hued skin and blue-black hair and a bit of dash to his red sash, dressed largely in white with shining black boots and piping, a fine black velvet cloak tossed over one shoulder. An escort of his private soldiers with familiar blue insignias loomed behind him as he met the king near the door of the expansive marbled hall. The king, a handsome fellow with a gray curly beard over tanned white skin, was dressed in fine robes of silk encrusted with sparkly bits and was handing Løcher a few envelopes. A gold scepter swung from his hip, informing everyone who held the kingly might.

"Mishdelivered posht," the drunken king was saying, his speech already slurred. "Thought I'd drop it by myshelf shince you said you had a casssh . . . k of Amon Tiyado you wanted to share. Hope's not an impozish (hic) . . . impo (urrrp) . . . any trouble."

Argabella piped up: "No trouble at all! I have the Amon Tiyado right here!"

Løcher, the king, and their assorted muscled lads all turned to look at the interlopers, and the chamberlain's pleasant expression melted into a scowl.

"Intruders!" Løcher shouted. "Protect your king! Kill them!" he added, not bothering to inquire who they were. He drew his wand out of a pocket in his cloak, a rather short and thin one to Fia's eye, bordering on inadequate, but perhaps he had some moves to make up for its disappointing appearance. In any case, Grinda was ready.

"Vumbi pua!" she screeched, and her spell directed every particle of dust in the room to fly straight up Løcher's nose. He sneezed and struggled to catch his breath and in the meantime would not be casting any spells. His bodyguards were unafflicted, however, and they advanced, swords drawn, in two groups of three while the king's escort surrounded him in a protective ring.

Fia had seen these men before with the circles on their armor, *these soldiers with profound vulnerabilities for all they thought they were protected. She had mown them down and drunk deeply of them.* And Fia thought she would never say that because she hadn't drunk of them even a little bit, so who's really thinking of this? But she *thirsted at the sight of those circles, more delicious paid fighters practically flinging themselves upon her, their hot flesh enveloping her and squeezing even as she tore through it and their blood spilling out, delicious, as they screamed once, sweetly, before they died.* And Fia thought that was crazier than a bag full of bug nuts and why was she even thinking stuff like that as she flourished her sword to intimidate her opponents and the song of it overwhelmed her, *so much delightful blood to be shed—*

Wait, what? Blood was many things, but delightful wasn't quite the—

—so many soft organs hiding in the spaces between the bones. There!

Yes! Oh, that was too quick. Another, sipping from the throat! Yes, yes, parry, bash to stun, and oh my goodness, what a fine dive into a brain through the eye! A delicacy to be sure, what a rare feast is laid out before me—

Fia faced the second trio of Løcher's men and growled at them. She spied an opening on the left and lashed out with a swift kick to the nearest set of ribs. In that vulnerable moment her sword was knocked free of her hand by one of the other soldiers and she fell from the shock of its absence more than from the strength of the blow. The sweetly insinuating song in her head went silent. She somersaulted backward, giving herself space, and came to her feet unarmed except for her pruning shears and bottle opener. That honestly relieved her, because the disturbing thoughts were gone. The magical sword she'd accepted from the Dread Necromancer Steve had grown far too strong on all the blood she'd fed it recently. The thing to do, she figured, was to pour lead around it and chuck it into the deepest part of the lake. She'd have to find a regular sword to use instead.

She didn't have to look far or long: one was thrusting at her vitals that very instant. She swept it away with a forearm and stepped in to ram the shears underneath the jaw of the soldier. His nerveless fingers obligingly surrendered the sword to her, which she caught in midair by the hilt in her left hand and then transferred it to the right. She sighed in relief when the sword offered no immediate soliloquies on blood. But these last two soldiers were more cautious. They had graphic proof of why they needed to be. And maybe, Fia thought, she could save them.

"Just drop your swords and walk away," she told them. "You can go home and see the sunrise tomorrow. You don't need to die."

"That's not how this works," one snarled. "*You* drop *your* sword."

"Look around, fellas. I'm much better at killing than you, but I don't enjoy it. I don't want to do it. I'm giving you this chance to live. Please take it."

They yelled and charged her, choosing death. As Fia cut them down, she thought that at least they'd have a clear shot at Løcher now. Except something on the ground moved.

It was her erstwhile sword, struggling to guide itself to the nearest fresh blood source. Which, at this point, was her. The melee between Løcher and the others still raged, but it was a safe distance away and she could worry about it later. Keeping her new sword poised in defense, she lunged forward and stepped down hard on the flat of her cursed sword's blade. It bucked underneath her boot and tried to slide free, and she shivered, realizing how close she'd come to the edge. That thing was far more dangerous than she'd supposed. It had nearly taken her over completely, and who knew, maybe one or two more deaths was all it would have needed to capture her forever, turning her into an unthinking killing machine. The sword was almost ready to become such an abomination without her.

Fia had no trouble imagining what she would have done once she'd lost herself to the sword. She would have killed everyone. Her friends. Her love. She would have become an avatar of war when all she wanted was a place to be at peace. She could not stop shuddering at the thought, and her cheeks were wet, her vision blurry.

She hesitated to pick it up without protective gloves, and so she felt trapped; she couldn't simply let the sword do whatever it wanted at that point, because it wanted to kill her. But she couldn't pick it up without losing herself.

Fia heard a horrible death scream and turned to see who had made it. Her jaw dropped in surprise at the carnage strewn behind her.

"Oh, no, Gustave . . . !"

28.

WHEREUPON DESTINY IS DELIVERED BY AN OVERLY CREDULOUS POSTMAN

Gustave could practically see the recipes the cooks were imagining as he trotted past them in the kitchen. Their cold eyes professionally appraised his haunches and calculated how many mouths his carcass could feed. As such, he couldn't wait to get away from the fires and the knives and the stew pots and the glass jars of spices. But he couldn't refrain from taunting them as he went past, either: "That's right. Curry on the hoof, baby. Curry you ain't ever gonna taste. Last two people who tried to cook me straight-up DIED. Think on that before you pick up your cleaver there. By the way, y'all smell bad and nobody likes you."

He supposed that last had not been strictly necessary to add, nor was it even close to being true since they smelled fantastic—or maybe that was the giant salad lounging on the counter. Such insults were unworthy of him, to be honest, but kitchens made him nervous. And there was a tiny fact hidden away in his morass of sass: Lord Toby and Poltro had both sought his death and had died instead. Not through anything he had personally done, of course, but it was sobering to think that this Chosen One aura made him effortlessly deadly.

Gustave became a bit dizzy when he took in the servant types bustling around in the dining room, just adding it all up: Løcher must possess tremendous wealth to have all these people preparing a meal for him and his friends, each one of them smelling clean and dressed smartly and double or triple the worth of a single pooboy. And what was Løcher doing with all this wealth? Nothing tangibly good for the people of Pell. He used a private army to kill folks and sent a pixie around to ruin the lives of farm boys.

He was mentally spooling up a wry commentary on excess and privilege when suddenly, everything happened. They entered a room with a marble floor on which his trotters clopped loudly and created echoes, and there was a drunk guy and a bunch of soldiers, and once the rabbit girl said something like "Look! I have wine," there was shouting and so much blood. A man in white with a black cloak said, "Protect your king!" and Gustave panicked. Which one was the king? Was it the man in white? Kings talked about themselves in the third person sometimes, he'd heard, and the fellow in white looked pretty regal. It couldn't be the guy so blistering drunk that he could hardly talk. That must be the evil chamberlain, because why would humans let themselves be led by someone so staggeringly incompetent and mentally absent? He thought he saw a diaper underneath the flowing silks. Yes, that had to be the chamberlain. Or was it the king after all?

Grinda had said something about the king drinking himself to death, but he hadn't paid close attention because he'd still been daydreaming about the nanny goats. Nah, that must have been some other king she was talking about because this guy, while drunk, wasn't dead yet. He had to be Løcher, a mean drunk wizard frustrated by his inability to seize the throne or dress in smart cloaks and boots. The drunk guy even had an abnormally large and ornate scepter strapped to his hip, which had to be his magic wand.

And then the fight broke out, and no one paid attention to saving the goat.

Gustave turned to head back the way he'd come but then remembered that the kitchen was back there and he didn't want to give the cooks either a second chance or the last laugh. He spun around again and saw Grinda spewing curses and firing bolts of eldritch energy at the man in white as he gasped and sneezed and fell awkwardly on his ass. Fia was straight up slaying dudes, her sword slicing and taking lives with juicy, crunchy noises. Some others were trying to draw the drunk guy away, but he shrugged them off and said, "Unhand me! They have my wine!" and added that one or more of them were, perhaps, cretins. Yep, that was Løcher, then. It was his wine because this was his house. He half staggered toward Argabella with a snarl, eyes crazed with madness and hands outstretched for the cask of Amon Tiyado. There was no telling what he'd do to that poor defenseless bunny, who was a vegetarian just like Fia and had never suggested that any harm should come to a saucy goat from the backward earldom of Borix. So Gustave lowered his head toward the drunk chamberlain and charged, intending to ram him out of the way and protect the bard from harm.

But so many things went wrong in those few seconds while he had his head down and his goatly arse-ramming course set.

Argabella, seeing the drunk man coming for her, shifted to the right a wee bit, and he adjusted course to match.

Grinda the possum sand witch unleashed some kind of spell that filled the air with more dust than a fluff-up in the Morningwood. Whatever it was, Gustave was blinded by it and didn't have hands with which to rub his eyes. While he blinked furiously and kept running toward the chamberlain, the humans threw their hands up to their eyes by reflex. That meant Løcher left his midsection unprotected at the approach of a charging billy goat.

The collision was not the sort that Gustave was used to. Normally there was a loud crack accompanying the impact and the sort of rebound one expects when bone hits bone. This was different. It was a tear and a squelch and a hot puddle on his noggin, followed by a horrible scream. Blood dripped down into his eyes and a heavy weight fell onto his head, dragging him to the marble floor. Gustave lowered his head even farther, the weight still on top of him, so he locked his knees and drew back, realizing with horror that he had not merely rammed the chamberlain as he'd intended but impaled him. Gustave's horns somehow had become mired in intestines, and his withdrawal yanked them out of the abdomen of the gurgling drunken man, who was no longer concerned with casks or indeed anything else but putting his parts back where they were supposed to be, his eyes panicked and his mouth a tiny *o* of surprise as he fell back, feebly clutching at his innards.

"Oh, gods! The king!" someone shouted, and Gustave looked around, shaking blood and entrails from his head. Where was the king? What had happened to him? There certainly were many dead people to choose from at this point. Where was the man in white? Ah, there he was! On the ground over there, coughing, with visible streams of dirt flowing into his nose and mouth. But no one appeared to be trying to help him. That was odd.

Fia was some distance away, surrounded by bodies, staring at him in horror. Argabella looked panicked about something seen over his shoulder. Gustave whirled around to see a cadre of armored guys who'd been trying to hold the drunk man back. Their expressions were distinctly unhappy. They looked not unlike Worstley's mother and father when they'd been intent on slaying him for exhibiting signs of evil magic. The men had sharp pointy things in their hands, and they were coming for him even though their eyes were watery and they were blinking furiously.

Gustave turned tail to run and a split second later had a portion of his tail sheared away by one of the mad soldiers. Another connected more effectively, a stinging cut to his right haunch that buckled his leg and sent him spinning spread-eagled on the slick stone floor. He grimly recalled that Grinda had warned him about this, that an aura didn't guarantee freedom from harm, that he'd probably be hurt and possibly crippled before he died so long as the spell fulfilled its purpose. She had said, in fact, that most Chosen Ones died very soon after removing the king, and from what he understood, that meant that the king was already dead or in dire straits. This might be the end. That chef in the kitchen might soon be butchering him for tomorrow's luncheon and gloating over his bones.

But the bunny woman threw the wine cask at the leading swordsman and hit him square in the face, knocking him out, bursting the cask, and spilling a supposed fortune in the process. The possum sand witch scurried past to clamber up pant legs and latch her sharp teeth on to the throat of the choking man in white, which told Gustave that he couldn't be the king after all, since Grinda would never do that—she'd been trying to protect the king from Løcher all this time! That man must've been the captain of the guard or something. Five more snarling madmen rushed for Gustave, determined to do more than slice at his back leg. It was the end of his time, he supposed, but at least it had been far more exciting and full of delicious boots than he would have enjoyed otherwise had he awaited his fate in Borix. At least, he thought, he wouldn't go out like that sow, resigned to her own slaughter. He'd seen the world, and he had no regrets except that he'd never get to party with Beatrix and her crew.

And then Fia landed among the soldiers, a sword scything through necks and plunging underneath arms into gaps in their armor, and Gustave understood that they all died not because Fia was honoring her oath to protect him but because they were vaguely threatening Argabella on their way to get to him. And the tall warrior did it with only one hand, for she kept her left clutched on the scabbard of her old sword, now sheathed, while she wielded a new one that painted death among the soldiers like a manic artist working in red.

And when they were all dead—all except for Grinda, Argabella, and Fia—Gustave felt distinctly uncomfortable deep in his belly, and he wondered if he'd been wounded there, too, even though it was his tail and his right leg that stung with the sharp pain of torn tissue. He was, for once, utterly devoid of pellets.

The discomfort grew into piercing agony, and he bleated in distress, but there was a strange warmth as well, and Gustave remembered the softly glowing boot of glory he'd eaten back at the Braided Beard: he had called it The Boot, in fact. It was coming back on him now like spoiled seafood.

"Oh, poo," he muttered, and he thought those were mighty fine last words compared with most others, like "Hey, what?" or "Ouch!" or "Wait, not yet!"

And then he felt more pain than he thought was possible, ripped what he hoped was the most explosive fart in history, and gave one last despairing bleat. A huge burst of light engulfed the room, a sudden wind lifted Gustave up in a tornado of golden sunbeams, and glitter rained down, sticking in the blood on the marble floor and drifting about everywhere, as glitter is wont to do.

But Gustave wasn't dead.

He felt distinctly strange as his eyes blinked open, giving him his first taste of binocular vision from eyeballs pointed in the same direction.

Gustave had utterly ceased to be a black billy goat.

He was instead something else that dropped back to the floor with a smacking sound.

Something without hooves.

Something with . . . fingers? And toes? Spread out facedown on the cold marble?

"Aw, newt poots," he said. "This is not good."

When he'd eaten The Boot, he had wished to be anything other than a billy goat. But not a pig and not a rooster. In that regard, his wish had come true.

He drew his new hands under his chest, pushed against the floor, and utterly failed to stand up. His right leg didn't work that well. He fell flat once more.

"Gah! This is dumber than Poltro! How do you people even function on two legs?"

"Gustave?" Argabella's voice quailed.

"Name's still the same. Help me up!"

"Your hair's all gone."

That wasn't precisely true, Gustave thought. It wasn't gone: it just wasn't on him anymore. He was surrounded by his former goat coat, his lush locks lying still and dead on the frigid marble of Løcher's entrance hall, mixed in with glitter and blood.

"Yes, and it's damn cold," he noted. "Now help me stand, will you?"

Argabella and Fia hooked arms under his and helped him to a pair of unsteady, fleshy feet. Both of the women were spattered with gallons of blood that rubbed off on him in the process of trying to get him upright.

He wobbled even with their support and instructions to lock his knees.

"This is a terrible idea," he said.

"What is?" Fia asked.

"Bipeds. Why are you not spending your lives wishing for four legs instead of these completely inadequate two?"

"Look down," Fia said. Gustave looked down and sighed in relief.

"Whew. At least I'm still black. Or dark brown, at least. And there appear to be some dangly bits."

"See?"

"Well, yes, I see, Fia. But I'm not impressed."

"Have you ever seen your dangly bits before?"

"Oh. Well, no, I guess I haven't."

"That's just one reason we don't mind two legs. You see things you wouldn't see otherwise. Plus, there are thumbs."

"What are they good for?"

"You'll find out." He supposed he would. The sow had said something about that. Humans had thumbs and weapons, and that, to her at least, settled the matter of who had the right to rule. Though many other peoples had thumbs and weapons, too. That couldn't be the only reason humans seemed to be running everything— jingly bits and thumbs. There had to be some other reason.

To his left, Grinda made some spitting and hacking noises, trying to get pieces of the now dead man's throat out of her teeth. "I'll have nightmares and dental bills for the rest of my life, but Løcher is dead, so it was worth it. Or it will be if we survive the aftermath."

"What aftermath?"

"We're going to be found soon, and we'll have to explain this. We're going to say Løcher planned to poison the king with bad wine and Gustave uncovered the plot and ran here to stop it. At that point Løcher ordered his men to attack, and one of them managed to dis-embowel the king. If they buy it, we stay. If they don't, we run."

"I don't think I can run on these legs," Gustave said. "Especially since one of them is sliced up a bit."

"Then lie convincingly."

"Lie? If it's on the floor, you got it. But just to clarify: Which one was the king?"

"The one you killed, of course."

"The drunk guy was the king, not the chamberlain?" Replaying the reactions to his accidental goring of that man, it made sense—and it fit with his role as the Chosen One. Løcher's plan had worked in that sense. And it also meant that he had committed regicide and no longer had any protections. Gustave's stupid knees buckled, and he would have fallen had Fia and Argabella not been supporting him. "Gah! See, I told you I shouldn't have come here! But you humans didn't listen to me."

"You're human now. How did you manage that, by the way?" Grinda asked.

"That magic boot I ate, probably."

"I don't suppose there was a matching one lying around? I could use a transformation myself."

"No, there wasn't—"

"Hellooo! I have the chamberlain's mail!" Someone knocked twice on the door and it swung open, revealing a grizzled postman with a heavy sack slung over his shoulder and a wad of letters in his hand. He drew up short when he spied a naked man, a mostly naked woman, a half rabbit, and a possum, all smeared with blood and sur-rounded by dead bodies.

"Ah. Palace intrigue is finally out in the open, I see. How refreshing! And who might you be? The leaders of a coup?"

"Oh, no, no," Grinda said, and the postman merely blinked at the talking possum. "It was Løcher who planned the coup, and we were here to foil it and save the king."

Grinda spun her tale after providing her bona fides as a trusted alderman of Malefic Beach, and the postman listened attentively, following along until she wound down, when he held up a finger. "One question," he said, and stared directly into Gustave's eyes. "Why are you naked and covered in glitter?"

"Oh. That. Well, I'd been recovering from one heck of a party the night before, you see, sleeping in until late, and once I heard the king was on his way to Løcher's, there was no time to get dressed. It was an emergency."

"Ah, yes, of course, of course," the postman said, smiling and nodding as if he remembered fondly the halcyon days of his youth, when he had regularly been awakened from a comfortable slumber to join in battle, all nude and sparkling.

"If it hadn't been for him," Argabella said, "these traitors would have gotten away with it!"

The postman's eyes shifted to the wide staring eyes of King Benedick and pointed his chin at the body. "Well, er . . . didn't they? The king's dead, after all."

Argabella jumped in. "Yes! Yes, he is! But so are the traitors! Gustave made sure they paid for their crimes! He prevented an evil cabal from taking over the entire realm! They were in cahoots with trolls, my good man. Trolls! Can you imagine the world run by trolls?" Argabella shook her furry fist at the sky. "Forbid it, ye gods! That's why I'm so glad Gustave arrived in time to prevent it. It's that kind of decisive, sober leadership that Pell needs right now! That's right: I said *sober*! You ask me, good sir, Gustave here should be the next king!"

"Hey, what?" Gustave said, forgetting that moments earlier he had thought they were among the worst possible last words a person could utter.

"I agree," Fia chimed in, making it worse. "Many's the time I've heard Gustave comment that postmen are underpaid and underappreciated. But that goes for most everyone. Most people don't get the credit they deserve, do they, Gustave?"

"No?" he guessed.

"That's right! Things will be different from now on. No, they'll be *better* with Gustave running things!" Fia asserted. Gustave couldn't help noticing that Argabella was singing softly under her breath; he only caught the chorus of "Forsooth, forsooth, it's all the truth!"

Hope bloomed on the postman's face like sun striking the tulip fields of Teabring. "You know what? I think they will. Things will be better without that drunken fool in charge. How could they not be? I'm going to tell everyone. The old king is dead. Long live King Gustave!"

The postman threw his handful of mail into the air, not caring since every letter was addressed to a dead man, and waved cheerily at them before departing. The letters fluttered down dramatically and sank into a bog of blood, innards, and glitter. Many a valiant catalog was lost that day. Gustave's knees gave out again, and he demanded that Fia and Argabella let him sit on the floor, his strength all gone.

"I'm doomed now," he told them. "I'm not the Chosen One anymore. Right, Grinda? The aura's all gone, isn't it?"

The possum squinted at him for a moment and confirmed, "It is."

"Great. So I'm just the guy who killed the king. And you know what happens to guys who kill the king? They get killed in turn. Dang it. I wanted to party with Beatrix."

"If by 'party' you mean what I think you mean, that's illegal for you now," the sand witch told him huffily.

"Unless you could transform her into a human?"

"Or you could just meet a nice girl who was actually born human."

"Oh, gross."

Grinda sighed. "You're going to have to stop thinking of yourself as a goat and start thinking of yourself as a human and a king," she said with great gravitas.

To everyone's surprise and disgust, Gustave rolled over and ejected what was no longer a harmless volley of pellets onto a floor already filthy with blood and glitter. His friends lurched back, disgusted. He smiled beatifically.

"It's good to be the king," he said.

29.

Uponst a Cushy Throne, Surrounded by Many Supple Leathers

Although Grinda's current friends, if friends they indeed were, made a fine traveling party, they weren't much of a junta. As soon as the postman set off to spread the word of Løcher's dastardly attempt at the throne, followed by his immediate and grisly murder by a pet possum, someone had to take charge. And even if Grinda was currently the smallest in stature, she was still the most well versed in power, politics, and ordering people around. She attempted to stalk into the dining room with authority but only managed an angry mincing gait once she squeezed through the door, where the sumptuous feast had been at least partially set. Still, her wrath, combined with her personal charisma and no doubt her bloodied muzzle, proved every bit as intimidating as the arrival of a giant.

"You there!" she shouted at a servant cowering under the grand table with a platter of butterflied Gorrible prawns bathed in ghee. "Bring every maid you can find, as well as the most senior ranking member of whatever guard remains." When the servant merely trembled, buttery shrimp dribbling down his jerkin, she snapped her tiny fingers. "Now! King Gustave requires it! Or do you want to be sacked?"

She smacked her teeth, and the servant sprinted out of the room, leaving the trembling tray of shellfish behind.

"And that's how we do it," she muttered, trundling over to the platter to lick up some shrimp and get the vinegarlike flavor of Løcher out of her mouth. It had been years since she'd bitten anyone to death, and the flavor of villains had not improved.

Gustave crawled into the room, obviously having heard what she said, followed by Fia and Argabella. "Uh, I don't think I plan on ruling through fear," Gustave said. "Not that I have any plans yet, but I suppose I should start making some. So: no fear, no threats of violence. It'll mean more arguments but fewer nightmares and guilty dreams. And all meals in the palace will be vegetarian. Oh, and I'm definitely going to need a pooboy, so please hire one. A heavy-duty one, judging by what just happened back there."

Grinda looked up, considering him. Gustave had been an altogether average goat, and he appeared to be an altogether average human. The magic he'd ingested hadn't turned him into a picture book king, tall and brawny and handsome and in complete control of his faculties. He was a somewhat gangly man with goatlike features, including a potbelly, knobby knees, and spindly arms. He appeared to be about forty, which was a reasonable enough age for a king, and he had a little scruff of a beard and ears that stuck out. Even his eyes, although no longer blessed with devilish horizontal pupils, were golden and a little bit off, as if they still yearned to be on the sides of his head. But dress him up, teach him to control his bodily functions, and he could be a good king. He was already predisposed to worry about the weak and helpless and distrust the powerful, and as such, Grinda was unlikely to find another leader who'd agree so readily to the kinds of changes she wished to make. For that, she supposed, she could forget that he'd once purposely pooped on her feet. Making him be the king would most likely be punishment enough.

"Well, that's settled, then. I will be your new chamberlain," she announced. "At least until the castle is well in hand. We must travel there immediately to distance ourselves from the scene of . . . this kerfuffle. Argabella, you'll handle propaganda, beginning with a song telling the True Tale of King Gustave's Triumph, which will in no way be true but will help us stay alive. Weave in some magic that suggests we are benign and good—because we are—but that also suggests we are honest, because we aren't. Sing it every step of the way as we journey to the castle."

Turning to Fia, the possum nodded sagely. "Fia, you'll be in charge of the king's guard. Round up whatever is left of Løcher's forces. Have Argabella sing them a song about loyalty to Gustave. Make sure they look smart, as appearance is almost more important than lethality. They must guard us for the journey."

"But what do I do?" Gustave asked, flailing a hand at his blood-soaked body as he clambered to his feet.

"Hmm." Grinda stroked her whiskers. "Here's what we say. You were hurt during your brave but ultimately fruitless defense of King Benedick and will need time for rehabilitation. On the way back to the castle, you'll ride in a closed palanquin due to your disfiguring injuries. You can't face your people until you've learned to walk—on your back legs only—and hold your . . . uh . . . well."

Grinda waited while Gustave urinated, the stream arcing straight up into the air and splashing into a bowl of lima beans, which may or may not have improved the dish.

"Man, I don't know why you guys wear clothes at all," Gustave enthused. "Your bodies do the funnest stuff!"

"Just not usually in public," Fia grumbled.

"And now I must hire a governess," Grinda broke in. "Very discreet. Very brawny. Willing to wash a lot of diapers. Don't do anything stupid until I'm back from town."

"What's considered stupid for humans?" Gustave asked. "Because I'm guessing it's considerably different from what's stupid for goats."

Grinda sighed deeply. The payoff was potentially huge, but this was going to be her hardest job yet.

They were soon on the road, King Gustave safely tucked into King Benedick's old coach, the shades drawn tight, his diaper fitted snugly just in case. Fortunately, thanks to Benedick's history of wetting himself in his drunken stupor and the reluctance of visiting earls to embarrass the king by not dressing as he did, the people of Songlen were used to seeing diapered heads of state.

Grinda curled across from him on the cushy bench, her possum fur sparkling after a hurried but refreshing trip to Løcher's spa. Argabella sat on the wagon box in a fine gown raided from a guest closet, strumming her polished lute and singing a song telling the story of how Good King Gustave had routed the terrible Løcher, leaping in front of poor King Benedick and taking a stab wound in his place before a completely different and entirely unavoidable stab wound felled the mighty monarch. The song also made it clear that King Benedick had died despite attempts to save him and that was in no way Gustave's fault. The chorus encouraged everyone to give King Gustave their loyalty. Fia rode outside on a splendid white mare the size of an elephant, leading a guard composed of remnants of Løcher's private army dressed in the uniforms of the king's bodyguard. They'd been promised a raise for loyalty to Gustave, and this ruse allowed them to get into the palace and install Gustave in the king's residence. Still, Grinda had her wand ready. Considering that Gustave was no longer the Chosen One, he could easily be felled by someone with political aspirations, and she'd gone to far too much trouble to let some annoying upstart upend all her plans.

Once he was installed in the castle nursery with his new governess, it took a week before King Gustave was ready for public consumption. Grinda visited him daily, and each morning he seemed a little less . . . goaty. He learned to sit up, to chew with his mouth closed, to hold a teacup, to hold his bowels, and, more important, to hold his tongue. His walk would wobble for quite some time, his hands reaching out as if to feel the solid earth crunching under his hooves. Every now and then, when startled, he would still bleat, but many a king had kept worse habits. Grinda was, overall, pleased.

Except by her own inability to become human again. The irony of serving a king who had once been a goat as a possum who had once been a human did not amuse her. Although she called upon every witch, wizard, and beard barber in Songlen, no one knew a spell to reverse what Grinda herself had wrought. Such was the curse of power, she thought: it often meant you made messes only you could clean up.

The day of King Gustave's coronation dawned sunny and warm and betokened a prosperous reign. Grinda had taken total control of the castle's operations and masterminded everything from the decorations to the guest list. Banners of Gustave's official sigil—a rampant and noble goat, for he'd lost the argument to make it a golden boot—hung from balconies overlooking the throne room, which was filled with every baronet, marquess, and earl in Songlen except for the sleeping Earl of Borix. They were all ready to pucker up to kiss the new king's slender but flat behind. Not that they would if they knew how recently it had required wiping by Hurlga the governess.

Gustave sat in the throne with fabulous posture wearing a serious expression he'd been practicing in the mirror all week. He was unused to keeping his tongue inside his mouth, but he'd finally mastered it, and he'd likewise ceased to scratch at his clothes as if they were a lice-infested stable blanket. Hurlga had done a magnificent job. Grinda was quite proud standing by Gustave's side as Argabella sang a beautiful song about kingly greatness, loyalty to the throne, definitely not being a goat, and being the sort of king who would never require any sort of beheading. Fia's corps of guards stood in perfect lines holding their halberds and flags, and the doddering old clergyman performing the coronation ceremony didn't muck anything up too terribly. At the end, everyone clapped, no one attempted an assassination, and they scored some elvish moose cheese as a gift from the Morningwood, so Grinda reckoned they had pulled off quite the coup.

After all hands had been shaken and babies had been kissed—not licked; Grinda had been very adamant with Gustave that there was a difference and people would notice if he did one and not the other—the friends sat around the king's table, enjoying the kitchen's finest vegetarian fixings. Argabella noted that Lord Toby would've approved the crispy sprout bouquets sprinkled with a plum wine vinaigrette.

The new king agreed. "Even though he wanted to eat me, the Dark Lord also helped save us all from the hooktongues that time. I feel I should do something to honor his life, so I wish to outlaw smoothies," Gustave announced. "Or apprentices who can't read basic signs like NOT COFFEE. Whichever you think is best, chamberlain."

"Got it." Grinda added that to the ever-growing list of his edicts, many of which she hoped he would forget, such as the requirement that eating goat was forever punishable by halving and that all old boots must in perpetuity be given to the king as birthday gifts.

But he also had some ideas worth pursuing. A modern, reliable post office as the foundation for good business throughout the realm. A housing and jobs program for trolls so they'd stop dwelling in dark places and ambushing people with their stupidity. A bone donor initiative in which humans would donate their bones upon their deaths to be ground into bonemeal flour for giant laborers who were building so much of the country's infrastructure—it might stop the strike south of Nockney and keep people from being turned into meat pretzels but also encourage more giants to work for the kingdom instead of fighting against it.

All Grinda had to do was keep Gustave clean and alive and they could perhaps do some truly good work in the world.

"I didn't know being a king would be so exhausting," Gustave said, lovingly eating delicate slices of a molasses oatmeal cake the cooks had shaped like a boot for old times' sake. Leather still tasted delicious, but he'd learned the hard way that it shouldn't be swallowed. The human bowel was a delicate thing.

"I don't know if it's being a king that's exhausting so much as being human is," Fia said. "It's certainly a lot of work, worrying about castle security. I kind of miss the road."

"I miss the earl's tower, believe it or not," Argabella said with a sigh. "Not so much the thorns and people who seemed dead all the time, but the roses and the peace."

"Yes! That's exactly what I want!" Fia said. "Roses and peace."

"Life isn't peaceful," Grinda said. "Anyone who tells you otherwise is trying to sell you an overpriced mattress."

"Wait!" Gustave stood and slammed his hands on the table. "I forgot! The main edict! I want Staph the pixie brought before me. She started this mess, and although Løcher has been punished, she's just running around, screwing up the lives of innocent goats and pooboys." He walked to the window, and although he was successful, it was by no means a graceful walk. Throwing open the shutters, he shouted to the street below. "Do you hear that, Songlen! I will reward whoever brings me Staph the pixie! With two—no, three old boots!" When he turned and saw the horrified expressions of his friends, he added, "Okay, four old boots, but really nice ones!"

Grinda waddled up behind him and whispered, "Try five gold pieces. Most people aren't moved to action by used footwear."

"Yes. Thank you, chamberlain." He shouted out the window, "Plus five gold pieces!"

Grinda found it quite satisfying how the populace outside scrambled to oblige, turning over rocks and opening doors, hoping to find the wayward pixie. But it took several days before Gustave's demand proved fruitful. They were accustomed now to allowing the castle to run itself, and most visitors never made it past the front door thanks to the stern demeanor of the king's new halfling butler, a cousin of Milieu Goobersnootch named Mondeux Goobersnootch the Third. But this time the bell rang, and they all hurried down to the throne room to see what kind of mastermind could scoot past a Goobersnootch.

Gustave took his seat and arranged his cloak of brown velvet.

"You may address me," he said to the elegantly attired elf waiting on the royal carpet.

This elf looked ever so slightly different from the elves of the Morningwood, with a wild air about him and his hair cut short and slicked back. He wore a blazer and carried a briefcase, and as soon as the king addressed him, he bowed and began his spiel.

"Good King Gustave, and I don't know why they call you that, because me? I would call you great. Great King Gustave. Or better yet, Best King Gustave. Can't get better than best, can you, King Gustave?"

"Er, no?"

"Excellent. Excellent. Now, Best King Gustave, I heard you were looking for Staph the pixie, and let's say I was able to get my hands on her. What do you think you'd pay for that?"

"The king has put the price of five gold pieces on the enemy of the crown known as Staph the pixie," Grinda broke in sharply.

"And a great number that is, too," the elf agreed. "Five is just a super number. But what if that number was ten? Wouldn't it be worth it to you, King Gustave, to never have to worry about Staph the pixie again?"

Gustave leaned over to where Fia stood at attention in a full suit of armor with his golden goat sigil emblazoned on the cuirass. "Can you threaten this guy and get it over with?" he asked. "Unless your thirsty sword is, uh, extra thirsty, and then maybe we shouldn't let it loose."

"It's gone," she whispered back. "I had lead poured over it and threw it in the lake."

"I've been wondering about that," Argabella said. "Isn't lead supposed to be kind of poisonous? And if so, maybe we shouldn't have put any in a lake full of fish?"

"Oh, no, it's still killing!" Fia wailed.

"Quiet," Grinda hissed. "We're in public."

The elf was still prattling on about numbers and return on investment and the cost of retaining a caught pixie as compared to finding a new pixie, and although Grinda knew she was being upsold and was somehow under the sinister influence of elf magic, she was nearly prepared to acquiesce and give this hardworking elf spellsman the fifteen gold pieces he deserved for being a superior entrepreneur.

But Gustave shouted, "Show me the pixie, and then we'll talk."

The elf grinned with a creepy amount of teeth and unbuckled his briefcase, which popped open to reveal a small cage containing none other than Staph the pixie. Grinda's possum tail immediately tightened on her wand, and she nearly blasted the meddling fairy into oblivion until she recognized that the cage was crafted from Titania's Two-Toe Titanium and thus immune to magic spells. That explained how the elf was able to contain someone as powerful as Staph. As for the pixie herself, she sprawled on the floor of the cage in a fug of liquor fumes, her red pants covered in foul stains and her nose hairs curling gently with each exhalation.

"Are you sure it's her?" Gustave asked. "The pixie I remember had one blue sock, and this pixie is wearing a hideous pair of mismatched galoshes."

At that, Staph stirred and sat up, rubbing warty fists into her bleary red eyes. When she looked around and saw Gustave, she did a comical double take and shrugged.

"That's right," the pixie said. "I'm not the one you want. This stank-face nutter kidnapped me while I was helping save a bunch of orphans from a troll! I'm innocent! This is an outrage! My good friend Løcher can sort this out." She peered around the throne room. "Løcher? Old buddy, old pal?"

"He's dead," Grinda hissed, waddling toward Staph with all her bristly gray fur standing on end and her lips pulled back over her teeth. "And soon you will be, too."

Staph stood and felt all over her body for a wand, a series of actions that made everyone else wince. "Where is it? Who took my wand?"

The elf, who had been watching the interchange with a pleased smile, held out a wand by the tips of his fingers and waggled it just out of Staph's reach. Grinda couldn't blame him for not wanting to touch it. Part of the pixie's magic derived from her mucus, and the wand was moist and gobbeted with boogers.

"So now that we've established that this is Staph the pixie and that you, the king, have requested Staph the pixie, let's talk about payment plans." The elf pulled out a sheaf of parchment as tall as half a halfling. "Now that we've mutually agreed on fifty gold pieces, if you'll just sign here—"

Grinda nodded and reached for the quill he held out. "Yes, that seems very reasonable."

"No!" Gustave shouted, startling everyone. "I don't know why you're all suddenly stupid, but this nincompoop is trying to swindle me, and as the king, I don't like that one bit. Guards, take him in hand. Bring me that cage and give the elf five boots or five gold pieces, his choice, and kick him out. And for the love of all that's goaty, put up a No Soliciting sign. Whenever he opens his mouth, I feel a part of me die."

Grinda shook herself, feeling the elf's spell partially broken and realizing that Gustave was immune to the charm the elf had used to ensnare her. What they needed was some hearing-impaired guards mixed in with the rest to protect them from spoken spells—and rival bardic spells—in the future. Before the elf could talk again, she flicked her wand and shouted, "Swige!"

The elf's mouth kept moving, but no sound came out. The phrases he shouted would've shocked anyone with the ability to read lips, and his hand gestures made his feelings clear to those without that skill. Gustave's guards moved in, taking the elf in hand, and one guard brought the cage to Gustave as the pixie beat herself against the bars, trying to squeeze through and failing.

"You started all this," Gustave marveled, staring at the nasty little creature. "If not for you, I'd probably be stew by now, and poorly seasoned, too, judging by the sorry herb garden Worstley's mother kept. So thanks a lot for that, both for real and sarcastically. Now, I'm not really in favor of anyone's execution—"

"What?" Grinda sputtered.

"—but I can't set you free, either. You've caused too much trouble, and I can't have you flying around, activating all sorts of Chosen Ones to come after me. What next, a talking shark? Just no." He turned to Grinda. "Any nonlethal suggestions, chamberlain? I have a strict no-slaughter policy for captives."

"You'll have to open the cage first. The metal is ensorcelled. And then cut off her wings," Grinda said. "That will nullify her magic. Since you're feeling kind."

King Gustave motioned Fia over. "Get your sword ready."

"No!" Staph shrieked. "Don't you dare!"

"On three," Gustave said, holding the clasp on the cage. Grinda grinned in anticipation, anxious to see her old foe rendered helpless.

"One."

Fia's sword was ready.

"Two."

Argabella closed her eyes.

"Three."

Gustave opened the cage, and Fia reached inside, grabbing the pixie by the wings. Staph struggled and shrieked, kicking and screaming as she was tugged through the door.

But the moment she was outside, a thunderclap shook the room, filling it with noxious green gas.

As the gas cleared, Fia called out in dismay.

The pixie had disappeared.

30.

OUTSIDE A DOOR HUNG WITH GNARLY KNOCKERS

Argabella choked on fairy gas and experienced a profound sense of incompletion. They'd come so far, and Staph had escaped. Even worse, Fia would blame herself for letting the pixie go even though it wasn't her fault.

"I should've known," Grinda said, examining the cage with her tiny possum hands. "Her wand wasn't her only source of power. Witches and wizards require an artifact to focus our magic, but pixies are fairies and fairies have their own sort of filthy, disgusting magic they can let rip, so to speak."

Beside her, the elf jumped up and down, shouting silently and pointing at his hand as if requesting the gold he'd come to claim. Argabella thought he looked more than a little ridiculous. It was funny how she'd once thought elves to be gracious, cultured, magical beings but had learned that they were all complete toerags.

"Drop him outside," Grinda instructed the guards. As they dragged him out, she shouted, "Gold is for closers!"

"But he brought me Staph the pixie, so don't I owe him five gold pieces?" Gustave asked, confused. "I mean, even if she got away by deploying a magical fart, he still did his job."

"So you're going to be *that* kind of king." Grinda smoothed down her fur and sighed yet again before shouting after the guards. "Fine. Give him five gold pieces and tell him never to come back here again." She turned to Gustave. "You're setting a dangerous precedent with that, you know. If the people think you can be trusted, they'll start asking for things. Living wages. Clean water. Proper health care."

"Oh. But . . . that sounds pretty reasonable, doesn't it? I mean, they're paying taxes, right?"

Grinda threw her possum hands in the air and sounded vexed, but Argabella saw her smiling a wee possum smile out of Gustave's vision. The witch was secretly pleased. "Benevolence. It had to be benevolence. You're never going to make it as king with a soft heart like that."

"I'm kind of worried about it, actually," Gustave admitted. "I mean, what am I going to do when you're gone? I don't really trust anyone but you guys. I still feel like most people want to eat me. Even Hurlga sometimes looks at me like I'm made of meat."

"You *are* still made of meat," Argabella said gently.

"I know! And it's terrifying!"

Grinda scampered up the throne and sat on the arm, patting Gustave's shoulder. "Being king is like being anything. At first it's scary, but then you get the hang of it. And then it gets boring and you want to spend a year on a boat, finding yourself. For now, you're still in the scary bit. But you have Hurlga and your guards and a bunch of cooks and maids, and—"

"Please stay."

Poor Gustave. As a goat, he could simply faint when he was frightened, but as a human, he had no choice but to hunch down in his throne and tremble. He looked around, meeting the eyes of each of his friends. Argabella found it a little disconcerting, considering it didn't quite feel like both of his eyes were meeting hers. But she read the desperation there and felt terribly bad for him.

"What did you say?" Grinda asked.

"Stay. Please. All of you. I've grown so accustomed to you. I'm a herd animal at heart, and . . . well . . . you're my herd. Beatrix and the nanny goats are still mad at me for tricking them and putting Blurt to sleep."

Argabella went to his other side and scratched behind his ear the way he liked, and Fia came up and put her arm around Argabella's waist.

"But there's still work to do," Argabella said gently. "My old castle is still enchanted." *As am I,* she thought but didn't say.

"And Worstley might still be saved," Fia added, "which I'd really like to do."

"And I'd like to not be a marsupial," Grinda said, one little pink hand going unconsciously to her pouch. Gustave made a strangled bleat, and she graciously added, "But I will come back to act as your adviser once my business is done if you wish."

Gustave sighed in relief. "Yes, please. Advise me. I'm starting to get the hang of forks, but I'm still clueless about how I'm supposed to rule. This nanny goat I was talking to said everyone's saying I'm screwing it up on purpose. That nobility aren't supposed to *care* about the people they've been entrusted to lead. I mean, what else am I supposed to do with taxes, hoard them? Sheesh."

"That can wait until I return. Mondeux will help you with the day-to-day business in the meantime," Grinda promised, "and Hurlga, of course, will help you with, uh—" Her eyes dropped to his diaper before she added, "Your other business. It will only be a few weeks if you lend us a coach. And then we can start cleaning up this mess of a kingdom."

"What a strange idea," Gustave said with a grin. "Me, cleaning something up."

They set out the next morning in the king's most luxurious coach. Gustave had given them many gifts, although he hadn't quite mastered gift giving yet on a human scale. They had a large bale of hay, five boots, several shoelaces, and a bouquet of thistles. Thankfully, Mondeux knew his way around a treasury, and he'd made sure they were truly well fortified for their journey. Argabella had a beautiful new lute carved of Morningwood birch and ensorcelled to always be in tune. Fia's fine new helmet was fitted with an enormous pair of carved wood goat horns to mark her as a member of Gustave's elite guard. Grinda had a bucket of wet cat food and a pashmina shawl to nest in. Together, they settled into the cushy seats and prepared to see the land in a new way: comfortably.

They were so accustomed to traveling as a party that there was little strife. They encountered neither trolls nor giants, and their horses had more sense than their old oxen. Four of the king's guards traveled with them, ensuring they were unmolested. Grinda kept a small notebook and made a list of which roads required attention, and they stopped in each town to take note of the general attitudes surrounding happiness, government, and goats. Argabella had once thought Grinda to be very selfish and somewhat cruel, but it seemed like having a purpose suited the witch. Perhaps that was the way of people: they just needed to matter. And it was hard to be relevant when all one did was sit on fantastic beaches, surrounded by sparkling crabs.

"Why do you like those shiny crabs so much?" Argabella asked, pointing to the ring glittering on Grinda's tail.

"They are tough and beautiful whether you are there to notice them or not. They're like people that way. For example, those years you spent in the tower due to this awful curse? Nobody saw you. And still you were tough and beautiful."

"What? No—" Argabella began, surprised that this was suddenly about her.

"Ask Fia."

She blushed furiously and slid her eyes to Fia, who grinned at her from inside her helmet. "You were, honey bunny."

"Anyway, they remind me of what I'm working for. The unseen

people, folks from Qul and Teabring and Burdell and the Skyr, the denizens of the eastern provinces, the dwarfs and elves and the giants, too. They're just like you and me, except they're out of common sight—well, except perhaps the giants are a little more cannibalistic than we are. Still, working for them is working for myself."

They rolled up to the thorny tower one afternoon on a properly sunny day, and Argabella was awed by how mysterious and sublime it looked from the outside. The sunlight slanted through glistening green leaves and beautiful magenta roses, the gray stone underneath forbidding and ancient. To think, for so long she'd been inside, letting the world pass by. And all because of one foul pixie, everything had changed. She didn't feel ashamed of her soft rabbit fur and long ears now. When she saw the way Fia looked at her, she was simply glad to exist at all.

The carriage jingled to a stop, and Argabella held the door open for Grinda. The sand witch clambered out and waddled up and down the base of the thorn-covered wall.

"Where is it?" she muttered. "Ah. Here."

She aimed her wand at a section of the wily thatch and thrust it forward, penetrating so deeply that the wand all but disappeared. The thorns rustled and shivered in response and then shuddered apart to reveal a wooden door with two gnarly old knockers hanging on it somewhat higher than a halfling's reach.

Fia groaned. "You've got to be kidding me. I climbed up a hank of nasty hair and killed a kid, and there was a door here all along?"

Grinda raised a whiskery eyebrow. "There's almost always a way in. You just have to know where to look. Or, you know, to have seen it originally, before you hid it. I can't reach them, Fia, so I want you to grab hold of those knockers and twist them."

Fia did so, and the door sighed and moaned as it swung open on the courtyard, a place Argabella knew well. When she saw Oxnard the guard, still asleep with his face buried in cherry pie, and then looked to the lady's tower, she felt a thrum of guilt. As if sensing her feelings, Fia slid a hand into hers.

"It's going to be fine," she said.

And Argabella believed her.

"Now show me your dead pooboy." Grinda stopped, mouth open, in shock at herself. "I mean, my dear nephew Worstley. My goodness, how that goat gets under one's skin."

"Don't you want to wake up the castle first?" Argabella urged.

"Mm. No. Let's do this first. Trust me: you don't want someone to wake up next to a dead body."

Fia led them to the tower and held Argabella's hand all the way up the steps. The Lady Harkovrita still lay in her bed, beautiful if a little creepy, her beard lustrous and shining, but Worstley was . . .

"Oh, goodness, my darlings. Yes, he's dead. Really, really dead. Way beyond my powers. Beyond anybody's powers," Grinda pronounced, tears slipping down her silver cheeks.

Argabella turned away and vomited carrots, and Fia silently wept. Although Argabella had seen many corpses recently and had almost become one herself on several occasions, she hadn't yet seen someone so supremely dead as Worstley, and she felt horrible for Fia, who had fought past trolls and hooktongues and soldiers and so much more in the hope that he might be saved. The tower's magic had done nothing to halt his . . . Deadfulness, and he was in fact in an advanced state of decay.

"What do we do with it? I mean him?" Argabella asked, wiping sour juice from her lips.

Grinda was panting, her little beady eyes bugging out. "Wrap him in something and stow him in that wardrobe over there. There will soon be brawnier people about to dig the grave, and we have business to attend to."

Fia's mouth gaped. "But . . . isn't he your nephew?"

"We weren't close," Grinda said. "I am sorry he's gone and very sorry for my sister's grief. It was a senseless tragedy, and the blame for it rests squarely on the shoulders of Løcher and Staph. You should bear no guilt for this. Now, let's all move past it and do some good in the world." She had that firm resolve that comes from a life of tragedy, and Argabella and Fia immediately set to rolling what was left of Worstley up inside what they now recognized as a priceless tapestry from Pickelangelo's Blue Period.

After visiting the washroom to clean up, Argabella strode out of the tower, gulped fresh air, and sucked in the scent of roses. She needed a break after that harrowing sight. Although she didn't think it would be quite as easy for Fia to move on from the crushing disappointment of Worstley's confirmed death, she felt a lift of hope as Grinda called her inside the castle to where the heart rose waited. Standing before it, she remembered the moment she'd first seen Fia and begged her not to hurt the leggy cultivar with its crumpled heart. But the possum had no such scruples about the tender flower.

"Fia, lift me up to the blossom, please," she said. "There's only one way to break this enchantment."

Fia obligingly picked Grinda up, and the possum stretched out her neck, snapping up the rose blossom in three quick bites. Once the last petal was swallowed, the thorns fell away from every surface of the castle walls and turned to dust, creating quite a cleanup project in the process.

Argabella didn't get to witness the castle waking up, however, as she was engulfed in a golden whirlwind of light and glitter. Her body lifted up in the center of a powerful vortex, and she went warm all over as if bathing in the summer sun. Spinning around, blinded by incandescent light, she could hear Fia shouting, "Hold on, love! I'm here!"

But then the warmth and light tore away from her as if someone had blown out the only candle in her bedroom and snatched away her blanket. Argabella shivered in the dark and cold and painfully banged her knees on the floor as she fell, seized by an epic fit of sneezing as the dust from all the enchanted thorns had been blown about in her own personal tornado. A hand landed on her shoulder.

"Are you okay?" Fia asked between her own sneezes.

"I think so."

But when she looked up, Fia gasped and touched her cheek.

"What is it? Am I a worse monster? Am I a goat? Or a marmoset? What happened?" Argabella wailed.

But Fia just helped her stand and turned her to face a mirror.

Argabella was human again. The fur and whiskers and long ears were gone, and when she reached around behind her, the fluffy tail was gone, too, leaving an awkward hole in her gown. She had never thought herself particularly pretty, yet she suddenly felt like herself, more like herself than she'd ever herselved.

"Am I . . . do I look okay?" she asked Fia. Because she was terrified that Fia might not like this version of who she was.

"You're still perfect," the fighter said, pulling her in for a kiss.

All around them, her friends and fellow castle denizens were waking up, shaking their heads in disbelief and yawning. And then fighting over privies. Argabella didn't really care. She only had eyes for Fia.

The next hour was a rush of questions and answers, and they carefully steered clear of the earl and countess and Argabella's pushy father to avoid any possible interrogation. Not that the gentry would know what questions to ask any better than the others. Mostly everyone asked everyone else, "What happened?" to which Argabella replied, "I don't know, but aren't you glad to be awake and alive?" What the castle denizens didn't know wouldn't hurt them—or make them attack the sand witch, who, Argabella believed, was going to do real good in the kingdom by Gustave's side.

They were attempting to edge toward the tower to check on Lady Harkovrita when a screech rang out from the top.

"The lady is dead!" someone shouted.

Hurrying up the stairs, they found a maid standing over the Lady Harkovrita, who lay still and waxy on her bed. She wasn't awake, but she was definitely breathing, Argabella noticed with great relief.

"She's not dead," she told the girl.

"But she's not moving! And the smell is so bad; somebody vomited carrots in here."

"Um, that was the possum," Argabella said. Grinda hissed.

But Argabella's eyes flitted to the closet. "You should probably go fetch a physician."

"This is highly abnormal," Grinda whispered after the frantic woman ran out the door, wailing. "The spell is broken. She should be awake. I mean, I'm glad she's not dead, but she shouldn't be half dead. This is not how the spell was supposed to work. I really do need my library." She held up a teeny possum hand to the light. "This form grows tiresome. I must return to my beach house to investigate. Will you two be fine if I take the coach?"

Argabella looked at Fia, and Fia looked at Argabella.

"We don't mind walking," Argabella said.

"You know, I was thinking." Fia smiled at Argabella like she was the most beautiful thing in the world. "Now that the heart rose is gone, I remember you saying Lord Toby had lovely roses. I might have even spied a few on my visit there."

"He does," Argabella said. "I mean, he did when he was alive. I suspect the roses are still there, but they'll need tending. Pruning, mulching, that sort of thing. Can't have them getting leggy."

"And I know he would want someone to keep his tower properly landscaped. He was the sort of fellow who would hate to think of his demesne gone amok."

"He would probably appreciate it if two kind souls took over his rose gardens and kept his chickens in check. And we know a goat— I mean a guy—who could grant us proper title to that land."

Fia grinned at her. "We should depart forthwith and enjoy the flowers in bloom."

"We should."

Grinda growled to get their attention, as they were just gazing into each other's eyes like complete ninnies as they murmured about roses and peace.

"Well, you two darlings seem to have a plan. I'll see you at King Gustave's birthday party next month, I suppose. Hopefully, I'll have proper hands by then. Oh, and don't even think of getting him a boot. I already got him one."

The possum sand witch left with the usual curtness that poorly hid her feelings, and Argabella and Fia wandered back down to the courtyard as everyone else rushed up the tower steps to fret over the sleeping lady. They were serene amidst the pandemonium. As they approached the door to leave, Argabella watched Oxnard the guard finally finish eating his cherry pie, look up, and exclaim, "Oi! Where's my crossbow?"

They managed to just barely contain their mirth until they exited, when their eyes met and they both burst out laughing.

Everyone lived happily ever after—or at least until King Gustave's birthday.

Except for the dead people, who remained dead.

And for the sleeping lady, who kept on sleeping.

Epilogue

King Gustave received many, many old boots for his birthday, which his human dentition and digestive system could no longer tolerate but which were very much appreciated by Beatrix and the nanny goats, and his regifting of said boots went a long way toward repairing the rift between them. He had already given Blurt a fresh jar of pickled herring and a new bed to nap in after eating it.

In the same dining hall where Gustave had once urinated into a bowl of lima beans, the now diaperless monarch reveled in a fine birthday feast with his friends. Grinda was there, triumphantly returned to her human form and efficiently organizing the dissemination of Gustave's policies while dealing ruthlessly (and quietly) with threats to his throne. He had successfully negotiated the end to the giant strike with the bone donor ploy and was thinking something similar might tempt Ol' Faktri to work in exchange for food and make much of Grunting habitable again. He had also made immediate improvements to the postal service, and when people remarked upon it, the postal workers were quick to credit King Gustave's canny mind. Not all of his initiatives were soaring, but these early successes were doing much to discourage challenges to his rule, and Grinda could deal with what little resistance she'd seen.

Fia and Argabella were there for the party, too, having come from a victorious visit to the Pell Smells Rose Show. Once they promised to spend at least part of the year in Songlen in service to the crown, Gustave immediately granted them title to Toby's tower at Malefic Reach. That way, they could continue to employ old Dementria and Poltro's brother Morvin while enjoying their peace and roses. King Gustave was all about caring for the pooboys of the world.

As the party progressed, they raised glasses and flagons of elvish mead to the dear memories of both Lord Toby and Poltro, and then the cake was brought out, a magnificently flaming baked meringue cake in the shape of a leather boot, its innards filled with delicious vegan custard that set their mouths to watering.

Argabella volunteered to slice the cake and serve everyone, and she sang a tiny happy cake tune while she distributed the treat:

> *"Cake is good, cake is fine,*
> *I'd eat cake all the time*
> *If I could, because cake is good.*
> *And so is King Gustave, knock on wood."*

Something blue and ethereal slid over the frosted expanse of the cake as she sang, and it took Argabella a moment to realize that it was a pair of feet. And when she looked up, she recognized that the owner of said feet was a vaporous and glowing Lord Toby, who said, "Wow, that looks pretty scrumptious!"

"What? Toby? Is anyone else seeing this?"

Judging by the exclamations of surprise, they all were. And then Poltro appeared next to him, similarly limned in blue. "Were any chickens harmed in the making of this cake?" the ghostly form asked. "Please say yes."

The ghosts were immediately peppered with a barrage of questions. "How are you here?"

"How did you die, Poltro?"

"Is this what happens after you die? You crash birthday parties?"

"Forget death. Can you even eat cake now?"

Lord Toby held up his hands for silence. "We merely heard your kind toast to our memories and thought it would be nice to visit. We've been quite busy otherwise, you know, haunting the Morningwood for fun. Those horrible cheese thieves have had cause to regret their actions, let me tell you."

Fia asked Poltro about Konnan. "Did he bury your body next to Lord Toby?"

"Oh, yes, he did, very polite and respectful of my bones, he was. Then, because for a bit I was attached to him and Lord Toby was attached to me, we followed him here to Songlen, where he spent a week in Testy Tom's asking everyone if they'd seen a girl who looked kind of like a rabbit, and he was feeling pretty testy and blue by the end of it."

"I'm glad I don't look like that anymore," Argabella said. "Lord Toby, did you take any revenge on Bigolo?"

"It proved not to be necessary. Indeed, I couldn't!" he cried, dramatically clutching a fist in the air. "Fate dealt with him first. The very troll for whom Belladonna had prepared that bog frog smoothie wound up eating him somewhere near the Grange."

The two ghosts were welcomed by all after that, even by King Gustave, who was fairly certain the ghosts could not make curry out of him now.

"This is all very merry, m'lord," Poltro said, "but I'm thinkin' it's probably time you got around to asking them that thing, you know."

"Ask us what?" Grinda wondered aloud.

"Well, you know what would go perfectly with this cake?" Toby asked.

"What?"

"Some flesh honey."

Argabella promptly vomited her entire meal on top of the king's birthday cake, and there was much wailing and gnashing of teeth. But then Lord Toby pressed his case.

"Seriously, I think just a dollop or two of—of that precious substance upon our bodies might serve to give me and Poltro another shot at living. And you know where to get some."

"Nonsense," Grinda said. "Fle—that stuff extends life, it doesn't resurrect it."

"Well, how would you know?" Toby demanded. "Have you ever tried what I suggest?"

"No, but—"

"Recall, if you will, who originally bred the necrobees: the Dread Necromancer Steve."

"Auggh! I hate Steve!" Fia cried.

The door to the dining room burst open, and the friends were instantly on guard even as the specters of Lord Toby and Poltro winked out of sight. It was a postman looking sharp and crisp in a new Pellican Poste uniform. He held aloft a wax-sealed envelope.

"Majesty, a message from Lord Ergot in Bruding. It's the first one sent at the new Super Big Way Huge Mega Important rate."

"Bruding?" Gustave looked at Grinda. "Is that in Borix?"

"It is. And I recognize that name." Grinda's expression was dark and smeared, but her power suit was impeccable.

"I think I do, too. Wasn't he the guy who stabbed my pooboy's older brother in the heart?"

"Yes. He killed my nephew Bestley."

"Huh. Might be time to find a new lord of Bruding. Well, let's see what he wants." He took the letter from the postman and dismissed him, then promptly handed over the missive to Grinda since he still had problems fiddling with paper because paper cuts are terrible. The sand witch tore open the envelope, fished out the letter, noted the date, and read aloud:

> "My Deare Goode King Gustave,
>
>   My Best Congratulations on your Recent Kingship. I have always known you wouldst make a Foine King, and I am sure you will keep our Realme in Foine Fettle. I wish to assure you

that my state of Bruding is likewise in Excellent Handes and
will require little of your Most Important Time. The Halflings
are Foine People, and the Gnomes are Under Control. No
problems to see Here!

If, on the Other Hande, you wouldst require an Aide to act
as Wise Adviser in your New Role, I wouldst welcome the
Opportunitye for Bro Times on the Town. And I did take care
of Borix while the earl slept, so I know Things about keeping
Order. Do send for Me soon!

Yours in service,

Lord Ergot of Bruding"

The first thing Gustave said was, "What the heck are Bro Times,
and why do they sound so terrible? Are they even legal?"

"More importantly, why is this lord spending so much gold to tell
us there are no problems?" Grinda asked. "I think this matter might
require our personal attention."

"Yeah? Okay, that's fine with me."

"We have to see to the Lady Harkovrita anyway," the sand witch
added. "I have researched some additional remedies that may cure
her condition."

"And, uh, there's Worstley to think about," Fia said. "Remember
we left his body wrapped up in the lady's wardrobe?"

Grinda waved her hand, dismissing it. "Don't worry about that.
I'm sure the people in the earl's castle have found him by now and
buried him somewhere. His body's just an empty husk of flesh, anyway." She looked at the ruined birthday cake and sniffled once, a tear
in her eye.

"Believe me, my friends: that farm boy is dead."

ACKNOWLEDGMENTS

U nlike perhaps all other humans in history, we are thankful for airport barbecue. Not because the barbecue was good but because the joint inside the Dallas–Fort Worth airport was strangely open at 10 a.m. in February 2016 and we could sit down and chat for an hour before we had to catch our flights home. It was during that discussion that we thought it was high time someone killed the farm boy. And by that we meant it was time to make fun of white male power fantasies, the formula for which almost always involves some kid in a rural area rising to power in the empire after he loses his parents, usually because somebody comes along and tells him not to worry, he's special. (For the record, we do not have anything against farmers of any gender.)

We didn't get started on writing it until a year later, when we discovered that skewering tropes was tremendous fun, and we wondered why we'd waited so long.

Thank you, airport barbecue. Thank you.

And epic thanks to Tricia Narwani, the Metal Editor, for believing in this project, providing golden insights (and golden corn pudding!), and taking pictures of us with goats.

Thanks also to the spiffy Del Rey peeps who help get our words into readers' hands: David Moench, Julie Leung, Ryan Kearney, Scott Shannon, and the Darths—Darth Internous and Darth Breakfast—plus the art mages Scott Biel and Craig Robertson and the myriad folks in sales who get our books on shelves.

You all deserve a luncheon with the Dark Lord Toby and a jar of invigorated ham jam.

Kevin would like to thank Kimberly & Kid for putting up with me during a year in which I wrote three different series. Your love and support keep me going.

Thank you, Delilah, for making me laugh all the time and being a bottomless well of inspiration. It is such a pleasure to work with you, D.

Thanks also to my agent, Evan Goldfried, for taking our proposal in stride and running with it and for introducing me to mushroom toast.

Delilah would like to thank Craig, her sweet babies, and her mom for putting up with me during a year in which I also wrote three different series. Your love and support likewise keep me going, as do the hugs, gluten-free pizza, and cookies you supply.

Thank you, Kevin, for being the ideal writing partner and friend. When people ask me what it's like to co-write a book, I tell them that for us, it's mostly drinking fizzy things, giggling, and trading compliments. You're the best, homey!

Thanks to my agent of awesome, Kate, for encouraging my hare-brained schemes and always taking me to the places that serve duck.

And merci beaucoup to all the people who read books and to booksellers and librarians. You're the best people walking the planet right now, you know.

Thanks for going to Pell with us!

ABOUT THE AUTHORS

DELILAH S. DAWSON is the author of the *New York Times* bestseller *Star Wars: Phasma*, as well as *Hit, Servants of the Storm*, the Blud series, *Star Wars: The Perfect Weapon*, a variety of short stories and comics, and *Wake of Vultures* (written as Lila Bowen). She lives in Florida with her family and a fat mutt named Merle.

whimsydark.com
Facebook.com/DelilahSDawson
Twitter: @DelilahSDawson

KEVIN HEARNE hugs trees, pets doggies, and rocks out to heavy metal. He also thinks tacos are a pretty nifty idea. He is the author of *A Plague of Giants* and the *New York Times* bestselling series The Iron Druid Chronicles.

kevinhearne.com
Facebook.com/authorkevin
Twitter: @KevinHearne

Please visit talesofpell.com for more.

ABOUT THE TYPE

This book was set in Caslon, a typeface first designed in 1722 by William Caslon (1692–1766). Its widespread use by most English printers in the early eighteenth century soon supplanted the Dutch typefaces that had formerly prevailed. The roman is considered a "workhorse" typeface due to its pleasant, open appearance, while the italic is exceedingly decorative.